Always gripping. Always new.

This is what NEW DESTINIES is all about:

. . . being stranded on a planet with only one way to escape: through a resurrected wildcat with a thousand-year itch. "Cathouse" by Dean Ing.

. . . mobile robots, artificial intelligence and time travel. Hans Moravec, Senior Research Scientist at the Carnegie-Mellon Robotics Institute, brings it all together in an article stuffy Harvard wouldn't publish.

. . . losing your reason for living, the center of your being and pressing on. "LaToya is Wounded" by Dafydd ab Hugh.

... the most exciting breakthrough in technology today. Charles Sheffield, on superconductors.

Not enough? Then try LET'S KILL NASA TODAY!

EDITED BY
JIM BAEN

Spring Edition 1988

EDITOR IN CHIEF
Jim Baen

SENIOR EDITOR
Elizabeth Mitchell

MANAGING EDITOR
Toni Weisskopf

NEW DESTINIES, Spring 1988

A Baen Books Original

Baen Publishing Enterprises
260 Fifth Avenue
New York, N.Y. 10001

First printing, February 1988

ISBN: 0-671-65385-7

Cover art by Gregory A. West

Printed in the United States of America

Distributed by
SIMON & SCHUSTER
1230 Avenue of the Americas
New York, N.Y. 10020

CONTENTS

EDITED BY
JIM BAEN

NEW DESTINIES

Spring Edition 1988

Introduction

Is it true that it's raining soup up there and all we need to do is build some soup bowls? Robert Heinlein thinks so. So do Jerry Pournelle and G. Harry Stine. I guess I think so too . . . though I can't seem to quite keep it straight why if the potential is so large the payoff has been so small. Yes, I know all about comsats and landsats; so did my grandfather—and anyway, we're talking serious business here—not a few measly billion. In any event, here is a cheap and foolproof way to find out once and for all. And remember: you read it first in New Destinies. (If you think this is grandiose, wait till next issue, when we detail a perversely Libertarian plan for dealing with the drug problem, the deficit, and organized crime, all in one swell foop.)

THE PURE SPACE ACT OF 1989

*A Modest Proposal for Harnessing the
Profit Motive for the Conquest of Space*

A principle to live by: a state should not be permitted to use taxation to modify the behavior of its populace, because such power will inevitably be abused, and so corrupt both the state and the people.

This I believe . . . .

Well, they say that everyone has a price, and I guess that I've found mine: peace and freedom for all humankind. No, *really*.

Today we are trapped in a place where the majority of us are mired in the most incredible poverty, and the race itself is under constant threat of extinction, both from its own activities and from cosmic chance. One "serious" nuclear exchange, one moderately large asteroid impact, and our species can bend over and kiss its only dirtball goodbye. But it need not be ever so, and indeed need not be so for much longer. Our children can know the freedom of the spaceways. All it would take is a teensy-weensy bit of tax policy. . . .

THE PLAN
Phase I

First we kill NASA.

Now that may seem a bit extreme. Even if NASA is about as efficient at delivering space as the Post Office is at delivering mail, surely it is better than *nothing*? Well, maybe so, but some people think that NASA has had a negative effect on American space achievements—that there would have been more progress with NASA simply factored out of the equation—not replaced with some other government entity that works better—just factored out.

Consider: Would our mail be delivered more slowly if the U.S. Post Office were to disappear? What then might the several hundred billion dollars and tens of thousands of our best and brightest engineers soaked up by NASA have accomplished in the private sector? Would you really want to stack up any government organization against Apple, or IBM, or Federal Express? Would you bet stock on it?

Certainly not on anything remotely resembling a level playing field, you wouldn't. But there is another downside to NASA: it doesn't *like* level playing fields—or competition under any circumstances, for that matter—and, being a government agency, what it doesn't like it has the power to squelch. Who can say what opportunities have gone undiscovered because our government has virtually banned private enterprise in space? What if it were to *subsidize* private enterprise in space instead?

Let me share an insight given to me by one of our most brilliant missile engineers. Consider for a moment what NASA-style management of commercial air traffic would be like. First, twelve thousand technicians per transcontinental "launch" (that's what the Shuttle has had) don't come cheap. Because of that expense, "launches" would be infrequent—ten or twenty per year? Two or three? Because there would not be much call for vehicles, the industry dedicated to their production would be marginal (each jumbo jet would be quite literally hand-crafted) and utterly dependent on its governmental masters.

The price of a ticket? Well, a shuttle launch runs about forty million and the vehicle is good for twenty-five to fifty flights; call a "fare share" of the vehicle cost another thirty million. Plus throw in something to amortize R&D; a small part of what an accountant would consider reasonable brings the launch price to one hundred million dollars. (*Newsweek* in a recent article put the price at *two* hundred million.) Divide the total among a hundred passengers and you get a million dollar ticket. Not much call for air transport at that rate. In contrast, certain space entrepreneurs claim they could make good money selling one-orbit "joyrides" for ten thousand dollars . . .

Remember the movie, "The Right Stuff," and Chuck Yeager's disdain for "spam in a can"? Some say that if it weren't for NASA smothering its funding, Yeager's program would have produced an orbit-capable hypersonic rocketjet, a "Gipper Clipper," by the mid '70s. What we got for a hundred times more money was the Shuttle.

Do I believe all that? I have no doubt that others could mount persuasive counterarguments, but clearly there are grounds for at least arguing that NASA is better dead, and many space professionals secretly wish that it were. On the other hand, I am not here to bury NASA but to rob it . . .

Phase II

Now that we've killed NASA we have all that lovely money to play with! Oh, in the normal course of things NASA's funding would disappear like mist in the morning sun, but that's where The Plan kicks in:

Lets's take NASA's average yearly budget and *give it back to the people*—but only to spend on pure space enterprises. I.e., every individual and corporate taxpayer would receive a 100% tax writeoff for "pure space" investments up to two percent of their taxes otherwise due (NASA's approximate share of government revenues over the years). Not the world. Less, in fact, than IRAs or many other current deductions—and anyway, we traded in NASA for it.

Individuals and corporations could both play by simply investing in "pure space" activities and by investing in Mutuals dedicated to pure space stocks. Megacorporations could also play by spinning off their own space-only divisions. To fulfill the criteria for being "space only" an enterprise's only profit would have to come either from activities carried on in space, ground-based support activities, or from developing, building and/or operating space transport systems. (I suppose we would need a—small!—government commission to keep a list of eligible companies.)

As for objections, aside from those offered by the inevitable infinitude of nattering nabobs of negativism, I see two that might be argued on the merits:

1. Won't this tax policy result in swarms of investment shelter scams and "moondoggles" galore?

Answer: Why should it? True, the invested money represents funds that would otherwise simply be handed over to the IRS, but income from such investments would be perfectly real. Investors would have every incentive to maximize returns. High-risk players looking for astronomical returns might take a flier (so to speak) on Gary Hudson's space transport company. Folks looking for maximum security might prefer stock in Comsat, or Charles Sheffield's Earthsat Corporation. Others might go for one of the Space Mutuals (U.S. Space Power and Minerals is a good one), and leave the thinking to professionals. Me, I think I might invest in GM's new Heavy Space Division. (Think of it: billions of dollars looking for the best possible space investment!)

2. What about all the decent hardworking folks at NASA—not uppity Top Management, but engineers, scientists, and laborers—many of whom got involved in the first place because they wanted a piece of the Dream? We can't just throw them away as if they don't matter any more.

Answer: indeed we can't. How's this: for the first year after dismantling, all unemployed ex-NASA employees will get their full salaries, pending transfer to other government work at the same level. After the first year those that have not found other work or been transferred will receive half the previous amount until they find work equivalent in income and prestige to what they were doing.

Even if we were to wind up supporting a large portion of the ex-NASA personnel roster forever, it would be cheap at the price (Postal Reformers take note!), but as The Plan kicks in we are going to see a space boom that will make the Europeans sigh, the Russians whimper, and the Japanese slaver. In such an environment experienced space-oriented workers and scientists are going to be in the catbird seat. How many of them will want to stay on the dole? None who are worth their pay, surely.

So there it is: A modest proposal for commencing the true Age of Space and freeing humankind forever from the bonds of gravity. If you believe that the market's invisible hand will point the way to whatever profits there may be, this is the Plan for you!

So what are we waiting for? Let's kill NASA today!

—BAEN

Introduction

It seems absurd that the loss of a single vehicle and seven lives could have put an end to our national space effort, and yet, as of this writing it is nearly two years since Challenger went down, since then nothing much of consequence has gone up. Except in the narrowest institutional sense there is no particular reason that this should be so: the reasons have far less to do with national will (whatever that is) and technology than with the dynamics of instititutional devolution as they apply to NASA. Dr. Sheffield has incisively diagnosed the problem, but by his own admission his prescription is forlorn. So let's try mine; Let's Kill Nasa Today!

ACROSS THE GREAT DIVIDE

Charles Sheffield.

Pain, rage, and trauma. This is a cry of pain; one of rage, too, and certainly one of frustration. The world is not doing what I want it to, and I don't like it.

In late January 1986, I flew out to JPL to be present at the Voyager-2 encounter with the Uranus system. It was a wonderful event, filled with new discoveries. I flew back to Washington on January 27. The next morning, January 28, the *Challenger* exploded.

At the time my first reactions were like yours: shock, horror, distress, and little rational thought. But when the hearings of the Rogers Commission began in February my feelings changed.

I know the critical moment for me, exactly. It came on the morning of Tuesday, February 25, when I was on WAMU, the radio station of American University. I was there to explain to the audience the significance of the testimony of witnesses called before the commission. There were, inevitably, lengthy discussions of

O-ring seals, of weather conditions, and of testing procedures that were or were not observed.

Allan McDonald, an engineer with Morton Thiokol, was a completely persuasive and poignant witness. He had recommended that the launch be postponed, for three distinct reasons: the temperature was well outside the range where the O-ring seals were rated safe (it was 20 degrees Fahrenheit, and the O-ring recommendation was for no launch below 53 degrees!); there was ice on the spacecraft, with icicles two feet long; and the weather in the ocean recovery zone was terrible, with 30-foot seas and gale-force winds.

McDonald added in testimony: "I made the direct statement that if anything happened to this launch, I told them I sure wouldn't want to be the person that had to stand in front of a board of inquiry to explain why a launch was outside of the qualification of the solid rocket motor or any Shuttle system."

McDonald's recommendation to postpone was overruled by Morton Thiokol and NASA management. Then, as the final insult, he was asked to sign off in writing, to OK the launch. He refused.

As he said in testimony to the commission, the *accuracy* of his statements was not challenged. It was simply that his statements were ignored.

His testimony was horrifying. But it was when the NASA officials appeared before the commission, and produced lengthy and self-serving statements justifying their actions, that my problems began. If I said what I thought, live on radio, I would probably be faced with libel suits. Because what I wanted to say was that NASA was done for; the gargoyles had finally taken over the cathedral. The long history of engineering excellence was winding down into a mass of tepid bureaucracy.

I don't want to give the impression that this was the first time I had wanted to criticize NASA. Quite the opposite. I had been saying bad things about them for years. But that had been for their conservative approach, their grey engineering excellence, their poor sense of public relations. This was different. When risks are taken consciously and knowingly, by brave men and women who know their chances, that is one thing; and it is not a bad thing. It's another matter when crews don't know the odds because the engineers have been ignored by the managers.

I was as forthright as I dared to be on radio, and I probably shocked the WAMU lady who was passing me listeners' questions. What I didn't realize was that I had not gone nearly far enough.

To go far enough, it is necessary to put both those January events together: Voyager, and *Challenger*. They fit. And when we put them together, and look at their aftermath, we find that in January 1986, the United States Space Program passed through a great transition point—one of the "singularities of the timeline" that I have analyzed in earlier issues of this publication. And that singularity spells trouble to anyone who believes that this country needs a strong civilian space program.

To make my point, I want to reproduce, verbatim, the text of a keynote speech that I made ten years ago, at the San Francisco annual meeting of the American Astronautical Society. (A memorable meeting for other reasons. It was the first time that I met Joe Haldeman and Jerry Pournelle; prior to that, Jerry and I had been limited to writing each other rude letters.) The theme of the meeting was the industrialization of space. The text that follows is an unedited transcript of an actual speech, so there are a few warts on it. But here it is, just as it was given:

KEYNOTE ADDRESS, OCTOBER 18, 1977.

A little more than twenty years ago, the then-Astronomer Royal of Great Britain, Richard Woolley (now Sir Richard Woolley) came to give a speech to the Cambridge University Astronomical Society. He prefaced that speech with a rather peculiar statement, thus: "After my talk I will be happy to answer general astronomical questions on any subject—with two exceptions.

The *other* subject is the expansion of the universe, about which I know nothing."

This cryptic pronouncement made good sense to the audience, and we all laughed. A few months earlier, Woolley had made a statement that was widely reported in the press: "Space travel is utter bilge."

Woolley is a respected astronomer and astrophysicist. He has done major work in both practical and theoretical astronomy. So it is ironic that he may well go down in history as the Astronomer Royal who made a curiously ill-timed remark, at the very moment that the Space Age was born.

As we all know, Sputnik was launched in October 1957, and we are now able to look back on twenty years of accomplishment that would have seemed incredible to even the boldest and most optimistic in 1957. Yet, in some ways, Woolley was right. I worked at the Royal Observatory for two summers in the late '50s, as a summer student, and had a chance to hear in more detail what Woolley had meant by his remark. (I did hand calculations, for months. Looking back on those efforts, and seeing today's electronic calculators, is enough to make me weep. We used machines that were mechanical or electro-mechanical, and looked up our trig functions in big volumes of tables. I estimate that I could now do those calculations, using a $50 calculator, between fifty and one hundred times as quickly. However, the progress in computers, though not unrelated to the progress in space exploration, is not today's topic of discussion.)

In what sense was Woolley correct? Remember, before the space program got underway, "space travel" referred to the very small body of factual writing about rocketry and orbital flight, and to the very large body of fiction. Science *fiction* had been happily exploring the universe for half a century and more, even if we discount such earlier writers as Kepler or Dean Swift. The ways they chose to handle the problem of space travel were (and are) various. Space warps, faster-than-light drives, hyperspace gateways, matter transmitters—they all tended to have one thing in common. They were easily developed, and they opened up, instantaneously and effortlessly, the whole universe for our exploration.

Woolley was a hard-headed and practical man, well used to the problems of something as "simple" as installing a large reflector here on Earth. He objected to the notion that we would easily explore space—not only the Solar System, but the stars too. I'm afraid I agree with him.

Are such things as space warps and faster-than-light drives impossible? It would need a rasher man than me to assert that they are. Less than a hundred years ago, respected scientists had *proved* that mechanical heavier-than-air flight was impossible. Theories change. Although relativity seems to be doing very well, and although the limits that it seems to impose are daunting, we don't *know* that the FTL drive will remain beyond our reach.

Are such things *improbable?* In the near future, the answer to that question is easier. In terms of our current understanding of the universe, there is no "royal road" to space. Unless some other civilization comes to see us, and tells us the easy way to do it (and that would be at best a mixed blessing) we'll have to do it the hard way. It will be the usual mixture: some inspiration, a lot of hard engineering, a lot of pushing both for and against by special interest groups, and an over-all stimulus that ranges from the desire to make money, to the desire to understand the heavens.

The universe is a big place, and the word "space" encompasses everything that is not the Earth. More than anything else, space exploration in the larger sense of interstellar movement is going to take a long time. To mentalities that are geared to rapid results, with everything fitted into a few (fiscal) years, the timescale for stellar exploration may seem intolerable. We are talking centuries, and millennia, of time (perhaps much less subjective time—here relativity can help a good deal, but that takes me too far astray). It is very hard for us to accept things that occupy a natural timescale much longer than our own lifetimes, or if we accept them we can't seem to get too interested in them.

This problem is arising in other fields, also. In the Leonard Schiff Memorial Lecture given this year, Sir Denys Wilkinson tackles the same problem in the field of theoretical physics. In a beautiful paper with the intriguing title of "The quarks and Captain Ahab," Wilkinson talks of the need for *dynastic* experiments, in which a scientist cannot hope to see the result himself, but must settle for the knowledge that his distant descendants will one day have the answer, and can incorporate it into their theories. Needless to say, most scientists would not be prepared to spend their life in such a mode, unless they were also to be in on the final stages of some earlier experiment.

Fortunately, there is plenty to do, and plenty of places to go, even if we confine ourselves to "near space" and stay within, say, six light-hours of the Sun. Here we are looking at timescales that we can comprehend and live with, particularly since we will be involved in a progressive program, in which most of our money and resources will go into the first few light-seconds from Earth. Now we are talking of the next twenty years, say up to the year 2000.

What propulsion system will be most widely used in that time frame? It is hard for many people to accept the idea that the vehicle that will take us into space will be anything as unromantic and unappealing as the chemical rocket. No denying it, the chemical rocket is an unattractive animal: noisy, wasteful and unesthetic. No one would *choose* to launch a spacecraft with a chemical rocket—just as no one would choose to begin space exploration at the bottom of Earth's deep gravity well. Unfortunately, right now there is only one game in town. In space, or on the Moon, we have other launch propulsion systems as options, but here and now we have nothing that can compete with the chemical rocket for Earth-launch. In the same way, it is no use complaining about the inefficiency of Earth as a starting point for space exploration. The old farmer, who, asked the way to Newbiggin, replied, "If I were going to Newbiggin, I wouldn't start from here," is accurate but unhelpful. We have to start from here, although the sooner we can get some launch capability in a more shallow potential well, the happier we will all be.

So far as the romance is concerned, that's a function of the times. What was romantic to one generation was often the bane of an earlier one. In the 1840s, Wordsworth wrote a sonnet objecting to the introduction of the steam railway ("On the projected Kendal and Windermere railway," composed October 12, 1844—he was in his seventies, and it isn't a sonnet you would particularly recommend to your friends—but it is worth reading because of the point it makes). Now, steam locomotives are considered part of the romance of the past and there are groups of enthusiasts who love steam trains. Remember, too, how people mourned the passing of the clipper sailing ships, when steam made them non-competitive. I have no doubt that in a hundred years we will look back nostalgically on the good old chemical rockets, and despise the functional and new-fangled ones powered by the intermediate vector boson or Kerr-Newman black hole drives. On this subject, as on many others, Rudyard Kipling said the final word, in the poem beginning "Farewell, Romance" (title: "The King," composed in 1894).

We can expect developments in chemical rockets, and we can expect ion propulsion and perhaps solar sailing and nuclear to help out on the long hauls. These tools, already, are quite enough to allow us to do many things—if we want to, and are willing to apply the resources. There are no engineering obstacles that we can see between us and a lunar colony, or a solar electric power satellite, or a colony at L5. Right now, if we wanted to, the United States could initiate a manned Mars program, and I am confident that it could be completed in the next decade. We have those tools, already. So why don't we do it? Well, the conventional answer is that we have other priorities. For myself, I regard the space program as the only major effort that the United States had undertaken in the past twenty years and *succeeded* in. The war on crime, the war on drugs, the increased expenditures on education, on welfare and on energy conservation—all these, looked at realistically, have failed. Not to mention the war in Vietnam, which took an incredible amount of our resources.

Some would answer the implied criticism of government thinking in the previous paragraph by saying, "Technical goals are easy to achieve, social goals are more difficult." A true statement, I think—but while we are trying to decide how to do the things we don't know how to do, why not spend more money on the things we can do successfully?

I won't belabor the point, since I suspect that I am preaching now to the converted.

In any case, I don't happen to regard space exploration as of lesser social importance than the other activities that currently occupy a big place in Federal thinking. To my mind, we need to move off-planet in significant numbers, sometime in the next hundred years. This is not particularly because of a Doomsday feeling about Earth, although it is hard to deny that we have spoiled large parts of it in our (successful) search for higher living standards. It is also undeniable that when I say "we" I am really speaking for the "haves," rather than the "have-nots." On the other hand, it is the "haves" who also possess the weapons to make the end a bang rather than a whimper, so this is one reason for a feeling of urgency. I don't think we have any real long-term alternative to moving out and expanding, and no one knows how urgent that need may prove to be.

There is an alternative view, quite popular at the moment, which decries technology as a solution, and emphasizes thinking small, conserving and contracting. I like two of those three very well. I would prefer to rephrase "think small" to "think the appropriate size," and I agree completely with "conserve." But I think that "contract," as a philosophy for the human race, is fatal. I can think of no example in which an organism has advanced up the evolutionary scale by decreasing its area of influence. The unwritten biological rule seems to be "expand and thrive"—almost, "expand or die." It may be dangerous to regard the human race as a whole as a single organism. Analogies of that type can certainly be misleading. On the other hand, to quote Samuel Butler, analogy may be misleading, but it's the least misleading thing we have.

Accepting this view of analogy, and being careful not to stretch it beyond reason, can we learn anything from earlier "expansion periods" of the human race, during which the unknown was beyond the seas, rather than out in space? What can we learn from the Polynesians, the Phoenicians, the Vikings, and the Spanish and Portuguese navigators?

Less perhaps than we might hope. The role of technology is so central to our current exploration, and was apparently so much less important in earlier efforts, that in this case analogy may well be misleading. A visit to the Greenwich Maritime Museum quickly convinces us that the determination of longitude, and hence of position, was central to British exploration. But the Vikings were much less worried by navigation—or else they had methods of navigation that have not been handed down to us. And if this is true of the Vikings, it is truer yet of the Polynesians, who sailed the Pacific using navigation methods that we can scarcely guess at.

Can we learn nothing, then, from this analogy? Well, consider the question of motivation. The motives of the Vikings are a little mysterious, and undocumented. They seem to have been driven by the need to get away from their own women folk, and the desire to indulge in a little rape, pillage and arson in foreign parts. On the other hand, the Spanish and Portuguese, while less flamboyant in their goals, had motives that we can easily recognize and relate to: *religious zeal*, and *financial zeal* (specifically, gold and silver).

Religious zeal may seem at first sight to be far from our modern interests, unless we realize that the religious wars of the 15th century have been replaced by the ideological wars of the 20th. Thus for religious zeal, we should substitute ideological zeal. Now do we see a familiar pattern emerging? Would Armstrong have walked on the Moon in 1969 if Sputnik had not flown in 1957? In short, the entire impetus of the U.S. space program, for its first ten years, was the ideological war with Russia. Without that, there would have been little or no U.S. space program.

More recently (since 1969, to be precise), the ideological thrust has diminished. Politically, the Russian lead in space has disappeared, and the U.S. drive to move ahead fast into space has gone with it. What has replaced it? Balboa, Pizarro, and Cortez could answer that for us, if we could find any way of asking them. When religious zeal diminishes, financial zeal takes over. But where in space are the equivalents of the treasures of the Incas, the Aztecs and the Mayans?

I wish I knew. NASA, with a shrinking budget, is looking hard for the treasure of the Incas, and is turning more and more to *Applications*—the profit motive—as the best answer that can be offered. As ideological drive lessens, the profit drive is taking over—just as it did in developing the Americas. Now, for the first time, industry can play a changed role in space development.

You see, as long as the thrust is ideology, industry can't do too much. Only a federal government can initiate and carry through a space program that has as its main *raison d'être* an ideological war. Industry comes into its own when the second stage ignites and the thrust becomes financial, based on profit objectives and subject to the rational scrutiny of cost-benefit calculations.

That, in my opinion, is where we stand now. At the crossroads, where U.S. policy for space development shifts from religious zeal to planned profit.

Many people who were active in the early days of the space program bemoan this change, this loss of public interest. They pine for the good old days, when budgets looked unlimited, and they are saddened by the lowly position that the space appropriation occupies in the Federal budget. Personally, I think this is a good thing. (I should no doubt be burned as a heretic for this view—but we are past the age of religious zeal, so I am safe.) A good thing, because space development needed to move beyond the gee-whiz stage, to the dull, boring stage of routine development, before it could amount to anything important. If the public yawns at Apollo-Soyuz and sleeps through the Shuttle while flocking to see "Star Wars," that is fine. It means that we are past the stage where a successful launch is a surprise, where even a rendezvous and docking is an unusual event. The prologue is over. We are ready for the real, routine work in space.

That stage had to come. It is not enough for perfect physical specimens to be able to take space travel. The day of people who can take ten gee without wincing must end. Space must become accessible to people like me—people with one good eye, who feel dizzy in high-speed elevators, who suffer motion sickness on a water-bed (in the right circumstances).

This new day will not arrive, until the commercial spirit can replace religious zeal. Wouldn't it be nice if the Federal expenditures on space were *irrelevant*—because the private investment was so large?

Could it happen?

The theme of the conference is the *Industrialization* of Space. This can be interpreted as the movement of the space program from the public to the private sector. In this context, we have clearly a long way to go. We have one small example, but an important one: the communications satellite business—and even this happened only with a strong boost from the U.S. government. Other examples still seem to be a long way off. There is no sign that the government is ready to get out of the weather satellite business, or the earth resources satellite business. Perhaps it is simply too early—or perhaps, as I rather fear, the process of public management has become so entrenched that industry will now be hard put to force the transition from public to private control.

One final word is in order. All new developments—

technological, artistic, spiritual or scientific—are led and promoted by a small fraction of the human race. Thus we should be neither surprised nor alarmed if discussions of this type occupy less space in the newspapers than Jimmy Carter's haircut or Elizabeth Taylor's tenth marriage. Bread and circuses have always been the opiate of the masses. If you are reading this, and feel discouraged by an inability to communicate to others your own feelings about the importance of an active space development effort, comfort yourself with this thought. If you want to be on the leading edge of anything, you have by definition to be a couple of standard deviations away from most people. That makes you an oddball. The trick is to learn to accept it, then to like it—and keep on making lots of noise for what you believe in. That's the only way that a minority group will be heard. *END*.

I couldn't deliver that talk today. There are too many built-in assumptions that have proved to be invalid and optimistic. Thus:

1) ". . . we can expect ion propulsion and perhaps solar sailing and nuclear to help out on the long hauls."

Can we, indeed? Today we have no program in ion propulsion, a negligible expenditure on solar sails, and the very word "nuclear" is frowned upon. We have, if anything, gone *backwards* in the past ten years on space propulsion systems.

2) ". . . the United States could initiate a manned Mars program, and I am confident that it could be completed in the next ten years."

Today the United States could initiate a manned Mars program—we show no sign of wanting to do so—and I am confident that it could *not* be completed in the next ten years. Did you know that NASA says it would take us longer to *return* to the Moon than it took to go there after Kennedy's original announcement of the Apollo Program? Again, we seem to have gone backwards.

3) "There is an alternative view, quite popular at the moment, which decries technology as a solution . . ."

Truer than ever. The average citizen sees technology as the source of multiple ills, and discounts the huge and varied benefits. Talk to Congress, and you find that the Science and Technology Committee is a shadow of its old self. It's not the fault of the committee members or their staffers, it's a reflection of public distrust in technology, which is equated with Three Mile Island, Chernobyl, Bhopal, and Love Canal. Technology, the American people seem to argue, is something for the Japanese, Koreans, Taiwanese and Europeans. Oddly enough, those other nations agree.

4) ". . . the profit drive is taking over—just as it did in developing the Americas . . . we stand now at the crossroads where U.S. policy for space development shifts from religious zeal to planned profit."

If only that were true! We are still waiting for a private launch capability and commercial space services. Most companies are interested in the potential of space only if the risks are underwritten by the Federal government. The one commercially successful activity of 1977—communications satellites—remains the solitary example. Commercial operation of the Earth resources satellites Is in trouble, with the failure of the government to provide promised transition funds to move it from public to private ownership. Transfer of the weather satellites to private ownership was dropped three years ago because of public protest.

5) ". . . I rather fear the process of public management has become so entrenched that industry will be hard put to force the transition from public to private control."

I feared it then, and I'm more convinced of it now. The brave new world of an industrial space program is farther away then ever. All space launches are government-controlled, and will be for the foreseeable future—see Harry Stine's articles, in *Far Frontiers* V and VI, if you want to see how unwilling the government is to let U.S. industry operate freely in space. As Stine says, this country may have given away the Solar System.

Problems and Pessimism. There could be other explanations as to why I couldn't give that 1977 talk today. For one thing, I am ten years older; with increasing age comes, as a general rule, increasing pessimism.

The pessimism of age is curiously limited. It is a *general* pessimism, a conviction that things are not as good as they used to be and are still getting worse. And yet it is a *conservative* pessimism, which cannot bring itself to believe how bad things might become. World War I would never have started, had the generals and politicians been able to imagine how horrible the combat would become. World War II would have begun years earlier if people had realized that Hitler meant exactly what he said. The principle of limited pessimism convinces me that all-out nuclear war is quite likely, simply because most people are reluctant to face up to what that would do to the world, and therefore do not take action to make that war impossible. And now I have to worry that the future I see for the U.S. space program may not be bleak enough.

However, I really don't think the problem is pessimism on my part. I think we have just been through a time of fundamental change. In 1986 we crossed a watershed, the great divide of the United States space program, and the landscape on the other side of it is quite different and less hospitable than it used to be.

The Voyager Uranus encounter, like the Jupiter and Saturn encounters before it, was a marvellous scientific feast. In some ways Uranus was best of all, because we knew less about that planet than we knew about its sunward neighbors. It was a three-day high at JPL, with unexpected treats like the off-axis magnetic field and the startlingly active satellites, while the expected (but still new and magnificent) images streamed in every hour or two.

But the euphoria was already beginning to fade on the flight back from Los Angeles to Washington. I found myself looking ahead to the rest of the '80s decade—and finding a great blank in space sciences. On that flight, I happened to be sitting across the aisle from Geoffrey Briggs, who runs NASA's planetary science programs. We couldn't help comparing the '70s and the '80s. The Voyager-2 Uranus encounter looked more and more like a watershed event, separating a period of dynamic activity from one of stagnation.

In the ten years from 1970 to 1979, we saw Pioneer spacecraft visit Mercury, Venus, Jupiter, and Saturn, with Pioneer 10 heading right out of the Solar System. We had Moon landings, Skylab, and the Apollo-Soyuz space hook-up. We had the Viking Orbiter and Lander, exploring Mars from close orbit and on the surface. And we had Voyager-1 and -2, launched in 1977 on the long journey of planetary exploration that Voyager-2 is still engaged in.

And for the 1980s? One major scientific spacecraft—the Infrared Astronomical Satellite—and that will be it, for the whole decade. No Halley's Comet mission, of course; we missed our chance there for the next seventy-six years. Fortunately, the Europeans, Japanese and Soviets seized that unique opportunity. In the 1980s we will see no Galileo, and no Hubble Telescope, while other missions, such as the Magellan Venus Radar Mapper, the Comet Rendezvous/Asteroid Flyby, the Mars Observer, and the Ulysses solar polar mission (which the European Space Agency may now undertake alone) look even farther off. The Galileo mission, by the way, is still officially scheduled for a November 1988 launch. You can believe that date if you want to, but I am very skeptical. I bet it will not be launched before 1990.

We have moved from the Golden Age of planetary exploration in the 1970s, to the Age of Austerity in the mid-1980s. To quote more (and better) Wordsworth: "To be a prodigal's favorite, then, worse truth, a miser's pensioner—behold our lot!"

Meanwhile, the USSR is preparing its Phobos mission, to the inner satellite of Mars, probably with two spacecraft and four Phobos landers. This will be followed, according to reports, by a Soviet Mars mission in 1992 with a lander, balloons, and an orbiter, and then a Mars surface rover two years later.

Like it or not, we will sit on the sidelines and watch. Even if we were given a go-ahead today (which will not happen) new programs cannot be designed and launched in a few weeks. When Geoffrey Briggs was asked, later in 1986, what someone ought to do in order to work on U.S. planetary sciences programs, he said: "Stop smoking, live cleanly, and exercise regularly." It sounds funny, but it is not a joke. And people like Briggs, who care about the U.S. planetary science programs, are driven apoplectic by public apathy and governmental inertia.

In NASA's mind the 1980's was to be remembered, fifty years from now, as the decade of the Space Shuttle and Space Station. Then came *Challenger*, and the plan for the '80s began to fall farther apart.

In retrospect, the *Challenger* explosion was more a symptom than a cause. For the real problems go far deeper than a single accident, which every sane person knows must happen sometime, somehow, to some unfortunate crew.

More Problems. Last week, it was announced that the cost estimate of the Space Station had increased. Increased? It *doubled*—to sixteen billion, up from eight billion. The main reason given by NASA is delay. Shortage of immediately available (appropriated) funds, plus the effects of the *Challenger* explosion, mean that the station will not be up by 1992 as originally planned, but by 1994.

On the face of it that may sound reasonable. But look at it a little more closely. Why does a two-year stretch in schedule imply an increase in cost?

Inflation? No. The calculations are all done in 1984 dollars, which means the new cost in current dollars will be even higher. The stated reason is "more comprehensive methods of accounting." The earlier estimates ignored such things as ground-based support for the station, test facilities, simulators, crew training, ongoing operational costs, shuttle flight costs to assemble the station, and the cost of experiments run on the station. In other words, the eight billion was for *hardware alone*, and not all the hardware at that. Any corporation that presented its future cost estimates in such misleading fashion would be liable to stockholder suit.

The new station cost figures tell me a couple of things. First, the original numbers for the cost of the space station were severely *and deliberately* underestimated—because NASA desperately wanted the program to start. Once started, it would have its own inertia and be harder to stop. Second, the development of the space station is being undertaken with no emphasis on tight, lean operations, and no emphasis on moving at maximum speed. For many in NASA, the first U.S. space station is not a dream come true; it is a ten-year guaranteed meal ticket. The longer NASA takes to complete the station, the better those marking time toward retirement will like it.

Bureaucratic placidity does not encourage good engineering, either. The same forces that permitted the *Challenger* launch against the advice of the technical specialists are now slowing progress on the space station.

If you really want to build a station, and you want it done fast and well—and maybe with some risks thrown in along the way—then you take it out of government hands as fast as you can. Because the first rule of a good government employee, the bureaucratic Prime Axiom, is this: never allow yourself to be associated with risk or failure. High-speed, high-intensity programs are by their nature dangerous.

How do you build it? Easy. You grab a couple of people like Ted Turner, of CNN, or Ross Perot, of EDS. You tell them what you want and when you want it, and you ask them if they can do the job for ten billion dollars, fixed price. If they say yes, you give them the money and get out of the way. You don't tell them how to spend the money, you don't ask them how they are going to manage the project, you don't ask them for endless reports on what they are doing, and you don't tell them how to do the job.

Why pick those two, or someone like them? That's easy, too. You need someone of proven management competence with a big ego, someone who will succeed or die trying. When James Webb was running NASA, he commented informally that Wernher von Braun was exactly the right man for the Apollo project, because his ego was too big to allow him to fail.

One reason for von Braun's success is that he never quite realized that he worked for the U.S. government. When he wanted a piece of equipment, he had it delivered and then let his assistants fight the battle of the paperwork. When necessary, he himself was suitably contrite to his bean-counters ("It is easier to obtain absolution than permission") but he never let rules get in the way of actions. And Apollo took us to the Moon, ahead of schedule.

That's not the way you do it in today's NASA, or in the Pentagon. If you want a hammer, you don't go out and buy one. Still less do you go around to other people, trying to scrounge the use of a hammer somebody else has and isn't using.

No. You start filling in forms, and sending them off through the "proper channels." And then, if you didn't miss a form, and you are lucky, six months or a year later you may have your hammer. By then you may have forgotten why you needed it.

It's a terrible thing to say, but the space station now looks like the biggest boondoggle in NASA's history. And what a shame, when so many space enthusiasts worked so hard to save it when it was in funding trouble. In the long run, we must have a permanent occupation of space. But the way we are going, we will find ourselves with a white elephant of a station, completed about 1997, at a bloated cost of twenty-five to thirty billion dollars. Or we will find the project being cancelled, around 1990, because no one in Congress will be able to find any public support for the idea.

Paradoxes. If you have been reading my articles in *New Destinies* and *Far Frontiers*, you may have noticed recent contradictions. In "Running Out" and "On Timeline Singularities," I said that the space program is vitally important to human affairs. But "Do You Really Want A Bigger U.S. Space Program?" argued that you can only achieve a bigger program by moving this country to the left; and this column seems to be saying that the government space program is in such a shambles that the last thing we want is more public participation in space.

I believe all those statements. What I'm suffering from is antinomy (one of Spider Robinson's favorite words, which is probably going to be mis-typed along the way as "antimony"). Antinomy is the simultaneous holding of strong but contradictory impulses, and it applies perfectly to this situation.

Here are three statements which, taken together, are antinomian:

1) A strong space program is vital to this country.

2) Private industry and the people of this country won't put up the money for a private space program, so the space program has to be a public effort.

3) The U.S. space program is in a disastrous condition, because it is being run by an uninspired government bureaucracy.

Unfortunately, I believe all three.

Looking For Solutions. What do those three statements tell us? Well, maybe they tell us that space will be developed, and in this century; but not by the United States—rather, by Europe, Japan, and the Soviet Union. It's tempting to say, if you want to work in space, that you should learn French, because it's the easiest of the foreign languages that will be used in space.

That's an answer I can't live with; that is why I said at the beginning that I am filled with anger, pain, and frustration. However, emotions do not solve problems. We need a positive agenda for action.

To guide us to that agenda, I return to something that I noted in 1977: the analogy between space development activities and particle physics research. The two are similar in many ways. Each requires multi-billion-dollar investment of funds, each is incomprehensible to many citizens (space has a definite edge here—try explaining a quark to your mother), and each is the subject of considerable international activity and competition.

There is at least one significant difference. Despite budget cuts and setbacks, the particle physics community keeps rolling along. President Reagan has just approved the Superconducting Super Collider (SSC) with a $4.4 billion price tag. What is being done right in particle physics that is being done wrong in space?

One thing, and one thing of paramount and central importance: the centers for particle physics research are run and managed by first-rate scientists. NASA certainly has many excellent scientists of its own, competent, innovative, and hard-working. Unfortunately, they are not running the show. If they were, the whole agency would behave very differently—because the scientists want to see those payloads flown, as soon and as safely as possible. They are waiting for data to come back so they can begin their analyses. The scientists are mostly in mid-level jobs. But NASA needs *at the top* its best research scientists and engineers, people who are the very antithesis of bureaucrats.

Suggesting such a change to NASA is much easier than making it happen. The pro-space community knows how to fight for a particular budget item or program these days. It followed the lead of the environmental movement and the special-interest lobbying programs, and now has the political process fairly well understood. But how do you accomplish a needed *internal* restructuring of a government agency? That is much trickier, because there is no analogy to aid us.

I don't know of any attempt to do it successfully. There were many who wanted to get rid of the egregious James Watt as Secretary of the Interior, but nothing happened until the man put his foot in his own mouth.

Here are my suggestions, and they are no more than

that: work on the *scientific aides* to the House and Senate. Make sure they know where the competence lies in NASA and who are the best people; make sure they are thoroughly briefed on the best scientific programs, and make sure they know why those programs are important.

It is less useful to work on the Congress itself. Other factors place too many demands on a senator's time to permit a full and detailed briefing of scientific issues. If you get the chance, certainly bend his or her ear. But remember that the aides, to a large extent, steer the House and Senate on questions of science.

Work the problem, but don't think you will get results quickly and easily. For we crossed the Great Divide, a little more than a year ago, and the things that used to work to advance the space program won't work now. Somehow I don't think we're in Kansas any more.

Introduction

At long last a pure science fiction shared universe is about to take flight. Created by Jerry Pournelle, WARWORLD is set in the same universe as the classic Niven/Pournelle novel, *The Mote in God's Eye*, *though the emissary from the Moties is not due for some centuries yet. The stories in WARWORLD take place in the hellish period from the fall of the eugenic Frankenstein creatures, the Sauron Supermen, through the rise of the Second Empire of Man. As for Brenda, you may or may not like her, but she is a true child of her times, a daughter of the WARWORLD.*

Volume I of WARWORLD, Eye of Fire *(Baen Books), is scheduled for publication in the Fall of 1988.*

BRENDA

Larry Niven

2656 AD, March (Firebee *clock time*)

Human-settled worlds all looked alike from high orbit. Terry thought that the CoDominium explorers must have had it easy.

Alderson jump. ZZZTT! One white pinpoint among myriads has become a flood of white light. Nerve networks throughout ship and crew are strummed in four dimensions. Wait for the blur to go away. You had a hangover this bad, once. It lasted longer.

Now search the ecliptic a decent distance from the sun. Look for shadows in the neudar screen: planets. Big enough? Small enough? Colors: blue with a white froth of clouds, if men are to breath the air. Is there enough land? How big are the ice caps? Three or four months to move close, and look.

Nuliajuk's ice caps had covered half the surface. If they ever melted, Nuliajuk would be all water. A cold world. Nobody else would settle, but what about Eskimos? So Terry Kakumee's ancestors had found a home, four centuries ago.

Tanith had no ice caps at all, and almost no axial tilt. Half land, but plenty of rainfall: the equatorial oceans boiled where they were shallow enough. Salt deserts around the equator. Swamps across both poles. Transportees had settled the north pole.

Terry Kakumee floated against the big window at *Firebee's* nose. It was sixteen years since he'd seen Tanith.

Tanith was a growing crescent, blue with white graffiti, and a blazing highlight across the northern pole. Summer. One serious mountain, the Warden, stood six kilometers tall. It had been white-tipped in winter. Dagon City would be in the foothills, south.

The clouds were sparse. The city itself didn't show, but he found a glare-point that had to be the old spaceport.

Brenda's farm would be south of that.

Sharon Hayes drifted up behind him. "I've been talking to the Dagon Port Authority. One George Callahan, no rank given, tells me they don't have much in the way of repair facilities, but we're intensely welcome. I've got a dinner date."

"Good." On a world this far from what civilization was left near Sparta, the population would feel cut off. Ships would be welcome. "What about fuel?"

"They can make liquid hydrogen. There's a tanker. Callahan gave me a course down. Four hours from now, and we'll have to lower *Firebee's* orbit. Time to move, troops. Are we all going down?"

She meant that for Charley. Charley Laine (Cargo and Purser) was almost covered in burn scars. His face was a smooth mask. There was an unmarred patch along his jaw that he had to shave, and good skin in strips along his back and the backs of his arms and legs, and just enough unburned scalp to grow a decent queue. Sometimes he didn't want to face strangers. He said, "Somebody'd better stay on duty, Captain Sharon. Did you ask about outies?"

"They haven't been raided since the Battle. They do have a couple of high-thrust mining ships. Charley, I think *Firebee's* safe enough."

Charley let out a breath. "I'll come. I can't be the only war vet on Tanith. There was—I wonder—"

"Brenda," Terry said.

"Yeah. I wonder about Brenda sometimes."

"I wonder too."

2640A, November (Tanith local time):

Lieutenant Kakumee had been Second Engineer aboard the recon ship *Firebee* during the destruction of the Sauron Second Fleet. The enemy's gene-tailored warriors were dead or fled, but they had left their mark. Damaged ships were limping in from everywhere in Tanith system. *Firebee* would orbit Tanith until she could be refitted or rifled for parts.

Firebee's midsection was a blob of metal bubbles where the Langston Field generator had vaporised itself and half melted the hull around it. It was the only hit *Firebee* had taken. Charley Laine had been caught in the flare.

They'd taken him to St. Agnes Hospital in Dagon City.

"The sky's full of ruined ships," Terry told him. "Most of them have damaged Langston Field generators. First thing that goes in a battle. We'll never get replacements."

Charley didn't answer. He might have heard; he might have felt the touch of Terry's hand. He looked like a tremendous pillow stuck with tubes in various places.

"Without a Langston Field we don't have a ship. I'd give *Firebee* a decent burial if I could get her down. You'll be healed a long time before any part of *her* flies again," Terry said. He believed that Charley would heal. He might never look quite human again, and if he walked he'd never run; but his central nervous system wasn't damaged, and his heart beat, and his lungs sucked air through the hole at one end of the pillow, while regeneration went on inside.

Terry heard urgent voices through the door. Patients healthy enough for curiosity stirred restlessly.

"Something's going on." Terry patted the padded hand. "I'll come back and tell you about it."

At first glance she wasn't that badly hurt.

She was slumped in an armchair in the lobby. Half a dozen people swarmed about her: a doctor, two nurses, two MPs and a thick-necked Marine in a full leg cast who was trying to stay out of the way and see too. She was wearing a bantar cloth coverall. It was a mess: sky blue with a green-and-scarlet landscape on the back, barely visible under several pounds of mud and swamp mold.

Bantar cloth had been restricted to Navy use up to eighty years ago. It was nearly indestructible. It wasn't high style, but farmers and others in high-risk jobs wore bantar cloth at half the price of a tractor. Whatever had happened to the woman, it would have been worse without that.

She had black ancestry with some white (skin like good milk chocolate, but weathered by fatigue and the elements) and oriental (the tilt of the eyes.) Thick, tightly coiled black hair formed a cushion around her head. It carried its own share of mud. A nasty gash cut through the hair. It ran from above her left eye back to the crown of her head. A nurse had cleaned it with alcohol; it was bleeding.

She drained a paper cup of water. A doctor—Charley's doctor, Lex Hartner—handed her another and she drained that too. "No more," Hartner said. "We'll get you some broth."

She nodded and said, "Uh." Her lip curled way up on the left. She tried to say something else. Stroke? Nonsense, she couldn't be past thirty. The head wound—

Poor woman.

Hartner said, "We'll get that soup into you before we look you over. How long were you out there?"

"Wumble." Her lip curled up; then half her face wrinkled in frustration. The other half remained slack. She held up one finger, then lifted another.

"A week or two?"

She nodded vigorously. Her eyes met Terry's. He smiled and turned away, feeling like an intruder. He went back to talk to Charley.

2656 AD, June, Tanith local time
The wrecked ships that had haloed the planet after

the Battle of Tanith were long gone. Shuttle #1 descended through a sky that seemed curiously empty.

What had been the Tanith spaceport still glared like a polished steel dish. Seen from low angle the crater became a glowing eye with a bright pupil.

The big Langston Field dome had protected Dagon City during the battle. The smaller dome at the spaceport had absorbed a stream of guided meteors, then given all of the energy back as the field collapsed.

A new port had grown around the crater's eastern rim. Terry and Charley, riding as passengers while Sharon flew, picked out a dozen big aircraft, then a horde of lighter craft. The crater must make a convenient airfield. The gleaming center was a small lake. Have to avoid that.

Both of *Firebee's* shuttles had lost their hover capability. They'd been looking for repair facilities for six years now. Shuttle #1 came in a little fast because of the way the crater dipped, coasted across and braked to a stop at the rim.

Tanith was hot and humid, with a smell of alien vegetation. The sun was low. Big autumn-colored flutterbys formed a cloud around them as they emerged. These were new to Terry. He'd never seen a Tanith summer.

They had drawn a crowd of twenty-odd, still growing. Terry noticed how good they looked: shorter than average, but all well muscled, none obtrusively fat. A year in Tanith's 1.14 gravity made anyone look good. The early strokes and heart attacks didn't show.

Terry was a round man; he felt rounder by contrast. Sharon Hayes fit right in. She was past fifty, and it showed in the deep wrinkle patterns around eyes and mouth; but regular exercise and a childhood in Tanith gravity had kept her body tight and muscular.

The airport bar was cool and dry, and crowded now.

George Callahan was a burly man in his forties, red hair going gray, red fur along his thick arms. He and Sharon seemed to like each other on sight. They settled at a smaller table, and there they dealt with entry forms on Callahan's pocket computer. (Cargo: a Langston Field generator big enough to shield a small city. Purpose of entry: trade.)

Terry and Charley drank at the crowd's expense and tried to describe sixteen years of interstellar trading.

Terry let Charley do most of the talking. Let him forget the fright mask he wore. "*Yes* we are heroes, by damn! We saved Phoenix from famine two years ago." He'd tried to hold his breath when *Firebee's* Langston Field generator blew up, but his voice still had a gravelly texture. "We'd just come from Hitchhiker's Rest. They've got a gene-tailored crop called kudzu grain. We went back and filled *Firebee* with kudzu grain, we were *living* in the stuff all the way back, and we strewed it across the Phoenix croplands. It came up before twenty-two million people quite ran out of stores. Then it died off, of course, because it isn't designed for Phoenix conditions, but by then they had their crops growing again. I never felt that good before or since."

The barmaids were setting out a free lunch, and someone brought them plates. Fresh food! Charley had his mouth full, so Terry said, "It's Hitchhiker's Rest that's in trouble. That kudzu grain is taking over everything. It really is wonderful stuff, but it eats the houses."

He bit into a sandwich: cheese and mystery meat and tomatoes and chili leaf between thick slices of bread. Sharon was working on another. She'd have little room for dinner . . . or was this lunch? The sun had looked like late afternoon. He asked somebody, "What time is it local?"

"Ten. Just short of noon." The woman grinned. "And nights are four hours long."

He'd forgotten: Dagon City was seven hundred kilometers short of the north pole. "Okay. I need to use a phone."

"I'll show you." She was a small brunette, wide at hips and shoulders. When she took his arm she was about Terry's height.

Charley was saying, "We don't expect to get rich.

There aren't any rich worlds. The war hurt everybody, and some are a long time recovering. We don't try to stop outies. We just go away, and I guess everyone else does too. That means a lot of worlds are cut off."

The brunette led him down a hall to a bank of computer screens. He asked, "How do I get Information?"

"You don't have a card? No, of course not. Here." She pushed plastic into a slot. The screen lit with data, and Terry noticed her name: Maria Montez. She tapped QQQ.

The operator had a look of bony Spartan aristocracy: pale skin, high cheekbones and a small, pursed mouth. "What region?"

"I don't know the region. Brenda Curtis."

The small mouth pursed in irritation. (Not a recording?) He said, "Try south-south. Then west." Brenda had inherited the farm. She might have returned there, or she might still be working at the hospital.

"South-south, Brenda Curtis." The operator tapped at her own keyboard. "Six-two-one-one-six-eight. Do you have that?"

She was alive! "Yes. Thank you." He jotted it on his pocket computer.

Maria was still there . . . naturally she'd want her card back. Did he care what she heard? He took his courage in both hands and tapped out the number.

A girl answered: ten years old, very curly blond hair, cute, with a serious look. "Brenda's."

"Can I talk to Brenda Curtis?"

"She's on the roof."

"Will you get her, please?"

"No, we don't bother her when she's on the roof."

"Oh. Okay. Tell her I called. Terry Kakumee. When should I call back?"

"After dinner. About eighteen."

"Thanks." Something about the girl . . . "Is Brenda your mother?"

"Yes. I'm Reseda Anderssen." The girl hung up.

Maria was looking at him. "You know Brenda Curtis?"

"I used to. How do you know her?"

"She runs the orphanage. I know one of her boys. Not hers, I mean, but one of the boys she raised."

"Tell me about her."

Maria shrug-sniffed. Maybe talking about another woman wasn't what she'd had in mind. "She moved to a swamp farm after the Battle of Tanith. The City paid her money to keep orphans, and I guess there were a lot of them. Not so many now. Lots of teenagers. They've got their own skewball team, and they've had the pennant two years running."

"She was in bad shape when I knew her. Head wound. Does her lip pull up on one side when she talks?"

"Not that I noticed."

"Well," he said, "I'm glad she's doing okay."

Thinking of her as a patient might have put a different light on things. Maria took his arm again. They made an interesting match, Terry thought. Same height, both rounded in the body, and almost the same shade of hair and skin. She asked, "Was she in the Navy? Like Mr. Laine—"

"No."

"How did she get hurt?"

"Maria, I'm not sure that's been declassified. She wasn't in the Navy, but she got involved with the Sauron thing anyway." And he wouldn't tell her any more.

2640A, November (Tanith local time):

He'd taken Dr. Hartner to dinner partly because he felt sorry for him, partly to get him talking.

Lex Hartner was thin all over, with a long, narrow face and wispy blond hair. Terry would always remember him as tired . . . but that was unfair. Every doctor on Tanith lived at the edge of exhaustion after the battle of Tanith.

"Your friend'll heal," he told Terry. "He was lucky. One of the first patients in after the battle. We still had eyes in stock, and we had a regeneration sleeve. His real problem is, we'll have to take it off him as soon as he can live without it."

"Scars be damned?"

"Oh, he'll scar. They wouldn't be as bad if we left the sleeve on him longer. But *Napoleon's* coming in with burn cases—"

"Yeah. I wouldn't want your job."

"This is the hardest part."

It was clear to Terry: there was no way to talk Lex into leaving Charley in the sleeve for a little longer. So he changed the subject. "That woman in the hall this morning—"

Lex didn't ask who he meant. "We don't have a name yet. She appeared at a swamp farm south of here. Mrs. Maddox called the hospital. We sent an ambulance. She must have come out of the swamps. From the look of her, she was there for some time."

"She didn't look good."

"She's malnourished. There's fungus all over her. Bantar cloth doesn't let air through. You have to wear net underwear, and hers was rotted to shreds. That head wound gouged her skull almost through the bone. Beyond that I just can't tell, Terry. I don't have the instruments."

Terry nodded; he didn't have to ask about that.

There had been one massive burn-through during the Battle of Tanith. Raw plasma had washed across several city blocks for three or four seconds. A hotel had been slagged, and shops and houses, and a stream of flame had rolled up the dome and hovered at the apex while it died. The hospital had lost most of its windows . . . and every piece of equipment that could be ruined by an electromagnetic pulse.

"There's just no way to look inside her head. I don't want to open her up. She's coming along nicely, she can say a few words, and she can draw and use sign language. And she tries so hard."

All of which Terry told to Charley the next day. They'd told him Charley wasn't conscious most of the time; but Terry pictured him going nuts from boredom inside that pillow.

2656, June (Tanith local time)

The bar had turned noisy. At the big table you could still hear Charley. "Boredom. You spend months getting to and from the Jump points. We've played every game program in ship's memory half to death. I think any one of us could beat anyone on Tanith at Rollerball, Chance, the Mirror Game—"

"We've got a Mirror Game," someone said. "It's in the Library."

"Great!"

Someone pushed two chairs into the pattern for Maria and Terry. Charley was saying, "We did find something interesting this trip. There's a Sauron ship in orbit around EST 1310. We knew it was there, we could hear it every time we used the jump points, but EST 1310 is a flare star. We didn't dare go after it. But this trip we're carrying a mucking great Langston Field generator in the cargo hold . . ."

Captain Sharon looked dubious. Charley was talking a lot. They'd pulled valuable data from the Sauron wreck, saleable data. But so what? Tanith couldn't reach the ship, and maybe they should be considered customers. And Brenda might hear. Let him talk.

"It was *Morningstar*, a Sauron hornet ship. The Saurons must have gutted it for anything they could use on other ships, then turned it into a signalling beacon. They'd left the computer. They had to have that to work the message sender. We disarmed some booby traps and managed to get into the programming . . ."

People drifted away, presumably to run the airport. Others came in. The party was shaping up as a long one. Terry was minded to stay. He'd maintained a pleasant buzz, and Brenda had waited for sixteen years. She'd wait longer.

At seven he spoke into Maria's ear. "I'd be pleased to take you to dinner, if you can guide me to a restaurant."

She said, "Good! But don't you like parties?"

"Oh, hell yes. Stick with the crowd?"

"Good. Till later."

"I still have to make that phone call."

She nodded vigorously and fished her card out of a pocket. He got up and went back to the public phones.

2640A, November (Tanith local time):

When *Firebee's* Shuttle #2 came down, there had been no repair facilities left on Tanith. There was little for a Second Engineer to do.

Napoleon changed that. *Napoleon* was an old Spartan troopship arriving in the wake of the Battle of Tanith. Word had it that it was loaded with repair equipment. Now *Napoleon's* shuttles were bringing stuff down, and *Napoleon's* Purser was hearing requests from other ships in need of repairs.

Captain Shu and the others would be cutting their own deals in orbit. Terry and Charley were the only ones on the ground. Terry spent four days going through Shuttle #2, listing everything the little GO craft would need. When he went begging to *Napoleon's* Spartan officers, he wanted to know exactly what to ask for. He made three lists: maximum repairs if he could get them, the minimum he could settle for, and a third list no other plaintiff would have made. He hoped.

He hadn't visited Charley in four days.

The tall dark woman in the corridor caught his attention. He would have remembered her. She was eight inches taller than Terry, in a dressing gown too short for her and a puffy shower cap. She was more striking than beautiful: square-jawed and lean enough to show ribs and hip bones where the cloth pulled taut.

She caught him looking and smiled with one side of her face. "He'o! I member you!" Her lip tugged way up on the left.

"Oh, it's you," Terry said. Six days ago: the head wound case. "Hey, you can talk! That's good. I'm Terry Kakumee."

"Benda Curris."

It was an odd name. "Benda?"

"Br, renda. Cur, tiss."

"Brenda. Sorry. What were you doing out there in the swamps?" He instantly added, "Does it tire you to talk?"

She spoke slowly and carefully. "Yes. I told my story to the Marines and Navy officers and Doctor Hartner. I don't like it. You wo—wouldn't like it. They smiled a lot when we all knew I wasn't pregnant." She didn't seem to see Terry's bewilderment. "You're Charley's friend. He'd out of the re-gener-ation sleeve."

"Can he have visitors?"

"Ssure. I'll take you."

Charley wasn't a pillow any more. He didn't look good, either. Wasted. Burned. He didn't move much on the water bed. His lips weren't quite mobile enough; he sounded a bit like Brenda. "There are four regeneration sleeves on Tanith, and one tank to make the goo, and when they wear out there's nothing. My sleeve is on a Marine from Tabletop. Burn patient, like me. I asked. I see you've met Brenda?"

"Yeah."

"She went through a hell of an experience. We don't talk about it. So how's the work coming?"

"I'll go to the Purser tomorrow. I want all my ducks in a row, but I don't want everyone getting their requests in ahead of me either. I made a list of things we could give up to other ships. That might help."

"Good idea. Very Eskimo."

"Charley, it isn't really. The old traditions have us giving a stranger what he needs whether we need it or not."

He noticed Brenda staring at him. She said, "How strange."

He laughed a little uncomfortably. "I suppose a stranger wouldn't ask for what the village had to have. Anyway, those days are almost gone."

Brenda listened while they talked about the ship. She wouldn't understand much of it, though both men tried to explain from time to time. "The Langston Field is your reentry shield and your weapons shield and your true hull. We'll never get it repaired, but *Firebee* could still function in the outer system. I'm trying to get the shuttles rebuilt. Maybe we can make her a trader. She sure isn't part of a Navy any more."

Charley said, "The Tanith asteroids aren't mined out."

"So?"

"Asteroids. Metal. Build a metal shell around *Firebee* for a hull."

"Charley, you'd double her mass!"

"We could still run her around the inner system. If we could get a tank from some wrecked ship, a detachable fuel tank, we'd be interstellar again." His eyes flicked to Brenda and he said, "With more fuel we could still get to the Jump points and back. Everything'd be slower, we couldn't outrun anything . . . have to stay away from bandits . . ."

"You're onto something. Charley, we don't really want to be asteroid miners for five years. But if we could find *two* good tanks—"

"Ahhh! One for a hull. Big. Off a battleship, say."

"Yeah."

"Terry, I'm tired," Charley said suddenly, plaintively. "Take Brenda to dinner? They let her out."

"Brenda? I'd be honored."

She smiled one-sided.

November was twelve days long on Tanith, and there wasn't any December. Every so often they put the same number on two consecutive years, to stay even with Spartan time.

In November Dagon City was dark eighteen hours out of twenty-one-plus. The street lighting was back, but snatchers were still a problem. Maybe Terry's uniform protected him; and he went armed, of course.

He took her to a place that was still passable despite the shortages.

He did most of the talking. She'd never heard of the Nuliajuk migration. He told her how the CoDominium had moved twenty thousand Eskimos, tribes all mixed together, to a world too cold for the comfort of other peoples.

They'd settled the equator, where the edges of the ice caps almost met. They'd named the world for a myth-figure common to all the tribes, though names differed: the old woman at the bottom of the sea who brought game or withheld it. There was native sea life, and the imported seals and walruses and bears throve too. Various tribes taught each other their secrets. Some had never seen a seal, some had never built an igloo.

The colony throve; but the men studied fusion and Langston Field engineering, and many wound up on Navy and merchant ships. Eskimos don't really like to freeze. The engine room of a Navy ship is a better place, and Eskimos of all tribes have a knack with tools.

Nuliajuk was near Sol and Sparta. It might still be part of the shrinking Empire, but Terry had never seen it. He was a half-breed, born in a Libertarian merchant ship. What he knew of Nuliajuk came from his father.

And Brenda had lived all her life on a Tanith farm. "I took my education from a TV wall. No hands-on, but I learned enough to fix our machines. We had a fusion plant and some Gaineses and Tofflers. Those are special tractors. Maybe the Saurons left them alone."

"Saurons?"

"Sorry." Her grimace twisted her whole face around. "I spent the last four days talking about nothing else. I own that farm now. I don't own anything else." She studied him thoughtfully. Her face in repose was symmetrical enough, square-jawed, strong even by Tanith standards. "Would you like to see it?"

"What?"

"Would you like to see my farm? Can you borrow a plane?"

They set it up for two days hence.

2656, June (Tanith local time)

Brenda's face lit when she saw him. "Terry! Have you gotten rich? Have you saved civilization? Have you had fun?"

"No, yes, yes. How are you?"

"You can see, can't you? It's all over, Terry. No more nightmares." He'd never seen her bubble like this. There was no slur in her voice . . . but he could see the twitch at the left side of her mouth. Her face was animated on the right, calmer on the left. Her hair bloomed around her head like a great black dandelion, teased, nearly a foot across. The scar must have healed completely. She'd gained some weight.

He remembered that he had loved her. (But he didn't remember her having nightmares.)

"They tell me you opened an orphanage."

"Yeah, I had twenty kids in one schlumph," she said. "The city gave me financing to put the farm back on its legs, and there were plenty of workmen to hire, but I thought I'd go nuts taking care of the children and the farm both. It's easier now. The older kids are my farmers, and they learn to take care of the younger ones. Two of them got married and went off to start their own farm. Three are in college, and the oldest boy's in the Navy. I'm back down to twenty kids."

"How many of your own? I met Reseda."

"Four. She's the youngest. And one who died."

"I guess I'm surprised you moved back to the farm."

She shook her head. "I did it right. The children took the curse off the memories. So how are you? You must have stories to tell. What are you doing now?"

"There's a party at the spaceport and we're the stars. Want to join us?"

"No. Busy."

"Can I come out there? Like tomorrow, noon or thereabouts?"

He was watching for hesitation, but it was too quick to be sure. "Good. Come. Noon is fine. You remember how to get here? And noon is just past eleven?"

"And midnight is twenty-two twenty."

"Right. See you then."

He hung up. Now: summon the Library function on the computer? He wondered how much of the Sauron story was still classified. But a party was running, and a spaceman learned to differentiate: there was a time for urgency and a time to hang loose.

When he pushed back into the crowd, Maria grabbed his arm and shouted in his ear. "Mayor Anderssen!" She pointed.

The Mayor nodded and smiled. He was tall, in his late thirties, with pale skin and ash-blond hair and a wispy beard. Terry reached across the table to offer his hand. The Mayor put something in it. "Card," he shouted. "Temporary."

"Thanks."

The Mayor circled the table and pulled up a chair next to him. "You're the city's guest while you're down. Restaurants, hotels, taxis, rentals."

"Very generous. How can we repay you?"

"Your Captain has already agreed to some interviews. Will you do the same? We're starved for news. I talked Purser Laine into speaking on radio."

"Fine by me. I'm busy tomorrow, though."

"I got a call from a friend of mine, a Brenda Curtis. She says she used to know you—"

"I just called her a minute ago. Hey, one of her kids—"

"Reseda. My daughter. Brenda isn't married, but she's had four children, and she's got something going with a neighbor, Bob Maddox. Anyway, she called to find out if I was getting you cards, which I already was."

Terry's memory told him that nuclear families were the rule on Tanith. "An unusual life style," he said.

"Not so unusual. We've got more men than women. Four hundred ships wrecked in the Battle. Lots of rescue action. Some of the crews reached Tanith and never went any further. We tend to be generous with child support, and there are specialized marriage contracts. Can you picture the crime rate if every woman thought she had to get married?"

Tanith had changed.

Maria handed Terry a drink, something with fruit and rum. He sipped, and wondered.

Brenda must have called the Mayor as soon as the little girl told her about his first call. He remembered an injured woman trying to put her life back together. She'd been in no position to do spur-of-the-moment favors for others. Brenda had changed too.

2640A, November (Tanith local time):

"We're trying to save civilization," *Napoleon's* Purser lectured Terry. "Not individual ships. If Tanith doesn't have *some* working spacecraft, it won't survive until the Empire gets things straightened out. So. We're giving you— *Firebee?*—if you want it. The terms say that you have to run it as a merchant ship or lose it. That's if we decide it's worth repairing. Otherwise—well. We'll have to give any working parts to someone else."

Arrogant, harassed, defensive. He was dispensing other people's property as charity. The way he used the word *give*—

They discussed details. Terry's third list surprised him. He studied it. "Your drives are intact? Alderson and fusion both?"

"Running like new. They are new, almost." Terry knew the danger here. *Firebee* was alive if her drives were alive . . . and some other ship might want those drives.

"Well. I don't know anyone who needs these spares, offhand, except . . . we'll record these diagnostic programs. Very bright of you to list these. Some of our ships lost most of their data to EMPs. Can I copy this list?"

"Yessir."

"I can give you a rebuilt fusion zap. You'd never leave orbit without that, would you? We can re-core the hover motors on your #2 boat. Spinner for the air plant if you can mount it. *Don't* tell me you can if you can't. Someone else might need it. You could ruin it trying to make it fit."

"I can fit it."

"I dare say. Nuliajuk?"

"Halfbreed. Libertarian mother."

"Look, our engineers aren't Esks *or* Scots, but they've been with us for years. So we can't hire you ourselves, but some other ship—"

"I'd rather make *Firebee* fly again."

"Good luck. I can't give you any more."

From the temporary port he went directly to the

hospital. Lex Hartner was in surgery. Terry visited with Charley until Lex came out.

"Brenda Curtis invited me to visit her farm with her. Anything I should know? What's likely to upset her?"

Lex stared at him in astonishment. He said, "Take a gun. A big gun."

"For what?"

"Man, you missed some excitement here. Brenda said something to a nurse a couple of days after she got here. You know what happened to her?"

"She doesn't want to talk about it."

"She sure doesn't, and I don't blame her, but the more she said the more the Navy wanted. She'd have died of exhaustion if I hadn't dragged her away a couple of times. She was kidnapped by two Saurons! They killed the whole family."

"On Tanith itself?"

"Yeah, a landing craft got down. More like a two-seater escape pod, I guess. I haven't seen pictures. It came down near an outback farm, way south. The Saurons killed off her family from ambush. They stayed on the farm for a month. She . . . belonged to one of them." Lex was wringing his hands. Likely he didn't know it. "We looked her over to see if she was pregnant."

"I should think you bloody would! Can they still breed with human beings?" Rumor had it that some of the Sauron genes had been borrowed from animals.

"We won't find out from Brenda. She's had a child, though. It probably died at the farm. She won't talk about that either."

"Lord. How did she get away?"

"One went off by himself. Maybe they fought over Brenda. The other one stayed. One day a Weem's beast came out of the water and attacked them in the rice paddy. It clawed her; that's how she got the head wound. When she got the blood out of her eyes the Sauron was dead and so was the Weem's beast. So she started walking. She had to live for two weeks in the swamps, with that wound. Hell of a woman."

"Yeah. You're telling me there's a Sauron loose on Tanith."

"Yup. They're hunting for him. She took the Marines to the farm, and they found the escape pod and the corpse. I've been doing the autopsy. You can see where they got the traits—"

"Animal?"

"No, that's just a rumor. It's all human, but the way it's put together . . . think of Frankenstein's monster. A bit here, a bit there, the shape changes a little. Maybe add an extra Y gene to turn it mean. I'm guessing there. The high-power microscope's down."

"The other one?"

"Could be anywhere. He's had almost a month."

"Not likely he'd stick around. Okay, I'll take a big gun. Anything else I should know?"

"I don't know how she'll react. Terry, I'll give you a trank spray. Put her out if she gets hysterical and get her back here fast. Other than that . . . watch her. See if you think she can live on that farm. Bad memories there. I think she should sell the place."

2656, June (Tanith local time)

Dinner expeditions formed and went off in three directions. The cluster that took Terry along still crowded the restaurant. A blackboard offered a single meal of several courses, Spartan cooking strangely mutated by local ingredients.

The time change caught up with him as desserts arrived. "I'm running out of steam," he told Maria Montez.

"Okay." She led him out and waved at a taxi. The gray-haired driver recognised him for what he was. She kept him talking all the way to Maria's apartment house. She wasn't interested in planets; it was the space between that held her imagination.

On the doorstep Maria carefully explained that Terry couldn't possibly presume on an acquaintanceship of one afternoon (though he hadn't asked yet.) She kissed him quickly and went inside.

Terry started down the steps, grinning. Customs differ. Now where the hell was he, and where was a taxi likely to be hiding?

So Brenda was alive and doing well. Friend of the Mayor. Running an orphanage. Four children. Well, well.

Maria came out running. "I forgot, you don't have a place to stay! Terry, you can come in and sleep on the couch if you promise to behave yourself."

"I can't really do that, Maria, but if you'll call me a taxi?"

She was affronted. "Why not?"

He went back up the steps. "I haven't set foot on a world for four months. I haven't held a woman in my arms in longer than that. Now, we heroes have infinite self-control—"

"But—"

"I could probably leave you alone all night. But I wouldn't sleep and I'd wake up depressed and frustrated. So what I want is a hotel."

She thought it over. "Come in. Have some coffee."

"Were you listening?"

"Come in."

They entered. The place was low-tech but roomy. He asked, "Was I supposed to lie?"

"It's not a lie, exactly. It just, just leaves things open. Like I could be telling you we could have some coffee and then get you a taxi, and we could wind up sniffing some borloi, and . . . you could be persuasive?"

"Nuliajuks lie. It's called tact. My mother made sure I knew how to keep a promise. She wasn't just a Libertarian. She was a Randist."

Maria smiled at him, much amused. "Four months, hey? But you should learn to play the game, Terry."

He shook his head. "There's a different game on every world, almost in every city. I can't sniff borloi with you either. I tried it once. That stuff could hook me fast. I just have to depend on charisma."

She had found a small bottle. "Take a couple of

these. Vitamins, hangover formula. Take lots of water. Does wonders for the charisma."

Maria made scrambled eggs with sausage and fungus, wrapped in chili leaves. It woke him up fast and made him forget his hangover. He'd been looking forward to Tanith cooking.

There were calls registered on his pocket computer. He used Maria's phone. Nobody answered at Polar Datafile or Other Worlds. When he looked at his watch it was just seven o'clock.

No wonder Maria was yawning. She'd woken when he did, and that must have been about six. "Hey, I'm sorry. It's the time change."

"No sweat, Terry. I'll sleep after you leave. Want to go back to bed?"

He tried again later. Polar Datafile wanted him tomorrow, five o'clock news. An interviewer for Other Worlds wanted all three astronauts for two days, maybe more. Good payment, half in gold, for exclusive rights. How exclusive? he asked. She reassured him: radio and TV spots would be considered as publicity. What she wanted was depth, and no other vidtapes competing. He set it up.

He called Information. "I need to rent a plane."

Maria watched him with big dark eyes. "Brenda Curtis?"

"Right." The number answered, and he dealt with it. A hoverplane would pick him up at the door. He was expected to return the pilot to the airport and then go about his business. How far did he expect to fly? About forty miles round trip.

Maria asked, "Were you in love with her?"

"For about two months."

"Are you going to tell her about us?"

That might put both women in danger. "No. In fact, I'm going to get a hotel room—"

"Damn your eyes, Terry Kakumee!"

"I'll be back tonight, Maria. I've got my reasons. No, I can't tell you what they are."

"All right. Are they honest?"

"I . . . dammit. They're right on the edge."

She studied his face. "Can you tell me after it's over?"

". . . No." Either way, he wouldn't be able to do that.

"Okay. Come back tonight." She wasn't happy. He didn't blame her.

The land had more color than he remembered. Fields of strange flowers bloomed in the swampland. Huge dark purple petals crowned plants the size of trees. A field of sunlovers, silver ahead of him, turned green in his rear view camera.

Farms were sparse pale patches in all that color. In the wake of the Battle of Tanith they had had a scruffy look. They were neater now, with more rice and fewer orange plots of borloi. The outworld market for the drug had disintegrated, of course.

He should be getting close. He took the plane higher. Farms all looked alike, but the crater wouldn't have disappeared.

It was there, several miles south, a perfect circle of lake . . .

2640B, January (Tanith local time)

. . . A perfect circle of lake surrounded by blasted trees lying radially outward. "A big ship made a big bang when it fell," Brenda said. She was wearing dark glasses, slacks and a chamois shirt. Her diction was as precise as she could make it, but he still had to listen hard. A Tanith farm girl's accent probably slurred it further. "We were on the roof. We wanted to watch the battle."

"Sauron or Empire ship?"

"We never knew. It was only a light. Bright enough to fry the eyeballs. It gave us enough warning. We threw ourselves flat. We would have been blown off the roof."

They turned east. Presently he asked, "Is that your farm?"

"No. There, beyond."

Four miles east of the fresh crater, a wide stretch of rice paddies. The other farm was miles closer. The Saurons must have gone around it. Why?

They'd passed other farms. Here the paddies seemed to be going back to the wild. The house nestled on a rise of ground. The roof was flat, furnished with tables and chairs and a swimming pool in the shape of a bloobby eagle. The walls sloped inward.

"You don't like windows?"

"No. It rains. When it doesn't, we work outside. On a good day we all went up on the roof."

The door showed signs of damage. It might have been blasted from its hinges, then re-hung.

Lights came on as they entered. Terry trailed Brenda as she moved through the house.

Pantry shelves were in neat array, but depleted. The fridge was empty. The freezer was working, but it stank. He told her, "There've been power failures. You'll have to throw all this out." She sniffed; half her face wrinkled.

He found few obvious signs of damage. Missing furniture had left its marks on the living room floor, and the walls had been freshly painted.

There were muddy footprints everywhere. "The Marines did that," Brenda said.

"Did they find anything?"

"Not here. Not even dry blood. Horatius made me clean up. They found the escape pod three miles away."

Beds in the master bedroom were neatly made. Brenda turned on the TV wall and got Dagon City's single station, and a picture of Boat #1 floating gracefully toward the landing field. "This works too."

Terry shook his head. "What did these Saurons look like?"

"Randus was bizarre. Horatius was more human—"

"It looks like he was ready to stay here. To pass himself off as a man, an ordinary farmer."

She paused. "He could have done that. It may be why he left. We never saw a Sauron on Tanith. He was

muscular. His bones were heavy. He looked . . . round
shoulders. His eyes had an epicanthic fold, and the
pupils were black, jet black." Pause. "He made sex like
an attack."

The smiling faces of *Firebee's* crew flashed and died.
The lights died too. Terry said, "Foo."

"Never mind." Brenda took his arm and led him two
steps backward through the dark. The bed touched his
knees and he sat.

"What did Randus look like?"

"A monster. I hated Horatius, but I wanted him to
protect me from Randus."

Could he pass as a farmer? He'd have to hide Randus
the monster and Brenda the prisoner, or kill them. But
he hadn't. Honor among Saurons? Or . . . leave the
monster to guard his woman. Find or carve a safe
house. Come back later, see if it worked. The risk
would not be to Horatius. So.

"Did Horatius think you were pregnant?"

"Maybe. Terry, I would like to take the taste of
Horatius out of my mind."

"Time will do that."

"Sex will do that."

He tried to look at her. He saw nothing. They were
sitting on a water bed in darkness like a womb.

"I haven't been with a woman in over a year. Brenda,
are you sure you're ready for this?" He hadn't thought
to ask Lex about *this!*

She pulled him to his feet, hands on his upper arms.
Strong! "You're a good man, Terry. I've watched you. I
couldn't do better. Do you maybe think I'm too tall for
you?" She pulled him against her, and his cheek was
against her breasts. "You can't do this with a short
woman."

"Not standing up." His arms went around her, but
how could he help that?

"Is it my face? We're in the dark." He could hear her
amusement.

"Brenda, I'm not exactly fighting. It's just, I still
think of you as a patient."

"So be patient."

She didn't need patience. She had none herself. He'd expected the aftereffects of the head wound to make her clumsy. She was, a little. She came on as if she would swallow him up and go looking for dessert. He was apalled, then delighted, then . . . exhausted, but she wouldn't let him go . . .

He woke in darkness. He wasn't tempted to move. The water bed was kind to his gravity-abused muscles. He felt the warmth of the woman in his arms, and presently knew that she was awake.

No warning: she attacked.

She disappeared into the dark like a vampire leaving her victim. She draped his clothes over him and dropped the heavy flechette gun on his belly. He giggled, and presently dressed.

She led him stumbling through a black maze and out into the dusk of a winter morning. "There. After all, I know the house."

"This is the trouble with not having windows," he groused.

"Weem's beasts like windows too. In rain they can come this far."

The graveyard was eight stone markers cut with a vari-saw, letters and numbers cut with a laser. "The names and dates are wrong, except these old ones," she said. "Horatius hoped it would look like they all died many years ago. I'll get a chisel or a laser to fix it."

There was no *small* grave. "Lex told me you had a child."

"Miranda. He took her with him."

"God." He took her in his arms. "Did you tell the Marines?"

"No. I . . . try not to think about Miranda."

There was nothing more to see. She told him that the Navy men had found Randus' skeleton and taken that, and sent out a big copter for the rescue pod. When the lights came on around noon, Terry helped Brenda clean up the mudstains and empty the freezer and fridge.

"I need money to run the farm," Brenda said. "Maybe someone will hire me for work in Dagon."

"Why not sell the place?"

"It was ours for too long. It won't be bad. You can see for yourself, the Saurons left no trace. No trace at all."

2656, June (Tanith local time)

Four miles east of the crater. He should be near. He was crossing extensive fields of rice. A dozen men and women worked knee-deep in water that glinted through the stalks like fragments of a shattered mirror. A man stood by with a gun. Terry swooped low, lowered his flaps, hovered. Several figures waved.

They were all children.

He set the plane down. The gun-carrier broke off work and came toward him. Terry waded to meet him; what the hell. "Brenda Curtis's?"

The boy had an oriental look despite the black, kinky hair. He grinned and said, "Where else would you find all these kids? I'm Tarzan Kakumee."

"Terry Kakumee. I'm visiting. You've be about sixteen?"

The boy's jaw dropped. "Seventeen, but that's Tanith time. Kakumee? Astronaut? You'd be my father!"

"Yeah. Can I stare a little?"

They examined each other. Tarzan was an inch or two taller than Terry, narrower in the hips and face and chest, and his square jaw was definitely Brenda's. Black eyes with an oriental slant: Terry and Brenda both had that. The foolish grins felt identical.

"I'm on duty," Tarzan said. "I'll see you later?"

"Can't you come with me? I'm due for lunch."

"No, I've got my orders. There are Weem's beasts and other things around here. I once shot a tax collector the size of my arm. It had its suckers in Gerard's leg and Gerard was screaming bloody murder." Tarzan grinned. "I blew it right off him."

Smaller fields of different colors surrounded a sprawling structure. If that was the farmhouse it had doubled

in size . . . right. He could make out the original farmhouse in the center. The additions had windows.

Fields of melons, breadfruit, and sugar cane surrounded the house. Three children in a mango grove
broke off work to watch him land.

Brenda came through the door with a man beside
her.

He knew her at once. (But was it her?) She waved
both arms and ran to meet him. (She'd changed.) "Terry,
I'm so glad to see you! The way you went off—my fault,
of course, but I kept wondering what had happened to
you out there and why you didn't come back!" Her
dress looked like current Tanith style, cut above the
knee and high at the neck. Her grip on his arm was
farmhand-strong. "You wouldn't have had to see me, it
just would have been good to know — Well, it *is* good to
know you're alive and doing all right! Bob, this is Terry
Kakumee the astronaut. Terry, Bob Maddox is my neighbor three miles southeast."

"Pleased to meet you." Bob Maddox was a brown-
haired white man, freckled and tanned. He was large
all over, and his hand was huge, big-knuckled and
rough with work. "Brenda's told me about you. How's
your ship?"

"Truth? *Firebee* is gradually and gracefully disinte-
grating. There's a double hull instead of a Langston
Field, and we have to patch it every so often. We got
Boat #1 repaired on Phoenix. Maybe we can hold it all
together till the Empire gets back out here. You interested in spaceflight?"

Maddox hesitated. "Not really. I mean, it's surprising
more of us don't want to build rocket ships, consider-
ing. We weren't all transportees, our ancestors."

Brenda turned at the door. She clapped her hands
twice and jerked her thumb. The children who had
been climbing over Terry's rental plane, dropped off
and scampered happily back toward the mangoes.

They went in. Reseda Anderssen, busy at a samovar,
smiled at them and went out through another door.
There was new furniture, couches and small tables and

piles of pillows, enough to leave the living room quite cluttered. Brenda saw him looking and said, "Some of the kids sleep in here."

It didn't look it. "You keep them neat." He noticed noises coming from what he remembered as the kitchen.

"I've got a real knack for teaching. Have some tea?"

"Borloi tea? I'd better not."

"I made Earl Grey." She poured three cups. She'd always had grace, even with the head injury to scramble the signals. He could see just a trace of her lip pulling up on the left when she spoke. She settled him and Bob on a couch and faced them. "Now talk. Where've you been?"

"Phoenix. Gafia. Hitchhiker's Rest. Medea. Uhura. We commute. We tried Lenin, but three outie ships came after us. We ran and didn't come back, and that cuts us off from the planets beyond. And we found a Sauron ship at EST 1310."

It was Maddox who stared. "Well, go on! What's left of it? Were there Saurons?"

"Bob, we were clever. We knew there was a ship there because we caught the signal every time we used the jump points to get to Medea. We couldn't get down there because the star's a flare star and we don't have a Langston Field.

"Only, this time we do. Phoenix sold us—actually, they *gave* us a mucking great Langston Field generator. We left it on. We moved in and matched orbit with the signal ship, and we expanded the field to put both ships inside."

"Clever, right. Terry, we Taniths are a little twitchy about Saurons—"

"Just one. Dead. They rifled it and left it for a message beacon. They left a Sauron on duty. Maybe a flare got him." The corpse had been a skewed man-shape, a bogie man. Like Randus? "I managed to get into the programming. Now we're thinking of going on to Sparta. We learned some things they might want to know."

"Let me just check on lunch," Brenda said, and she went.

It left Terry feeling awkward. Maddox said, "So there are still Sauron supermen out there?"

"Just maybe. The beacon was set to direct Saurons to a Jump point in that system. Maybe nobody ever got the message. If they did, I don't know where they went. I ran the record into *Firebee's* memory and ran a translation program on it, but I didn't look at the result. I'd have to go back to *Firebee*, then come back here."

Maddox grimaced. "We don't have ships to do anything about it. Sparta might. I'd be inclined to leave them the hell alone."

"Did they ever catch—"

"Nope. Lot of excitement. Every so often some nut comes screaming that he saw a Sauron in the marshes. The Mayor's got descriptions of a Sauron officer, and he says they don't check out. How the hell could that thing still be hiding?"

"Those two must have gone right past your place to get here."

"Yeah. Brenda had to backtrack to get to my place. Weeks in the wild, fungus and tax collectors, polluted water, God knows what she ate . . . Well, yeah, I've wondered. Maybe they saw we had guns."

"That's not it."

Bob hesitated. "Okay, why?"

He'd spoken without thinking. "You'd think I'm crazy. Anyway, I could be wrong."

"Kakumee, everyone knows more about Saurons than the guy he's talking to. It's like skewball scores. What I want to know about is, I never saw Brenda's lip curl up like that when she talks."

"Old head injury."

"I haven't seen her face do that since the day she staggered through my gate. I wonder if meeting you again might be upsetting her."

Bob Maddox was coming on like a protective husband. Terry asked, "Have you thought of marriage?"

"That's none of your business, Kakumee—"

"Brenda's—"

"—But I've asked, and she won't." His voice was still

low and reasonably calm. "She'd rather live alone, and I don't know why. Ventura's mine."

"I haven't met her."

"I guess I don't mind you worrying over Brenda. Have you met any of the kids?"

"Yeah—"

Brenda was back. "We can serve any time you get hungry. Terry, can you stay for dinner? You could meet the rest of the children. They'll be coming in around five."

"I'd like that. Bob, feel like lunchtime?"

"Yeah."

The men hung back for a moment. "I'll leave after dinner," Terry said. "I tell you, though, I don't think anything's bothering Brenda. She's tougher than that."

Bob nodded. "Tough lady. Kakumee, I think she's working on how to tell you one of the kids is yours."

2640B, January to March (Tanith local time)

Their idyll lasted two months.

They made an odd couple. Tall and lean; short and round. He could see it in the mirror, he could see the amusement in strangers and friends too.

Terry's rented room was large enough for both. Brenda began buying clothes and other things after she had a job, but she never crowded the closets. Brenda cleaned. Terry did all the cooking. It was the only task he'd ever seen her fail at.

He was busy much of the time. In a week the work on Boat #2 was finished. There were parts for Boat #1, and he carried them to orbit to work. Boat #1 still wouldn't be able to make a reentry.

He talked *Napoleon's* Purser out of a ruined battleship's hydrogen tank. Over a period of three weeks (with two two-day leaves in Dagon) Terry and the rest of the crew moved *Firebee* into it. Had Charley been thinking in terms of a regeneration sleeve for the ship?

Firebee was now the silliest-looking ship since the original Space Shuttle, and too massive for interstellar capability. Without an auxiliary tank she couldn't even use a Jump point with any hope of reaching a planet on the far side.

Captain Shu had done something about that. *Firebee* now owned a small H2 tank aboard *Armadillo*, but they'd have to wait for it to arrive. Terry went back down to Dagon City.

Brenda was still attending the clinic every two days. She was working there too, and trying to arrange something with the local government. She wouldn't talk about that; she wasn't sure it would work.

He made her a different offer. "Four of our crew want to stay. Cropland doesn't cost much on Tanith. But you've got a knack for machines. Let me teach you how to make repairs on *Firebee*. Come as my apprentice."

"Terry—"

"And wife."

"I get motion sickness."

"*Damn*." There had never been a lover like Brenda. She could play his nervous system like a violin. She knew his moods. She maintained civilization around him. The thought of leaving her made him queasy.

Armadillo had won an expensive victory in the outer Tanith system. The hulk was just capable of thrust, and it didn't reach Tanith until months after the battle. Then crews from other ships swarmed over it and took it apart. *Firebee's* crew came back with an intact tank and fuel feed system. Terry had to tear that apart and put it together different, in vacuum. It would ride outside the second hull.

Firebee was fragile now, fit to be a trader, but never a warship or a miner.

Charley was in decent shape by then and working out in a local gym. He came up to help weld the fuel tank. He seemed fit for space. "Captain Shu wants to go home, but we've got you and me and Sharon Hayes and that kid off *Napoleon*, Murray Weiss. I say we go interstellar."

"I know you do, but think about it, Charley. No defenses. We can haul cargo back and forth between the mining asteroids, and if outies ever come to take over we'd have someplace to run to."

"And you could see Brenda every couple of months."

The argument terminated when Terry returned to Dagon.

Brenda was gone. Brenda's clothes were gone. There was a phone message from Lex Hartner; he looked grim and embarrassed.

Phoning him felt almost superfluous, but Terry did it.

"We've been seeing each other," Lex said. "I think she's carrying my child. Terry, I want to marry her."

"Good luck to you." The days in which an Ihalmiut hunter might gather up a band of friends and hunt down a bride were long ago, far away. He considered it anyway. And went to the stars instead.

2656, June (Tanith local time)

Reseda and three younger children served lunch, then joined them at the table. Three more came in from the fields. There was considerable chatter. Terry found he was doing a lot of the talking.

Dessert was mangos still hot from the sun.

Brenda went away and came back wearing a bantar cloth coverall. It was the garment she'd worn the day she reached the hospital, like as not, but much cleaner. The three adults spent the afternoon pulling weeds in the sugar cane. Brenda and Bob Maddox instructed him by turns.

Terry had never done field work. He found he was enjoying himself, sweating in the sun.

The sun arced around the horizon, dropping gradually. Other children came flocking from the rice fields shortly after five. The adults pulled weeds for a little longer, then joined the children in the courtyard. He could smell his own sweat, and Bob's, different by race or by diet.

Twenty children all grinned at some shared joke. Brenda must have briefed them. When?

"Brenda, I can sort them out," Terry said.

"Go ahead."

"The Mayor already told me Reseda was his. The freckled girl must be Ventura Maddox. Hello, Ventura!" She was big for twelve, tanned dark despite the freckles, and round in the face, like Bob himself. A tall girl, older, had Brenda's tightly kinked black hair, pale skin and a pointed chin. "I don't know her name, but she's . . . Lex's?" Lex's face, but it would still be a remarkable thing.

"Yes, that's Sepulveda."

"Hello, Sepulveda. And the boy—" Tarzan grinned at him but didn't wave. Tactful: he didn't know whether they were supposed to have met. "—is mine."

"Right again. Terry, meet Tarzan."

"Hello, Tarzan. Brenda, I set down in the rice field before I got here."

She laughed. "Dammit, Terry! I had it all planned."

"And they're named for suburbs of some city on Earth."

"I never thought you'd see *that*."

A different crew served dinner. Bob and Brenda took one end of the table. Terry and Tarzan talked as if nobody else was present, but every so often he noticed how the other children were listening.

But tracks in his mind ran beneath what he was saying. *They look good together. He's spent time with these children, probably watched them grow up. She should marry him.*

She can't! Unless I'm all wrong from beginning to end.

Wouldn't that be nice? "We've been carrying kudzu grain in the cargo ever since. Someday we'll find another famine—"

She must have been carrying Tarzan when she took up with Lex. She held his attention while she carried Tarzan to term, and she held him after Lex knew Tarzan wasn't his, and *then* she had Sepulveda. She could have held him if she'd married him, but she didn't. Held him anyway.

Quite a woman. And then she gave him up. Why?

* * *

Terry took the car up into the orange sunset glow and headed north. En route he used his card and the car phone to get a hotel room. By nine he had checked into the Arco-Elsewhere and was calling Maria.

"Want to see the best hotel on the planet? Or shall I get a cab and come to you?"

"I guess I'll come there. Hey, why not? It's close to work."

He used an operator to track down Charley and Sharon, and wasn't surprised to find they had rooms in the same hotel. "Call me for breakfast," Sharon said groggily. "I'm not on Dagon time yet."

Charley seemed alert. "Terry! How's Brenda?"

"Brenda's running the planet, or at least twenty kids' worth of planet. One of the boys is mine. She looks wonderful. Got a burly protector, likeable guy, wants to be her fiance but isn't."

"You've got a kid! What's he like?"

Terry had to sort out his impressions. "She raised 'em all well. He's self-confident, delighted to see me, taller than me . . . if he saves civilization I'll take half the credit."

"That good, huh?"

"Easily."

"I've been working. We've sold the big Langston Field generator. Farmer, lots of land, he may be thinking about becoming a suburb for the wealthy. I got a good price, Terry. He thought he could beat me at the Mirror Game—"

"He bet you?"

"He did. And I've signed up for eight tons of borloi, but I'll have to see how much bulk that is before—"

"Borloi!"

"Sure, Terry, borloi has medical uses too. We'll deal with a government at our next stop, give it plenty of publicity too. That way it'll be used right."

"I'm glad to see you've put some brain sweat into this. What occurs to me is—"

The door went *bingbong.*

"Company." Terry went to open the door. Maria was in daytime dress, with a large handbag. "Come on in. Check out the bathroom, it's really sybaritic. I'm on the phone." He returned. "Borloi, right? It's not worth stealing on the way out, but after we jump we tell the whole population of Gaea about it? Shrewd. We'll be a target for any thief who wants to *sell* eight tons of borloi on the black market."

"Good point. What do you think?"

"Oh, I think we raise the subject with Sharon, and then I think we'll do it anyway."

"Let's meet for breakfast. Eight? Someone I want you to meet."

"Good." He hung up. He called, "I can offer you three astronauts for breakfast."

Maria came out to the sound of bathwater running. "Sounds delicious. It has to be early, Terry. Tomorrow's a working day."

"Oh, it'll be early. Early to bed?" He'd wanted to use the city computer files, but he was tired too. It wasn't the time change; the shorter days would have caught him up by now. It was stoop labor in high G.

Maria said, "I want to try that spa. Come with me? You look like you need it. And tell me about your day."

They all met for breakfast in Charlie's suite.

Charley had a groupie. Andrea Soucek was a university student, stunningly beautiful, given to cliches. She was goshwowed-out by the presence of *three* star-travellers. Sharon had George Callahan. Terry had Maria.

The conversation stayed general for awhile. Then George had to leave, and so did Maria. Over coffee it degenerated into shop talk, while Andrea Soucek listened in half-comprehending awe.

Eight tons of dry borloi (they'd freeze-dry it by opening the airlock) would fill more than half the cargo hold. Not much mass, though. The rest of the cargo space could go to heavy machinery. Their next stop, Gaea, had a small population unlikely to produce much for export, unlikely to buy much of the borloi. Most of it would be with them on two legs of their route.

Sharon asked, "Tanith doesn't manufacture much heavy machinery, do they?"

"I haven't found any I can buy. I'm working on it," Charley said.

Terry had an idea. "We want to freeze-dry the borloi anyway. We could pack it between the hull and the sleeve. Plenty of room for light stuff in the cargo hold."

"Hmm. Yeah! Any drug-running raider attacks us, his first shot would blow the borloi all across the sky! No addicts on our conscience."

"Rape the addicts. Evolution in action," Sharon said. "What kind of idiot would hook himself on borloi when the source is light years away? Get 'em out of the gene pool."

Andrea began to give her an argument. All humans were worthwhile, all could be saved. And borloi was a harmless vice—

Terry returned to his room carrying a mug of coffee.

The aristocratic phone operator recognised him by now. "Mr. Kakumee! Who may I track down for you?"

"Lex Hartner, MD, surgeon. Lived in Dagon City, Dryland sector, fifteen years ago."

"Fifteen years? Thanks a lot." But she'd stopped showing irritation. "Mmm. Not Dryland . . . he doesn't appear to be anywhere in Dagon."

"Try some other cities, please. He won't be outside a city."

Almost a minute crawled by. "I have a Lex Hartner in Coral Beach."

"I'll try that. Thanks."

It was Lex. He was older, grayer; his cheeks sagged in Tanith gravity. "Terry Kakumee?"

"Hello. I met your daughter yesterday."

The sagging disappeared. "How is she?"

"She's wonderful. All of Brenda's kids are wonderful. Are you wondering whether to tell me I've got a boy?"

"Yeah."

"He's wonderful too."

"Of course he is." Lex smiled at last. "How's Brenda?"

"She's wonderful. I asked her to marry me too, Lex. I mean sixteen years ago."

"Who else has she turned down?"

"Brawny farmer type named Maddox. Lex, I don't think she needs a man."

"How are you?"

"I'm fine. Would you believe Charley Laine is fine too? He looks like you'd expect, but his groupie is prettier than mine if not as smart."

"I did a good job there, didn't I?"

"That's what I'm telling you."

"Is it too late to say I'm sorry?"

"No, forget that. She didn't need me. Lex, have you got a moment? I've got some questions."

"About Brenda?"

"No. Lex, you did an autopsy on the corpse of a Sauron superman. Remember?"

"A man isn't likely to forget that. They rot fast in the swamps. It was pretty well chewed, too."

"Was there enough left for a gene analysis?"

"Some. Not enough to make me famous. It matched what the Navy already knew. I didn't find anything inhuman, anything borrowed from animals."

"Yeah. Anything startling?"

"Nope. It's all in the records."

"A Sauron and a Weem's beast, you don't expect them to go to a photo finish."

"It must have been something to see. From a distance, that is. Brenda never wanted to talk about it, but that was a long time ago. Maybe she'd talk now."

"Okay, thanks. Lex, I still think of you as a friend. I won't be on Tanith very long. Everything I do is on the city account for awhile—"

"Maybe I'll come into town."

"Call me when and if, and everything goes on the card. I'm at the Arco-Elsewhere."

Next he linked into the Dagon City computer files.

Matters relating to Saurons had been declassified. Navy ships had transferred much of their data to city computers on Tanith and other worlds. Terry found a picture he'd seen before: a Sauron, no visible wounds, gassed in an attack on Medea. It rotated before him, a monster out of a nightmare. Randus?

An XYY, the text said. All of the Sauron soldiers, any who had left enough meat to be analyzed, had had freaky gene patterns—males with an extra Y gene, where XY was male and XX was female—until the Battle of Tanith. There they'd found some officers.

Those pictures were of slides and electron-microscope photographs. No officer's corpse had survived unshredded. Their gene patterns included the XY pair, but otherwise resembled those of the XYY berserkers.

Results of that gene pattern were known. Eyes that saw deep into the infrared; the altered eye structure could be recognised. Blood that clotted fast to block a wound. Rapid production of endorphins to block pain. Stronger bones. Bigger adrenal glands. Powerful muscles. Skin that changed color fast, from near-white (to make vitamin D in cold, cloudy conditions, where a soldier had to cover most of his skin or die) to near-black (to prevent lethal sunburn in field conditions under a hotter sun.) Officers would have those traits too.

Nothing new yet.

Ah, here was Lex Hartner's autopsy report on Randus himself. XYY genes. Six-times-lethal damage from a Weem's beast's teeth, and one wound . . . one narrow wound up through the base of the skull into the cerebellum, that must have paralyzed or killed him at once.

A Sauron superman working in a rice paddy might not expect something to come at him out of the water.

Terry studied some detail pictures of a Weem's beast. It was something like a squat crocodile, with huge pads for front paws, claws inward-pointing to hold prey, a single dagger of a front tooth . . . That might have made the brain puncture if the thing was biting Randus's head. Wouldn't the lower teeth have left other marks on, say, the forehead?

So.

And a stranger, human-looking but with big bones and funny eyes, had run loose on Tanith for sixteen years. Had a man with a small daughter appeared somewhere, set up a business, married perhaps? By now he would have an identity and perhaps a position of power.

Saurons were popularly supposed to have been exterminated. Terry had never found any record of an attack on whatever world had bred the monsters, and he didn't now, though it must have happened. No mention of further attempts to track down fleets that might have fled across the sky. The Navy had left some stuff classified.

Early files on the Curtis family had been scrambled. He found a blurred family picture: a dark man, a darker woman, five children; he picked out a gawky eleven-year-old (the file said) who might have grown to be Brenda. The file on the Maddoxes was bigger, with several photographs. The men all looked like Bob Maddox, all muscle and confidence and freckled tans. The women were not much smaller and tended to be freckled and burly.

So.

An XY officer, a male, might have wanted children. Might have had children. They were gene-tailored, but the doctors had used mostly human genes; maybe all-human, despite the tales. They weren't a different species, after all. What would such children look like? How would they grow up?

The Polar Datafile interview was fun. The Other Worlds interview the next day felt more like work. Charley's voice gave out, so they called it off for a few days.

The borloi arrived in several planeloads. Terry didn't notice any special attempts at security. On many worlds there would have been a police raid followed by worldwide publicity. Memo: call all possible listeners in Gaea system *immediately* after jump. Sell to government only. Run if anything looks funny.

They flew half the borloi to orbit and packed it into

Firebee's outer hull, with no objection from Sharon. The work went fast. The next step was taken slowly, carefully.

The Langston Field generator from Phoenix system was too big for either boat.

Sharon put *Firebee* in an orbit that would intersect the atmosphere. With an hour to play with, they moved the beast out of the cargo hold with an armchair-type pusher frame and let it get a good distance away. They all watched as Terry beamed the signal that turned it on.

The generator became a black sphere five hundred meters across.

Charley and Terry boarded Shuttle #1. Sharon set *Firebee* accelerating back to orbit.

When the black sphere intersected the atmosphere there was little in the way of reentry flame. Despite the massive machine at the center, the huge sphere was a near-vacuum. It slowed rapidly and drifted like a balloon. Boat #1 overshot, then circled back.

Air seeped through the black force field to fill the vacuum inside. It ceased to be a balloon.

It touched down in the marshes south and east of Dagon City, more or less as planned. No signal would penetrate the field. Terry and Charley had to go into the Field with a big inflatable cargo raft, mount it beneath the generator and turn it off.

At that point it became the owner's problem. He'd arranged for two heavy-lift aircraft. *Firebee's* crew waited until the planes had landed, then took Boat #1 back to Dagon.

They were back at the hotel thirty-six hours after they'd left. Maria found the door open and Terry lolling in the spa. "I think I'm almost dissolved," he told her.

Lex didn't call. Brenda didn't call.

They ferried the rest of the borloi up a day later. Some went into the outer hull. The rest they packed around the cargo hold, leaving racks open in the center.

Dried borloi for padding, to shield whatever else Charley found to carry.

It was morning when they landed, with time for sightseeing. Andrea and Charley opted to rent equipment and do some semiserious mountain climbing in the foothills of the Warden. Terry called Maria, but she couldn't get off work, and couldn't see him tonight either. That made mountain climbing less attractive. Terry hiked around Dagon City for awhile, looked through the major shopping mall, then went back to the hotel.

He was half asleep with his shoes off when the phone chimed.

The face was Brenda's. Terry rubbed his palms together and tapped the answer pad.

"Hi, Terry. I'm in the lobby. Can I come up?"

"Sure, Brenda. Can I order you a drink? Lunch?"

"Get me a rum collins."

Terry rang off, then ordered from room service. His palms were sweating.

I ran the record into Firebee's *memory and ran a translation program on it, but I didn't look at the result. I'd have to go back to* Firebee, *then come back here.* Had Bob Maddox told her? Probably not.

She walked in like she owned the hotel, smiling as if nobody was supposed to know. Her dress was vivid orange; it went well with her color. The drink trolley followed her in. When it had rolled out she asked, "How long are you going to be on Tanith?"

"Two weeks, give or take a week. Charley has to find us something to sell. Besides borloi, that is."

"Have you tried bantar cloth? It's just about the only hi-tech stuff we make enough of. Don't take clothing. Styles change. Get bolts, and be sure you've got the tools to shape it."

"Yeah . . . Brenda, is there anything you can't do?"

"Cook. And I'm not the marrying type."

"I know that now."

"But I have children. Do you like Tarzan?"

He smiled and relaxed a little. "Good job there. I'm glad I met him."

"Let's do it again."

His drink slopped. Somehow he hadn't expected this. "Hold it, Brenda. I'm with another woman this trip."

"Maria? Terry, Maria's with Fritz Marsden tonight and all tomorrow. Fritz is one of mine. He works at the fusion plant at Randall's Point, and he only gets into town every couple of weeks. Maria isn't going to give *him* up for a, well, a transient."

He sipped at his drink to give himself time to think. When he took the glass from his lips, she pulled it out of his hand without spilling it and set it down. She pulled him to his feet with a fist in his belt. "I'm not asking for very much, am I?"

"Ah, no. Child support? We'll be leaving funds behind us anyway. Are you young enough?" Was she *serious*?

"I don't know. What's the worst that can happen?" She had unzipped his shirt and was pulling it loose. And with wild hope he thought, *It could be*!

She stripped him naked, then stepped back to examine him. "I don't think you've gained or lost an ounce. Same muscle tone too. You people don't even wrinkle."

"We wrinkle all at once. You've changed incredibly."

"I wanted to. I needed to. Terry, am I coming on too strong? You're tense. Let me show you something else I learned. Face down on the bed—" She helped him irresistibly. "I'll keep my dress on. Okay? And if you've got anything like massage oil around, tell me now."

"I've never had a massage of any kind."

The next hour was a revelation. She kept telling him to relax, and somehow he did that, while she tenderized muscles he'd strained moving borloi bags in free fall. He wondered if he'd been wrong; he wondered if he was going to die; he wondered why he'd never tried this before.

"I took massage training after you left. I used it at the hospital. I never had to work through a Nuliajuk's fat padding before . . . no sweat, I can reach the muscle underneath."

"Hell, you could reach through the ribs!"

"Is this too hard? Were you having trouble in orbit?"

"Nope. Everything went fine."

"Then why the tension? Turn over." She rolled him over and resumed work on his legs, then his arms and shoulders. "You didn't used to be shy with me."

"Am I shy now?"

"You keep tensing up." Her skirt was hiked up and she straddled his hips to work on his belly. "Good muscle here. Ease up— Well."

He had a respectable erection.

She caressed him. "I was afraid you'd changed." She slid forward and, hell, she didn't have panties.

"I kept my promise," she gloated.

"True," he croaked. "Take it off."

She pulled her dress over her head. There was still a brassiere; no woman would go without one in Tanith gravity. She took that off too.

She was smoothly dark, with no pale areas anywhere. His hands remembered her breasts as smaller. Four kids—and it had been too long, far too long. He cried out, and it might have been ecstasy or grief or both.

She rolled away, then slid up along the length of him. "And that was a massage."

"Well, I've been missing something."

"I did you wrong all those years ago. Did you hate me? Is that why you're so tense?"

"That wasn't it." He felt good: relaxed, uncaring. She'd come here only to seduce him, to mend fences, to revive memories. Or she already knew, and he might as well learn. "There's a Sauron message sender, galactic south of the Coal Sack. It was there to send Sauron ships to a certain Jump point."

"So?"

"Would you like to know where they were supposed to go? I could find out."

"No."

"Flat-out no? Suppose they come back?"

"Cut the crap, Terry. Hints and secrets. You never did *that* to me before."

"I'm sorry, love—"

"Why did two Saurons go around the Maddox farm and straight to us? You told Bob you knew."

"Because they're white."

Brenda's face went uncannily blank. Then she laughed. "Poor Bob! He'd think you were absolutely loony."

"He sure would. I didn't *want* to know this, Brenda. Why don't you want to find the Saurons?"

"What would I want with them? I want to see my children safe—"

"Send them."

"Not likely! Terry, how much have you figured out?"

"I think I've got it all. I keep testing it, Brenda, and it fits every time."

She waited, her nose four centimeters from his, her breath on his face. The scent of her was very faint.

He said, "You saw to it that three of your own children were out in the rice paddy, including Tarzan. The girl you kept at the house was Reseda, the blond, the girl with the least obvious of Sauron genes. You invited Bob over. Maybe he'd get rid of me before the kids came back."

"Just my luck. He likes you."

"They took away your scent. No enemy could smell you out. They gave you an epicanthic fold to protect your eyes. The flat, wide nose is less vulnerable and pulls in more air." He pushed his fingers into her hair. Spongy, resilient, thick. She didn't flinch; she smiled in pleasure. "And this kind of hair to protect your skulls. It's take an impact. You grow your own skewball helmets!"

"How gracefully you put it."

"But it looks like a black woman's hair, so you want black skin. So you spend an hour on the roof every afternoon. Naked?" There were no white areas.

"Sure."

"There was a burn-through over Dagon City, and the EMP destroyed most of the records, but maybe not all. Whatever was left had to say that the Curtis family was mostly black."

"Whereas the Maddoxes are white," she said.

"That burn-through was important. You had to be sure. I'm betting you caused it yourself. It didn't have any serious military importance, did it? The pulse wiped out hospital equipment too, so they couldn't look inside you. Couldn't see that you aren't built—"

"If you say, 'Not quite like a woman,' I'll turn you upside down." She reached down to grip his ankle.

"You came down in a two-man escape pod. One XYY Sauron, and you. There wasn't any Horatius loose for fifteen years. No Miranda either."

"Only an XX," she said. Oh, she felt good lying alongside him. The Saurons weren't a different species. Gene-tailored, but human, quite human.

He said, "But you didn't speak Anglic. Here you were on Tanith with some chance of passing for a . . . citizen. But you couldn't speak a word, and you were with a Sauron berserker—"

"We say soldier. Soldiers and officers. We don't say Sauron."

"Okay."

"We killed a family and took over the house. It was still war, Terry. We cleaned up as best we could. Hid one body, a girl about my size, and buried the rest. I painted our bantar cloth armor. Turned on the TV wall and left it on. It didn't tell me what they were talking about, but I got the accents. Worked naked in the fields, but that didn't help. It left my feet white up to the knees!"

"The soldier couldn't hide, so you had to kill him. Lex found the knife wound. He wouldn't tell me about it, Brenda."

"Lex knows. He delivered Van, our second. Van was a soldier."

He couldn't think of anything to say. Brenda said, "I killed Randus. I found a Weems beast and gave him to it. We don't think much of the soldiers, Terry. I cut a claw off the Weem's beast and made the wound—"

"Almost through your skull."

"It had to be done in one stroke. And kept septic. And in the jungle I had to climb a tree when I had daylight and take off all my clothes to keep the tan. I waved at a plane once. Too late to hide. If the pilot saw me he must have thought he was hallucinating."

"What'd you eat out there?"

"Everything! What good is a soldier who gets food poisoning? Anything a De Lap's Ghoul can eat, I can eat."

"*That's* not in the records."

"That's why I can't cook. I can't tell when it tastes wrong, I can't tell when meat's rotten. I used recipes till I could teach some of the kids to cook."

"You couldn't talk, but you could fake the symptoms of a stroke. That's the part I just couldn't believe—God damn!"

The left side of her face had gone slack as a rubber mask. She grinned with the other side. "Brenda Curris," she said.

"Don't do that."

She reached across him and finished the collins in two swallows. "How long have you known?"

"Maybe fifteen years, but I didn't *know*, Brenda. I was still angry. There's a lot of time to think between the stars. I made up this tale. And worked on the kinks, and then I started thinking I must be crazy, because I couldn't pick a hole in it. You told the Marines about the Saurons to make them talk to you. They wouldn't notice how fast your speech improved. They were hanging on every word, trying to get a line on the escaped Sauron, and chattering away to each other. They taught you Anglic.

"I used to wonder what you saw in me. I'm an outworlder. I couldn't recognise a Tanith accent. You made love to me in the dark because you'd lost too much of your tan in the hospital—"

He stopped because her hand had closed hard on his arm. "I wanted your child! I wanted children, and Tarzan would *look* like he was half outworlder. I didn't plan the power failure, Terry. Hell, it probably tipped you off."

"Yeah, you moved like you could almost see in the dark. And wore dark glasses in daylight. The Tanith sun doesn't get that bright, love."

"Bright enough."

"Tanith must have been perfect for you. The sun never gets high. In this gravity *everybody's* got muscles."

"True, but I didn't pick Tanith. Tanith was where the ships went. What else did you notice?"

"Nothing you could have covered up. I talked marriage at you so you switched to Lex. While you were carrying my child."

"But I *can't* get married. In winter the tan goes away, I have to use tanning lotion and do everything by phone."

"What was it like for . . . you? Before?"

Brenda sat up. "For Sauron women? All right. I'm second generation. Test tube children, all of us. Women are kept in . . . it's like a laboratory and a harem both. The first generation didn't work out. The women didn't like being brood mares, so to speak, and one day they killed half the doctors and ran loose."

"Good."

"There's nothing good about any of this. They were hunted down and shot, and I got all of this by rumor. Maybe it's true and maybe it isn't."

"They made you a brood mare too, didn't they?"

"Oh, sure. The second generation Sauron women, we like having children. I don't know if they fiddled with our genes or if they just kept the survivors for, for breeding after the revolt. They gave us a TV wall and let us learn. I think the first group was suffering from sensory deprivation. Most of the children were bottled, but we tended them, and every so often they'd let us carry a child to term, after they were sure it'd survive. I had two. One was Miranda."

"Survive?" He was sitting up now too, with the remains of his collins.

"Mating two Saurons is a bad idea. The doctors don't give a shit about side effects. Out of ten children you get a couple of soldiers and an officer and a couple of girls. They're the heterozygotes. The homozygotes die. Paired genes for infrared eyes give blindness. Paired genes for fast blood clotting gets you strokes and heart attacks in your teens. You get albinos. You get freaks who die of shock just because the adrenal glands got too big."

"Yuk."

"Can you see why I don't want to find the Saurons? But these are good genes—" Her hands moved down her body, inviting him to witness: good genes, yes. "As long as you don't backbreed. My children are an asset to the human race, Terry."

"I—"

"Six of us escaped. We killed some doctors on the way. Once we reached the barracks it was easy. The XYYs will do anything for us. They smuggled us into four of the troop ships. I don't know what happened to the others. I got aboard *Deimos* as a soldier. None of the officers ever saw me. We were part of the attack on Tanith. When I saw we had a good burn-through in the Dagon City shield, the whole plan just popped into my mind. I grabbed a soldier and we took an escape pod and ran it from there."

"You're incredible." He pulled back to look at her. Not quite a woman . . . not quite *his* woman, ever.

"Terry, did you wonder if I might kill you?"

"Yeah. I thought you'd want to know where the Saurons went first."

"You bet your life on that?"

"I bet on you."

"Fool."

"I'm not dead yet," he pointed out.

"Bad bet, love. When I knew you knew, I assumed you'd made a record somewhere, somehow, that would spill it all if you died. I couldn't find it in the city records. But suppose I decided to wipe out everyone who might know? Everyone you might have talked to. Charley, Sharon, Maria—"

Oh my God.

"—Lex, Bob because you might have talked to him, George Callahan in case Sharon talked, maybe a random lawyer; do you think I can't trace your phone calls? Okay, calm down now." Hands where his neck joined his shoulders, fingers behind the shoulder blades, rubbing smooth and hard. The effort distorted her voice. "We Saurons . . . we have to decide . . . *not* to kill. I've decided. But you've got a . . . real blind spot there, Terry. You put some people in danger."

"I guess I just don't think that way. I had to *know* whether you'd kill me, before I told you anything useful. I had to know what you are."

"What am I?" she asked.

"I'm not dead. Nobody's dead since you reached the hospital."

"Except Van."

"Yeah. Van. But if any of this got out, you'd be dead and Tarzan would be dead and, hell, they'd probably kill every kid who ever lived with you, just in case you trained them somehow. So."

"So," she said. "Now what?"

2656 AD, April (Firebee *clock time*)

Firebee approached the Alderson jump point with a load of borloi and bantar cloth.

Tanith's sun had turned small. Terry searched the sky near that hurtingly bright point for some sign of Tanith itself. But stars don't waver outside an atmosphere, and he couldn't find the one point among many.

"We made some good memories there," Sharon said. "Another two minutes . . . Troops, are we really going to try to reach Sparta?"

Charley called from aft. "Sparta's a long way away. See what they buy on Gaea first."

Terry said, "I'm against it. Sparta's got six Alderson points. If they're not at war they'll be the center of all local trade. This beloved wreck won't be worth two kroner against that competition. We might have to join a guild too, if they let us."

"Isn't there a chance the Emperor would buy the data we got from *Morningstar?*"

"I'll run through those records, Captain, but my guess is we've got nothing to sell. There won't be anything Sparta doesn't have."

She nodded. "Okay. Jumping *now.*"

And *Firebee* was gone.

Introduction

One of the problems with trying to publish a quarterly magazine in paperback format and marketed through paperback channels is that the lag time from composition to publication is ridiculous. For instance, when this article was commission (April of 1987) warm superconduction was the hottest topic in science. During the next four months things kept popping; see in the addendum to this article, prepared in July.

As of this writing (October 22, 1987) several weeks have passed with no major annoncements (other than the awarding of the Nobel in physics going to IBM's superconductor researchers) and while there is still time I would like to make an off-the-wall prediction. There is a very close correlation between electrical conductivity and heat transfer; I predict that the most important application of superconductors will not be electrical or electronic, but thermal. Think about it. While most fossil fuels are burned to warm us up or cool us down, not far beneath the surface of any planet on earth the tempaerature is 76 degrees Fahrenheit. But that is another article. . . .

THE WINDING ROAD:

TO ROOM-TEMPERATURE SUPER-CONDUCTIVITY VIA ABSOLUTE ZERO

Charles Sheffield

At a dinner a month ago, the man next to me bemoaned the way that scientists "keep secret" what they are doing, failing to explain their work in ways that "normal people can understand."

I disagreed, insisted that was true only of *bad* science, and quoted Lord Rutherford, who said, "You should be able to explain any important scientific work to a barmaid."

"Lord Rutherford, whoever he is, can say what he likes," replied my neighbor. "And maybe he can do it. But most people can't do it. I bet you can't do it."

"He died in 1937," I said. "In the sort of way I'd like to die—he fell out of a tree he was pruning, when he was an old man. Anyway, I bet I can."

The wrong reply, perhaps, because he said at once:

"All right. There's been all this talk in the papers for the past couple of months about high-temperature superconductors. I know what a superconductor does—it lets electrical currents flow without resistance—but I don't know *why*. Explain to me what superconductivity is, how a superconductor works, so I can understand it, and why it's so important. *And* explain why it's easier to do it at low temperatures."

"Sure. Piece of cake." I started to talk. After about ten minutes he said that I had succeeded—that now he understood superconductors. But I don't think he did. I think he had simply heard all that he could stand, because by that time, I was convinced that I didn't understand superconductors, either.

Here, four weeks and some thought later, is the answer that I wish I had given him.

LOW TEMPERATURES. Superconductivity was first observed in materials at extremely low temperatures, and is best understood there, so that is a logical place to begin.

The whole field is relatively new. Ten thousand years ago, people already knew how to make things hot. It was easy. You put a fire underneath them. But as recently as two hundred years ago, it was difficult to make things cold. There was no "cold generator" that corresponded to fire as a heat generator. Low temperatures were something that came naturally; they were not man-made.

The Greeks and Romans knew that there were ways of lowering the temperature of materials, although they did not use that word, by using such things as the mixture of salt and ice. But they had no way of seeking progressively lower temperatures. That had to wait for the early part of the nineteenth century, when Humphrey Davy and others found that you could liquefy many gases merely by compressing them. The resulting liquid will be warm, because turning gas to liquid gives off the gas's so-called "latent heat of liquefaction."

If you now allow this liquid to reach a thermal balance with its surroundings, and then reduce the pressure on it, the liquid boils; and in so doing, it drains heat from its surroundings—including itself. The same result can be obtained if you take a liquid at atmospheric pressure, and put it into a partial vacuum. Some of the liquid boils, and what's left is colder. This technique, of "boiling under reduced pressure," was a practical and systematic way of pursuing lower temperatures. It first seems to have been used by a Scotsman, William Cullen, who cooled ethyl ether this way in 1748, but it took another three-quarters of a century before the method was applied to science (and to commerce; the first refrigerator was patented by Jacob Perkins in 1834).

Another way to cool was found by James Prescott Joule and William Thomson (later Lord Kelvin) in 1852. Named the Joule-Thomson Effect, or the Joule-Kelvin Effect, it relies on the fact that a gas escaping from a valve into a chamber of lower pressure will, under the right conditions, suffer a reduction in temperature. If the gas entering the valve is first passed in a tube through that lower-temperature region, we have a cycle that will move the chamber to lower and lower temperatures.

Through the nineteenth century the Joule-Thomson Effect and boiling under reduced pressure permitted the exploration of lower and lower temperatures. The natural question was, how low could you go?

A few centuries ago, there seemed to be no answer to that question. There seemed to be no limit to how cold something could get, just as today there is no practical limit to how hot something can become.

(A digression: I will actually offer a theoretical [and highly bogus] upper limit on how hot something can get. Suppose we could turn all the universe except one gram of water into energy, and use that energy to heat the water. Taking the mass of the universe as 6×10^{52} kgms, which is a number just enough to give a closed universe, the temperature of that gram of water would be about 1.3×10^{69} degrees Celsius. If we use a smaller amount of water, say one hundredth of a gram, the temperature would be a hundred times as high. Taking that to its limit, we will use the whole universe to heat a single electron, which is the lightest particle of accepted mass. It is meaningless to talk of temperature in such a case, because temperature is a group property of a large number of particles; however, the calculated result, which is 1.4×10^{96} degrees Celsius, is some sort of upper bound to all temperatures to be experienced in this universe. If the neutrino has a rest mass of 1/140,000th of an electron, as suggested by analysis of data from the recent supernova in the Magellanic Cloud, we might use our energy to heat that. The upper limit on temperature then becomes 2×10^{101} degrees Celsius—a number that ought to be big enough to satisfy the most demanding reader.)

The problem of reaching low temperatures was clarified when scientists finally realized, after huge intellectual efforts, that heat is nothing more than motion at the atomic and molecular scale. "Absolute zero" could then be identified as no motion—the temperature of an object when you "took out all the heat." (Purists will object to this statement since even at absolute zero, quantum theory tells us that an object still has a zero point energy; the thermodynamic definition of absolute zero is done in terms of reversible isothermal processes).

Absolute zero, it turns out, is reached at a temperature of −273.16 degrees Celsius. Temperatures measured with respect to this value are all positive, and are said to be in *degrees Kelvin* (written °K). One degree Kelvin is the same *size* as one degree Celsius, but it is measured with respect to a reference point of absolute zero, rather than to the Celsius zero value of the freezing point of water. We will use the two scales interchangeably, whichever is the more convenient at the time.

Is it obvious that this absolute zero temperature must be the same for all materials? Suppose that you had two materials which reached their zero heat state at different temperatures. Put them in contact with each other. Then thermodynamics requires that heat should flow from the higher temperature body to the other one, until they both reach the same temperature. Since there is by assumption no heat in either material (each is at its own absolute zero), no heat can flow; and when no heat flows between two bodies in contact, they must be at the same temperature. Thus absolute zero is the same temperature for every material.

Even before an absolute zero point of temperature was identified, people were trying to get down as low in temperature as they could, and also trying to liquefy gases. Sulfur dioxide (boiling point $-10°C$) was the first to go, when Monge and Clouet liquefied it in 1799 by cooling it in a mixture of ice and salt. De Morveau produced liquid ammonia (boiling point $-33°C$) later in that year using the same method, and in 1805 Northmore claimed to have produced liquid chlorine (boiling point $-35°C$) by simple compression.

In 1834, Thilorier produced carbon dioxide snow (dry ice; melting point $-78.5°C$) for the first time using gas expansion. Soon after that, Michael Faraday, who had earlier (1823) liquefied chlorine, employed a carbon dioxide and ether mixture to reach the record low temperature of $-110°$ Celsius ($163°K$). He was able to liquefy many gases, but not hydrogen, oxygen, or nitrogen.

In 1877, Louis Cailletet used gas compression to several hundred atmospheres, followed by expansion through a jet, to produce liquid mists of methane (boiling point $-164°C$), carbon monoxide (boiling point $-192°C$), and oxygen (boiling point $-183°C$). He did not, however, manage to collect a volume of liquid from any of these substances.

Liquid oxygen was finally produced in quantity in 1883, by Wroblewski and Olszewski, who reached the lowest temperature to date (− 136°C). Two years later they were able to go as low as − 152°C, and liquefied both nitrogen and carbon monoxide. In that same year, Olszewski reached a temperature of − 225°C (48°K), which remained a record for many years. He was able to produce a small amount of liquid hydrogen for the first time. In 1886, Joseph Dewar invented the Dewar flask (which we think of today as the thermos bottle) that allowed cold, liquefied materials to be stored for substantial periods of time at atmospheric pressure. In 1898, Dewar liquefied hydrogen in quantity and reached a temperature of 20°K. At that point, all known gases had been liquefied.

What about helium, which has not so far been mentioned?

In the 1890s, helium was still a near-unknown quantity. The gas had been observed in the spectrum of the Sun by Janssen and Lockyer, in 1868, but it had not been found on earth until the early 1890s. Its properties were not known. It is only with hindsight that we can find good reasons why the gas, when available, proved unusually hard to liquefy.

The periodic table had already been formulated by Mendeleyev, in 1869. He listed all the elements, in terms of their *atomic number*, a value that was eventually shown to correspond to the number of protons in the nucleus of each element.

As other gases were liquefied, a pattern emerged. Table 1 shows the temperatures where a number of gases change from the gaseous to the liquid state, under normal atmospheric pressure, together with their atomic number and molecular weights.

What happens when we plot the boiling point of the element against its atomic number in the periodic table? This is shown in Figure 1.

There are clearly two different groups of gases in the diagram. Radon, xenon, krypton, argon, and neon remain gases to much lower temperatures than other materials of similar atomic number. This is even more

TABLE 1

Gas	Boiling point		Atomic number	Molecular weight
	(°C)	(°K)		
Radon	− 61.8	211.4	86	222
Xenon	− 107.1	166.1	54	131
Krypton	− 152.3	120.9	36	84
Argon	− 185.7	87.5	18	40
Chlorine	− 34.6	238.6	17	71
Neon	− 246.1	27.1	10	20
Fluorine	− 188.1	85.1	9	38
Oxygen	− 183.0	90.2	8	32
Nitrogen	− 195.8	77.3	7	28
Hydrogen	− 252.8	20.4	1	2

noticeable if we add a number of other common gases, such as ammonia, acetylene, carbon dioxide, methane, and sulfur dioxide, and look at the variation of their boiling points with their molecular weights (see Table 2). They are also shown in Figure 1.

Radon, xenon, krypton, and the others of the low-boiling-point group are all inert gases, often known as noble gases, that rarely participate in any chemical reactions. Figure 1 also shows that the inert gases of lower atomic number and molecular weight liquefy at lower temperatures. Helium, the second-lightest element, is the final member of the inert gas group, and the one with the lowest atomic number. Hel-

TABLE 2

Gas	Boiling point (°C)	(°K)	Molecular weight
Methane	− 164	109	16
Ammonia	− 33	240	17
Acetylene	− 75	198	26
Carbon dioxide	− 78	195	44
Sulfur dioxide	− 10	263	64

ium should therefore have an unusually low boiling point.

It does. All through the late 1890s and early 1900s, attempts to liquefy it failed.

When the Dutch scientist Kamerlingh Onnes finally succeeded, in 1908, the reason for other people's failures became clear. Helium remains liquid until − 268.9 Celsius—16 degrees lower than liquid hydrogen, and only 4.2 degrees above absolute zero. As for solid helium, not even Onnes' most strenuous efforts could produce it. When he boiled helium under reduced pressure, the liquid helium went to a new form—but it was a new and strange *liquid* phase, now known as Helium II, that exists only below 2.2°K. It turns out that the solid phase of helium does not exist at atmospheric pressure, or at any pressure less than 25 atmospheres. It was first produced in 1926, by P. H. Keeson.

The liquefaction of helium looked like the end of the story; it was, in fact, the beginning.

SUPER PROPERTIES. Having produced liquid helium, Kamerlingh Onnes set about determining its properties. History does not record what he expected to find, but it is fair to guess that he was amazed.

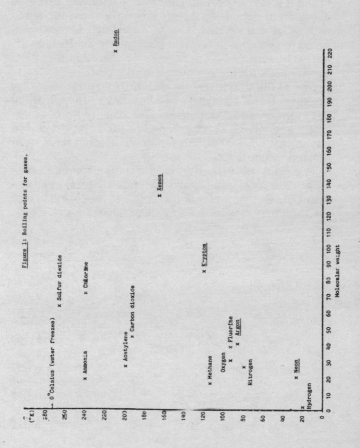

Figure 1: Boiling points for gases.

Science might be defined as guessing something you don't know using what you do know, and then measuring to see if it is true or not. The biggest scientific advances often occur when what you measure does not agree with what you predict. What Kamerlingh Onnes measured for liquid helium, and particularly for Helium II, was so bizarre that he must have wondered at first what was wrong with his measuring equipment.

One of the things that he measured was the viscosity. Viscosity is the gooeyness of a substance, though there are more scientific definitions. We usually think of viscosity as applying to something like oil or molasses, but non-gooey substances like water and alcohol have well-defined viscosities.

The unit of viscosity is the *poise* (named after Poiseuille, who established the fundamental relationship between rate of volume flow and viscosity). Here are the viscosities of some familiar substances:

Liquid	Viscosity (in poises)
Olive oil (at 20 C)	8.40
Machine oil (at 15 C)	6.61
Glycerine (at 20 C)	14.90
Benzene (at 20 C)	0.007
Water (at 20 C)	0.011
Ethyl alcohol (at 20 C)	0.012

Onnes tried to determine a value of viscosity for Helium II down around 1°K. He failed. It was too small to measure. As the temperature goes below 2°K, the viscosity of Helium II goes rapidly toward zero. It will flow with no measurable resistance through narrow capillaries and closely packed powders. Above 2.2°K, the other form of liquid helium, known as Helium I, does have a measurable viscosity, low but highly temperature-dependent.

Helium II also conducts heat amazingly well. At about 1.9°K, where its conductivity is close to a maximum, this form of liquid helium conducts heat about eight hundred times as well as copper at room temperature—and copper is usually considered an excellent conductor. Helium II is, in fact, by far the best known conductor of heat.

More disturbing, perhaps, from the experimenter's point of view, is Helium II's odd reluctance to be confined. In an open vessel, the liquid creeps in the form of a thin film up the sides of the container, slides out over the rim, and runs down to the lowest available level. This phenomenon can be readily explained, in terms of the very high surface tension of Helium II; but it remains a striking effect to observe.

Liquid helium is not the end of the low-temperature story, and the quest for absolute zero is an active and fascinating field that continues today. New methods of extracting energy from test substances are still being developed, with the most effective ones employing a technique known as *adiabatic demagnetization*. Invented independently in 1926 by a German, Debye, and an American, Giauque, it was first used by Giauque and MacDougall in 1933, to reach a temperature of 0.25°K. A more advanced version of the same method was applied to nuclear adiabatic demagnetization in 1956 by Simon and Kurti, and they achieved a temperature within a hundred thousandth of a degree of absolute zero. With the use of this method, temperatures as low as thirty billionths of a degree have recently been reported from Finland.

However, the pursuit of absolute zero is not our main objective, and to pursue it further would take us too far afield. We are interested in another effect that Kamerlingh Onnes found in 1911, when he examined the electrical properties of selected materials immersed in a bath of liquid helium. He discovered that certain pure metals exhibited what is known today as *superconductivity*.

Below a few degrees Kelvin, the resistance to the passage of an electrical current in these metals drops suddenly to a level too small to measure. Currents that are started in wire loops under these conditions continue to flow, apparently forever, with no sign of dissipation of energy. For pure materials, the cut-off temperature between normal conducting and superconducting is quite sharp, occurring within a couple of hundredths of a degree.

Superconductivity today is a familiar phenomenon. At the time it was discovered, it was an absolutely astonishing finding—a physical impossibility, less plausible than anti-gravity. Frictional forces must slow all motion, including the motion represented by the flow of an electrical current. Such a current could not therefore keep running, year after year, without dissipation. That seemed like a fundamental law of nature.

Of course, there is no such thing as a law of nature. There is only the universe, going about its business, while humans scurry around trying to put everything into neat little intellectual boxes. It is amazing that the tidying-up process called physics works as well as it does, and perhaps even more astonishing that mathematics seems important in every box. But the boxes have no reality or permanence; a "law of nature" is useful until we discover cases where it doesn't apply.

In 1911, the general theories that could explain superconductivity were still decades in the future. The full explanation did not arrive until 1957, forty-six years after the initial discovery.

To understand superconductivity, and to explain its seeming impossibility, it is necessary to look at the nature of electrical flow itself.

ELECTRICITY. While techniques were being developed to reach lower and lower temperatures, the new field of electricity and magnetism was being explored in parallel—sometimes by the same experimenters. Just three years before the Scotsman, William Cullen, found how to cool ethyl ether by boiling it under reduced pressure, von Kleist of Pomerania and van Musschenbroek in Holland independently discovered a way to store electricity. Van Musschenbroek did his work at the University of Leyden—the same university where, 166 years later, Kamerlingh Onnes would discover superconductivity. The *Leyden Jar*, as the storage vessel soon became known, was an early form of electrical capacitor. It allowed the flow of current through a wire to take place under controlled and repeatable circumstances.

Just what it was that constituted the current through that wire would remain a mystery for another century and a half. But it was already apparent to Ben Franklin by 1750 that *something* material was flowing. The most important experiments took place three-quarters of a century later. In 1820, just three years before Michael Faraday liquefied chlorine, the Danish scientist Oersted and then the Frenchman Ampère found that there was a relation between electricity and magnetism—a flowing current would make a magnet move. In the early 1830s, Faraday himself then showed that the relationship was a reciprocal one, by producing an electric current from a moving magnet. However, from our point of view, an even more significant result had been established a few years before, when in 1827 the German scientist Georg Simon Ohm discovered *Ohm's Law*: that the current in a wire is given by the ratio of the voltage between the ends of the wire, divided by the wire's resistance.

This result seemed too simple to be true. When Ohm announced it, no one believed him. He was discredited, resigned his position as a professor at Cologne University, and lived in poverty and obscurity for several years. Finally, he was vindicated, recognized, and fourteen years later began to receive awards and medals for his work.

Ohm's Law is important to us because it permits the

relationship between the resistance and temperature of a substance to be explored, without worrying about the starting value of the voltage or current. It turns out that the resistance of a conducting material is roughly proportional to its absolute temperature. Just as important, materials vary enormously in their conducting power. For instance, copper allows electricity to pass through it 10^{20} times as well as quartz or rubber. The obvious question is, why? What makes a good conductor, and what makes a good insulator? And why should a conductor pass electricity more easily at lower temperatures?

The answers to these questions were developed little by little through the rest of the nineteenth century. First, heat was discovered to be no more than molecular and atomic motion. Thus, changes of electrical resistance had somehow to be related to those same motions.

Second, in the 1860s, James Clerk Maxwell, the greatest physicist of the century, developed Faraday and Ampère's experimental results into a consistent and complete mathematical theory of electricity and magnetism, finally embodied in four famous differential equations. All observed phenomena of electricity and magnetism must fit into the framework of that theory.

Third, scientists began to realize that metals, and many other materials that conduct electricity well, have a regular structure at the molecular level. The atoms and molecules of these substances are arranged in a regular three-dimensional grid pattern, termed a lattice, and held in position by inter-atomic electrical forces.

Finally, in 1897, J.J. Thomson found the elusive carrier of the electrical current. He originally termed it the "corpuscle," but it soon found its present name, the *electron*. All electrical currents are carried by electrons.

With these tools in hand, we are in a position to understand the flow of electricity through conductors—but not yet, as we shall see, to explain superconductivity.

Electricity is caused by the movement of electrons. Thus, a good conductor must have plenty of electrons readily able to move, which are termed *free electrons*.

An insulator has few or no free electrons, and the electrons in such materials are all bound to atoms.

If the atoms of a material maintain exact, regularly spaced positions, it is very easy for free electrons to move past them, and hence for current to flow. In fact, electrons are not interfered with at all if the atoms in the material stand in a perfectly regular array. However, if the atoms in the lattice can move randomly, or if there are imperfections in the lattice, the electrons are then impeded in their progress, and the resistance of the material increases.

This is exactly what happens when the temperature goes up. Recalling that heat is random motion, we expect that atoms in hot materials will jiggle about on their lattice sites with the energy provided by increased heat. The higher the temperature, the greater the movement, and the greater the obstacle to free electrons. Therefore, the resistance of conducting materials increases with increasing temperature.

This was all well known by the 1930s. Electrical conduction could be calculated very well by the new quantum theory, thanks largely to the efforts of Arnold Sommerfeld, Felix Bloch, Rudolf Peierls, and others. However, those same theories predicted a *steady* decline of electrical resistance as the temperature went toward absolute zero. Nothing predicted, or could explain, the precipitous drop to zero resistance that was encountered in some materials at their critical temperature. Superconductivity remained a mystery for another quarter of a century. To provide its explanation, it is necessary to delve a little further into quantum theory itself.

SUPERCONDUCTIVITY AND STATISTICS. Until late 1986, superconductivity was a phenomenon encountered only at temperatures below 23°K, and usually at just a couple of degrees Kelvin. Even 23°K is below the boiling point of everything except hydrogen (20°K) and helium (4.2°K). Most superconductors become so only at far lower temperatures (see Table 3). Working with them is thus a tiresome business, since such low temperatures are expensive to achieve and hard to maintain. Let us term superconductivity below 20°K "classical superconductivity," and for the moment, confine our attention to it.

For another fifteen years after the 1911 discovery of

TABLE 3: The critical temperature T_c at which selected materials become superconducting when no magnetic field is present.

Material	Temperature (T_c, °K)
Titanium	0.39
Zinc	0.93
Uranium	1.10
Aluminum	1.20
Tin	3.74
Mercury	4.16
Lead	7.22
Niobium	8.90
Technetium	11.20

Note that all these temperatures are below the temperature of liquid hydrogen (20°K), which means that superconductivity cannot be induced by bathing the metal sample in a liquid hydrogen bath, although such an environment is today readily produced. For many years, the search was for a material that would sustain superconductivity above 20°K.

superconductivity, there seemed little hope of explaining it. However, in the mid-1920s, a new tool, quantum theory, encouraged physicists to believe that they at last had a theoretical framework that would explain all phenomena of the sub-atomic world. In the late 1920s and 1930s, hundreds of previously intractable problems yielded to a quantum mechanical approach. And the importance of a new type of statistical behavior became clear.

On the atomic and nuclear scale, particles and systems of particles can be placed into two well-defined and separate groups. Electrons, protons, neutrons, positrons, muons, and neutrinos all satisfy what is known as Fermi-Dirac statistics, and they are collectively known as *fermions*. For our purposes, the most important point about such particles is that their behavior is subject to the Pauli Exclusion Principle, which states that no two identical particles obeying Fermi-Dirac statistics can have the same values for all physical variables (so, for example, two electrons in an atom cannot have the same spin, and the same energy level). The Pauli Exclusion Principle imposes very strong constraints on the motion and energy levels of identical fermions, within atoms and molecules, or moving in an atomic lattice.

The other kind of statistics is known as Bose-Einstein statistics, and it governs the behavior of photons, alpha particles (*i.e.*, helium nuclei), and mesons. These are all termed *bosons*. The Pauli Exclusion Principle does not apply to systems satisfying Bose-Einstein statistics, so bosons are permitted to have the same values of all physical variables; in fact, since they seek to occupy the lowest available energy level, they will group around the same energy.

In human terms, fermions are loners, each with its own unique state; bosons love a crowd, and they all tend to jam into the same state.

Single electrons are, as stated, fermions. At normal temperatures, above a few degrees Kelvin, electrons in a metal are thus distributed over a range of energies and momenta, as required by the Pauli Exclusion Principle.

In 1950, H. Fröhlich suggested a strange possibility: that the fundamental mechanism responsible for superconductivity was somehow the interaction of free electrons with the atomic lattice. This sounds at first hearing highly improbable, since it is exactly this lattice that is responsible for the resistance of metals at normal temperatures. However, Fröhlich had theoretical reasons for his suggestion, and in that same year, 1950, there was experimental evidence—unknown to Fröhlich—that also suggested the same thing: superconductivity is caused by electron-lattice interactions.

This does not, of course, explain superconductivity. The question is, what does the lattice do? What can it possibly do that would give rise to superconducting materials? Somehow, the lattice must affect the free electrons in a fundamental way, but in a way that is able to produce an effect only at low temperatures.

The answer was provided by Leon Cooper, John Bardeen, and Robert Schrieffer, in 1957 (they got the physics Nobel Prize for this work in 1972). They showed that the atomic lattice causes free electrons to *pair off*. Instead of single electrons, moving independently of each other, the lattice encourages the formation of electron couplets, which can then each be treated as a unit. The coupling force is tiny, and if there is appreciable thermal energy available, it is enough to break the bonds between the electron pairs. Thus, any effect of the pairing should be visible only at very low temperatures. The role of the lattice in this pairing is absolutely fundamental, yet at the same time, the lattice does not participate in the pairing—it is more as if the lattice is a catalyst, which permits the electron pairing to occur but is not itself affected by that pairing.

The pairing does not mean that the two electrons are close together in space. It is a pairing of angular momentum, in such a way that the total angular momentum of a pair is zero. The two partners may be widely separated in space, with many other electrons between them. Like husbands and wives at a crowded party, paired electrons remain paired, even though they may be widely separated, and have many other electrons between them.

Now for the fundamental point implied by the work of Bardeen, Cooper, and Schrieffer. Once two electrons are paired, that pair behaves like a *boson*, not a fermion. Any number of these electron pairs can be in the same low-energy state. More than that, when a current is flowing (so all the electron pairs are moving), it takes more energy to stop the flow than to continue it. To stop the flow, some boson (electron pair) will have to move to a different energy level; and as we already remarked, bosons like to be in the same state.

To draw the chain of reasoning again: superconductivity is a direct result of the boson nature of electron pairs; electric current is carried by these electron pairs; electron pairs are the direct result of the mediating effect of the atomic lattice; and the energy holding the pairs together is very small, so that they exist only at very low temperatures, when no heat energy is around to break up the pairing.

HIGH-TEMPERATURE SUPERCONDUCTORS. We now have a very tidy explanation of classical superconductivity, one that suggests we will never find anything that behaves as a superconductor at more than a few degrees above absolute zero. Thus, the discovery of materials that turn into superconductors at much higher temperatures is almost an embarrassment. Let's look at them and see what is going on.

The search for high-temperature superconductors began as soon as superconductivity itself was discovered. Since there was no good theory before the 1950s to explain the phenomenon, there was also no reason to assume that a material could not be found that exhibited superconductivity at room temperature, or even above it. That, however, was not the near-term goal. The main hope of researchers in the field was more modest—to find a material with superconductivity well above the temperature of liquid hydrogen. Scientists would certainly have loved to find something better yet—perhaps a material that remained superconducting above the temperature of liquid nitrogen (77°K). That would have allowed superconductors to be readily used in many applications, from electromagnets to power transmission. But as recently as December 1986, that looked like an impossible dream.

The first signs of the breakthrough had come early that year. In January 1986, Alex Müller and Georg Bednorz, at the IBM Research Division in Zurich, Switzerland, produced superconductivity in a ceramic sample containing barium, copper, oxygen, and lanthanum (one of a group of elements, atomic numbers 58 to 71, known as the rare-earth elements). The temperature was 11°K, which was not earth-shaking, but much higher than anyone might have expected. Müller and Bednorz knew they were on to something good. They produced new ceramic samples, and little by little worked the temperature for the onset of superconductivity up to 30°K. The old record, established in 1973, had been 23°K. By November, Paul Chu and colleagues at the University of Houston, and Tanaka and Kitazawa at the University of Tokyo, had repeated the experiments, and also found the material superconducting at 30°K.

Once those results were announced, every experimental team engaged in superconductor research jumped onto the problem. In December, Robert Cava, Bruce van Dover, and Bertram Batlogg at Bell Labs had produced superconductivity in a strontium-lanthanum-copper-oxide combination at 36°K. Also in December 1986, Chu and colleagues had positive results over 50°K.

In January 1987, there was another astonishing breakthrough. Chu and his fellow workers substituted yttrium, a metal with many rare-earth properties, for lanthanum in the ceramic pellets they were making. The resulting samples went superconducting at 90°K. The researchers could hardly believe their result, but within a few days they had pushed up to 93°K, and had a repeatable, replicable procedure. Research groups in

Tokyo and in Beijing also reported results above 90°K in February.

Recall that liquid nitrogen boils at 77°K. For the first time, superconductors had passed the "nitrogen barrier." In a bath of that liquid, a ceramic wire using yttrium, barium, copper, and oxygen was superconducting.

The end of the road had still not been reached. In early March 1987, a team at the University of California reported signs of superconductive behavior at 234°K. This is only −40°C, just a few degrees below the temperature at which ammonia boils. A group at Wayne State University found signs of superconductivity at −33°C, right at the temperature of liquid ammonia.

Once these results are understood, room-temperature superconductors seem to be just around the corner. Samples are being made using all the rare-earth elements, in hundreds or thousands of different combinations. More progress seems almost inevitable.

Unfortunately, the experimental results are not yet understood. The research teams have systematic procedures by which they select new materials to use as samples, and it would be totally unfair to suggest that they proceed by trial and error. However, they would agree that there is no accepted model as to what is going on, and it would not be unfair to say that at the moment, experiment is well ahead of theory.

The Bardeen, Cooper, and Schrieffer theory of superconductivity leads to a very weak binding force between electron pairs. Thus, according to this theory, the phenomenon ought not to occur at 90°K, still less at 240°K. At the same time, the theory tells us that *any* superconductivity, high-temperature or otherwise, is almost certainly the result of free electrons forming into pairs, and then behaving as bosons. In classical superconductivity, at just a few degrees above absolute zero, the mediating influence that operates to form electron pairs can be shown to be the atomic lattice itself. That result, in quantitative form, comes from the Bardeen, Cooper, and Schrieffer approach. The natural question

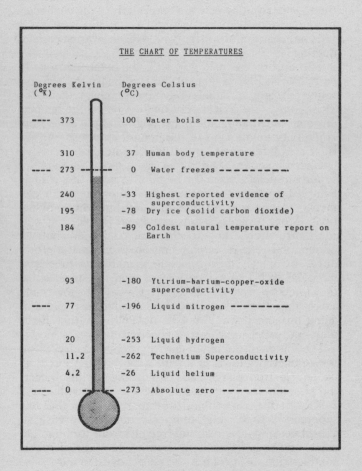

THE CHART OF TEMPERATURES

Degrees Kelvin (°K)	Degrees Celsius (°C)	
---- 373	100	Water boils -------------
310	37	Human body temperature
---- 273	0	Water freezes ----------
240	-33	Highest reported evidence of superconductivity
195	-78	Dry ice (solid carbon dioxide)
184	-89	Coldest natural temperature report on Earth
93	-180	Yttrium-barium-copper-oxide superconductivity
---- 77	-196	Liquid nitrogen --------
20	-253	Liquid hydrogen
11.2	-262	Technetium Superconductivity
4.2	-26	Liquid helium
---- 0	-273	Absolute zero ----------

to ask is, What other factor could work to produce electron pairs? To be useful, it must produce strong bonding of electron pairs; otherwise, they would be dissociated by the plentiful thermal energy at higher temperatures. And any electron pairs so produced must be free to move, in order to carry the electric current.

There are theories—several of them. A plausible one is offered by Philip Anderson of Princeton University. In this case, the mediating influence that permits the formation of electron pairs is not interaction with the atomic lattice; rather, it is suggested that the electron pairs already exist in the material. "Doping" the ceramic material with small amounts of other substances, such as lanthanum or yttrium, allows the pairs to move freely through it.

Other workers believe that a new explanation of electron pair occurrence is not necessary—only a better understanding of how electrons and the atomic lattice can interact to permit high-temperature pairing. Yet another view is that it is the existence of electron-hole pairs that mediates the bonding of free electrons.

The one thing on which everyone agrees is that at the moment there is no generally accepted theory. Because of this uncertainty, no one is keen to say at how high a temperature superconductivity may eventually occur. But Philip Anderson offered a tentative upper limit, placing it at the antiferromagnetic transition temperature. For some materials this is as high as $330°C$—a temperature that will melt lead. If that number is at all likely, the story of superconductivity has only just begun.

MAKING IT WORK. Does this mean that we now have useful, work-horse superconductors above the temperature of liquid nitrogen, ready for industrial applications? It looks like it. But there are still possible complications.

Soon after Kamerlingh Onnes discovered superconductivity, he also discovered (in 1913) that superconductivity was destroyed when he sent a large current through the material. This is a consequence of the effect that Oersted and Ampère had noticed in 1820; namely, that an electric current creates a magnetic field. The temperature at which a material goes superconducting is *lowered* when it is placed in a magnetic field. That is why the stipulation was made in Table 3 that those temperatures apply only when no magnetic field is present. A large current creates its own magnetic field, so it may itself destroy the superconducting property.

For a superconductor to be useful in power transmission, it must remain superconducting even though the current through it is large. Thus we want the critical temperature, T_c, to be insensitive to the current through the sample. One concern was that the new high-temperature superconductors might perform poorly here, and the first samples made were in fact highly affected by imposed magnetic fields. However, some of the new superconductors have now been found to remain superconducting at currents up to 1,000 amperes per square millimeter, and this is more than adequate for power transmission.

A second concern is a practical one: can the new materials be worked with, to make wires and coils that are not too brittle or too variable in quality? Again the answers are positive. The ceramics can be formed into loops and wires, and they are not unduly brittle or fickle in behavior.

The only thing left is to learn where the new capability of high-temperature superconductors will be most useful. Some applications are already clear.

First, we will see smaller and faster computers, where the problem of carrying off heat caused by dissipation of energy from electrical currents in small components is a big problem. This application will exist, even if the highest temperature superconductors cannot tolerate high current densities.

Second, as Faraday discovered, any tightly wound coil of wire with a current running through it becomes an electromagnet. Superconducting coils can produce very powerful magnets of this type, ones that will keep their magnetic properties without using any energy or needing any cooling. Today's electromagnets that operate at room temperature are limited in their strength, because very large currents through the coils also produce large heating effects.

Third, superconductors have another important property that we have not so far mentioned; namely, they do not allow a magnetic field to be formed within them. In the language of electromagnetic theory, they are *perfectly diamagnetic*. This is known as the Meissner Effect, and it was discovered in 1933. It could have easily been found in 1913, but it was considered so unlikely a possibility that no one did the experiment to test superconductor diamagnetism for another twenty years.

As a consequence of the Meissner Effect, a superconductor that is near a magnet will form an electric current layer on its surface. That current layer is such that the superconductor is then strongly *repelled* by the magnetic field, rather than being attracted to it. This permits a technique known as *magnetic levitation* to be used to lift and support heavy objects. Magnets, suspended above a line of superconductors, will remain there without needing any energy to hold them up. Friction-free support systems are the result, and they should be useful in everything from transportation to factory assembly lines. For many years, people have talked of super-speed trains, suspended by magnetic fields and running at a fraction of the operating costs of today's locomotives. When superconductors could operate only when cooled to liquid hydrogen temperatures and below, such transportation ideas were hopelessly expensive. With high-temperature superconductors, they become economically attractive.

And, of course, there is the transmission of electrical power. Today's transmission grids are full of transformers that boost the electrical signal to hundreds of thousands of volts for sending the power through the lines, and then bring that high-voltage signal back to a hundred volts or so for household use. However, the only reason for doing this is to minimize energy losses. Line heating is less when electrical power is transmitted at low current and high voltage, so the higher the voltage, the better. With superconductors, however, there are no heat dissipation losses at all. Today's elaborate system of transformers will be unnecessary. The implications of this are enormous: the possible replacement of the entire electrical transmission systems of the world by a less expensive alternative, both to build and to operate.

However, before anyone embarks on such an effort, they will want to be sure that the technology has gone as far as it is likely to go. It would be crazy to start building a power-line system based on the assumption that the superconductors need to be cooled to liquid nitrogen or liquid ammonia temperatures, if next year sees the discovery of a material that remains superconducting at room temperature and beyond.

Supercomputers, heavy lift systems, magnetically cushioned super-trains, cheap electrical power transmission—these are the obvious prospects. Are there other important uses that have not yet been documented?

Almost certainly, there are. Everything has been happening so fast, and every worker in the field has been so desperately busy, that no one has had time to think through all the possible applications. But everyone probably agrees on one thing: in the next ten years, there are billions of dollars and several Nobel Prizes waiting for somebody in the field of high-temperature superconductors.

Post Script. The ball is still rolling, and rolling fast. What you have read so far was written in April 1987. Today is July 29, 1987, and already there are enough new results that an update is necessary.

Superconductors at more than 90°K have now been reported by many groups—the preparation is easy and reliable enough that it is becoming a high-school experiment! In addition, a variety of different rare earths are being used in place of yttrium, and many of them also form superconductors. The basic mixture rare-earth + barium + copper + oxygen seems to admit superconductivity in many different combinations.

The structure of the yttrium-based superconducting materials is steadily being revealed. It appears to have a strongly asymmetrical form, like a set of sandwich layers, and the superconducting effect is seen only in certain directions. The presence of "defects" in the structure, where oxygen atoms are absent, seems to be central to the superconducting property.

There have also been tantalizing new hints of superconductivity at 260°K, at 280°K, at 292°K (62° Fahrenheit, a rather chill room temperature) and even some indications at 360°K (nearly hot enough to boil water). Pinning down these cases has proved difficult, but enough people have seen evidence that this seems to be just a matter of time—and in this field, we are talking months, not years. Almost certainly, sporadic superconductivity shows the presence of small superconducting parts embedded in a non-conducting whole. Purification and removal of impurities may be all that is needed for a full-fledged room-temperature superconductor.

The first useful device using a superconductor that operates above liquid nitrogen temperatures has already been built, by James Zimmerman at the National Bureau of Standards in May 1987. It is a SQUID, a Superconducting Quantum Interference Device, and it is capable of measuring extremely low magnetic fields. Can you think of a place with a very low magnetic field? You can't think without one—the human brain generates just such fields, and SQUIDs will be useful in monitoring brain activity.

How important is this whole field of research going to be in the next decade? Very important. But don't take my word for it; look at some other evidence. I just came back from an unprecedented event: a physics conference where Nobel prizewinners and research workers held the stage until midday, discussing the present state of experimental and theoretical high-temperature superconductivity, and then handed over to a second and quite different group.

That second party included President Ronald Reagan, Secretary of Defense Caspar Weinberger, Secretary of State George Shultz, Secretary of Energy John Herrington, the President's Science Advisor, William Graham, and the head of the National Science Foundation, Erich Bloch. In his keynote speech, President Reagan announced the formation of a Council on Superconductivity, headed by George Keyworth (former Science Advisor to the President) and intended to promote American industrial leadership in using superconductors.

The President quoted Ben Franklin, who said, "I have sometimes almost wished it had been my destiny to be born two or three centuries hence. For invention and improvement are prolific, and beget more of their kind." If we have that same feeling today, we can take comfort that in the field of superconductivity we won't have to wait for centuries. As Edward Teller said, "We've seen discoveries in the last eight months that the *optimists* thought we wouldn't make for two hundred years."

Introduction

A few decades ago "eugenics," the proposed appliction of the science of genetics to the bredding of people, was all the rage in some circles. Fun and games with Hitler and the Master Race pretty much cured us of that particular social disease, but now, as we thunder down the home stretch to total understanding and consequent control of our own heredity, the question of what we are will inevitably merge with what we should be, taking on a terrible force in the process. If Dean Ing is right the result of controlling the genetic structure of our descendants is less likely to result in superhumans than in people who embody a sort of burlesque of our most desired charcteristics. Certainly that's what happened to the Kzin.

"Cathouse" will appear in Book One of Larry Niven's shared universe series, THE MAN-KZIN WARS (June 1988, Baen Books).

CATHOUSE

Dean Ing

Sampling war's minor ironies: Locklear knew so little about the *Weasel* or wartime alarms, he thought the klaxon was hooting for planetfall. That is why, when the *Weasel* winked into normal space near that lurking kzin warship, little Locklear would soon be her only survivor. The second irony was that, while the Interworld Commission's last bulletin had announced sporadic new outbursts of kzin hostility, Locklear was the only civilian on the *Weasel* who had never thought of himself as a warrior and did not intend to become one.

Moments after the *Weasel's* intercom announced completion of their jump, Locklear was steadying himself next to his berth, waiting for the ship's gravity-polarizer to kick in and swallowing hard because, like ancient French wines, he traveled poorly. He watched with envy as Herrera, the hairless, whipcord-muscled Belter in the other bunk, swung out with one foot planted on the deck and the other against the wall. "Like a cat," Locklear said admiringly.

"That's no compliment anymore, flatlander," Herrera said. "It looks like the goddam tabbies want a fourth war. You'd think they'd learn," he added with a grim headshake.

Locklear sighed. As a student of animal psychology in general, he'd known a few kzinti well enough to admire the way they learned. He also knew Herrera was on his way to enlist if, as seemed likely, the Kzinti were

117

spoiling for another war. And in that case, Locklear's career was about to be turned upside down. Instead of a scholarly life puzzling out the meanings of Grog forepaw gestures and kzin ear-twitches, he would probably be conscripted into some warren full of psych warfare pundits, for the duration. These days, an ethologist had to be part historian, too—Locklear remembered more than he liked about the three previous man-kzin wars.

And Herrera was ready to fight the kzinti already, and Locklear had called *him* a cat. Locklear opened his mouth to apologize but the klaxon drowned him out. Herrera slammed the door open, vaulted into the passageway reaching for handholds.

"What's the matter," Locklear shouted. "Where are you—?"

Herrera's answer, half-lost between the door-slam and the klaxon, sounded like 'atta nation' to Locklear, who did not even know the drill for a deadheading passenger during battle stations. Locklear was still waiting for a familiar tug of gravity when that door sighed, the hermetic seal swelling as always during a battle alert, and he had time to wonder why Herrera was in such a hurry before the *Weasel* took her fatal hit amidships.

An energy beam does not always sound like a thunderclap from inside the stricken vessel. This one sent a faint crackling down the length of the *Weasel's* hull, like the rustle of pre-space parchment crushed in a man's hand. Sequestered alone in a two-man cabin near the ship's aft galley, Locklear saw his bunk leap toward him, the inertia of his own body wrenching his grip from his handhold near the door. He did not have time to consider the implications of a blow powerful enough to send a twelve-hundred-ton Privateer-class patrol ship tumbling like a pinwheel, nor the fact that the blow itself was the reaction from most of the *Weasel's* air, exhausting to space in explosive decompression. And because his cabin had no external viewport, he could not see the scatter of human bodies into the void. The last thing he saw was the underside of his bunk, and the metal brace that caught him above the left cheekbone. Then he knew only a mild curiosity: wondering why he heard something like the steady sound of a thin whistle underwater, and why that yellow flash in his head was followed by an infrared darkness crammed with pain.

It was the pain that brought him awake, that, and the sound of loud static. No, more like the zaps of an arc welder in the hands of a novice—or like a catfight. And then he turned a blurred mental page and *knew* it, the way a Rorschach blot suddenly becomes a face half-forgotten but always feared. So it did not surprise him, when he opened his eyes, to see two huge kzinti standing over him.

To a man like Herrera they would merely have been massive. To Locklear, a man of less than average height, they were enormous; nearly half again his height. The broadest Kzin, with the notched right ear and the black horizontal fur-mark like a frown over his eyes, opened his mouth in what, to humans, might be a smile. But Kzinti smiles showed dagger teeth and always meant immediate threat. This one was saying something that sounded like, 'Clash-rowll whuff, rurr fitz'.

Locklear needed a few seconds to translate it, and by that time the second kzin was saying it in Interworld: "Grraf-Commander says, 'Speak when you are spoken to.' For myself, I would prefer that you remained silent. I have eaten no monkeymeat for too long."

While Locklear composed a reply, the big one—the Grraf-Commander, evidently—spoke again to his fellow. Something about whether the monkey knew his posture was deliberately obscene. Locklear, lying on his back on a padded table as big as a Belter's honeymoon bed, realized his arms and legs were flung wide. "I am not very fluent in the Hero's tongue," he said in passable kzin, struggling to a sitting position as he spoke.

As he did, some of that pain localized at his right collarbone. Locklear moved very slowly thereafter. Then, recognizing the dot-and-comma-rich labels that graced much of the equipment in that room, he decided not to ask where he was. He could be nowhere but an emergency surgical room for Kzin warriors. That meant he was on a kzin ship.

A faint slitting of the smaller kzin's eyes might have meant determination, a grasping for patience, or—if Locklear recalled the texts, and if they were right, a small 'if' followed by a very large one—a pause for relatively cold calculation. The smaller kzin said, in his own tongue, "If the monkey speaks the hero's tongue, it is probably as a spy."

"My presence here was not my idea," Locklear pointed out, surprised to find his memory of the language returning so quickly. "I boarded the *Weasel* on command to leave a dangerous region, not to enter one. Ask the ship's quartermaster, or check her records."

The commander spat and sizzled again: "The crew are all carrion. As you will soon be, unless you tell us why, of all the monkeys on that ship, you were the only one so specially protected."

Locklear moaned. This huge kzin's partial name and his scars implied the kind of warrior whose valor and honor forbade lies to a captive. All dead but himself? Locklear shrugged before he thought, and the shrug sent a stab of agony across his upper chest. "Sonofabitch," he gasped in agony. The navigator kzin translated. The larger one grinned, the kind of grin that might fasten on his throat.

Locklear said in kzin, very fast, "Not you! I was cursing the pain."

"A telepath could verify your meanings very quickly," said the smaller kzin.

"An excellent idea," said Locklear. "He will verify that I am no spy, and not a combatant, but only an ethologist from Earth. A kzin acquaintance once told me it was important to know your forms of address. I do not wish to give offense."

"Call me Tzak-Navigator," said the smaller kzin abruptly, and grasped Locklear by the shoulder, talons sinking into the human flesh. Locklear moaned again, gritting his teeth. "You would attack? Good," the navigator went on, mistaking the grimace, maintaining his grip, the formidable kzin body trembling with intent.

"I cannot speak well with such pain," Locklear managed to grunt. "Not as well protected as you think."

"We found you well-protected and sealed alone in that ship," said the commander, motioning for the navigator to slacken his hold. "I warn you, we must rendezvous the *Raptor* with another Ripping-Fang class cruiser to pick up a full crew before we hit the Eridani worlds. I have no time to waste on such a scrawny monkey as you, which we have caught nearer our home worlds than to your own."

Locklear grasped his right elbow as support for that aching collarbone. "I was surveying life-forms on purely academic study—in peacetime, so far as I knew," he said. "The old patrol craft I leased didn't have a weapon on it."

"You lie," the navigator hissed. "We saw them."

"The *Weasel* was not my ship, Tzak-Navigator. Its commander brought me back under protest; said the Interworld Commission wanted noncombatants out of harm's way—and here I am in its cloaca."

"Then it was already well-known on that ship that we are at war. I feel better about killing it," said the commander. "Now, as to the ludicrous cargo it was carrying: what is your title and importance?"

"I am scholar Carroll Locklear. I was probably the least important man on the *Weasel*—except to myself. Since I have nothing to hide, bring a telepath."

"Now it gives orders," snarled the navigator.

"Please," Locklear said quickly.

"Better," the commander said.

"It knows," the navigator muttered. "That is why it issues such a challenge."

"Perhaps," the commander rumbled. To Locklear he said, "A skeleton crew of four rarely includes a telepath. That statement will either satisfy your challenge, or I can satisfy it in more—conventional ways." That grin again, feral, willing.

"I meant no challenge, Grraf-Commander. I only want to satisfy you of who I am, and who I'm not."

"We know *what* you are," said the navigator. "You are our prisoner, an important one, fleeing the Patriarchy rim in hopes that the monkeyship could get you to safety." He reached again for Locklear's shoulder.

"That is pure torture," Locklear said, wincing, and saw the navigator stiffen as the furry orange arm dropped. If only he had recalled the kzinti disdain for torture earlier! "I am told you are an honorable race. May I be treated properly as a captive?"

"By all means," the commander said, almost in a purr. "We eat captives."

Locklear, slyly: "Even important ones?"

"If it pleases me," the commander replied. "More likely you could turn your coat in the service of the Patriarchy. I say you could; I would not suggest such an obscenity. But that is probably the one chance your sort has for personal survival."

"My sort?"

The commander looked Locklear up and down, at the slender body, lightly muscled with only the deep chest to suggest stamina. "One of the most vulnerable specimens of monkeydom I have ever seen," he said.

That was the moment when Locklear decided he was at war. "Vulnerable, and important, and captive. Eat me," he said, wondering if that final phrase was as insulting in kzin as it was in Interworld. Evidently not . . .

"Gunner! Apprentice Engineer," the commander called suddenly, and Locklear heard two responses through the ship's intercom. "Lock this monkey in a wiper's quarters." He turned to his navigator. "Perhaps Fleet Commander Skrull-Rrit will want this one alive. We shall know in an eight-squared of duty watches." With that, the huge kzin commander strode out.

After his second sleep, Locklear found himself roughly hustled forward in the low-polarity ship's gravity of the

Raptor by the nameless Apprentice Engineer. This smallest of the crew had been a kitten not long before and, at two-meter height, was still filling out. The transverse mustard-tinted band across his abdominal fur identified Apprentice Engineer down the full length of the hull passageway.

Locklear, his right arm in a sling of bandages, tried to remember all the mental notes he had made since being tossed into that cell. He kept his eyes downcast to avoid a challenging look—and because he did not want his cold fury to show. These orange-furred monstrosities had killed a ship and crew with every semblance of pride in the act. They treated a civilian captive at best like playground bullies treat an urchin, and at worst like food. It was all very well to study animal behavior as a detached ethologist. It was something else when the toughest warriors in the galaxy attached you to their food chain.

He slouched because that was as far from a military posture as a man could get—and Locklear's personal war could hardly be declared if he valued his own pelt. He would try to learn where hand weapons were kept, but would try to seem stupid. He would . . . he found the last vow impossible to keep with the Grraf-Commander's first question.

Wheeling in his command chair on the *Raptor*'s bridge, the commander faced the captive. "If you piloted your own monkeyship, then you have some menial skills." It was not a question; more like an accusation. "Can you learn to read meters if it will lengthen your pathetic life?"

Ah, there *was* a question! Locklear was on the point of lying, but it took a worried kzin to sing a worried song. If they needed him to read meters, he might learn much in a short time. Besides, they'd know bloody well if he lied on this matter. "I can try," he said. "What's the problem?"

"Tell him," spat Grraf-Commander, spinning about again to the holo screen.

Tzak-Navigator made a gesture of agreement, stand-

ing beside Locklear and gazing toward the vast humped
shoulders of the fourth kzin. This nameless one was of
truly gigantic size. He turned, growling, and Locklear
noted the nose scar that seemed very appropriate for a
flash-tempered gunner. Tzak-Navigator met his gaze
and paused, with the characteristic tremor of a kzin
who prided himself on physical control. "Ship's Gunner, you are relieved. Adequately done."

With the final phrase, Ship's Gunner relaxed his ear
umbrellas and stalked off with a barely creditable sa-
lute. Tzak-Navigator pointed to the vacated seat, and
Locklear took it. "He has got us lost," muttered the
navigator.

"But you were the navigator," Locklear said.

"Watch your tongue!"

"I'm just trying to understand crew duties. I asked
what the problem was, and Grraf-Commander said to
tell me."

The tremor became more obvious, but Tzak-Navigator
knew when he was boxed. "With a four-kzin crew, our
titles and our duties tend to vary. When I accept duties
of executive officer and communications officer as well,
another member may prove his mettle at some simple
tasks of astrogation."

"I would think Apprentice Engineer might be good
at reading meters," Locklear said carefully.

"He has enough of them to read in the engine room.
Besides, Ship's Gunner has superior time in grade; to
pass him over would have been a deadly insult."

"Um. And I don't count?"

"Exactly. As a captive, you are a nonperson—even if
you have skills that a gunner might lack."

"You said it was adequately done," Locklear pointed
out.

"For a gunner," spat the navigator, and Locklear
smiled. A kzin, too proud to lie, could still speak with
mental reservations to an underling. The navigator went
on: "We drew first blood with our chance sortie to the
galactic West, but Ship's Gunner must verify gravitational blips as we pass in hyperdrive."

Locklear listened, and asked, and learned. What he learned initially was fast mental translation of octal numbers to decimal. What he learned eventually was that, counting on the gunner to verify likely blips of known star masses, Grraf-Commander had finally realized that they were monumentally lost, light-years from their intended rendezvous on the rim of known space. *And that rendezvous is on the way to the Eridani worlds*, Locklear thought. He said, as if to himself but in kzin, "Out Eridani way, I hear they're always on guard for you guys. You really expect to get out of this alive?"

"No," said the navigator easily. "Your life may be extended a little, but you will die with heroes. Soon."

"Sounds like a suicide run," Locklear said.

"We are volunteers," the navigator said with lofty arrogance, making no attempt to argue the point, and then continued his instructions.

Presently, studying the screen, Locklear said, "That gunner has us forty parsecs from anyplace. Jump into normal space long enough for an astrogation fix and you've got it."

"Do not abuse my patience, monkey. Our last Fleet Command message on hyperwave forbade us to make unnecessary jumps."

After a moment, Locklear grinned. "And your commander doesn't want to have to tell Fleet Command you're lost."

"What was that thing you did with your face?"

"Uh,—just stretching the muscles," Locklear lied, and pointed at one of the meters. "There; um, that was a field strength of, oh hell, three eights and four, right?"

Tzak-Navigator did not have to tremble because his four-fingered hand was in motion as a blur, punching buttons. "Yes. I have a star mass and," the small screen stuttered its chicken-droppings in Kzinti, "here are the known candidates."

Locklear nodded. In this little-known region, some star masses, especially the larger ones, would have been recorded. With several fixes in hyperdrive, he could make a strong guess at their direction with respect to the galactic core. But by the time he had his second group of candidate stars, Locklear also had a scheme.

Locklear asked for his wristcomp, to help him translate octal numbers—his chief motive was less direct—and got it after Apprentice Engineer satisfied himself that it was no energy weapon. The engineer, a suspicious churl quick with his hands and clearly on the make for status, displayed disappointment at his own findings by throwing the instrument in Locklear's face. Locklear decided that the kzin lowest on the scrotum pole was most anxious to advance by any means available. And that, he decided, just might be common in all sentient behavior.

Two hours later by his wristcomp, when Locklear tried to speak to the commander without prior permission, the navigator backhanded him for his trouble and then explained the proper channels. "I will decide whether your message is worth Grraf-Commander's notice," he snarled.

Trying to stop his nosebleed, Locklear told him.

"A transparent ruse," the navigator accused, "to save your own hairless pelt."

"It would have that effect," Locklear agreed. "Maybe. But it would also let you locate your position."

The navigator looked him up and down. "Which will aid us in our mission against your own kind. You truly disgust me."

In answer, Locklear only shrugged. Tzak-Navigator wheeled and crossed to the commander's vicinity, stiff and proper, and spoke rapidly for a few moments. Presently, Grraf-Commander motioned for Locklear to approach.

Locklear decided that a military posture might help this time, and tried to hold his body straight despite his pains. The commander eyed him silently, then said, "You offer me a motive to justify jumping into normal space?"

"Yes, Grraf-Commander; to deposit an important captive in a lifeboat around some steller body."

"And why in the name of the Patriarchy would I want to?"

"Because it is almost within the reach of plausibility that the occupants of this ship might not survive this mission," Locklear said with irony that went unnoticed. "But en route to your final glory, you can inform Fleet Command where you have placed a vitally important captive, to be retrieved later."

"You admit your status at last."

"I have a certain status," Locklear admitted. *It's damned low, and that's certain enough.* "And while you were doing that in normal space, a navigator might just happen to determine exactly where you are."

"You do not deceive me in your motive. If I did not locate that spot," Tzak-Navigator said, "no Patriarchy ship could find you—and you would soon run out of food and air."

"And you would miss the Eridani mission," Locklear reminded him, "because we aren't getting any blips and you may be getting farther from your rendezvous with every breath."

"At the least, you are a traitor to monkeydom," the navigator said. "No kzin worthy of the name would assist an enemy mission."

Locklear favored him with a level gaze. "You've decided to waste all nine lives for glory. Count on me for help."

"Monkeys are clever where their pelts are concerned," rumbled the commander. "I do not intend to miss rendezvous, and this monkey must be placed in a safe cage. Have the crew provision a lifeboat but disable its drive, Tzak-Navigator. When we locate a steller mass, I want all in readiness for the jump."

The navigator saluted and moved off the bridge. Locklear received permission to return to his console, moving slowly, trying to watch the commander's furry digits in preparation for a jump that might be required at any time. Locklear punched several notes into the wristcomp's memory; you could never tell when a scholar's notes might come in handy.

Locklear was chewing on kzin rations, reconstituted meat which met human teeth like a leather brick and tasted of last week's oysters, when the long-range meter began to register. It was not much of a blip but it got stronger fast, the vernier meter registering by the time Locklear called out. He watched the commander, alone while the rest of the crew were arranging that lifeboat, and used his wristcomp a few more times before Grraf-Commander's announcement.

Tzak-Navigator, eyeing his console moments after the jump and still light-minutes from that small stellar mass, was at first too intent on his astrogation to notice that there was no nearby solar blaze. But Locklear noticed, and felt a surge of panic.

"You will not perish in solar radiation, at least," said Grraf-Commander in evident pleasure. "You have found yourself a black dwarf, monkey!"

Locklear punched a query. He found no candidate stars to match this phenomenon. "Permission to speak, Tzak-Navigator?"

The navigator punched in a final instruction and, while his screen flickered, turned to the local viewscreen. "Wait until you have something worth saying," he ordered, and paused, staring at what that screen told him. Then, as if arguing with his screen, he complained, "But known space is not old enough for a completely burnt-out star."

"Nevertheless," the commander replied, waving toward the screens, "if not a black dwarf, a very, very brown one. Thank that lucky star, Tzak-Navigator; it might have been a neutron star."

"And a planet," the navigator exclaimed. "Impossible! Before its final collapse, this star would have converted any nearby planet into a gas shell. But there it lies!" He pointed to a luminous dot on the screen.

"That might make it easy to find again," Locklear said with something akin to faint hope. He knew, watching the navigator's split concentration between screens, that the kzin would soon know the *Raptor*'s position. No chance beyond this brown dwarf now, an unheard-of anomaly, to escape this suicide ship.

The navigator ignored him. "Permission for proximal orbit," he requested.

"Denied," the commander said. "You know better than that. Close orbit around a dwarf could rip us asunder with angular acceleration. That dwarf may be only the size of a single dreadnaught, but its mass is enormous enough to bend distant starlight."

While Locklear considered what little he knew of collapsed star matter, a cupful of which would exceed the mass of the greatest warship in known space, the navigator consulted his astrogation screen again. "I have our position," he said at last. "We were on the way to the galactic rim, thanks to that untrained—well, at least he is a fine gunner. Grraf-Commander, I meant to ask permission for orbit around the planet. We can discard this offal in the lifeboat there."

"Granted," said the commander. Locklear took more notes as the two kzinti piloted their ship nearer. If lifeboats were piloted with the same systems as cruisers, and if he could study the ways in which that lifeboat drive could be energized, he might yet take a hand in his fate.

The maneuvers took so much time that Locklear feared the kzin would drop the whole idea, but, "Let it be recorded that I keep my bargains, even with monkeys," the commander grouched as the planet began to grow in the viewport.

"Tiny suns, orbiting the planet? Stranger and stranger," the navigator mused. "Grraf-Commander, this is—not natural."

"Exactly so. It is artificial," said the commander. Brightening, he added, "Perhaps a special project, though I do not know how we could move a full-sized planet into orbit around a dwarf. Tzak-Navigator, see if this tallies with anything the Patriarchy may have on file." No sound passed between them when the navigator looked up from his screen, but their shared glance did not improve the commander's mood. "No? Well, backup records in triplicate," he snapped. "Survey sensors to full gain."

Locklear took more notes, his heart pounding anew with every added strangeness of this singular discovery. The planet orbited several light-minutes from the dead star, with numerous satellites in synchronous orbits, blazing like tiny suns—or rather, like spotlights in imitation of tiny suns, for the radiation from those satellites blazed only downward, toward the planet's surface. Those satellites, according to the navigator, seemed to be moving a bit in complex patterns, not all of them in the same ways—and one of them dimmed even as they watched.

The commander brought the ship nearer, and now Tzak-Navigator gasped with a fresh astonishment. "Grraf-Commander, this planet is dotted with force-cylinder generators. Not complete shells, but open to space at orbital height. And the beam-spread of each satellite's light flux coincides with the edge of each force cylinder. No, not all of them; several of those circular areas are not bathed in any light at all. Fallow areas?"

"Or unfinished areas," the commander grunted. "Perhaps we have discovered a project in the making."

Locklear saw blazes of blue, white, red, and and yellow impinging in vast circular patterns on the planet's surface. *Almost as if someone had placed small models of Sirius, Sol, Fomalhaut, and other suns out here,* he thought. He said nothing. If he orbited this bizarre mystery long enough, he might probe its secrets. If he orbited it too long, he would damned well die of starvation.

Then, "Homeworld," blurted the astonished navigator, as the ship continued its close pass around this planet that was at least half the mass of Earth.

Locklear saw it too, a circular region that seemed to be hundreds of kilometers in diameter, rich in colors that reminded him of a kzin's fur. The green expanse of a big lake, too, as well as dark masses that might have been mountain crags. And then he noticed that one of the nearby circular patterns seemed achingly familiar in its colors, and before he thought, he said it in Interworld: "Earth!"

The commander leaped to a mind-numbing conclusion the moment before Locklear did. "This can only be a galactic prison—or a zoo," he said in a choked voice. "The planet was evidently moved here, after the brown dwarf was discovered. There seems to be no atmosphere outside the force walls, and the planetary surface between those circular regions is almost as cold as interstellar deeps, according to the sensors. If it is a prison, each compound is well-isolated from the others. Nothing could live in the interstices."

Locklear knew that the commander had overlooked something that could live there very comfortably, but held his tongue awhile. Then, "Permission to speak," he said.

"Granted," said the commander. "What do you know of this—this thing?"

"Only this: whether it is a zoo or a prison, one of those compounds seems very Earthlike. If you left me there, I might find air and food to last me indefinitely."

"And other monkeys to help in Patriarch-knows-what," the navigator put in quickly. "No one is answering my all-band queries, and we do not know who runs this prison. The Patriarchy has no prison on record that is even faintly like this."

"If they are keeping heroes in a kzinti compound," grated the commander, "this could be a planet-sized trap."

Tzak-Navigator: "But whose?"

Grraf-Commander, with arrogant satisfaction: "It will not matter whose it is, if they set a vermin-sized trap and catch an armed lifeboat. There is no shell over these circular walls, and if there were, I would try to blast through it. Re-enable the lifeboat's drive. Tzak-Navigator, as Executive Officer you will remain on alert in the *Raptor*. For the rest of us: sound planetfall!"

*   *   *

Caught between fright and amazement, Locklear could only hang on and wait, painfully buffeted during re-entry because the kzin-sized seat harness would not retract to fit his human frame. The lifeboat, the size of a flatlander's racing yacht, descended in a broad spiral, keeping well inside those invisible force-walls that might have damaged the craft on contact. At last the commander set his ship on a search pattern that spiraled inward while maintaining perhaps a kilometer's height above the yellow grassy plains, the kzin-colored steaming jungle, the placid lake, the dark mountain peaks of this tiny, synthesized piece of the kzin homeworld.

Presently, the craft settled near a promontory overlooking that lake and partially protected by the rise of a stone escarpment—the landfall of a good military mind, Locklear admitted to himself. "Apprentice-Engineer: report on environmental conditions," the commander ordered. Turning to Locklear, he added, "If this is a zoo, the zookeepers have not yet learned to capture heroes—nor any of our food animals, according to our survey. Since your metabolism is so near ours, I think this is where we shall deposit you for safekeeping."

"But without prey, Grraf-Commander, he will soon starve," said Apprentice Engineer.

The heavy look of the commander seemed full of ironic amusement. "No, he will not. Humans eat monkeyfood, remember? This specimen is a *kshat*."

Locklear colored but tried to ignore the insult. Any creature willing to eat vegetation was, to the kzinti, *kshat*, a herbivore capable of eating offal. And capable of little else. "You might leave me some rations anyway," he grumbled. "I'm in no condition to be climbing trees for food."

"But you soon may be, and a single monkey in this place could hide very well from a search party."

Apprentice-Engineer, performing his extra duties proudly, waved a digit toward the screen. "Grraf-Commander, the gravity constant is exactly home normal. The temperature, too; solar flux, the same; atmosphere and micro-organisms as well. I suspect that the builders of this zoo planet have buried gravity polarizers with the force cylinder generators."

"No doubt those other compounds are equally equipped to surrogate certain worlds," the commander said. "I think, whoever they are—or were—, the builders work very, very slowly."

Locklear, entertaining his own scenario, suspected the builders worked very slowly, all right—and in ways, with motives, beyond the understanding of man or kzin. But why tell his suspicions to Scarface? Locklear had by now given his own private labels to these infuriating kzin, after noting the commander's face-mark, the navigator's tremors of intent, the gunner's brutal stupidity and the engineer's abdominal patch: to Locklear, they had become Scarface, Brick-shitter, Goon, and Yellowbelly. Those labels gave him an emotional lift, but he knew better than to use them aloud.

Scarface made his intent clear to everyone, glancing at Locklear from time to time, as he gave his orders. Water and rations for eight duty watches were to be offloaded. Because every kzin craft has special equipment to pacify those kzinti who displayed criminal behavior, especially the Kdaptists with their treasonous leanings toward humankind, Scarface had prepared a *zzrou* for their human captive. The *zzrou* could be charged with a powerful soporific drug, or—as the commander said in this case—a poison. Affixed to a host and tuned to a transmitter, the *zzrou* could be set to inject its material into the host at regular intervals—or to meter it out whenever the host moved too far from that transmitter.

Scarface held the implant device, no larger than a biscuit with vicious prongs, in his hand, facing the captive. "If you try to extract this, it will kill you instantly. If you somehow found the transmitter and smashed it,—again you would die instantly. Whenever you stray two steps too far from it, you will suffer. I shall set it so that you can move about far enough to feed yourself, but not far enough to make finding you a difficulty."

Locklear chewed his lip for a moment, thinking. "Is the poison cumulative?"

"Yes. And if you do not know that honor forbids me to lie, you will soon find out to your sorrow." He turned and handed a small device to Yellowbelly. "Take this transmitter and place it where no monkey might stumble across it. Do not wander more than eight-cubed paces from here in the process—and take a side-arm and a transceiver with you. I am not absolutely certain the place is uninhabited. Captive! Bare your back."

Locklear, dry-mouthed, removed his jacket and shirt. He watched Yellowbelly bound back down the short passageway and, soon afterward, heard the sigh of an airlock. He turned casually, trying to catch sight of him as Goon was peering through the viewport, and then he felt a paralyzing agony as Scarface impacted the prongs of the *zzrou* into his back just below the left shoulder blade.

His first sensation was a chill, and his second was a painful reminder of those *zzrou* prongs sunk into the muscles of his back. Locklear eased to a sitting position and looked around him. Except for depressions in the yellowish grass, and a terrifyingly small pile of provisions piled atop his shirt and jacket, he could see no evidence that a kzin lifeboat had ever landed here. "For all you know, they'll never come back," he told himself aloud, shivering as he donned his garments. Talking to himself was an old habit born of solitary researches, and made him feel less alone.

But now that he thought on it, he couldn't decide which he dreaded most, their return or permanent solitude. "So let's take stock," he said, squatting next to the provisions. A kzin's rations would last three times as long for him, but the numbers were depressing: within three flatlander weeks he'd either find water and food, or he would starve—if he did not freeze first.

If this was really a compound designed for kzin, it would be chilly for Locklear—and it was. The water would be drinkable, and no doubt he could eat kzin game animals if he found any that did not eat him first. He had already decided to head for the edge of that lake, which lay shining at a distance that was hard to judge, when he realized that local animals might destroy what food he had.

Wincing with the effort, he removed his light jacket again. They had taken his small utility knife but Yellowbelly had not checked his grooming tool very well. He deployed its shaving blade instead of the nail pincers and used it to slit away the jacket's epaulets, then cut carefully at the triple-folds of cloth, grateful for his accidental choice of a woven fabric. He found that when trying to break a thread, he would cut his hand before the thread parted. Good; a single thread would support all of those rations but the water bulbs.

His wristcomp told him the kzin had been gone an hour, and the position of that ersatz 61 Ursa Majoris hanging in the sky said he should have several more hours of light, unless the builders of this zoo had fudged on their timing. "Numbers," he said. "You need better numbers." He couldn't eat a number, but knowing the right ones might feed his belly.

In the landing pad depressions lay several stones, some crushed by the cruel weight of the kzin lifeboat. He pocketed a few fragments, two with sharp edges, tied a third stone to a twenty-meter length of thread and tossed it clumsily over a branch of a vine-choked tree. But when he tried to pull those rations up to suspend them out of harm's way, that thread sawed the pulpy branch in two. Sighing, he began collecting and stripping vines. Favoring his right shoulder, ignoring the pain of the *zzrou* as he used his left arm, he finally managed to suspend the plastic-encased bricks of leathery meat five meters above the grass. It was easier to cache the water, running slender vines through the carrying handles and suspending the water in two bundles. He kept one brick and one water bulb, which contained perhaps two gallons of the precious stuff.

And then he made his first crucial discovery, when a

trickle of moisture issued from the severed end of a
vine. It felt cool, and it didn't sting his hands, and
taking the inevitable plunge he licked at a droplet, and
then sucked at the end of that vine. Good clean water,
faintly sweet; but with what subtle poisons? He decided
to wait a day before trying it again, but he was smiling a
ferocious little smile.

Somewhere within an eight-cubed of kzin paces lay
the transmitter for that damned thing stuck into his
back. No telling exactly how far he could stray from it.
"Damned right there's some telling," he announced to
the breeze. "Numbers, numbers," he muttered. And
straight lines. If that misbegotten son of a hairball was
telling the truth—and a kzin always did—then Locklear
would know within a step or so when he'd gone too far.
The safe distance from that transmitter would probably
be the same in all directions, a hemisphere of space to
roam in. Would it let him get as far as the lake?

He found out after sighting toward the nearest edge
of the lake and setting out for it, slashing at the trunks
of jungle trees with a sharp stone to blaze a straight-line
trail. Not exactly straight, but nearly so. He listened
hard at every step, moving steadily downhill, wondering what might have a menu with his name on it.

That careful pace saved him a great deal of pain, but
not enough of it to suit him. Once, studying the heat-
sensors that guided a captive rattlesnake to its prey
back on Earth, Locklear had been bitten on the hand.
It was like that now behind and below his left shoulder,
a sudden burning ache that kept aching as he fell forward, writhing, hurting his right collarbone again.
Locklear scrambled backward five paces or so and the
sting was suddenly, shockingly, absent. That part wasn't
like a rattler bite, for sure. He cursed, but knew he had
to do it: moved forward again, very slowly, until he felt
the lancing bite of the *zzrou*. He moved back a pace and
the sting was gone. "But it's cumulative," he said aloud.
"Can't do this for a hobby."

He felled a small tree at that point, sawing it with a
thread tied to stones until the pulpy trunk fell, held at

an angle by vines. Its sap was milky. It stung his finger. Damned if he would let it sting his tongue. He couldn't wash the stuff off in lake water because the lake was perhaps a klick beyond his limit. He wondered if Yellowbelly had thought about that when he hid the transmitter.

Locklear had intended to pace off the distance he had moved from his food cache, but kzin gravity seemed to drag at his heels and he knew that he needed numbers more exact than the paces of a tiring man. He unwound all of the thread on the ball, then sat down and opened his grooming tool. Whatever forgotten genius had stamped a five-centimeter rule along the length of the pincer lever, Locklear owed him. He measured twenty of those lengths and then tied a knot. He then used that first one-meter length to judge his second knot; used it again for the third; and with fingers that stung from tiny cuts, tied two knots at the five-meter point. He tied three knots at the ten-meter point, then continued until he had fifteen meters of surveying line, ignoring the last meter or so.

He needed another half-hour to measure the distance, as straight as he could make it, back to the food cache: four hundred and thirty-seven meters. He punched the datum into his wristcomp and rested, drinking too much from that water bulb, noting that the sunlight was making longer shadows now. The sundown direction was 'West' by definition. And after sundown, what? Nocturnal predators? He was already exhausted, cold, and in need of shelter. Locklear managed to pile palmlike fronds as his bed in a narrow cleft of the promontory, made the best weapon he could by tying fist-sized stones two meters apart with a thread, grasped one stone and whirled the other experimentally. It made a satisfying whirr—and for all he knew, it might even be marginally useful.

The sunblaze fooled him, dying slowly while it was still halfway to his horizon. He punched the time into his wristcomp, and realized that the builders of this zoo might be limited in the degree to which they could surrogate a planetary surface, when other vast circular

cages were adjacent to this one. It was too much to ask
that any zoo cage be, for its specimens, the best of all
possible worlds.

Locklear slept badly, but he slept. During the times
when he lay awake, he felt the silence like a hermetic
seal around him, broken only by the rasp and slither of
distant tree fronds in vagrant breezes. Kzin-normal mi-
croorganisms, the navigator had said; maybe, but
Locklear had seen no sign of animal life. Almost, he
would have preferred stealthy footfalls or screams of
nocturnal prowlers.

The next morning he noted on his wristcomp when
the ersatz kzinti sun began to blaze—not on the horizon, but seeming to kindle when halfway to its zenith—
rigged a better sling for his right arm, then sat scratching
in the dirt for a time. The night had lasted thirteen
hours and forty-eight minutes. If succeeding nights were
longer, he was in for a tooth-chattering winter. But
first: FIND THAT DAMNED TRANSMITTER.

Because it was small enough to fit in a pocket. And
then, ah then, he would not be held like a lap-dog on a
leash. He pounded some kzin meat to soften it and took
his first sightings while swilling from a water bulb.

The extension of that measured line, this time in the
opposite direction, went more quickly except when he
had to clamber on rocky inclines or cut one of those
pulpy trees down to keep his sightings near-perfect. He
had no spirit level, but estimated the inclines as well as
he could, as he had done before, and used the wristcomp's trigonometric functions to adjust the numbers
he took from his surveying thread. That damned kzin
engineer was the kind who would be half-running to do
his master's bidding, and an eight-cubed of his paces
might be anywhere from six hundred meters to a kilometer. Or the hidden transmitter might be almost un-
derfoot at the cache; but no more than a klick at most.
Locklear was pondering that when the *zzrou* zapped
him again.

He stiffened, yelped, and whirled back several paces,
then advanced very slowly until he felt its first half-

hearted bite, and moved back, punching in the datum, working backward using the same system to make doubly sure of his numbers. At the cache, he found his two new numbers varied by five meters and split the difference. His southwest limit had been 437 meters away, his northeast limit 529; which meant the total length of that line was 966 meters. It probably wasn't the full diameter of his circle, but those points lay on its circumference. He halved the number: 483. That number, minus the 437, was 46 meters. He measured off forty-six meters toward the northeast and piled pulpy branches in a pyramid higher than his head. This point, by God, *was* one point on the full diameter of that circle perpendicular to his first line! Next he had to survey a line at a right angle to the line he'd already surveyed, a line passing through that pyramid of branches.

It took him all morning and then some, lengthening his thread to be more certain of that crucial right-angle before he set off into the jungle, and he measured almost seven hundred meters before that bloody damned *zzrou* bit him again, this time not so painfully because by that time he was moving very slowly. He returned to the pyramid of branches and struck off in the opposite direction, just to be sure of the numbers he scratched in the dirt using the wristcomp. He was filled with joy when the *zzrou* faithfully poisoned him a bit over 300 meters away, within ten meters of his expectation.

Those first three limit points had been enough to rough out the circle, the fourth was confirmation. Locklear knew that he had passed the transmitter on that long northwest leg; calculated quickly, because he knew the exact length of that diameter, that it was a bit over two hundred meters from his pyramid; and measured off the distance after lunch.

"Just like that fur-licking bastard," he said, looking around him at the tangle of orange, green and yellow jungle growth. "Probably shit on it before he buried it."

Locklear spent a fruitless hour clearing punky shrubs and man-high ferns from the soft turf before he saw it, and of course it was not where he had been looking at all. 'It' was not a telltale mound of dirt, nor a kzin footprint. It was a group of three globes of milky sap, no larger than water droplets, just about knee-high on the biggest palm in the clearing. And just about the right pattern for a kzin's toe-claws.

He moved around the trunk, as thick as his body, staring up the tree, now picking out other sets of milky puncture marks spaced up the trunk. More kzin claw-marks. Softly, feeling the gooseflesh move down his arms, he called, "Ollee-ollee-all's-in-free," just for the hell of it. And then he cut the damned tree down, carefully, letting the breeze do part of the work so that the tree sagged, buckled, and came down at a leisurely pace.

The transmitter, which looked rather like a wristcomp without a bracelet, lay in a hole scooped out by Yellow-belly's claws in the tender young top of the tree. It was sticky with sap, and Locklear hoped it had stung the kzin as it was stinging his own fingers. He wiped it off with vine leaves, rinsed it with dribbles of water from severed vines, wiped it off again, and then returned to his food cache.

"Yep, the shoulder hurts, and the damned gravity doesn't help but," he said, and yelled it at the sky, "Now I'm loose, you rat-tailed sons of bitches!"

He spent another night at the first cache, now with little concern about things that went boomp in the ersatz night. The sunblaze dimmed thirteen hours and forty-eight minutes after it began, and Locklear guessed that the days and nights of this synthetic arena never changed. "It'd be tough to develop a cosmology here," he said aloud, shivering because his right shoulder simply would not let him generate a fire by friction. "Maybe that was deliberate." If he wanted to study the behavior of intelligent species without risking their learning too much, and had not the faintest kind of ethics about it, Locklear decided he might imagine just such a vast enclosure for the kzinti. Only they were already a spacefaring race, and so was humankind, and he could have *sworn* the adjacent area on this impossible zoo planet was a ringer for one of the wild areas back on Earth. He cudgeled his memory until he recalled the lozenge shape of that lake seen from orbit, and the earthlike area.

"Right—about—there," he said, nodding to the southwest, across the lake. "If I don't starve first."

He knew that any kzinti searching for him could simply home in on the transmitter. Or maybe not so simply, if the signal was balked by stone or dirt. A cave with a kink in it could complicate their search nicely. He could test the idea—at the risk of absorbing one zap too many from that infuriating *zzrou* clinging to his back.

"Well, second things second," he said. He'd attended to the first things first. He slept poorly again, but the collarbone seemed to be mending.

Locklear admitted an instant's panic the next morning (he had counted down to the moment when the ersatz sun began to shine, missing it by a few seconds) as he moved beyond his old limit toward the lake. But the *zzrou* might have been a hockey puck for its inert ness. The lake had small regular wavelets—*easy enough to generate if you have a timer on your gravity polarizer,* he mused to the builders—and a narrow beach that alternated between sand and pebbles. No prints of any kind, not even birds or molluscs. If this huge arena did not have extremes of weather, a single footprint on that sand might last a geologic era.

The food cache was within a stone's throw of the kzin landing, good enough reason to find a better place. Locklear found one, where a stream trickled to the lake (pumps, or rainfall? Time enough to find out), after cutting its passage down through basalt that was half-hidden by foliage. Locklear found a hollow beneath a low waterfall and, in three trips, portaged all his meagre stores to that hideyhole with its stone shelf. The water tasted good, and again he tested the trickle from slashed vines because he did not intend to stay tied to that lakeside forever.

The channel cut through basalt by water told him that the stream had once been a torrent and might be again. The channel also hinted that the stream had been cutting its patient way for tens of centuries, perhaps far longer. "Zoo has been here a long time," he said, startled at the tinny echo behind the murmur of water, realizing that he had begun to think of this planet as 'Zoo'. It might be untenanted, like that sad remnant of a capitalist's dream that still drew tourists to San Simeon on the coast of Earth's California. Cages for exotic fauna, but the animals long since gone. *Or never introduced?* One more puzzle to be shelved until more pieces could be studied.

During his fourth day on Zoo, Locklear realized that the water was almost certainly safe, and that he must begin testing the tubers, spiny nuts, and poisonous-looking fruit that he had been eyeing with mistrust. Might as well test the stuff while circumnavigating the lake, he decided, vowing to try one new plant a day. Nothing had nibbled at anything beyond mosslike growths on some soft-surfaced fruit. He guessed that the growths meant that the fruit was over-ripe, and judged ripeness that way. He did not need much time deciding about plants that stank horribly, or that stung his hands. On the seventh day on Zoo, while using a brown plant juice to draw a map on plastic food wrap (a pathetic left-handed effort), he began to feel distinct localized pains in his stomach. He put a finger down his throat, bringing up bits of kzin rations and pieces of the nutmeats he had swallowed after trying to chew them during breakfast. They had gone into his mouth like soft rubber capsules, and down his throat the same way.

But they had grown tiny hair-roots in his belly, and while he watched the nasty stuff he had splashed on stone, those roots continued to grow, waving blindly. He applied himself to the task again and finally coughed up another. How many had he swallowed? Three, or four? He thought four, but saw only three, and only after smashing a dozen more of the nutshells was he satisfied that each shell held three, and only three, of the loathesome things. Not animals, perhaps, but they would eat you nonetheless. Maybe he should've named the place 'Herbarium'. The hell with it: 'Zoo' it remained.

On the ninth day, carrying the meat in his jacket, he began to use his right arm sparingly. That was the day he realized that he had rounded the broad curve of the lake and, if his brief memory of it from orbit was accurate, the placid lake was perhaps three times as long as it was wide. He found it possible to run, one of his few athletic specialties, and despite the wear of kzin gravity he put fourteen thousand running paces behind him before exhaustion made him gather high grasses for a bed.

At a meter and a half per step, he had covered twenty-one klicks, give or take a bit, that day. Not bad in this gravity, he decided, even if the collarbone was aching again. On his abominable map, that placed him about midway down the long side of the lake. The following morning he turned west, following another stream through an open grassy plain, jogging, resting, jogging. He gathered tubers floating downstream and ate one, fearing that it would surely be deadly because it tasted like a wild strawberry.

He followed the stream for three more days, living mostly on those delicious tubers and water, nesting warmly in thick sheaves of grass. On the next day he spied a dark mass of basalt rising to the northwest, captured two litres of water in an empty plastic bag, and risked all. It was well that he did for, late in the following day with heaving chest, he saw clouds sweeping in from the north, dragging a gray downpour as a bride drags her train. That stream far below and klicks distant was soon a broad river which would have swept him to the lake. But now he stood on a rocky escarpment, seeing the glisten of water from those crags in the distance, and knew that he would not die of thirst in the highlands. He also suspected, judging from the shredded-cotton roiling of cloud beyond those crags, that he was very near the walls of his cage.

*　　*　　*

Even for a runner, the two-kilometer rise of those crags was daunting in high gravity. Locklear aimed for a saddleback only a thousand meters high where sheets of rain had fallen not long before, hiking beside a swollen stream until he found its source. It wasn't much as glaciers went, but he found green depths of ice filling the saddleback, shouldering up against a force wall that beggared anything he had ever seen up close.

The wall was transparent, apparent to the eye only by its effects and by the eldritch blackness just beyond it. The thing was horrendously cold, seeming to cut straight across hills and crags with an inner border of ice to define this kzin compound. Locklear knew it only seemed straight because the curvature was so gradual. When he tossed a stone at it, the stone slowed abruptly and soundlessly as if encountering a meters-deep cushion, then slid downward and back to clatter onto the minuscule glacier. Uphill and down, for as far as he could see, ice rimmed the inside of the force wall. He moved nearer, staring through that invisible sponge, and saw another line of ice a klick distant. Between those ice rims lay bare basalt, as uncompromisingly primitive as the surface of an asteroid. Most of that raw surface was so dark as to seem featureless, but reflections from ice lenses on each side dappled the dark basalt here and there. The dapples of light were crystal clear, without the usual fuzziness of objects a thousand meters away, and Locklear realized he was staring into a vacuum.

"So visitors to Zoo can wander comfortably around with gravity polarizer platforms between the cages," he said aloud, angrily because he could see the towering masses of ponderosa pines and blue spruce in the next compound. It was an Earth compound, all right—but he could see no evidence of animals across that distance, and that made him fiercely glad for some reason. He ached to cross those impenetrable barriers, and his vision of lofty conifers blurred with his tears.

His feet were freezing, now, and no vegetation grew as near as the frost that lined the ice rim. "You're good, but you're not perfect," he said to the builders. "You can't keep the heat in these compounds from leaking away at the rims." Hence frozen moisture and the lack of vegetation along the rim, and higher rainfall where clouds skirted that cold force wall.

Scanning the vast panoramic arc of that ice rim, Locklear noted that his prison compound had a gentle bowl shape, though some hills and crags surged up in the lowlands. *Maybe using the natural contours of old craters? Or maybe you made those craters.* It was an engineering project that held tremendous secrets for humankind, and it had been there for one hell of a long time. Widely spaced across that enormous bowl were spots of dramatic color, perhaps flowers. *But they won't scatter much without animal vectors to help the wind disperse seeds and such. Dammit, this place wasn't finished!*

He retraced his steps downward. There was no point in making a camp in this inclement place, and with every sudden whistle of breeze now he was starting to look up, scanning for the kzin ship he knew might come at any time. He needed to find a cave, or to make one, and that would require construction tools.

Late in the afternoon, while tying grass bundles at the edge of a low rolling plain, Locklear found wood of the kind he'd hardly dared to hope for. He simply had not expected it to grow horizontally. With a thin bark that simulated its surroundings, it lay mostly below the surface with shallow roots at intervals like bamboo. Kzinti probably would've known to seek it from the first, damn their hairy hides. The stuff—he dubbed it shamboo—grew parallel to the ground and arrow-straight, and its foliage popped up at regular intervals too. Some of its hard, hollow segments stored water, and some specimens grew thick as his thighs and ten meters long, tapering to wicked growth spines on each end. Locklear had been walking over potential hiking staffs, construction shoring, and rafts for a week without noticing. He pulled up one the size of a javelin and clipped it smooth. His grooming tool would do precision work, but

Locklear abraded blisters on his palms fashioning an
axehead from a chertlike stone common in seams where
basalt crags soared from the prairie. He spent two days
learning how to socket a handaxe in a shamboo handle,
living mostly on tuberberries and grain from grassheads,
and elevated his respect for the first tool-using creatures in the process.

By now, Locklear's right arm felt almost as good as
new, and the process of rediscovering primitive technology became a compelling pastime. He was so intent
on ways to weave split shamboo filaments into cordage
for a firebow, while trudging just below the basalt heights,
that he almost missed the most important moment of
his life.

He stepped from savannah grass onto a gritty surface
that looked like other dry washes, continued for three
paces, stepped up onto grassy turf again, then stopped.
He recalled walking across sand-sprinkled tiles as a
youth, and something in that old memory made him
look back. The dry wash held wavelike patterns of grit,
pebbles, and sand, but here and there were bare patches.

And those bare patches were as black and as smooth
as machine-polished obsidian.

Locklear crammed the half-braided cord into a pocket
and began to follow that dry wash up a gentle slope,
toward the cleft ahead, and toward his destiny.

His heart pounding with hope and fear, Locklear
stood five meters inside the perfect arc of obsidian that
formed the entrance to that cave. No runoff had ever
spilled grit across the smooth broad floor inside, and he
felt an irrational concern that his footsteps were defiling
something perfectly pristine, clean and cold as an ice
cavern. But a far, *far* more rational concern was the
portal before him, its facing made of the same material
as the floor, the opening itself four meters wide and just
as high. A faint flickering luminescence, as of gossamer
film stretched across the portal, gave barely enough
light to see. Locklear saw his reflection in it, and wanted
to laugh aloud at this ragged, skinny, barrel-chested

apparition with the stubble of beard wearing stained flight togs. And the apparition reminded him that he might not be alone.

He felt silly, but after clearing his throat twice he managed to call out: "Anybody home?"

Echoes; several of them, more than this little entrance space could possibly generate. He poked his sturdy shamboo hiking staff into the gossamer film and jumped when stronger light flickered in the distance. "Maybe you just eat animal tissue," he said, with a wavering chuckle. "Well,—." He took his grooming pincers and cut away the dried curl of skin around a broken blister on his palm, clipped away sizeable crescents of fingernails, tossed them at the film.

Nothing but the tiny clicks of cuticles on obsidian, inside; *that*'s how quiet it was. He held the pointed end of the staff like a lance in his right hand, extended the handaxe ahead in his left. He *was* right-handed, after all, so he'd rather lose the left one . . .

No sensation on his flesh, but a sudden flood of light as he moved through the portal, and Locklear dashed backward to the mouth of the cave. "Take it easy, fool," he chided himself. "What did you see?"

A long smooth passageway; walls without signs or features; light seeming to leap from obsidian walls, not too strong but damned disconcerting. He took several deep breaths and went in again, standing his ground this time when light flooded the artificial cave. His first thought, seeing the passageway's apparent end in another film-spanned portal two hundred meters distant, was, *Does it go all the way from Kzersatz to Newduvai?* He couldn't recall when he'd begun to think of this kzin compound as Kzersatz and the adjoining, Earthlike, compound as Newduvai.

Footfalls echoing down side corridors, Locklear hurried to the opposite portal, but frost glistened on its facing and his staff would not penetrate more than a half-meter through the luminous film. He could see his exhalations fogging the film. The resistance beyond it felt spongy but increasingly hard, probably an extension of that damned force wall. If his sense of direction was right, he should be just about beneath the rim of Kzersatz. No doubt someone or something knew how to penetrate that wall, because the portal was there. But Locklear knew enough about force walls and screens to despair of getting through it without better understanding. Besides, if he did get through he might punch a hole into vacuum. If his suspicions about the builders of Zoo were correct, that's exactly what lay beyond the portal.

Sighing, he turned back, counting nine secondary passages that yawned darkly on each side, choosing the first one to his right. Light flooded it instantly. Locklear gasped.

Row upon row of cubical, transparent containers stretched down the corridor for fifty meters, some of them tiny, some the size of a small room. And in each container floated a specimen of animal life, rotating slowly, evidently above its own gravity polarizer field. Locklear had seen a few of the creatures; had seen pictures of a few more; all, every last one that he could identify, native to the kzin homeworld. He knew that many museums maintained ranks of pickled specimens, and told himself he should not feel such a surge of anger about this one. *Well, you're an ethologist, you twit,* he told himself silently. *You're just pissed off because you can't study behaviors of dead animals.* Yet, even taking that into consideration, he felt a kind of righteous wrath toward builders who played at godhood without playing it perfectly. It was a responsibility he would never have chosen. He did not yet realize that he was surrounded with similar choices.

He stood before a floating *vatach*, in life a fast-moving burrower the size of an earless hare, reputedly tasty but too mild-mannered for kzinti sport. No symbols on any container, but obvious differences among the score of *vatach* in those containers.

How many sexes? He couldn't recall. "But I bet you guys would," he said aloud. He passed on, shuddering at the critters with fangs and leathery wings, marveling at the stump-legged creatures the height of a horse and the mass of a rhino, all in positions that were probably fetal though some were obviously adult.

Retracing his steps to the *vatach* again, Locklear leaned a hand casually against the smooth metal base of one container. He heard nothing, but when he withdrew his hand the entire front face of the glasslike container levered up, the *vatach* settling gently to a cage floor that slid forward toward Locklear like an offering.

The *vatach* moved.

Locklear leaped back so fast he nearly fell, then darted forward again and shoved hard on the cage floor. Back it went, down came the transparent panel, up went the *vatach*, inert, into its permanent rotating waltz.

"Stasis fields! By God, they're alive," he said. The animals hadn't been pickled at all, only stored until someone was ready to stock Kzersatz. *Vatach* were edible herbivores—but if he released them without natural enemies, how long before they overran the whole damned compound? And did he really want to release their natural enemies, even if he could identify them?

"Sorry, fellas. Maybe I can find you an island," he told the little creatures, and moved on with an alertness that made him forget the time. He did not consider time because the glow of illumination did not dim when the sun of Kzersatz did, and only the growl of his empty belly sent him back to the cave entrance where he had left his jacket with his remaining food and water. Even then he chewed tuberberries from sheer necessity, his hands trembling as he looked out at the blackness of the Kzersatz night. Because he had passed down each of those eighteen side passages, and knew what they held, and knew that he had some godplaying of his own to ponder.

He said to the night and to himself, "Like for instance, whether to take one of those goddamned kzinti out of stasis."

*   *   *

His wristcomp held a hundred megabytes, much of it concerning zoology and ethology. Some native kzin animals were marginally intelligent, but he found nothing whatever in memory storage that might help him communicate abstract ideas with them. "Except the tabbies themselves, eighty-one by actual count," he mused aloud the next morning, sitting in sunlight outside. "Damned if I do. Damned if I don't. Damn if I know which is the damnedest," he admitted. But the issue was never very much in doubt; if a kzin ship did return, they'd find the cave sooner or later because they were the best hunters in known space. He'd make it expensive in flying fur, maybe—but there seemed to be no rear entrance. Well, he didn't have to go it alone; Kdaptist kzinti made wondrous allies. Maybe he could convert one, or win his loyalty by setting him free.

If the kzin ship didn't return, he was stuck with a neolithic future or with playing God to populate Kzersatz, unless—"Aw shitshitshit," he said at last, getting up, striding into the cave. "I'll just wake the smallest one and hope he's reasonable."

But the smallest ones weren't male; the females, with their four small but prominent nipples and the bushier fur on their tails, were the runts of that exhibit. In their way they were almost beautiful, with longer hindquarters and shorter torsos than the great bulky males, all eighty-one of the species rotating nude in fetal curls before him. He studied his wristcomp and his own memory, uncomfortably aware that female kzin were, at best, morons. Bred for bearing kits, and for catering to their warrior males, female kzinti were little more than ferociously protected pets in their own culture.

'Maybe that's what I need anyhow," he muttered, and finally chose the female that bulked smallest of them all. When he pressed that baseplate, he did it with grim forebodings.

She settled to the cage bottom and slid out, and Locklear stood well away, axe in one hand, lance in the other, trying to look as if he had no intention of using either. His adam's apple bobbed as the female began to uncoil from her fetal position.

Her eyes snapped open so fast, Locklear thought they should have clicked audibly. She made motions like someone waving cobwebs aside, mewing in a way that he found pathetic, and then she fully noticed the little man standing near, and she screamed and leaped. That leap carried her to the top of a nearby container, *away* from him, cowering, eyes wide, ear umbrellas folded flat.

He remembered not to grin as he asked, "Is this my thanks for bringing you back?"

She blinked. "You (something, something) a devil, then?"

He denied it, pointing to the scores of other kzin around her, admitting he had found them this way.

If curiosity killed cats, this one would have died then and there. She remained crouched and wary, her eyes flickering around as she formed more questions. Her speech was barely understandable. She used a form of verbal negation utterly new to him, and some familiar words were longer the way she pronounced them. The general linguistic rule was that abstract ideas first enter a lexicon as several words, later shortened by the impatient.

Probably her longer words were primitive forms; God only knew how long she had been in stasis! He told her who he was, but that did not reduce her wary hostility much. She had never heard of men. Nor of any intelligent race other than kzinti. Nor, for that matter, of spaceflight. But she was remarkably quick to absorb new ideas, and from Locklear's demeanor she realized all too soon that *he*, in fact, was scared spitless of *her*. That was the point when she came down off that container like a leopard from a limb, snatched his handaxe while he hesitated, and poked him in the gut with its haft.

It appeared, after all, that Locklear had revived a very, *very* old-fashioned female.

*   *   *

"You (something or other) captive," she sizzled, un-sheathing a set of shining claws from her fingers as if to remind him of their potency. She turned a bit away from him then, looking sideways at him. "Do you have sex?"

His adam's apple bobbed again before he intuited her meaning. Her first move was to gain control, her second to establish sex roles. A bright female; yeah, that's about what an ethologist should expect . . . "Humans have two sexes just as kzinti do," he said, "and I am male, and I won't submit as your captive. You people eat captives. You're not all that much bigger than I am, and this lance is sharp. I'm your benefactor. Ask yourself why I didn't spear you for lunch before you awoke."

"If you could eat me, I could eat you," she said. "Why do you cut words short?"

Bewildering changes of pace but always practical, he thought. Oh yes, an exceedingly bright female. "I speak modern Kzinti," he explained. "One day we may learn how many thousands of years you have been asleep." He enjoyed the almost human widening of her yellow eyes, and went on doggedly. "Since I have honorably waked you from what might have been a permanent sleep, I ask this: what does your honor suggest?"

"That I (something) clothes," she said. "And owe you a favor, if nakedness is what you want."

"It's cold for me, too." He'd left his food outside but was wearing the jacket, and took it off. "I'll trade this for the axe."

She took it, studying it with distaste, and eventually tied its sleeves like an apron to hide her mammaries. It could not have warmed her much. His question was half disbelief: "That's it? Now you're clothed?"

"As (something) of the (something) always do," she said. "Do you have a special name?"

He told her, and she managed 'Rockear'. Her own name, she said, was (something fiendishly tough for humans to manage), and he smiled. "I'll call you 'Miss Kitty'."

"If it pleases you," she said, and something in the way that phrase rolled out gave him pause.

He leaned the shamboo lance aside and tucked the axe into his belt. "We must try to understand each other better," he said. "We are not on your homeworld, but I think it is a very close approximation. A kind of incomplete zoo. Why don't we swap stories outside where it's warm?"

She agreed, still wary but no longer hostile, with a glance of something like satisfaction toward the massive kzin male rotating in the next container. And then they strolled outside into the wilderness of Kzersatz which, for same reason, forced thin mewling *miaows* from her. It had never occurred to Locklear that a kzin could weep.

As near as Locklear could understand, Miss Kitty's emotions were partly relief that she had lived to see her yellow fields and jungles again, and partly grief when she contemplated the loneliness she now faced. *I don't count,* he thought. *But if I expect to get her help, I'd best see that I do count.*

Everybody thinks his own dialect is superior, Locklear decided. Miss Kitty fumed at his brief forms of Kzinti, and he winced at her ancient elaborations, as they walked to the nearest stream. She had a temper, too, teaching him genteel curses as her bare feet encountered thorns. She seemed fascinated by this account of the kzin expansion, and that of humans, and others as well through the galaxy. She even accepted his description of the planet Zoo though she did not seem to understand it.

She accepted his story so readily, in fact, that he hit on an intuition. "Has it occurred to you that I might be lying?"

"Your talk is offensive," she flared. "My benefactor a criminal? No. Is it common among your kind?"

"More than among yours," he admitted, "but I have no reason to lie to you. Sorry," he added, seeing her react again. *Kzinti don't flare up at that word today;*

maybe all cusswords have to be replaced as they weaken from overuse. Then he told her how man and kzin got along between wars, and ended by admitting it looked as if another war was brewing, which was why he had been abandoned here.

She looked around her. "Is Zoo your doing, or ours?"

"Neither. I think it must have been done by a race we know very little about: Outsiders, we call them. No one knows how many years they have traveled space, but very, very long. They live without air, without much heat. Just beyond the wall that surrounds Kzersatz, I have seen airless corridors with the cold darkness of space and dapples of light. They would be quite comfortable there."

"I do not think I like them."

Then he laughed, and had to explain how the display of his teeth was the opposite of anger.

"Those teeth could not support much anger," she replied, her small pink ear umbrellas winking down and up. He learned that this was her version of a smile.

Finally, when they had taken their fill of water, they returned as Miss Kitty told her tale. She had been trained as a palace *prret*; a servant and casual concubine of the mighty during the reign of *Rrawlrit* Eight and Three. Locklear said that the 'Rrit' suffix mean high position among modern kzinti, and she made a sound very like a human sniff. *Rrawlrit* was the arrogant son of an arrogant son, and so on. He liked his females, lots of them, especially young ones. "I was (something) than most," she said, her four-digited hand slicing the air at her ear height.

"Petite, small?"

"Yes. Also smart. Also famous for my appearance," she added without the slightest show of modesty. She glanced at him as though judging which haunch might be tastiest. "Are you famous for yours?"

"Uh—not that I know of."

"But not unattractive?"

He slid a hand across his face, feeling its stubble. "I

am considered petite, and by some as, uh, attractive."
Two or three are 'some'. Not much, but some . . .

"With a suit of fur you would be (something)", she
said, with that ear-waggle, and he quickly asked about
palace life because he damned well did not want to
know what that final word of hers had meant. It made
him nervous as hell. Yeah, but what *did* it mean?
Mud-ugly? Handsome? Tasty? *Listen to the lady, idiot,
and quit suspecting what you're suspecting.*

She had been raised in a culture in which females
occasionally ran a regency, and in which males fought
duels over the argument as to whether females were
their intellectual equals. Most thought not. Miss Kitty
thought so, and proved it, rising to palace prominence
with her backside, as she put it.

"You mean you were no better than you should be,"
he commented.

"What does that mean?"

"I haven't the foggiest idea, just an old phrase." She
was still waiting, and her aspect was not benign. "Uh, it
means nobody could expect you to do any better."

She nodded slowly, delighting him as she adopted
one of the human gestures he'd been using. "I did too
well to suit the males jealous of my power, Rockear.
They convinced the regent that I was conspiring with
other palace *prrets* to gain equality for our sex."

"And were you?"

She arched her back with pride. "Yes. Does that
offend you?"

"No. Would you care if it did?"

"It would make things difficult, Rockear. You must
understand that I loathe, admire, hate, desire kzintosh—
male kzin. I fought for equality because it was common
knowledge that some were planning to breed *kzinrret*,
females, to be no better than pets."

"I hate to tell you this, Miss Kitty, but they've done
it."

"Already?"

"I don't know how long it took, but—." He paused,
and then told her the worst. Long before man and kzin

first met, their females had been bred into brainless docility. Even if Miss Kitty found modern sisters, they would be of no help to her.

She fought the urge to weep again, strangling her miaows with soft snarls of rage.

Locklear turned away, aware that she did not want to seem vulnerable, and consulted his wristcomp's encyclopedia. The earliest kzin history made reference to the downfall of a *Rrawlrit* the fifty-seventh—Seven Eights and One, and he gasped at what that told him. "Don't feel too bad, Miss Kitty," he said at last. "That was at least forty thousand years ago; do you understand eight to the fifth power?"

"It is very, very many," she said in a choked voice.

"It's been more years than that since you were brought here. How did you get here, anyhow?"

"They executed several of us. My last memory was of grappling with the lord high executioner, carrying him over the precipice into the sacred lagoon with me. I could not swim with those heavy chains around my ankles, but I remember trying. I hope he drowned," she said, eyes slitted. "Sex with him had always been my most hated chore."

A small flag began to wave in Locklear's head; he furled it for further reference. "So you were trying to swim. Then?"

"Then suddenly I was lying naked with a very strange creature staring at me," she said with that ear-wink, and a sharp talon pointed almost playfully at him. "Do not think ill of me because I reacted in fright."

He shook his head, and had to explain what *that* meant, and it became a short course in subtle nuances for each of them. Miss Kitty, it seemed, proved an old dictum about downtrodden groups: they became highly expert at reading body language, and at developing secret signals among themselves. It was not Locklear's fault that he was constantly, and completely unaware, sending messages that she misread.

But already, she was adapting to his gestures as he had to her language. "Of all the kzinti I could have taken from stasis, I got you," he chuckled finally, and because her glance was quizzical, he told a gallant half-lie; "I went for the prettiest, and got the smartest."

"And the hungriest," she said. "Perhaps I should hunt something for us."

He reminded her that there was nothing to hunt. "You can help me choose animals to release here. Meanwhile, you can have this," he added, offering her the kzinti rations.

The sun faded on schedule, and he dined on tuberberries while she devoured an entire brick of meat. She amazed him by popping a few tuberberries for dessert. When he asked her about it, she replied that certainly kzinti ate vegetables in her time; why should they not?

"Males want only meat," he shrugged.

"They would," she snarled. "In my day, some select warriors did the same. They claimed it made them ferocious and that eaters of vegetation were mere *kshauvat*, dumb herbivores; we *prret* claimed their diet just made them hopelessly aggressive."

"The word's been shortened to *kshut* now," he mused. "It's a favorite cussword of theirs. At least you don't have to start eating the animals in stasis to stay alive. That's the good news; the bad news is that the warriors who left me here may return at any time. What will you do then?"

"That depends on how accurate your words have been," she said cagily.

"And if I'm telling the plain truth?"

Her ears smiled for her: "Take up my war where I left it," she said.

Locklear felt his control slipping when Miss Kitty refused to wait before releasing most of the *vatach*. They were nocturnal with easily-spotted burrows, she insisted, and yes, they bred fast—but she pointed to specimens of a winged critter in stasis and said they would control the *vatach* very nicely if the need arose. By now he realized that this kzin female wasn't above trying to vamp him; and when that failed, a show of fang and talon would succeed.

He showed her how to open the cages only after she threatened him, and watched as she grasped waking *vatach* by their legs, quickly releasing them to the darkness outside. No need to release the (something) yet, she said; Locklear called the winged beasts 'batowls'. "I hope you know what you're doing," he grumbled. "I'd stop you if I could do it without a fight."

"You would wait forever," she retorted. "I know the animals of my world better than you do, and soon we may need a lot of them for food."

"Not so many; there's just the two of us."

The cat-eyes regarded him shrewdly. "Not for long," she said, and dropped her bombshell. "I recognized a friend of mine in one of those cages."

Locklear felt an icy needle down his spine. "A male?"

"Certainly not. Five of us were executed for the same offense, and at least one of them is here with us. Perhaps those Outsiders of yours collected us all as we sank in that stinking water."

"Not *my* Outsiders," he objected. "Listen, for all we knew they're monitoring us, so be careful how you fiddle with their setup here."

She marched him to the kzin cages and purred her pleasure on recognizing two females, both *prret* like herself, both imposingly large for Locklear's taste. She placed a furry hand on one cage, enjoying the moment. "I could release you now, my sister in struggle," she said softly. "But I think I shall wait. Yes, I think it is best," she said to Locklear, turning away. "These two have been here a long time, and they will keep until—."

"Until you have everything under your control?"

"True," she said. "But you need not fear, Rockear. You are an ally, and you know too many things we must know. And besides," she added, rubbing against him sensuously, "you are (something)."

There was that same word again, *t'rralap* or some such, and now he was sure, with sinking heart, that it meant 'cute'. He didn't feel cute; he was beginning to feel like a Pomeranian on a short leash.

More by touch than anything else, they gathered bundles of grass for a bower at the cave entrance, and Miss Kitty showed no reluctance in falling asleep next to him, curled becomingly into a buzzing ball of fur. But when he moved away, she moved too, until they were touching again. He knew beyond doubt that if he moved too far in the direction of his lance and axe, she would be fully awake and suspicious as hell.

And she'd call my bluff, and I don't want to kill her, he thought, settling his head against her furry shoulder. *Even if I could, which is doubtful. I'm no longer master of all I survey. In fact, now I have a mistress of sorts, and I'm not too sure what kind of mistress she has in mind. They used to have a word for what I'm thinking. Maybe Miss Kitty doesn't care who or what she diddles; hell, she was a palace courtesan, doing it with males she hated. She thinks I'm t'rralap. Yeah, that's me, Locklear, Miss Kitty's trollop; and what the hell can I do about it? I wish there were some way I could get her back in that stasis cage . . .* And then he fell asleep.

To Locklear's intense relief, Miss Kitty seemed uninterested in the remaining cages on the following morning. They foraged for breakfast and he hid his astonishment as she taught him a dozen tricks in an hour. The root bulb of one spiny shrub tasted like an apple; the seed pods of some weeds were delicious; and she produced a tiny blaze by rapidly pounding an innocent-looking nutmeat between two stones. It occurred to him that nuts contained great amounts of energy. A pile of these firenuts, he reflected, might be turned into a weapon . . .

Feeding hunks of dry brush to the fire, she announced that those root bulbs baked nicely in coals. "If we can find clay, I can fire a few pottery dishes and cups, Rockear. It was part of my training, and I intend to have everything in domestic order before we wake those two."

"And what if a kzin ship returns and spots that smoke?"

That was a risk they must take, she said. Some woods burned more cleanly than others. He argued that they should at least build their fires far from the cave, and while they were at it, the cave entrance might be better disguised. She agreed, impressed with his strategy, and then went down on all-fours to inspect the dirt near a dry-wash. As he admired her lithe movements, she shook her head in an almost human gesture. "No good for clay."

"It's not important."

"It is vitally important!" Now she wheeled upright, impressive and fearsome. "Rockear, if any kzintosh return here, we must be ready. For that, we must have the help of others—the two *prret*. And believe me, they will be helpful only if they see us as their (something)."

She explained that the word meant, roughly, 'paired household leaders'. The basic requirements of a household, to a kzin female, included sleeping bowers—easily come by—and enough pottery for that household. A male kzin needed one more thing, she said, her eyes slitting: a *wtsai*.

"You mean one of those knives they all wear?"

"Yes. And you must have one in your belt." From the waggle of her ears, he decided she was amused by her next statement: "It is a—badge, of sorts. The edge is usually sharp but I cannot allow that, and the tip must be dull. I will show you why later."

"Dammit, these things could take weeks!"

"Not if we find the clay, and if you can make a *wtsai* somehow. Trust me, Rockear; these are the basics. Other kzinrret will not obey us otherwise. They must see from the first that we are proper providers, proper leaders with the pottery of a settled tribe, not the wooden implements of wanderers. And they must take it for granted that you and I," she added, "are (something)." With that, she rubbed lightly against him.

He caught himself moving aside and swallowed hard. "Miss Kitty, I don't want to offend you, but, uh, humans and kzinti do not mate."

"Why do they not?"

"Uhm. Well, they never have."

Her eyes slitted, yet with a flicker of her ears: "But they could?"

"Some might. Not me."

"Then they might be able to," she said as if to herself. "I thought I felt something familiar when we were sleeping." She studied his face carefully. "Why does your skin change color?"

"Because, goddammit, I'm upset!" He mastered his breathing after a moment and continued, speaking as if to a small child, "I don't know about kzinti, but a man can *not*, uh, mate unless he is, uh,—"

"Unless he is intent on the idea?"

"Right!"

"Then we will simply have to pretend that we do mate, Rockear. Otherwise, those two kzinrret will spend most of their time trying to become your mate and will be useless for work."

"Of all the," he began, and then dropped his chin and began to laugh helplessly. Human tribal customs had been just as complicated, once, and she was probably the only functioning expert in known space on the customs of ancient kzinrret. "We'll pretend, then, up to a point. Try and make that point, ah, not too pointed."

"Like your *wtsai*," she retorted. "I will try not to make your face change color."

"Please," he said fervently, and suggested that he might find the material for a *wtsai* inside the cave while she sought a deposit of clay. She bounded away on all-fours with the lope of a hunting leopard, his jacket a somehow poignant touch as it flapped against her lean belly.

When he looked back from the cave entrance, she was a tiny dot two kilometers distant, coursing along a shallow creekbed. "Maybe you won't lie, and I've got no other ally," he said to the swift saffron dot. "But you're not above misdirection with your own kind. I'll remember that."

Locklear cursed as he failed to locate any kind of tool chest or lab implements in those inner corridors. But he blessed his grooming tool when the tip of its pincer handle fitted screwheads in the cage that had held Miss Kitty prisoner for so long. He puzzled for minutes before he learned to turn screwheads a quarter-turn, release pressure to let the screwheads emerge, then another quarter-turn, and so on, nine times each. He felt quickening excitement as the cage cover detached, felt it stronger when he disassembled the base and realized its metal sheeting was probably one of a myriad stainless steel alloys. The diamond coating on his nailfile proved the sheet was no indestructible substance. It was thin enough to flex, even to be dented by a whack against an adjoining cage. It might take awhile, but he would soon have his *wtsai* blade.

And two other devices now lay before him, ludicrously far advanced beyond an ornamental knife. The gravity polarizer's main bulk was a doughnut of ceramic and metal. Its switch, and that of the stasis field, both were energized by the sliding cage floor he had disassembled. The switches worked just as well with fingertip pressure. They boasted separate energy sources which Locklear dared not assault; anything that worked for forty thousand years without harming the creatures near it would be more sophisticated than any fumble-fingered mechanic.

Using the glasslike cage as a test load, he learned which of the two switches flung the load into the air. The other, then, had to operate the stasis field—and both devices had simple internal levers for adjustments. When he learned how to stop the cage from spinning, and then how to make it hover only a hand's breadth above the device or to force it against the ceiling until it creaked, he was ecstatic. Then he energized the stasis switch with a chill of gooseflesh. Any prying paws into those devices would not pry for long, unless someone knew about that inconspicuous switch. Locklear could see no interconnects between the stasis generator and the polarizer, but both were detachable. If he could get that polarizer outside,—. Locklear strode out of the cave laughing. It would be the damnedest vehicle ever, but its technologies would be wholly appropriate. He hid the device in nearby grass; the less his ally knew about such things, the more freedom he would have to pursue them.

Miss Kitty returned in late afternoon with a sopping mass of clay wrapped in greenish yellow palm leaves. The clay was poor quality, she said, but it would have to serve—and why was he battering that piece of metal with his stone axe?

If she knew a better way to cut off a *wtsai*-sized strip of steel than bending it back and forth, he replied, he'd love to hear it. Bickering like an old married couple, they sat near the cave mouth until dark and pursued their separate stone-age tasks. Locklear, whose hand calluses were still forming, had to admit that she had been wonderfully trained for domestic chores; under those quick four-digited hands of hers, rolled coils of clay soon became shallow bowls with thin sides, so nearly perfect they might have been turned on a pot-ter's wheel. By now he was calling her 'Kit', and she seemed genuinely pleased when he praised her work. Ah, she said, but wait until the pieces were sun-dried to leather hardness; then she would make the bowls lovely with talon-etched decoration. He objected that decoration took time. She replied curtly that kzinrret did not live for utility alone.

He helped pull flat fibers from the stalks of palm leaves, which she began to weave into a mat. For bedding, he asked? Certainly not, she said imperiously: for the clothing which modesty required of kzinrret. He pursued it: would they really care all that much with only a human to see them? A human *male*, she re-minded him; if she considered him worthy of mating, the others would see him as a male first, and a non-kzin second. He was half amused but more than a little uneasy as they bedded down, she curled slightly facing away, he crowded close at her insistence, "—For companionship," as she put it.

Their last exchange that night implied a difference between the rigorously truthful male kzin and their females. "Kit, you can't tell the others we're mated unless we are."

"I can ignore their questions and let them draw their own conclusions," she said sleepily.

"Aren't you blurring that fine line between half-truths and, uh, non-truths?"

"I do not intend to discuss it further," she said, and soon was purring in sleep with the faint growl of a predator.

He needed two more days, and a repair of the handaxe, before he got that jagged slice of steel pounded and, with abrasive stones, ground into something resembling a blade. Meanwhile, Kit built her open-fired kiln of stones in a ravine some distance from the cave, ranging widely with that leopard lope of hers to gather firewood. Locklear was glad of her absence; it gave him time to finish a laminated shamboo handle for his blade, bound with thread, and to collect the thickest poles of shamboo he could find. The blade was sharp enough to trim the poles quickly, and tough enough to hold an edge.

He was tying crosspieces with plaited fiber to bind thick shamboo poles into a slender raft when, on the third day of those labors, he felt a presence behind him. Whirling, he brandished his blade. "Oh," he said, and lowered the *wtsai*. "Sorry, Kit. I keep worrying about the return of those kzintosh."

She was not amused. "Give it to me," she said, thrusting her hand out.

"The hell I will. I need this thing."

"I can see that it is too sharp."

"I need it sharp."

"I am sure you do. I need it dull." Her gesture for the blade was more than impatient.

Half straightening into a crouch, he brought the blade up again, eyes narrowed. "Well, by God, I've had about all your whims I can take. You want it? Come and get it."

She made a sound that was deeper than a purr, putting his hackles up, and went to all-fours, her furry tail-tip flicking as she began to pace around him. She was a lovely sight. She scared Locklear silly. "When I take it, I will hurt you," she warned.

"If you take it," he said, turning to face her, moving the *wtsai* in what he hoped was an unpredictable pattern. *Dammit, I can't back down now. A puncture wound might be fatal to her, so I've got to slash lightly.* Or maybe he wouldn't have to, when she saw he meant business.

But he did have to. She screamed and leaped toward his left, her own left hand sweeping out at his arm. He skipped aside and then felt her tail lash against his shins like a curled rope. He stumbled and whirled as she was twisting to repeat the charge, and by sheer chance his blade nicked her tail as she whisked it away from his vicinity.

She stood erect, holding her tail in her hands, eyes wide and accusing. "You—you insulted my tail," she snarled.

"Damn' tootin'," he said between his teeth.

With arms folded, she turned her back on him, her tail curled protectively at her backside. "You have no respect," she said, and because it seemed she was going to leave, he dropped the blade and stood up, and realized too late just how much peripheral vision a kzin boasted. She spun and was on him in an instant, her hands gripping his wrists, and hurled them both to the grass, bringing those terrible ripping foot talons up to his stomach. They lay that way for perhaps three seconds. "Drop the *wtsai*," she growled, her mouth near his throat. Locklear had not been sure until now whether a very small female kzin had more muscular strength than he. The answer was not just awfully encouraging.

He could feel sharp needles piercing the skin at his

stomach, kneading, releasing, piercing; a reminder that
with one move she could disembowel him. The blade
whispered into the grass. She bit him lightly at the
juncture of his neck and shoulder, and then faced him
with their noses almost touching. "A love bite," she
said, and released his wrists, pushing away with her
feet.

He rolled, hugging his stomach, fighting for breath,
grateful that she had not used those fearsome talons
with her push. She found the blade, stood over him,
and now no sign of her anger remained. *Right; she's in
complete control,* he thought.

"Nicely made, Rockear. I shall return it to you when
it is presentable," she said.

"Get the hell away from me," he husked softly.

She did, with a bound, moving toward a distant wisp
of smoke that skirled faintly across the sky. If a kzin
ship returned now, they would follow that wisp immediately.

Locklear trotted without hesitation to the cave, cursing, wiping trickles of blood from his stomach and neck,
wiping a tear of rage from his cheek. There were other
ways to prove to this damned tabby that he could be
trusted with a knife. One, at least, if he didn't get
himself wasted in the process.

She returned quite late, with half of a cooked *vatach*
and tuberberries as a peace offering, to find him weaving a huge triangular mat. It was a sail, he explained,
for a boat. She had taken the little animal on impulse,
she said, partly because it was a male, and ate her half
on the spot for old times' sake. He'd told her his distaste for raw meat and evidently she never forgot
anything.

He sulked awhile, complaining at the lack of salt,
brightening a bit when she produced the *wtsai* from his
jacket which she still wore. "You've ruined it," he said,
seeing the colors along the dull blade as he held it.
"Heated it up, didn't you?"

"And ground its edge off on the stones of my hot

kiln," she agreed. "Would you like to try its point?" She placed a hand on her flank, where a man's kidney would be, moving nearer.

"Not much of a point now," he said. It was rounded like a formal dinner knife at its tip.

"Try it here," she said, and guided his hand so that the blunt knifetip pointed against her flank. He hesitated. "Don't you want to?"

He dug it in, knowing it wouldn't hurt her much, and heard her soft miaow. Then she suggested the other side, and he did, feeling a suspicious unease. That, she said, was the way a *wtsai* was best used.

He frowned. "You mean, as a symbol of control?"

"More or less," she replied, her ears flicking, and then asked how he expected to float a boat down a drywash, and he told her because he needed her help with it. "A skyboat? Some trick of man, or kzin?"

"Of man," he shrugged. It was, so far as he knew, uniquely his trick—and it might not work at all. He could not be sure about his other trick either, until he tried it. Either one might get him killed.

When they curled up to sleep again, she turned her head and whispered, "Would you like to bite my neck?"

"I'd like to bite it off."

"Just do not break the skin. I did not mean to make yours bleed, Rockear. Men are tender creatures."

Feeling like an ass, he forced his nose into the fur at the curve of her shoulder and bit hard. Her miaow was familiar. And somehow he was sure that it was not exactly a cry of pain. She thrust her rump nearer, sighed, and went to sleep.

After an eternity of minutes, he shifted position, putting his knees in her back, flinging one of his hands to the edge of their grassy bower. She moved slightly. He felt in the grass for a familiar object; found it. Then he pulled his legs away and pressed with his fingers. She started to turn, then drew herself into a ball as he scrambled further aside, legs tingling.

He had not been certain the stasis field would operate properly when its flat field grid was positioned

beneath sheaves of grass, but obviously it was working.
Indeed, his lower legs were numb for several minutes,
lying in the edge of the field as they were when he
threw that switch. He stamped the pins and needles
from his feet, barely able to see her inert form in the
faint luminosity of the cave portal. Once, while fum-
bling for the *wtsai*, he stumbled near her and dropped
to his knees.

He trembled for half a minute before rising. "Fall
over her now and you could lie here for all eternity," he
said aloud. Then he fetched the heavy coil of fiber he'd
woven, with those super-strength threads braided into
it. He had no way of lighting the place enough to make
sure of his work, so he lay down on the sail mat inside
the cave. One thing was sure: she'd be right there the
next morning.

He awoke disoriented at first, then darted to the cave
mouth. She lay inert as a carven image. The Outsiders
probably had good reason to rotate their specimens, so
he couldn't leave her there for the days—or weeks!—
that temptation suggested. He decided that a day
wouldn't hurt, and hurriedly set about finishing his
airboat. The polarizer was lashed to the underside of his
raft, with a slot through the shamboo so that he could
reach down and adjust the switch and levers. The crosspieces, beneath, held the polarizer off the turf.

Finally, with a mixture of fear and excitement, he sat
down in the middle of the raft-bottomed craft and
snugged fiber straps across his lap. He reached down
with his left hand, making sure the levers were pulled
back, and flipped the switch. Nothing. Yet. When he
had moved the second lever halfway, the raft began to
rise very slowly. He vented a whoop—and suddenly
the whole rig was tipping before he could snap the
switch. The raft hit on one side and crashed flat like a
barn door with a tooth-loosening impact.

Okay, the damn' thing was tippy. He'd need a keel—a
heavy rock on a short rope. Or a little rock on a long
rope! He erected two short lengths of shamboo upright

with a crosspiece like goalposts, over the seat of his raft, enlarging the hole under his thighs. Good; now he'd have a better view straight down, too. He used the cord he'd intended to bind Kit, tying it to a twenty-kilo stone, then feeding the cord through the hole and wrapping most of its fifteen-meter length around and around that thick crosspiece. Then he sighed, looked at the westering sun, and tried again.

The raft was still a bit tippy, but by paying the cordage out slowly he found himself ten meters up. By shifting his weight, he could make the little platform slant in any direction, yet he could move only in the direction the breeze took him. By adjusting the controls he rose until the heavy stone swung lazily, free of the ground, and then he was drifting with the breeze. He reduced power and hauled in on his keel weight until the raft settled, and then worked out the needed improvements. Higher skids off the ground, so he could work beneath the raft; a better method for winding that weight up and down; and a sturdy shamboo mast for his single sail—better still, a two-piece mast bound in a narrow A-frame to those goalposts. It didn't need to be high; a short catboat sail for tacking was all he could handle anyhow. And come to think of it, a pair of shamboo poles pivoted off the sides with small weights at their free ends just might make automatic keels.

He worked on that until a half-hour before dark, then carried his keel cordage inside the cave. First he made a slip noose, then flipped it toward her hands, which were folded close to her chin. He finally got the noose looped properly, pulled it tight, then moved around her at a safe distance, tugging the cord so that it passed under her neck and, with sharp tugs, down to her back. Then another pass. Then up to her neck, then around her flexed legs. He managed a pair of half-hitches before he ran short of cordage, then fetched his shamboo lance. With the lance against her throat, he snapped off the stasis field with his toe.

She began her purring rumble immediately. He pressed lightly with the lance, and then she waked, and needed a moment to realize that she was bound. Her ears flattened. Her grin was nothing even faintly like enjoyment. "You drugged me, you little *vatach*."

"No. Worse than that. Watch," he said, and with his free hand he pointed at her face, staring hard. He toed the switch again and watched her curl into an inert ball. The half-hitches came loosed with a tug, and with some difficulty he managed to pull the cordage away until only the loop around her hand remained. He toed the switch again; watched her come awake, and pointed dramatically at her as she faced him. "I loosened your bonds," he said. "I can always tie you up again. Or put you back in stasis," he added with a tight smile, hoping this paltry piece of flummery would be taken as magic.

"May I rise?"

"Depends. Do you see that I can defeat you instantly, anytime I like?" She moved her hands, snarling at the loop, starting to bite it asunder. "Stop that! Answer my question," he said again, stern and unyielding, the finger pointing, his toe ready on the switch.

"It seems that you can," she said grudgingly.

"I could have killed you as you slept. Or brought one of the other *prret* out of stasis and made her my consort. Any number of things, Kit." Her nod was slow, and almost human, "Do you swear to obey me hereafter, and not to attack me again?"

She hated it, but she said it: "Yes. I—misjudged you, Rockear. If all men can do what you did, no wonder you win wars."

He saw that this little charade might get him in a mess later. "It is a special trick of mine; probably won't work for male kzin. In any case, I have your word. If you forget it, I will make you sorry. We need each other, Kit; just like I need a sharp edge on my knife." He lowered his arm then, offering her his hand. "Here, come outside and help me. It's nearly dark again."

She was astonished to find, from the sun's position, that she had 'slept' almost a full day. But there was no doubting he had spent many hours on that airboat of his. She helped him for a few moments, then remem-

bered that her kiln would now be cool, the bowls and
water jug waiting in its primitive chimney. "May I
retrieve my pottery, Rockear?"

He smiled at her obedient tone. "If I say no?"

"I do it tomorrow."

"Go ahead, Kit. It'll be dark soon." He watched her
bounding away through high grass, then hurried into
the cave. He had to put that stasis gadget back where
he'd got it or, sure as hell, she'd figure it out and one
fine day *he* would wake up hogtied. Or worse.

Locklear's praise of the pottery was not forced; Kit
had a gift for handcrafts, and they ate from decorated
bowls that night. He sensed her new deference when
she asked, "Have you chosen a site for the manor?"

"Not until I've explored further. We'll want a hidden
site we can defend and retreat from, with reliable sources
of water, firewood, food—not like this cave. And I'll
need your help in that decision, Kit."

"It must be done before we wake the others," she
said, adding as if to echo his own warnings, "And soon,
if we are to be ready for the kzintosh."

"Don't nag," he replied. He blew on blistered palms
and lay full-length on their grassy bower. "We have to
get that airboat working right away," he said, and patted the grass beside him. She curled up in her usual
way. After a few moments he placed a hand on her
shoulder.

"Thank you, Rockear," she murmured, and fell asleep.
He lay awake for another hour, gnawing the ribs of two
sciences. The engineering of the airboat would be largely
trial and error. So would the ethology of a relationship
between a man and a kzin female, with all those nuances he was beginning to sense. How, for example,
did a kzin make love? Not that he intended to—*unless*,
a vagrant thought nudged him, *I'm doing some of it
already*. . .

Two more days and a near-disastrous capsizing later,
Locklear found the right combination of ballast and sail.
He found that Kit could sprint for short distances faster

than he could urge the airboat, but over long distances he had a clear edge. Alone, tacking higher, he found stronger winds that bore him far across the sky of Kzersatz, and once he found himself drifting in cross-currents high above that frost line that curved visibly, now, tracing the edge of the force cylinder that was their cage.

He turned after a two-hour absence to find Kit weaving more mats, more cordage, for furnishings. She approached the airboat warily, mistrusting its magical properties but relieved to see him. "You'll be using this thing yourself, pretty soon, Kit," he confided. "Can you make us some decent ink and paper?"

In a day, yes, she said, if she found a scroll-leaf palm, to soak, pound, and dry its fronds. Ink was no problem. Then hop aboard, he said, and they'd go cruising for the palm. *That* was a problem; she was plainly terrified of flight in any form. Kzinti were fearless, he reminded her. Females were not, she said, adding that the sight of him dwindling in the sky to a scudding dot had "drawn up her tail"—a fear reaction, he learned.

He ordered her, at least, to mount the raft, sitting in tandem behind him. She found the position somehow obscene, but she did it. Evidently it was highly acceptable for a male to crowd close behind a female, but not the reverse. Then Locklear recalled how cats mated, and he understood. "Nobody will see us, Kit. Hang on to these cords and pull only when I tell you." With that, he levitated the airboat a meter, and stayed low for a time—until he felt the flexure of her foot talons relax at his thighs.

In another hour they were quartering the sky above the jungles and savannahs of Kzersatz, Kit enjoying the ride too much to retain her fears. They landed in a clearing near the unexplored end of the lake, Kit scrambling up a thick palm to return with young rolled fronds. "The sap stings when fresh," she said, indicating a familiar white substance. "But when dried and reheated it makes excellent glue." She also gathered fruit like purple leather melons, with flesh that smelled faintly of seafood, and stowed them for dinner.

The return trip was longer. He taught her how to tack upwind and later, watching her soak fronds that night inside the cave, exulted because soon they would have maps of this curious country. In only one particular was he evasive.

"Rockear, what is that thing I felt on your back under your clothing," she asked.

"It's, uh, just a thing your warriors do to captives. I have to keep it there," he said, and quickly changed the subject.

In another few days, they had crude air maps and several candidate sites for the manor. Locklear agreed to Kit's choice as they hovered above it, a gentle slope beneath a cliff overhang where a kzinrret could sun herself half the day. Fast-growing hardwoods nearby would provide timber and firewood, and the stream burbling in the throat of the ravine was the same stream where he had found that first waterfall down near the lake, and had conjectured on the age of Kzersatz. She rubbed her cheek against his neck when he accepted her decision.

He steered toward the hardwood grove, feeling a faint dampness on his neck. "What does that mean?"

"Why,—marking you, of course. It is a display of affection." He pursued it. The ritual transferred a pheromone from her furry cheeks to his flesh. He could not smell it, but she maintained that any kzin would recognize her marker until the scent evaporated in a few hours.

It was like a lipstick mark, he decided—"Or a hickey with your initials," he told her, and then had to explain himself. She admitted he had not guessed far off the mark. "But hold on, Kit. Could a kzin warrior track me by my scent?"

"Certainly. How else does one follow a spoor?"

He thought about that awhile. "If we come to the

manor and leave it always by air, would that make it harder to find?"

Of course, she said. Trackers needed a scent trail; that's why she intended them to walk in the nearby stream, even if splashing in water was unpleasant. "But if they are determined to find you, Rockear, they will."

He sighed, letting the airboat settle near a stand of pole-straight trees, and as he hacked with the dulled *wtsai*, told her of the new weaponry: projectiles, beamers, energy fields, bombs. "When they do find us, we've got to trap them somehow; get their weapons. Could you kill your own kind?"

"They executed me," she reminded him and added after a moment, "Kzinrret weapons might be best. Leave it to me." She did not elaborate. Well, women's weapons had their uses.

He slung several logs under the airboat and left Kit stone-sharpening the long blade as he slowly tacked his way back to their ravine. Releasing the hitches was the work of a moment, thick poles thudding onto yellow-green grass, and soon he was back with Kit. By the time the sun faded, the *wtsai* was biting like a handaxe and Kit had prepared them a thick grassy pallet between the cliff face and their big foundation logs. It was the coldest night Locklear had spent on Kzersatz, but Kit's fur made it endurable.

Days later, she ate the last of the kzin rations as he chewed a fishnut and sketched in the dirt with a stick. "We'll run the shamboo plumbing out here from the kitchen," he said, "and dig our escape tunnel out from our sleep room parallel with the cliff. We'll need help, Kit. It's time."

She vented a long purring sigh. "I know. Things will be different, Rockear. Not as simple as our life has been."

He laughed at that, reminding her of the complications they had already faced, and then they resumed notching logs, raising the walls beyond window height. Their own work packed the earthen floors, but the roofing would require more hands than their own.

That night, Kit kindled their first fire in the central room's hearth, and they fell asleep while she tutored him on the ways of ancient kzin females.

Leaning against the airboat alone near the cave, Locklear felt new misgivings. Kit had argued that his presence at the awakenings would be a Bad Idea. Let them grow used to him slowly, she'd said. Stand tall, give orders gently, and above all don't smile until they understand his show of teeth. *No fear of that*, he thought, shifting nervously a half-hour after Kit disappeared inside. *I don't feel like smiling*.

He heard a shuffling just out of sight; realized he was being viewed covertly; threw out his chest and flexed his pectorals. Not much by kzin standards, but he'd developed a lot of sinew during the past weeks. He felt silly as hell, and those other kzinrret had not made him any promises. The *wtsai* felt good at his belt.

Then Kit was striding into the open, with an expression of strained patience. Standing beside him, she muttered, "Mark me." Then, seeing his frown: "Your cheek against my neck, Rockear. *Quickly*."

He did so. She bowed before him, offering the tip of her tail in both hands, and he stroked it when she told him to. Then he saw a lithe movement of orange at the cave and raised both hands in a universal weaponless gesture as the second kzinrret emerged, watching him closely. She was much larger than Kit, with transverse stripes of darker orange and a banded tail. Close on her heels came a third, more reluctantly but staying close behind as if for protection, with facial markings that reminded Locklear of an ocelot and very dark fur at hands and feet. They were admirable creatures, but their ear umbrellas lay flat and they were not yet his friends.

Kit moved to the first, urging her forward to Locklear. After a few tentative sniffs the big kzinrret said, in that curious ancient dialect, "I am (something truly unpronounceable), prret in service of Rockear." She bent toward him, her stance defensive, and he marked her as Kit had said he must, then stroked her tabby-banded tail. She moved away and the third kzinrret approached, and Locklear's eyes widened as he performed the greeting ritual. She was either potbellied, or carrying a litter!

Both of their names being beyond him, he dubbed the larger one Puss; the pregnant one, Boots. They accepted their new names as proof that they were members of a very different kind of household than any they had known. Both wore aprons of woven mat, Kit's deft work, and she offered them water from bowls.

As they stood eyeing one another speculatively, Kit surprised them all. "It is time to release the animals," she said. "My lord Rockear-the-magician, we are excellent herders, and from your flying boat you can observe our work. The larger beasts might also distract the kzintosh, and we will soon need meat. Is it not so?"

She *knew* he couldn't afford an argument now—and besides, she was right. He had no desire to try herding some of those big critters outside anyhow, and kzinti had been doing it from time immemorial. *Damned clever tactic, Kit; Puss and Boots will get a chance to work off their nerves, and so will I*. He swept a permissive arm outward and sat down in the airboat as the three kzin females moved into the cave.

The next two hours were a crash course in zoology for Locklear, safe at fifty meter height as he watched herds, coveys, throngs and volleys of creatures as they crawled, flapped, hopped and galumphed off across the yellow prairie. A batowl found a perch atop his mast, trading foolish blinks with him until it whispered away after another of its kind. One huge ruminant with the bulk of a rhino and murderous spikes on its thick tail sat down to watch him, raising its bull's muzzle to issue a call like a wolf. An answering howl sent it lumbering off again, and Locklear wondered whether they were to be butchered, ridden, or simply avoided. He liked the last option best.

When at last Kit came loping out with shrill screams of false fury at the heels of a collie-sized, furry tyrannosaur, the operation was complete. He'd half-expected to see a troop of more kzinti bounding outside, but Kit was as good as her word. None of them recognized any of the other stasized kzinti, and all seemed content to let the strangers stay as they were.

The airboat did not have room for them all, but by now Kit could operate the polarizer levers. She sat ahead of Locklear for decorum's sake, making a show of her pairing with him, and let Puss and Boots follow beneath as the airboat slid ahead of a good breeze toward their tacky, unfinished little manor. "They will be nicely exhausted," she said to him, "by the time we reach home."

Home. My God, it may be my home for the rest of my life, he thought, watching the muscular Puss bound along behind them with Boots in arrears. *Three kzin courtesans for company; a sure 'nough cathouse! Is that much better than having those effing warriors to return? And if they don't, is there any way I could get across to my own turf, to Newduvai?* The gravity polarizer could get him to orbit, but he would need propulsion, and a woven sail wasn't exactly de rigueur for travel in vacuum, and how the hell could he build an airtight cockpit anyhow? Too many questions, too few answers, and two more kzin females who might be more hindrance than help, hurtling along in the yellowsward behind him. One of them pregnant.

And kzin litters were almost all twins, one male. Like it or not, he was doomed to deal with at least one kzintosh. The notion of killing the tiny male forced itself forward. He quashed the idea instantly, and hoped it would stay quashed. *Yeah, and one of these days it'll weigh three times as much as I do, and two of these randy females will be vying for mating privileges.* The return of the kzin ship, he decided, might be the least of his troubles.

That being so, the least of his troubles could kill him.

Puss and Boots proved far more help than hindrance. Locklear admitted it to Kit one night, lying in their small room off the 'great hall', itself no larger than five meters by ten and already pungent with cooking smokes. "Those two hardly talk to me, but they thatch a roof like crazy. How well can they tunnel?"

This amused her. "Every pregnant kzinrret is an expert at tunneling, as you will soon see. Except that you will not see. When birthing time nears, a mother digs her secret birthing place. The father sometimes helps, but oftener not."

"Too lazy?"

She regarded him with eyes that reflected a dim flicker from the fire dying in the next room's hearth, and sent a shiver through him. "Too likely to eat the newborn male," she said simply.

"Good God. Not among modern kzinti, I hope."

"Perhaps. Females become good workers; males become aggressive hunters likely to challenge for household mastery. Which would *you* value more?"

"My choice is a matter of record," he joked, adding that they were certainly shaping the manor up fast. That, she said, was because they knew their places and their leaders. Soon they would be butchering and curing meat, making (something) from the milk of ruminants, cheese perhaps, and making ready for the kittens. Some of the released animals seemed already domesticated. A few *vatach*, she said, might be trapped and released nearby for convenience.

He asked if the others would really fight the returning kzin warriors, and she insisted that they would, especially Puss. "She was a highly valued *prret*, but she hates males," Kit warned. "In some ways I think she wishes to be one."

"Then why did she ask if I'd like to scratch her flanks with my *wtsai*," he asked.

"I will claw her eyes out if you do," she growled. "She is only negotiating for status. Keep your blade in your belt," she said angrily, with a metaphor he could not miss.

That blade reminded him (as he idly scratched her flanks with its dull tip to calm her) that the cave was now a treasury of materials. He must study the planting of the fast-growing vines which, according to Kit, would soon hide the roof thatching; those vines could also hide the cave entrance. He could scavenge enough steel for lances, more of the polarizers to build a whopping big airsloop, maybe even—. He sat up, startling her. "Meat storage!"

Kit did not understand. He wasn't sure he wanted her to. He would need wire for remote switches, which might be recovered from polarizer toroids if he had the nerve to try it. "I may have a way to keep meat fresh, Kit, but you must help me see that no one else touches my magics. They could be dangerous." She said he was the boss, and he almost believed it.

Once the females began their escape tunnel, Locklear rigged a larger sail and completed his mapping chores, amassing several scrolls which seemed gibberish to the others. And each day he spent two hours at the cave. When vines died, he planted others to hide the entrance. He learned that polarizers and stasis units came in three sizes, and brought trapped *vatach* back in large cages he had separated from their gravity and stasis devices. Those clear cage tops made admirable windows, and the cage metal was then reworked by firelight in the main hall.

Despite Kit's surly glances, he bade Puss sit beside him to learn metalwork, while Boots patiently wove mats and formed trays of clay to his specifications for papermaking. One day he might begin a journal. Meanwhile he needed awls, screwdrivers, pliers—and a longbow with arrows. He was all thumbs while shaping them.

Boots became more shy as her pregnancy advanced. Locklear's new social problem became the casual nuances from Puss that, by now, he knew were sexual. She rarely spoke unless spoken to, but one day while resting in the sun with the big kzinrret he noticed her tailtip flicking near his leg. He had noticed previously that a moving rope or vine seemed to mesmerize a kzin; they probably thought it fascinated him as well.

"Puss, I—uh—sleep only with Kit. Sorry, but that's the way of it."

"Pfaugh. I am more skilled at *ch'rowl* than she, and I could make you a pillow of her fur if I liked." Her gaze was calm, challenging; to a male kzin, probably very sexy.

"We must all work together, Puss. As head of the household, I forbid you to make trouble."

"My Lord," she said with a small nod, but her ear-flick was amused. "In that case, am I permitted to help in the birthing?"

"Of course," he said, touched. "Where is Boots, anyway?"

"Preparing her birthing chamber. It cannot be long now," Puss added, setting off down the ravine.

Locklear found Kit dragging a mat of dirt from the tunnel and asked her about the problems of birthing. The hardest part, she said, was the bower—and when males were near, the hiding. He asked why Puss would be needed at the birthing.

"Ah," said Kit. "It is symbolic, Rockear. You have agreed to let her play the mate role. It is not unheard-of, and the newborn male will be safe."

"You mean, symbolic like our pairing?"

"Not quite that symbolic," she replied with sarcasm as they distributed stone and earth outside. "Prret are flexible."

Then he asked her what *ch'rowl* meant.

Kit vented a tiny miaow of pleasure, then realized suddenly that he did not know what he had said. Furiously: "She used that word to you? I will break her tail!"

"I forbid it," he said. "She was angry because I told her I slept only with you." Pleased with this, Kit subsided as they moved into the tunnel again. Some kzin words, he learned, were triggers. At least one seemed to be blatantly lascivious. He was deflected from this line of thought only when Kit, digging upward now, broke through to the surface.

They replanted shrubs at the exit before dark, and lounged before the hearthfire afterward. At last Locklear yawned; checked his wristcomp. "They are very late," he said.

"Kittens are born at night," she replied, unworried.

"But—I assumed she'd tell us when it was time."

"She has not said eight-cubed of words to you. Why should she confide that to a male?"

He shrugged at the fire. Perhaps they would always treat him like a kzintosh. He wondered for the hundredth time whether, when push came to shove, they would fight with him or against him.

In his mapping sorties, Locklear had skirted near enough to the force walls to see that Kzersatz was adjacent to four other compounds. One, of course, was the tantalizing Newduvai. Another was hidden in swirling mists; he dubbed it Limbo. The others held no charm for him; he named them Who Needs It, and No Thanks. He wondered what collections of life forms roamed those mysterious lands, or slept there in stasis. The planet might have scores of such zoo compounds.

Meanwhile, he unwound a hundred meters of wire from a polarizer, and stole switches from others. One of his jury-rigs, outside the cave, was a catapult using a polarizer on a sturdy frame. He could stand fifty meters away and, with his remote switch, lob a heavy stone several hundred meters. Perhaps a series of the gravity polarizers would make a kind of mass driver—a true space drive! There was yet hope, he thought, of someday visiting Newduvai.

And then he transported some materials to the manor where he installed a stasis device to keep meat fresh indefinitely; and late that same day, Puss returned. Even Kit, ignoring their rivalry, welcomed the big kzinrret.

"They are all well," Puss reported smugly, paternally. To Locklear's delighted question she replied in severe tones, "You cannot see them until their eyes open, Rockear."

"It is tradition," Kit injected. "The mother will suckle them until then, and will hunt as she must."

"I am the hunter," Puss said. "When we build our own manor, will your household help?"

Kit looked quickly toward Locklear, who realized the implications. *By God, they're really pairing off for another household,* he thought. After a moment he said, "Yes, but you must locate it nearby." He saw Kit relax and decided he'd made the right decision. To celebrate the new developments, Puss shooed Locklear and Kit outside to catch the late sun while she made them an early supper. They sat on their rough-hewn bench above the ravine to eat, Puss claiming she could return to the birthing bower in full darkness, and Locklear allowed himself to bask in a sense of well-being. It was not until Puss had headed back down the ravine with food for Boots, that Locklear realized she had stolen several small items from his storage shelves.

He could accept the loss of tools and a knife; Puss had, after all, helped him make them. What caused his cold sweat was the fact that the tiny *zzrou* transmitter was missing. The *zzrou* prongs in his shoulder began to itch as he thought about it. Puss could not possibly know the importance of the transmitter to him; maybe she thought it was some magical tool—and maybe she would destroy it while studying it. "Kit," he said, trying to keep the tremor from his voice, "I've got a problem and I need your help."

She seemed incensed, but not very surprised, to learn the function of the device that clung to his back. One thing was certain, he insisted: the birthing bower could not be more than a klick away. Because if Puss took the transmitter farther than that, he would die in agony. Could Kit lead him to the bower in darkness?

"I might find it, Rockear, but your presence there would provoke violence," she said. "I must go alone." She caressed his flank gently, then set off slowly down the ravine on all-fours, her nose close to the turf until she disappeared in darkness.

Locklear stood for a time at the manor entrance, wondering what this night would bring, and then saw a long scrawl of light as it slowed to a stop and winked out, many miles above the plains of Kzersatz. Now he knew what the morning would bring, and knew that he had not one deadly problem, but two. He began to check his pathetic little armory by the glow of his memocomp, because that was better than giving way entirely to despair.

When he awoke, it was to the warmth of Kit's fur nestled against his backside. *There was a time when she called this obscene*, he thought with a smile—and then he remembered everything, and lit the display of his memocomp. Two hours until dawn. How long until death, he wondered, and woke her.

She did not have the *zzrou* transmitter. "Puss heard my calls," she said, "and warned me away. She will return this morning to barter tools for things she wants."

"I'll tell you who else will return," he began. "No, don't rebuild the fire, Kit. I saw what looked like a ship stationing itself many miles away overhead, while you were gone. Smoke will only give us away. It might possibly be a Manship, but—expect the worst. You haven't told me how you plan to fight."

His hopes fell as she stammered out her ideas, and he countered each one, reflecting that she was no planner. They would hide and ambush the searchers—but he reminded her of their projectile and beam weapons. Very well, they would claim absolute homestead rights accepted by all ancient Kzinti clans—but modern Kzinti, he insisted, had probably forgotten those ancient immunities.

"You may as well invite them in for breakfast," he grumbled. "Back on earth, women's weapons included poison. I thought you had some kzinrret weapons."

"Poisons would take time, Rockcar. It takes little time, and not much talent, to set warriors fighting to the death over a female. Surely they would still respond with foolish bravado?"

"I don't know; they've never seen a smart kzinrret. And ship's officers are very disciplined. I don't think they'd get into a free-for-all. Maybe lure them in here and hit 'em while they sleep . . ."

"As you did to me?"

"Uh no, I—yes!" He was suddenly galvanized by the idea, tantalized by the treasures he had left in the cave. "Kit, the machine I set up to preserve food is exactly the same as the one I placed under you, to make you sleep when I hit a foot switch." He saw her flash of anger at his earlier duplicity. "An ancient sage once said anything that's advanced enough beyond your understanding is indistinguishable from magic, Kit. But magic can turn on you. Could you get a warrior to sit or lie down by himself?"

"If I cannot, I am no *prret*," she purred. "Certainly I can *leave* one lying by himself. Or two. Or . . ."

"Okay, don't get graphic on me," he snapped. "We've got only one stasis unit here. If only I could get more— but I can't leave in the airboat without that damned little transmitter! Kit, you'll have to go and get Puss now. I'll promise her anything within reason."

"She will know we are at a disadvantage. Her demands will be outrageous."

"We're *all* at a disadvantage! Tell her about the Kzin warship that's hanging over us."

"Hanging magically over us," she corrected him. "It is true enough for me."

Then she was gone, loping away in darkness, leaving him to fumble his way to the meat storage unit he had so recently installed. The memocomp's faint light helped a little, and he was too busy to notice the passage of time until, with its usual sudden blaze, the sunlet of Kzersatz began to shine.

He was hiding the wires from Puss's bed to the foot switch near the little room's single doorway when he heard a distant roll of thunder. No, not thunder: it grew to a crackling howl in the sky, and from the nearest window he saw what he most feared to see. The Kzin lifeboat left a thin contrail in its pass, circling just inside the force cylinder of Kzersatz, and its wingtips slid out as it slowed. No doubt of the newcomer now, and it disappeared in the direction of that first landing, so long ago. If only he'd thought to booby-trap that landing zone with stasis units! Well, he might've, given time.

He finished his work in fevered haste, knowing that time was now his enemy, and so were the kzinti in that ship, and so, for all practical purposes, was the traitor Puss. *And Kit? How easy it will be for her to switch sides! Those females will make out like bandits wherever they are, and I may learn Kit's decision when these goddamned prongs take a lethal bite in my back. Could be any time now.* And then he heard movements in the high grass nearby, and leaped for his longbow.

Kit flashed to the doorway, breathless. "She is coming, Rockear. Have you set your sleeptrap?"

He showed her the rig. "Toe it once for sleep, again for waking, again for sleep," he said. "Whatever you do, don't get near enough to touch the sleeper, or stand over him, or you'll be in the same fix. I've set it for maximum power."

"Why did you put it here, instead of our own bed?"

He coughed and shrugged. "Uh,—I don't know. Just seemed like—well, hell, it's *our* bed, Kit! I, um, didn't like the idea of your using it, ah, the way you'll have to use it."

"You are an endearing beast," she said, pinching him lightly at the neck, "to bind me with tenderness."

They both whirled at Puss's voice from the main doorway: "Bind who with tenderness?"

"I will explain," said Kit, her face bland. "If you brought those trade goods, display them on your bed."

"I think not," said Puss, striding into the room she'd shared with Boots. "But I will show them to you." With that, she sat on her bed and reached into her apron pocket, drawing out a *wtsai* for inspection.

An instant later she was unconscious. Kit, with

Locklear kibitzing, used a grass broom to whisk the knife safely away. "I should use it on her throat," she snarled, but she let Locklear take the weapon.

"She came of her own accord," he said, "and she's a fighter. We need her, Kit. Hit the switch again."

A moment later, Puss was blinking, leaping up, then suddenly backing away in fear. "Treachery," she spat.

In reply, Locklear tossed the knife onto her bed despite Kit's frown. "Just a display, Puss. You need the knife, and I'm your ally. But I've got to have that little gadget that looks like my wristcomp." He held out his hand.

"I left it at the birthing bower. I knew it was important," she said with a surly glance as she retrieved the knife. "For its return, I demand our total release from this household. I demand your help to build a manor as large as this, wherever I like. I demand teaching in your magical arts." She trembled, but stood defiant; a dangerous combination.

"Done, done, and done," he said. "You want equality, and I'm willing. But we may all be equally dead if that Kzin ship finds us. We need a leader. Do you have a good plan?"

Puss swallowed hard. "Yes. Hunt at night, hide until they leave."

Sighing, Locklear told her that was no plan at all. He wasted long minutes arguing his case: Puss to steal near the landing site and report on the intruders; the return of his *zzrou* transmitter so he could try sneaking back to the cave; Kit to remain at the manor preparing food for a siege—and to defend the manor through what he termed guile, if necessary.

Puss refused. "My place," she insisted, "is defending the birthing bower."

"And you will not have a male as a leader," Kit said. "Is that not the way of it?"

"Exactly," Puss growled.

"I have agreed to your demands, Puss," Locklear reminded her. "But it won't happen if the Kzin warriors get me. We've proved we won't abuse you. At least give me back that transmitter. Please," he added gently.

Too late, he saw Puss's disdain for pleading. "So that is the source of your magic," she said, her ears lifting in a kzinrret smile. "I shall discover its secrets, Rockear."

"He will die if you damage it," Kit said quickly, "or take if far from him. You have done a stupid thing; without this manbeast who knows our enemy well, we will be slaves again. To males," she added.

Puss sidled along the wall, now holding the knife at ready, menacing Kit until a single bound put her through the doorway into the big room. Pausing at the outer doorway she stuck the *wtsai* into her apron. "I will consider what you say," she growled.

"Wait," Locklear said in his most commanding tone, the only one that Puss seemed to value. "The kzintosh will be searching for me. They have magics that let them see great distances even at night, and a big metal airboat that flies with the sound of thunder."

"I heard thunder this morning," Puss admitted.

"You heard their airboat. If they see you, they will probably capture you. You and Boots must be very careful, Puss."

"And do not hesitate to tempt males into (something) if you can," Kit put in.

"Now you would teach me my business," Puss spat at Kit, and set off down the ravine.

Locklear moved to the outer doorway, watching the sky, listening hard. Presently he asked, "Do you think we can lay siege to the birthing bower to get that transmitter back?"

"Boots is a suckling mother, which saps her strength," Kit replied matter-of-factly. "So Puss would fight like a crazed warrior. The truth is, she is stronger than both of us."

With a morose shake of his head, Locklear began to fashion more arrows while Kit sharpened his *wtsai* into a dagger, arguing tactics, drawing rough conclusions. They must build no fires at the manor, and hope that the searchers spread out for single, arrogant sorties.

The lifeboat would hold eight warriors, and others might be waiting in orbit. Live captives might be better for negotiations than dead heroes—"But even as captives, the bastards would eat every scrap of meat in sight," Locklear admitted.

Kit argued persuasively that any warrior worth his *wtsai* would be more likely to negotiate with a potent enemy. "We must give them casualties," she insisted, "to gain their respect. Can these modern males be that different from those I knew?"

Probably not, he admitted. And knowing the modern breed, he knew they would be infuriated by his escape, dishonored by his shrewdness. He could expect no quarter when at last they did locate him. "And they won't go until they do," he said. On that, they agreed; some things never changed.

Locklear, dog-tired after hanging thatch over the gleaming windows, heard the lifeboat pass twice before dark but fell asleep as the sun faded.

Much later, Kit was shaking him. "Come to the door," she urged. "She refuses to come in."

He stumbled outside, found the bench by rote, and spoke to the darkness. "Puss? You have nothing to fear from us. Had a change of heart?"

Not far distant: "I hunted those slopes where you said the males left you, Rockear."

It was an obvious way to avoid saying she had reconnoitered as he'd asked, and he maintained the ruse. "Did you have good hunting?"

"Fair. A huge metal thing came and went and came again. I found four warriors, in strange costume and barbaric speech like yours, with strange weapons. They are making a camp there, and spoke with surprise of seeing animals to hunt." She spoke slowly, pausing often. He asked her to describe the males. She had no trouble with that, having lain in her natural camouflage in the jungle's verge within thirty paces of the ship until dark. *Must've taken her hours to get here in the dark over rough country*, he thought. *This is one tough bimbo*.

He waited, his hackles rising, until she finished. "You're sure the leader had that band across his face?" She was. She'd heard him addressed as 'Grraf-Commander'. One with a light-banded belly was called 'Apprentice Something'. And the other two tallied, as well. "I can't believe it," he said to the darkness. "The same foursome that left me here! If they're all down here, they're deadly serious. Damn their good luck."

"Better than you think," said Puss. "You told me they had magic weapons. Now I believe it."

Kit, leaning near, whispered into Locklear's ear. "If she were injured, she would refuse to show her weakness to us."

He tried again. "Puss, how do you know of their weapons?"

With dry amusement and courage, the disembodied voice said, "The usual way: the huge sentry used one. Tiny sunbeams that struck as I reached thick cover. They truly can see in full darkness."

"So they've seen you," he said, dismayed.

"From their shouts, I think they were not sure what they saw. But I will kill them for this, sentry or no sentry."

Her voice was more distant now. Locklear raised his voice slightly: "Puss, can we help you?"

"I have been burned before," was the reply.

Kit, moving into the darkness quietly: "You are certain there are only four?"

"Positive," was the faint reply, and then they heard only the night wind.

Presently Kit said, "It would take both of us, and when wounded she will certainly fight to the death. But we might overpower her now, if we can find the bower."

"No. She did more than she promised. And now she knows she can kill me by smashing the transmitter. Let's get same sleep, Kit," he said. Then, when he had nestled behind her, he added with a chuckle, "I begin to see why the kzinti decided to breed females as mere pets. Sheer self-defense."

"I would break your tail for that, if you had one," she replied in mock ferocity. Then he laid his hand on her flank, heard her soft miaow, and then they slept.

Locklear had patrolled nearly as far as he dared down the ravine at midmorning, armed with his *wtsai*, longbow, and an arrow-filled quiver rubbing against the *zzrou* when he heard the first scream. He knew that Kit, with her short lance, had gone in the opposite direction on her patrol, but the repeated kzin screams sent gooseflesh up his spine. Perhaps the tabbies had surrounded Boots, or Puss. He notched an arrow, half climbing to the lip of the ravine, and peered over low brush. He stifled the exclamation in his throat.

They'd found Puss, all right—or she'd found them. She stood on all-fours on a level spot below, her tail erect, its tip curled over, watching two hated familiar figures in a tableau that must have been as old as kzin history. Almost naked for this primitive duel, ebony talons out and their musky scent heavy on the breeze, they bulked stupefyingly huge and ferocious. The massive gunner, Goon, and engineer Yellowbelly circled each other with drawn stilettoes. What boggled Locklear was that their modern weapons lay ignored in neat groups. Were they going through some ritual?

They were like hell, he decided. From time to time, Puss would utter a single word, accompanied by a tremor and a tail-twitch; and each time, Yellowbelly and Goon would stiffen, then scream at each other in frustration.

The word she repeated was *ch'rowl*. No telling how long they'd been there, but Goon's right forearm dripped blood, and Yellowbelly's thigh was a sodden red mess. Swaying drunkenly, Puss edged nearer to the weapons. As Yellowbelly screamed and leaped, Goon screamed and parried, bearing his smaller opponent to the turf. What followed then was fast enough to be virtually a blur in a roil of Kzersatz dust as two huge tigerlike bodies thrashed and rolled, knives flashing, talons ripping, fangs sinking into flesh.

Locklear scrambled downward through the grass, his progress unheard in the earsplitting caterwauls nearby. He saw Puss reach a beam rifle, grasp it, swing it experimentally by the barrel. That's when he forgot all caution and shouted, "No, Puss! Put the stock to your shoulder and pull the trigger!"

He might as well have told her to bazzfazz the shimstock; and in any case, poor valiant Puss collapsed while trying to figure the rifle out. He saw the long ugly trough in her side then, caked with dried blood. A wonder she was conscious, with such a wound. Then he saw something more fearful still, the quieter thrashing as Goon found the throat of Yellowbelly, whose stiletto handle protruded from Goon's upper arm.

Ducking below the brush, Locklear moved to one side, nearer to Puss, whose breathing was as labored as that of the males. Or rather, of one male, as Goon stood erect and uttered a victory roar that must have carried to Newduvai. Yellowbelly's torn throat pumped the last of his blood onto alien dust.

"I claim my right," Goon screamed, and added a Word that Locklear was beginning to loathe. Only then did the huge gunner notice that Puss was in no condition to present him with what he had just killed to get. He nudged her roughly, and did not see Locklear approach with one arrow notched and another held between his teeth.

But his ear umbrellas pivoted as a twig snapped under Locklear's foot, and Goon spun furiously, the big legs flexed, and for one instant man and kzin stood twenty paces apart, unmoving. Goon leaped for the nearest weapon, the beam rifle Puss had dropped, and saw Locklear release the short arrow. It missed by a full armspan and now, his bloodlust rekindled and with no fear of such a marksman, Goon dropped the rifle and pulled Yellowbelly's stiletto from his own arm. He turned toward Locklear, who was unaccountably running *toward* him instead of fleeing as a monkey should flee a leopard, and threw his head back in a battle scream.

Locklear's second arrow, fired from a distance of five paces, pierced the roof of Goon's mouth, its stainless steel barb severing nerve bundles at the brain stem. Goon fell like a jointed tree, knees buckling first, arms hanging, and the ground's impact drove the arrow tip out the back of his head, slippery with gore. Goon's head lay two paces from Locklear's feet. He neither breathed nor twitched.

Locklear hurried to the side of poor, courageous, ill-starred Puss and saw her gazing calmly at him. "One for you, one for me, Puss. Only two more to go."

"I wish—I could live to celebrate that," she said, more softly than he had ever heard her speak.

"You're too tough to let a little burn," he began.

"They shot tiny things, too," she said, a finger migrating to a bluish perforation at the side of her ribcage. "Coughing blood. Hard to breathe," she managed.

He knew then that she was dying. A spray of slugs, roughly aimed at night from a perimeter-control smoothbore, had done to Puss what a beam rifle could not. Her lungs filling slowly with blood, she had still managed to report her patrol and then return to guard the birthing bower. He asked through the lump in his throat, "Is Boots all right?"

"They followed my spoor. When I—came out, twitching my best *prret* routine,—they did not look into the bower."

"Smart, Puss."

She grasped his wrist, hard. "Swear to protect it— with your life." Now she was coughing blood, fighting to breathe.

"Done," he said. "Where is it, Puss?"

But her eyes were already glazing. Locklear stood up slowly and strode to the beam rifle, hefting it, thinking idly that these weapons were too heavy for him to carry in one trip. And then he saw Puss again, and quit thinking, and lifted the rifle over his head with both hands in a manscream of fury, and of vengeance unappeased.

The battle scene was in sight of the lake, fully in the open within fifty paces of the creek, and he found it impossible to lift Puss. Locklear cut bundles of grass and spread them to hide the bodies, trembling in delayed reaction, and carried three armloads of weapons to a hiding place far up the ravine just under its lip. He left the dead kzinti without stripping them; perhaps a mistake, but he had no time now to puzzle out tightband comm sets or medkits. Later, if there was a later . . .

He cursed his watery joints, knowing he could not carry a kzin beam rifle with its heavy accumulator up to the manor. He moved more cautiously now, remembering those kzin screams, wondering how far they'd carried on the breeze which was toward the lake. He read the safety legends on Goon's sidearm, found he could handle the massive piece with both hands, and stuck it and its twin from Yellowbelly's arsenal into his belt, leaving his bow and quiver with the other weapons.

He had stumbled within sight of the manor, planning how he could unmast the airboat and adjust its buoyancy so that it could be towed by a man afoot to retrieve those weapons, when a crackling hum sent a blast of hot air across his cheeks. Face down, crawling for the lip of the ravine, he heard a shout from near the manor.

"Grraf-Commander, the monkey approaches!" The reply, deep-voiced and muffled, seemed to come from inside the manor. So they'd known where the manor was. Heat or motion sensors, perhaps, during a pass in the lifeboat—not that it mattered now. A classic pincers from down and up the ravine, but one of those pincers now lay under shields of grass. They could not know that he was still tethered invisibly to that *zzrou* transmitter. But where was Kit?

Another hail from Brickshitter, whose tremors of impatience with a beam rifle had become Locklear's ally: "The others do not answer my calls, but I shall drive the monkey down to them." Well, maybe he'd intended merely to wing his quarry, or follow him.

You do that, Locklear thought to himself in cold rage as he scurried back in the ravine toward his weapons cache; *you just do that, Brickshitter.* He had covered two hundred meters when another crackle announced the pencil-thin beam, brighter than the sun, that struck a ridge of stone above him.

White-hot bees stung his face, back and arms; tiny smoke trails followed fragments of superheated stone into the ravine as Locklear tumbled to the creek, splashing out again, stumbling on slick stones. He turned, intending to fire a sidearm, but saw no target and realized that firing from him would tell volumes to that big sonofabitchkitty behind and above him. Well, they wouldn't have returned unless they wanted him alive, so Brickshitter was just playing with him, driving him as a man drives cattle with a prod. Beam weapons were limited in rate of fire and accumulator charge; maybe Brickshitter would empty this one with his trembling.

Then, horrifyingly near, above the ravine lip, the familiar voice: "I offer you honor, monkey."

Whatthehell: the navigator knew where his quarry was anyhow. Mopping a runnel of blood from his face, Locklear called upward as he continued his scramble. "What, a prisoner exchange?" He did not want to be more explicit than that.

"We already have the beauteous kzinrret," was the reply that chilled Locklear to his marrows. "Is that who you would have sacrificed for your worthless hide?"

That tears it; no hope now, Locklear thought. "Maybe I'll give myself up if you'll let her go," he called. *Would I? Probably not. Dear God, please don't give me that choice because I know there would be no honor in mine . . .*

"We have you caged, monkey," in tones of scorn. "But Grraf-Commander warned that you may have some primitive hunting weapon, so we accord you some little honor. It occurs to me that you would retain more honor if captured by an officer than by a pair of rankings."

Locklear was now only a hundred meters from the precious cache. *He's too close; he'll see the weapons cache when I get near it and that'll be all she wrote. I've got to make the bastard careless and use what I've got.* He thought carefully how to translate a nickname into kzin and began to ease up the far side of the ravine. "Not if the officer has no honor, you trembling shitter of bricks," he shouted, slipping the safety from a sidearm.

Instantly a scream of raw rage and astonishment from above at this unbelievably mortal insult, followed by the head and shoulders of an infuriated navigator. Locklear aimed fast, squeezed the firing stud, and saw a series of dirt clods spit from the verge of the ravine. The damned thing shot low!

But Brickshitter had popped from sight as though propelled by levers, and now Locklear was climbing, stuffing the sidearm into his belt again to keep both hands free for the ravine, and when he vaulted over the lip into low brush, he could hear Brickshitter babbling into his comm unit.

He wanted to hear the exchange more than he wanted to move. He heard: ". . . has two kzin handguns— of course I saw them, and heard them; had I been slower he would have an officer's ears on his belt now!—Nossir, no reply from the others. How else would he have hero's weapons? What do you think?—I think so, too."

Locklear began to move out again, below brushtops, as the furious Brickshitter was promising a mansack to his commander as a trophy. *And they won't get that while I live,* he vowed to himself. In fact, with his promise, Brickshitter was admitting they no longer wanted him alive. He did not hear the next hum, but saw brush spatter ahead of him, some of it bursting into flame, and then he was firing at the exposed Brickshitter who now stood with brave stance, seven and a half feet tall and weaving from side to side, firing once a second, as fast as the beam rifle's accumulator would permit.

Locklear stood and delivered, moving back and forth. At his second burst, the weapon's receiver locked open.

He ducked below, discarded the thing, and drew its twin, estimating he had emptied the first one with thirty rounds. When next he lifted his head, he saw that Brickshitter had outpaced him across the ravine and was firing at the brush again. Even as the stuff ahead of him was kindling, Locklear noticed that the brush behind him flamed higher than a man, now a wildfire moving in the same direction as he, though the steady breeze swept it away from the ravine. His only path now was along the ravine lip, or in it.

He guessed that this weapon would shoot low as well, and opened up at a distance of sixty paces. Good guess; Brickshitter turned toward him and at the same instant was slapped by an invisible fist that flung the heavy rifle from his grasp. Locklear dodged to the lip of the ravine to spot the weapons, saw them twenty paces away, and dropped the sidearm so that he could hang onto brush as he vaulted over, now in full view of Brickshitter.

Whose stuttering fire with his good arm reminded Locklear, nearly too late, that Brickshitter had other weapons beside that beam rifle. Spurts of dirt flew into Locklear's eyes as he flung himself back to safety. He crawled back for the sidearm, watching the navigator fumble for his rifle, and opened up again just as Brickshitter dropped from sight. More wasted ammo.

Behind him, the fire was raging downslope toward their mutual dead. Across the ravine, Brickshitter's enraged voice: "Small caliber flesh wound in the right shoulder but I have started brush fires to flush him. I can see beam rifles, close-combat weapons and other things almost below him in the ravine.—Yessir, he is almost out of ammunition and wants that cache.—Yessir, a few more bolts. An easy shot."

Locklear had once seen an expedition bundle burn with a beam rifle in it. He began to run hard, skirting still-smouldering brush and grass, and had already passed the inert bodies of their unprotesting dead when the ground bucked beneath him. He fell to one knee, seeing a cloud of debris fan above the ravine, echoes of the explosion shouldering each other down the slopes, and he knew that Brickshitter's left-armed aim had been as good as necessary. Good enough, maybe, to get himself killed in that cloud of turf and stone and metal fragments, yes, and good wooden arrows that had made a warrior of Locklear. Yet any sensible warrior knows how to retreat.

The ravine widened now, the creek dropping in a series of lower falls, and Locklear knew that further headlong flight would send him far into the open, so far that the *zzrou* would kill him if Brickshitter didn't. And Brickshitter could track his spoor—but not in water. Locklear raced to the creek, heedless of the mis-step that could smash a knee or ankle, and began to negotiate the little falls.

The last one faced the lake. He turned, recognizing that he had cached his pathetic store of provisions behind that waterfall soon after his arrival. It was flanked by thick fronds and ferns, and Locklear ducked into the hideyhole behind that sheet of water streaming wet, gasping for breath.

A soft inquiry from somewhere behind him. He whirled in sudden recognition. *It's REALLY a small world,* he thought idiotically. "Boots?" No answer. Well, of course not, to his voice, but he could see the dim outline of a deep horizontal tunnel, turning left inside its entrance, with dry grasses lining the floor. "Boots, don't be afraid of me. Did you know the kzin males have returned?"

Guarded, grudging it: "Yes. They have wounded my mate."

"Worse, Boots. But she killed one,"—*it was her doing as surely as if her fangs had torn out Yellowbelly's throat*—and I killed another. She told me to—to retrieve the things she took from me." It seemed his heart must burst with this cowardly lie. He was cold, exhausted, and on the run, and with the transmitter he could escape to win another day, and, and—. And he wanted to slash his wrists with his *wtsai*.

"I will bring them. Do not come nearer," said the

soft voice, made deeper by echoes. He squatted under the overhang, the plash of water now dwindling, and he realized that the blast up the ravine had made a momentary check dam. He distinctly heard the mewing of tiny kzin twins as Boots removed the security of her warm, soft fur. A moment later, he saw her head and arms. Both hands, even the one bearing a screwdriver and the transmitter, had their claws fully extended and her ears lay so flat on her skull that they might have been caps of skin. Still, she shoved the articles forward.

Pocketing the transmitter with a thrill of undeserved success, he bade her keep the other items. He showed her the sidearm. "Boots, one of these killed Puss. Do you see that it could kill you just as easily?"

The growl in her throat was an illustrated manual of counterthreat.

"But I began as your protector. I would never harm you or your kittens. Do you see that now?"

"My head sees it. My heart says to fight you. Go."

He nodded, turned away, and eased himself into the deep pool that was now fed by a mere trickle of water. Ahead was the lake, smoke floating toward it, and he knew that he could run safely in the shallows hidden by smoke without leaving prints. And fight another day. And, he realized, staring back at the once-talkative little falls, leave Boots with her kittens where the cautious Brickshitter would almost certainly find them because now the mouth of her birthing bower was clearly visible.

No, I'm damned if you will!

"So check into it, Brickshitter," he muttered softly, backing deep into the cool cover of yellow ferns. "I've still got a few rounds here, if you're still alive."

He was alive, all right. Locklear knew it in his guts when a stone trickled its way down near the pool. He knew it for certain when he felt soft footfalls, the almost silent track of a big hunting cat, vibrate the damp grassy embankment against his back. He eased forward in water that was no deeper than his armpits, still hidden, but when the towering kzin warrior sprang to the verge of the water he made no sound at all. He carried only his sidearm and knife, and Locklear fired at a distance of only ten paces, actually a trifling space.

But a tremendous trifle, for Brickshitter was well-trained and did not pause after his leap before hopping aside in a squat. He was looking straight at Locklear and the horizontal spray of slugs ceased before it reached him. Brickshitter's arm was a blur. Foliage shredded where Locklear had hidden as the little man dropped below the surface, feeling two hot slugs trickle down his back after their velocity was spent underwater.

Locklear could not see clearly, but propelled himself forward as he broke the surface in a desperate attempt to reach the other side. He knew his sidearm was empty. He did not know that his opponent's was, until the kzin navigator threw the weapon at him, screamed, and leaped.

Locklear pulled himself to the bank with fronds as the big kzin strode toward him in water up to his belly. Too late to run, and Brickshitter had a look of cool confidence about him. *I like him better when he's not so cool.* "Come on, you *kshat*, you *natach*'s ass," he chanted, backing toward the only place where he might have safety at his back—the stone shelf before Boots's bower, where great height was a disadvantage. "Come on, you fur-licking, brickshitting hairball, do it! Leaping and screaming, screaming and leaping, you stupid no-name," he finished, wondering if the last was an insult.

Evidently it was. With a howling scream of savagery, the big kzin tried to leap clear of the water, falling headlong as Locklear reached the stone shelf. Dagger now in hand, Brickshitter floundered to the bank spitting, emitting a string of words that doubled Locklear's command of kzinti curses. Then, almost as if reading Locklear's mind, the navigator paused a few paces away and help up his knife. And his voice, though quivering, was exceedingly mild. "Do you know what I am going to do with this, monkey?"

To break through this facade, Locklear made it off-handed. "Cut your *ch'rowl*ing throat by accident, most likely," he said.

The effect was startling. Stiffening, then baring his fangs in a howl of frustration, the warrior sprang for the shelf, seeing in mid-leap that Locklear was waiting for exactly that with his *wtsai* thrust forward, its tip made needle-sharp by the same female who had once dulled it. But a kzin warrior's training went deep. Pivoting as he landed, rolling to one side, the navigator avoided Locklear's thrust, his long tail lashing to catch the little man's legs.

Locklear had seen that one before. His blade cut deeply into the kzin's tail and Brickshitter vented a yelp, whirling to spring. He feinted as if to hurl the knife and Locklear threw both arms before his face, seeing too late the beginning of the kzin's squatting leap in close quarters, like a swordsman's balestra. Locklear slammed his back painfully against the side of the cave, his own blade slashing blindly, and felt a horrendous fiery trail of pain down the length of his knife arm before the graceful kzin moved out of range. He switched hands with the *wtsai*.

"I am going to carve off your maleness while you watch, monkey," said Brickshitter, seeing the blood begin to course from the open gash on Locklear's arm.

"One word before you do," Locklear said, and pulled out all the stops. "*Ch'rowl* your grandmother. *Ch'rowl* your patriarch, and *ch'rowl* yourself."

With each repetition, Brickshitter seemed to coil into himself a bit farther, his eyes not slitted but saucer-round, and with his last phrase Locklear saw something from the edge of his vision that the big kzin saw clearly. Ropelike, temptingly bushy, it was the flick of Boots's tail at the mouth of her bower.

Like most feline hunters from the creche onward, the kzin warrior reacted to this stimulus with rapt fascination, at least for an instant, already goaded to insane heights of frustration by the sexual triggerword. His eyes rolled upward for a flicker of time, and in that flicker Locklear acted. His headlong rush carried him in a full body slam against the navigator's injured shoulder, the *wtsai* going in just below the ribcage, torn from Locklear's grasp as his opponent flipped backward in agony to the water. Locklear cartwheeled into the pool, weaponless, choosing to swim because it was the fastest way out of reach.

He flailed up the embankment searching wildly for a loose stone, then tossed a glance over his shoulder. The navigator lay on his side, half out of the water, blood pumping from his belly, and in his good arm he held Locklear's *wtsai* by its handle. As if his arm were the only part of him still alive, he flipped the knife, caught it by the tip, forced himself erect.

Locklear did the first thing he could remember from dealing with vicious animals: reached down, grasped a handful of thin air, and mimicked hurling a stone. It did not deter the navigator's convulsive move in the slightest, the *wtsai* a silvery whirr before it thunked into a tree of pace from Locklear's breast. The kzin's motion carried him forward into water, face down. He did not entirely submerge, but slid forward inert, arms at his sides. Locklear wrestled his blade from the tree and waited, his chest heaving. The navigator did not move again.

Locklear held the knife aloft, eyes shut, for long moments, tears of exultation and vengeance coursing down his cheeks, mixing with dirty water from his hair and clean blood from his cheek. His eyes snapped open at the voice.

"May I name my son after you, Rockear?" Boots, just inside the overhang, held two tiny spotted kittens protectively where they could suckle. It was, he felt, meant to be an honor merely for him to see them.

"I would be honored, Boots. But the modern kzin custom is to make sons earn their names, I think."

"What do I care what they do? We are starting over here."

Locklear stuffed the blade into his belt, wiping wet stuff from his face again. "Not unless I can put away that scarfaced commander. He's got Kit at the manor—

unless she has him. I'm going to try and bias the results," he said grimly, and scanned the heights above the ravine.

To his back, Boots said, "It is not traditional, but—if you come for us, we would return to the manor's protection."

He turned, glancing up the ravine. "An honor. But right now, you'd better come out and wait for the waterfall to resume. When it does, it might flood your bower for a few minutes." He waved, and she waved back. When next he glanced downslope, from the upper lip of the ravine, he could see the brushfire dwindling at the jungle's edge, and water just beginning to carve its way through a jumble of debris in the throat of the ravine, and a small lithe orange-yellow figure holding two tiny spotted dots, patiently waiting in the sunlight for everything he said to come true.

"Lady," he said softly to the waiting Boots, "I sure hope you picked a winner."

He could have disappeared into the wilds of Kzersatz for months but Scarface, with vast advantages, might call for more searchers. Besides, running would be reactive, the act of mindless prey. Locklear opted to be *proactive*—a hunter's mindset. Recalling the violence of that exploding rifle, he almost ignored the area because nothing useful could remain in the crater. But curiosity made him pause, squinting down from the heights, and excellent vision gave him an edge when he saw the dull gleam of Brickshitter's beam rifle across the ravine. It was probably fully discharged, else the navigator would not have abandoned it. But Scarface wouldn't know that.

Locklear doubled back and retrieved the heavy weapon, chuckling at the sharp stones that lay atop the turf. Brickshitter must have expended a few curses as those stones rained down. The faint orange light near the scope was next to a legend in Kzinti that translated as 'insufficient charge'. He thought about that a moment, then smeared his own blood over the light until its gleam was hidden. Shouldering the rifle, he set off again, circling high above the ravine so that he could come in from its upper end. Somehow the weapon seemed lighter now, or perhaps it was just his second wind. Locklear did not pause to reflect that his decision for immediate action brought optimism, and that optimism is another word for accumulated energy.

The sun was at his back when he stretched prone behind low cover and paused for breath. The zoom scope of the rifle showed that someone had ripped the thatches from the manor's window bulges, no doubt to give Scarface a better view. *Works both ways, hotshot,* he mused; but though he could see through the windows, he saw nothing move. Presently he began to crawl forward and down, holding the heavy rifle in the crooks of his arms, abrading his elbows as he went from brush to outcrop to declivity. His shadow stretched before him. Good; the sun would be in a watcher's eyes and he was dry-mouthed with awareness that Scarface must carry his own arsenal.

The vines they had planted already hid the shaft of their escape tunnel but Locklear paused for long moments as its mouth, listening, waiting until his breath was quiet and regular. What if Scarface were waiting in the tunnel? He ducked into the rifle sling, put his *wtsai* in his teeth, and eased down feet-first using remembered hand and footholds, his heart hammering his ribs. Then he scuffed earth with his knee and knew that his entry would no longer be a surprise if Scarface was waiting. He dropped the final two meters to soft dirt, squatting, hopping aside as he'd seen Brickshitter do.

Nothing but darkness. He waited for his panting to subside and then moved forward with great caution. It took him five minutes to stalk twenty meters of curving tunnel, feeling his way until he saw faint light filtering from above. By then, he could hear the fitz-rowr of kzin voices. He eased himself up to the opening and peered through long slits of shamboo matting that Boots had woven to cover the rough walls.

". . . Am learning, milady, that even the most potent

Word loses its strength when used too often," a male voice was saying. Scarface, in tones Locklear had never expected to hear. "As soon as this operation is complete, rest assured I shall be the most gallant of suitors."

Locklear's view showed only their legs as modern warrior and ancient courtesan faced each other, seated on benches at the rough-hewn dining table. Kit, with a sulk in her voice, said, "I begin to wonder if your truthfulness extends to my attractions, milord."

Scarface, fervently: "The truth is that you are a warrior's wildest fantasies in fur. I cannot say how often I have wished for a mate I could actually talk to! Yet I am first Grraf-Commander, and second a kzintosh. Excuse me," he added, stood up, and strode to the main doorway, now in full view of Locklear. His belt held ceremonial *wtsai*, a sidearm and God knew what else in those pockets. His beam rifle lay propped beside the doorway. Taking a brick-sized device from his broad belt, he muttered, "I wonder if this rude hut is interfering with our signals."

A click and then, in gruff tones of frustrated command, he said, "Hunt leader to all units: report! If you cannot report, use a signal bomb from your beltpacs, dammit! If you cannot do that, return to the hut at triple time or I will hang your hides from a pennant pole."

Locklear grinned as Scarface moved back to the table with an almost human sigh. *Too bad I didn't know about those signal bombs. Warm this place up a little. Maybe I should go back for those beltpacs.* But he abandoned the notion as Scarface resumed his courtship.

"I have hinted, and you have evaded, milady. I must ask you now, bluntly: will you return with me when this operation is over?"

"I shall do as the commander wishes," she said demurely, and Locklear grinned again. She hadn't said 'Grraf-Commander'; and even if Locklear didn't survive, *she* might very well wind up in command. Oh sure, she'd do whatever the commander liked.

"Another point on which you have been evasive,"

Scarface went on; "your assessment of the monkey, and what relationship he had to either of you." Locklear did not miss this nuance; Scarface knew of two kzinrret, presumably an initial report from one of the pair who'd found Puss. He did not know of Boots, then.

"The manbeast ruled us with strange magic forces, milord. He made us fearful at times. At any time he might be anywhere. Even now." *Enough of that crap,* Locklear thought at her, even though he felt she was only trying to put the wind up Scarface's backside. *Fat chance! Lull the bastard, put him to sleep.*

Scarface went to the heart of his question. "Did he act honorably toward you both?"

After a long pause: "I suppose he did, as a manbeast saw honor. He did not *ch'rowl* me, if that is—"

"Milady! You will rob the Word of its meaning, or drive me mad."

"I have an idea. Let me dance for you while you lie at your ease. I will avoid the term and drive you only a little crazy."

"For the eighth-squared time, I do not need to lie down. I need to complete this hunt; duty first, pleasure after. I—what?"

Locklear's nose had brushed the matting. The noise was faint, but Scarface was on his feet and at the doorway, rifle in hand, in two seconds. Locklear's nose itched, and he pinched his nostrils painfully. It seemed that the damned tabby was never completely off-guard, made edgy as a *wtsai* by his failure to contact his crew. Locklear felt a sneeze coming, sānk down on his heels, rubbed furiously at his nose. When he stood up again, Scarface stood a pace outside, demanding a response with his comm set while Kit stood at the doorway. Locklear scratched carefully at the mat, willing Kit alone to hear it. No such luck.

Scarface began to pace back and forth outside, and Locklear scratched louder. Kit's ear-umbrellas flicked, lifted. Another scratch. She turned, and saw him move the matting. Her mouth opened slightly. *She's going to warn him,* Locklear thought wildly.

"Perhaps we could stroll down the ravine, milord," she said easily, taking a few steps outside.

Locklear saw the big kzin commander pass the doorway once, twice, muttering furiously about indecision. He caught the words, ". . . Return to the lifeboat with you now if I have not heard from them very soon," and knew that he could never regain an advantage if that happened. He paced his advance past the matting to coincide with Scarface's movements, easing the beam rifle into plain sight on the floor, now with his head and shoulders out above the dusty floor, now his waist, now his—his—his sneeze came without warning.

Scarface leaped for the entrance, snatching his sidearm as he came into view, and Locklear gave himself up then even though he was aiming the heavy beam rifle from a prone position, an empty threat. But a bushy tail flashed between the warrior's ankles, and his next bound sent him skidding forward on his face, the sidearm still in his hand but pointed away from Locklear.

And the muzzle of Locklear's beam rifle poked so near the commander's nose that he could only focus on it cross-eyed. Locklear said it almost pleasantly: "Could even a monkey miss such a target?"

"Perhaps," Scarface said, and swallowed hard. "But I think that rifle is exhausted."

"The one your nervous brickshitting navigator used? It probably was," said Locklear, brazening it out, adding the necessary lie with, "I broiled him with this one, which doesn't have that cute little light glowing, does it? Now then: skate that little shooter of yours across the floor. Your crew is all bugbait, Scarface, and the only thing between you and kitty heaven is my good humor."

Much louder than need be, unless he was counting on Kit's help: "Have you no end of insults? Have you no sense of honor? Let us settle this as equals." Kit stood at the doorway now.

"The sidearm, Grraf-Commander. Or meet your ancestors. Your crew tried to kill me—and monkey see, monkey do."

The sidearm clattered across the rough floor mat. Locklear chose to avoid further insult; the last thing he needed was a loss of self-control from the big kzin. "Hands behind your back. Kit, get the strongest cord we have and bind him; the feet, then the hands. And stay to one side. If I have to pull this trigger, you don't want to get splattered."

Minutes later, holding the sidearm and sitting at the table, Locklear studied the prisoner who sat, legs before him, back against the doorway, and explained the facts of K'zersatz life while Kit cleaned his wounds. She murmured that his cheek scar would someday be *t'rralap* as he explained the options. "So you see, you have nothing to lose by giving your honorable parole, because I trust your honor. You have everything to lose by refusing, because you'll wind up as barbecue."

"Men do not eat captives," Scarface said. "You speak of honor and yet you lie."

"Oh, I wouldn't eat you. But *they* would. There are two kzinrret here who, if you'll recall, hate everything you stand for."

Scarface looked glumly at Kit. "Can this be true?"

She replied, "Can it be true that modern kzinrret have been bred into cattle?"

"Both can be true," he conceded. "But monk—men are devious, false, conniving little brutes. How can a kzinrret of your intelligence approve of them?"

"Rockear has defeated your entire force—with a little help," she said. "I am content to pledge my honor to a male of his resourcefulness, especially when he does not abuse his leadership. I only wish he were of our race," she added wistfully.

Scarface: "My parole would depend on your absolute truthfulness, Rockear."

A pause from Locklear, and a nod. "You've got it as of now, but no backing out if you get some surprises later."

"One question, then, before I give my word: *are all my crew truly casualties?*"

"Deader than this beam rifle," Locklear said, grinning, holding its muzzle upward, squeezing its trigger.

Later, after pledging his parole, Scarface observed reasonably that there was a world of difference between an insufficient charge and *no* charge. The roof thatching burned slowly at first; slowly enough that they managed to remove everything worth keeping. But at last the whole place burned merrily enough. To Locklear's surprise, it was Scarface who mentioned safe removal of the *zzrou*, and pulled it loose easily after a few deft manipulations of the transmitter.

Kit seemed amused as they ate al fresco, a hundred meters from the embers of their manor. "It is a tradition in the ancient culture that a major change of household leadership requires burning of the old manor," she explained with a smile of her ears.

Locklear, still uneasy with the big kzin warrior so near and now without his bonds, surreptitiously felt of the sidearm in his belt and asked, "Am I not still the leader?"

"Yes," she said. "But what kind of leader would deny happiness to his followers?" Her lowered glance toward Scarface could hardly be misunderstood.

The ear umbrellas of the big male turned a deeper hue. "I do not wish to dishonor another warrior, Locklear, but—if I am to remain your captive here as you say, um, such females may be impossibly overstimulating."

"Not to me," Locklear said. "No offense, Kit; I'm half in love with you myself. In fact, I think the best thing for my own sanity would be to seek, uh, females of my own kind."

"You intended to take us back to the manworlds, I take it," said Scarface with some smugness.

"After a bit more research here, yes. The hell with wars anyhow. There's a lot about this planet you don't know about yet. Fascinating!"

"You will never get back in a lifeboat," said Scarface, "and the cruiser is now only a memory."

"You didn't!"

"I assuredly did, Locklear. My first act when you released my bonds was to send the self-destruct signal."

Locklear put his head between his hands. "Why didn't we hear the lifeboat go up?"

"Because I did not think to set it for destruct. It is not exactly a major asset."

"For me it damned well is," Locklear growled, then went on. "Look here: I won't release Kit from any pair-bonding to me unless you promise not to sabotage me in any way. And I further promise not to try turning you over to some military bunch, because I'm the, uh, mayor of this frigging planet and I can declare peace on it if I want to. Honor bound, honest injun, whatever the hell that means, and all the rigamarole that goes with it. Goddammit, I could have blown your head off."

"But you did not know that."

"With the sidearm, then! Don't *ch'r*—don't fiddle me around. Put your honor on the line, mister, and put your big paw against mine if you mean it."

After a long look at Kit, the big kzin commander reached out a hand, palm vertical, and Locklear met it with his own. "You are not the man we left here," said the vanquished kzin, eyeing Locklear without malice. "Brown and tough as dried meat—and older, I would say."

"Getting hunted by armed kzinti tends to age a feller," Locklear chuckled. "I'm glad we found peace with honor."

"Was any commander," the commander asked no one in particular, "ever faced with so many conflicts of honor?"

"You'll resolve them," Locklear predicted. "Think about it: I'm about to make you the head captive of a brand new region that has two newborn babes in it, two intelligent kzinrret at least, and over an eight-squared other kzinti who have been in stasis for longer than you can believe. Wake 'em, or don't, it's up to you, just don't interfere with me because I expect to be here part of the time, and somewhere else at other times. Kit, show him how to use the airboat. If you two can't figure out how to use the stuff in this Outsider zoo, I miss my—"

"Outsiders?" Scarface did not seem to like the sound of that.

"That's just my guess," Locklear shrugged. "Maybe they have hidden sensors that tell 'em what happens on the planet Zoo. Maybe they don't care. What I care about, is exploring the other compounds on Zoo, one especially. I may not find any of my kind on Newduvai, and if I do they might have foreheads a half-inch high, but it bears looking into. For that I need the lifeboat. Any reason why it wouldn't take me to another compound on Zoo?"

"No reason." After a moment of rumination, Scarface put on his best negotiation face again. "If I teach you to be an expert pilot, would you let me disable the hyperwave comm set?"

Locklear thought hard for a similar time. "Yes, if you swear to leave its local functions intact. Look, fella, we may want to talk to one another with it."

"Agreed, then," said the kzin commander.

That night, Locklear slept poorly. He lay awake for a time, wondering if Newduvai had its own specimen cave, and whether he could find it if one existed. The fact was that Kzersatz simply lacked the kind of company he had in mind. *Not even the right kind of cathouse,* he groused silently. He was not enormously heartened by the prospect of wooing a Neanderthal nymphet, either. Well, that was what field research was for. *Please, God, at least a few Cro-Magnons! Patience, Locklear, and earplugs,* because he could not find sleep for long.

It was not merely that he was alone, for the embers near his pallet kept him as toasty as kzinrret fur. No, it was the infernal yowling of those cats somewhere below in the ravine.

Introduction

Long, long ago, in a different Galaxy, so to speak, I coined a phrase "speculative fact." Admittedly I did so in a spirit of mild derision directed at those who were busy attempting to geld my beloved science fiction and convert it into a perfect little literary trotter called Speculative Fiction. (And wasn't it cute that the two terms shared initials?) But while I was busy fighting the Good Fight in a lighthearted sort of way, I was also trying to pin down something real.

There is a kind of non-fiction that is more than simple explication of accepted facts, theories and co-nundrums, and it is the perfect companion to science fiction. Just as science fiction at its best must attempt to give us at least a glimpse of the magic inherent in the nature of reality, so too must this special flavor of scientific inquiry; just as science fiction transcends the natural boundaries of mundane fiction, speculative fact momentarily illuminates the mundane world with magic.

Of course enchantment bears a price. Science fiction really isn't very good at conveying all the grainy details of ordinary reality, and speculative fact isn't so great at minor details either. But for those of us to whom trival details are not of the essence, aren't they are a fine pair, our SF and SF? And for my part I am just delighted that Harvard doesn't publish science fiction— and so leaves the best for us!

Harvard Doesn't Publish Science Fiction

Hans Moravec

Mea culpa: reality and fantasy blend in my mind. My major source of income is as a scientist and, fortunately for all involved, on my very best behavior I can pass as such. What's more, it's fun. Working out problems slowly, carefully, and rigorously gives insight, a sense of solidity, and of a job well done. Often it sheds light in unexpected directions, and opens new doors. But it has limitations. To do it, you must already understand the problem in a detailed way. But many interesting questions are too nebulous and slippery for such intimacy. My burden is that often I'm insensitive to the difference.

Consider the question of intelligent machines. While the entire idea was once viewed suspiciously by most of the scientific community, the research has, by now, spun off enough practical results to be reasonably tolerated. On my best behavior, for my Ph.D. thesis, I wrote a program that enabled a robot to see well enough to cross a cluttered room, building a map of it along the way [there's a joke here—it took the robot five hours to make the transit, its million-dollar computer brain churning furiously the whole time]. At the same time I couldn't help extrapolating that modest reality to very immodest lengths. Why are robots so much worse than animals at the simplest things? When can we expect that to change? Will they ever be as good as humans at most things? Will they be better? Cheaper? Will they be able to carry on their own further improvement without our help? Is there some way we can avoid being left in the dust? What will the world be like after this happens?

By making some tentative assumptions and calculations, I was able to conclude: The computers are too small—insectlike now. Slowly but steadily, 1000-fold every 20 years. Yes, in about 40 years. Yes, rapidly thereafter. Certainly, much. Especially without our help. Only if we join them by rebuilding ourselves in their image. Very different—much bigger and more interesting. While many of my colleagues saw a big difference between the reasoning behind the robot driving program and the futurism, I found little distinction. Maybe it's the result of reading too much science fiction. In any case, several papers and essays on both subjects were published, with the robot results showing up mainly in technical literature, and the futurism in science fiction outlets. But there was crossover, in both directions.

Which brings us to Harvard. A new editor at Harvard University Press had read several of the futurism articles, and in January of 1985 invited me to submit an outline for a book expanding on the theme. His timing was excellent—I'd just started writing such a book, after ten years of procrastination. It was an opportunity to develop many new ideas. Some were about the evolution of our machines, but others were about surprises in the universe that might await our superintelligent progeny. When my editor read a first draft he explained that the book would have to be passed by an academic review committee, and Harvard, by policy, does not publish science fiction. He felt also that many of the physics and astronautics chapters impeded the theme of the book. So the second draft abandoned several ideas. Fortunately, Jim Baen *does* publish science fiction, and some of the orphan chapters have found a foster home here.

The first article addresses the possibility of computers so fast they violate apparent physical limits. The secret is exotic materials science.

SUPERDENSE COMPUTERS

Computers are usually characterized by their speed (or power) and their memory capacity. At a next level of detail, the amount of parallelism is a key measure. Here's a helpful metaphor: Computing is like a sea voyage in a motorboat. How fast a given journey can be completed depends on the power of the boat's engine, while the maximum length of any journey is limited by the capacity of its fuel tank. Some computations are like a trip to a known location on a distant shore; others resemble a mapless search for a lost island. Parallel computing is like having a fleet of small boats—it helps in searches, and in reaching multiple goals, but not very much in problems that require a distant sprint.

The calculation speed of computers has been increasing at a slightly accelerating pace averaging a thousand-fold every twenty years. This can be sustained for a considerable time even without great increases in raw switching speed by increasing parallelism—almost all computations have parts that can be sped up somewhat by this strategy. But some destinations cannot be reached in a given time by any number of slow boats.

What is the ultimate speed limit of computer logic? Quantum mechanics demands a minimum energy to localize an event to a given time:

$$Energy = \frac{h'}{time}$$

where h is Planck's constant, the basic scale of quantum mechanics. Higher speeds require greater energy. Above the frequency of light, about 10^{15} transitions per second, the energy reaches one electron volt—close to the energy of the chemical bonds holding solid matter together. Attempts to switch faster will tear apart the switches. The fastest switches in laboratories today, electronic or optical, operate at a mere 10^{11} transitions per second, so we can expect a further ten thousandfold speedup before our switches blow up. But things will be increasingly difficult as the limit is approached (by the year 2010, if our projection holds), aggravated by the fact that in 10^{-15} second, signals can cover a distance of only 30 atoms. Is there any hope of breaching this "light barrier?"

Neutronium and Heavy Electrons

The tendency of energetic signals to disintegrate matter can be overcome by increasing the restraining forces, internal or external. Necessarily, the matter will be pulled (or pushed) closer together and will become more dense, incidentally reducing the travel distances of signals. Conventional pressures, such as the three or four million atmospheres achieved in diamond anvil presses (large nutcrackers concentrating their force on sub-millimeter faces of two opposing gem-quality diamonds), make almost no difference. The additional forces are weaker than the chemical bonds. Much greater pressures are known to exist in the interior of large astronomical bodies. In normal stars the effects of extreme pressure are cancelled by equally extreme temperatures. This is not the case in the burnt out remnants of some supernovas. There, the fusion reactions that power the stars have ceased for lack of fuel, and the atoms in the interior are crushed to the size of their nuclei by the weight of the overlying layers. A star initially ten million kilometers in diameter may be squeezed into a ball ten kilometers across. In the interior, protons combine with electrons to form neutrons, which, with the neutrons in the original nuclei, form an undifferentiated, superfluid sea of neutrons, and a material that has been named Neutronium. If this matter, or the slightly looser packed nuclei on the surface, could be organized into some kind of integrated circuit, perhaps by high-energy versions of present methods, we would expect to be able to switch a million times as fast, 10^{21} times per second, using photons that are hard gamma rays. The residual heat of the neutron star would provide some power, which could be augmented from outside by beaming in gamma rays, dropping fusion fuel or simple dead weight, or orbiting dense, tide-raising bodies.

Someday, neutron stars may be the preferred location for monster supercomputers, since they are common and large. For the immediate future they are too far away, the nearest being thousands of light-years from us. Is there any hope for smaller, more immediate, ultraspeed gadgets? After all, we're going to reach the speed limit of conventional matter in a mere 25 years.

The size of an atom depends on the charge and mass of the electrons orbiting it. If electrons could be made twice as massive, atomic diameters would shrink by half and the density of matter would increase eightfold. Chemical binding energies, which depend on the inverse square law of electric forces, would quadruple, as would the maximum switching speed. Electrons are unlikely to get heavier, but perhaps something could be substituted for them. Heavier particles would bind to nuclei more tightly than electrons, and so would naturally displace them if introduced (just stand back so you're not fried by the liberated energy!). Protons, found in all atomic nuclei, weigh about 2,000 times as much as electrons, but they have the wrong charge to also serve for electrons. Antiprotons—protons' mirror images—have the right charge, but combine catastrophically with protons in trillionth-second fireballs of mutual annihilation. Particle physicists long ago discovered heavy cousins of electrons, the *mu* and (more recently) *tau* particles, 200 and 3,600 times as massive. Unfortunately, they are unstable and so unsuitable for constructing long-lasting matter. The muon lasts two microseconds before decaying into an electron; the tau much less time. In fact, no particle definitively observed so far will do. Stable charged particles should be very easy to detect in accelerator experiments, and since none have been seen, it's highly probable that none exist up to the energy range of present accelerators. This is over 50,000 times the electron's mass, unfortunately. It means the step beyond normal matter is likely to be big and difficult.

Higgsinium

The theoretical physicists make some tentative promises. Supersymmetry is a class of theories that predicts "spin-reflected" analogs of all of the known (and some merely predicted) particles. The theories are not well enough along to assign exact masses to these new particles, but, constrained by already performed experiments, do set bounds. Accelerators being completed now may produce some of these before 1990. One possibility is that the peculiarly named *negative Higgsino* particle is stable, and has a mass about 75 times that of a proton (or 150,000 electrons).

Suppose we start with a mass of hydrogen, the simplest atom. In it one electron orbits one proton. Since Higgsinos are heavier than protons, substituting one for the electron will turn the atom inside out: the massive Higgsino will become the nucleus, and the proton will do most of the orbiting, and will set the size of the atom, about 2,000 times smaller in diameter than a normal one. The force between adjacent atoms would be $2,000^2$ or four million times as great. Only astronomical temperatures would break those bonds—the material would remain a solid under any earthly conditions, and there would be $2,000^3$ or eight billion times as many atoms per cubic centimeter. Because Higgsinos are heavy, each atom will weigh 75 times as much, so the density would be about 10^{12} times that of normal matter. But there's a surprise. Each Higgsino added will itself generate about 20,000 electron volts of energy as it captures a proton—enough to radiate gamma rays. That's minor. But then the exposed orbiting protons of adjacent resulting "Higgsino Hydrogen" atoms will be in an optimum position to combine with one another in fours to form Helium nuclei in a fusion reaction. Each fusion liberates a whopping 10 million electron volts, and frees the Higgsinos to catalyze more fusions. This will continue until the resulting nuclear explosion blows the material apart. The Higgsinos may cause fusion of heavier elements as well, and perhaps fission of very heavy nuclei. Great opportunities here, but not quite what we had in mind!

Iron nuclei are prone neither to fusion nor fission—it takes energy either to break them down or to build them up—and so can (perhaps) be combined safely with Higgsinos. Each iron nucleus contains 26 protons, and must be neutralized by 26 negative Higgsinos. But it's unlikely that the Higgsinos can overcome their mutual repulsion to neatly form the right sized nuclei. A different, more condensed arrangement is probable. Suppose we mix small amounts of hydrogen and Higgsinos very slowly and carefully, taking away waste energy (perhaps to help power the Higgsino manufacturing accelerator). The resulting mass will settle down to some lowest energy configuration—probably a crystal of Higgsinos and protons, electrically neutralizing each other, and some neutrons, bound by other electromagnetism and the strong nuclear force. If there are too many neutrons, some will decay radioactively until a stable mix is reached. The protons and neutrons, being the lighter and fuzzier of the particles, will determine the spacing—about that found in neutron stars. The millionfold speed-ups possible there will apply here also.

The final material (let's call it Higgsinium) would be 10^{18} times as dense as water; a thimbleful would have the weight of a mountain. It'll be a while before that much of it is manufactured. A cubical speck a micron on a side weighs a gram, and should be enough to make thousands of very complex integrated circuits—analogous to a cubic centimeter of silicon. Their speed would be a millionfold greater, as would their power consumption and operating temperature. It may be possible to build the circuits with high energy versions of the optical and particle beam methods used to construct today's ICs, though the engineering challenges are huge! And in the long run, tiny machines of Higgsinium might be dropped onto neutron stars to seed the construction of immense Neutronium minds.

Magetic Monopoles

Higgsinos, and the rest of the supersymmetric stable, were "invented" only recently. An equally plausible, and even more interesting kind of particle was theorized in 1930, by Paul Dirac. In a calculation that combined quantum mechanics with special relativity, Dirac deduced the existence of the positrons, mirror images of the electrons. This was the first indication of antimatter, and positrons were actually observed in 1932. The same calculation predicted the existence of a magnetic monopole, a stable particle carrying a charge like an isolated north or south pole of a magnet. Dirac's calculation did not give the monopole's mass, but it did specify the magnitude of its "charge." Recent "gauge" theories, in which the forces of nature are treated as distortions in higher dimensional spaces, also predict monopoles (as knots in spacetime), and even assign masses. Unfortunately, there are competing versions with different mass predictions, ranging from 1,000 to 10^{16} times that of a proton. These masses are beyond the energy of existing and planned particle accelerators. Some cosmic rays are energetic enough.

For over forty years, searches for monopoles all came up empty-handed, and there was great skepticism about their existence. But they may have been fleetingly observed three times in the last decade, though none has yet been caught for extended observation. In 1973 a Berkeley cosmic ray experiment was lofted above most of the scattering atmosphere in a high-altitude balloon. In 1975, after two years of study, a very heavy track bearing the stigmata of a monopole was noted in the lexan sheets that served as three-dimensional detecting film. Calculations suggested it had twice Dirac's predicted charge, and a mass over 600 times that of a proton. Since monopoles had never been observed before, there was much skepticism. Other, more elaborate but more conventional possibilities were devised, and the incident was shelved.

On Valentine's Day in 1982, a modest experiment in Blas Cabrera's Stanford physics lab registered a clean, persistent, steplike jump in the current in a superconducting loop. The size of the step was just what a monopole with Dirac's quantum of magnetic charge would have caused had it passed through the loop. The only alternative explanation was mechanical failure in the experimental apparatus. Subsequent prodding and banging produced no effect—everything seemed shipshape. The result was so exciting that many groups around the world, including Cabrera's, built larger detectors, hoping to confirm the observation. For four years there was silence. By then the cumulative experience of the new detectors (collecting area multiplied by time) was over a thousand times that of Cabrera's original experiment. Once again the possibility of monopoles faded. Then, on May 22, 1986, a detector at Imperial College, London, whose experience was over four hundred times as large as Cabrera's original, registered another event. Until a monopole is caught and held, its existence will be in question. Yet each additional detection greatly increases the odds that the others were not mistakes.

Magnetism and electricity are right-angle versions of the same thing. A monopole waved up and down will cause a nearby electric charge to move side to side (and vice versa). A current of monopoles flowing in one wire will induce an electric current at right anles to itself. An electric current in a loop of conductor will flow in lock step with a current of monopoles in a monopole-conducting loop chain linked with it. Two coils of wire wrapped around a monopole loop make a DC transformer—a current started in one coil will induce a monopole current in the loop, which will produce an electric current in the other coil's circuit. If good DC transformers had existed in the late nineteenth century, Thomas Edison and George Westinghouse would have had less to fight about, and all our electrical outlets would produce direct current. With monopoles, we might refrain from making electrical connections at the plug at all, and draw power simply by passing the two ends of our power cords through a partially exposed monopole loop.

But let's get serious. If there are monopoles, they're not very common, and few will simply be picked out of the air. If they're very heavy, they will be hard to stop. Perhaps a few can be found already trapped here and there, and can be coaxed out (such a search was conducted worldwide by Kenneth Ford of Brandeis University, armed with a portable electromagnetic solenoid, in the early 1960s). Many things are possible given a few monopoles. Physicists routinely build superconducting solenoids with powerful magnetic fields several hundred thousand times as strong as Earth's. A monopole accelerates along magnetic field lines (for instance, a "North" monopole is strongly attracted to the south pole of a magnet). A monopole riding the field lines down the center of a powerful solenoid will gain an energy equivalent to the mass of several protons for every centimeter of travel. Ten meters of solenoid will impart an energy matching that of the most powerful existing accelerators. A few kilometers of solenoids will produce energies equal to millions of proton masses. The fireball resulting from a head-on collision of two monopoles moving thusly is intense enough to produce some number of additional monopoles, in North/South matching pairs. These can be sorted out magnetically, and so monopoles can be harnessed to breed more monopoles.

Detectors of the Cabrera type do not measure the mass of passing monopoles, and the theories are little help. Monopoles can't be too light or they would have been created in existing accelerators. As mentioned above, the theoretical range of uncertainty is enormous. Things are especially interesting if there are at least two kinds of non-mutually-annihilating stable monopole, analogous to the proton and electron in normal matter (the North/South pairs mentioned above don't count—the two are antiparticles of each other, and annihilate when brought in contact). Here's a real leap of ignorance: let's suppose there are two kinds and that they are near the low end of the possible mass range. Let's suppose the lighter variety weighs 1,000 protons, and the heavier 1,000,000 protons. If two kinds don't exist, or if monopoles turn out to be much heavier, many of the following proposals will become more extreme, or impossible. Others may open in their place.

An atom of *Monopolium* has a light monopole of one polarity (let's say North) bound to a heavy monopole of the opposite pole. Its size is set by the fuzzier light monopole. We assumed this has a mass of 1,000 protons (or two million electrons), making the monopole atom about two million times smaller than a normal one. The particle spacing in Monopolium is thus comparable to that in Neutronium or Higgsinium. Its density, however, will be a million times beyond those because of the great mass of the central, heavy monopole. This makes it 10^{25} times as heavy as normal matter. A thimbleful weighs as much as the Moon. Dirac's calculation found the magnetic quantum of charge to be 68.5 times as intense as the electric quantum. Two monopoles a certain distance apart would attract or repel each other 68.5^2 or 4,692 times as strongly as two equally separated electric particles. Combining this with the (inverse square) effects of much closer spacing and the increased density makes Monopolium ten thousand times as strong for its weight as normal matter, though this number changes radically with changes in the assumed masses of the two kinds of monopole. The limiting switching speeds may be a thousand times higher than those we found for Higgsinium.

Other Applications

If Higgsinium or Monopolium can be made, they may have applications beyond circuitry. Both materials are very tightly held together, and have no mechanism for absorbing small amounts of energy such as those found in photons, or even soft gamma rays. This should make the materials very transparent. Yet the internal electromagnetic fields are huge, making for a tremendous index of refraction. Submicroscopic gamma ray microscopes, telescopes, and lasers merely hint at the possibilities. In larger optics, gravitational effects will become important. If the materials can host loose electric or magnetic charges, they would almost certainly be superconductors up to very high temperatures, because the tremendous binding forces would limit the number of states that the conducting particles can assume. To them, the surface of the sun would still be very close to absolute zero in temperature. Superconducting versions of the materials should be nearly perfect mirrors, again up to gamma ray energies.

Macroscopic extents of these substances are possible in *very* thin fibers or sheets. An (utterly invisible) Higgsinium strand one conventional atom ($=10^6$ particles) in diameter masses 100 grams per centimeter of length. It may be able to support a 100 million tonnes, being about ten thousand times stronger for its weight than normal materials. Although it would slice through conventional matter as through a cloud (but sometimes the extremely thin cut would heal itself immediately), properly mounted, it would make gargantuan engineering projects such as orbital elevators trivial. A single-particle-thick layer of Higgsinium would weigh about ten kilograms per square centimeter. Overlaid on structures of conventional matter, the superconducting version especially would make powerful armor that would shield against essentially all normal projectiles, temperatures into the nuclear range, and all but the highest energy radiation. (But it could be penetrated by even denser Monopolium-tipped bullets. Arms races are relentless!)

The same armor could be used to line the combustion chamber and expansion bell of a matter-antimatter rocket. Normal matter is instantly disintegrated by the violence of the reaction, but Higgsinium would easily bounce the pions, gamma rays and X rays produced when hydrogen meets antihydrogen. Single-particle-thick Monopolium, at a hundred tonnes per square centimeter, may be too heavy to use as a veneer at macroscopic scales. But it might be just the thing for constructing microscopic interstellar ships. A ship with two tiny tanks crammed with ultra-compressed hydrogen and antihydrogen could rapidly propel itself at high acceleration to a few percent of the speed of light. Unaffected by either protons or antiprotons, Monopolium would be better for building the engine and tanks than Higgsinium. The ship's front end might house a superfast mind, and tiny robot arms. It could probably land on a neutron star and start raising Neutronium crops and children.

Combining electrically conducting matter and Monopolium is interesting. Our Monopolium is about 10,000 times as strong for its weight as normal matter. Properly exploited, it can store 10,000 times as much energy in mechanical or electromagnetic form. Monopolium superconductor plated in a ring around a copper rod should make a lovely storage battery. To charge it, pass a current through the rod, thus setting up a monopole supercurrent in the ring. The magnetic current remains when you break the electrical connection, and causes the ends of the rod to keep the voltage you had applied. When you connect a load to the rod ends, a current flows, and the voltage gradually drops toward zero as the monopole current slowly converts to electrical power. A kilogram of Monopolium should be able to store a fantastic one million watt hours. *Caution: Do Not Overcharge!* If the monopole current becomes too large, the electric field it generates will burst the ring, and all of the stored energy will be released at once in an explosion equal to a ton of TNT. There are other possibilities, especially involving intimate mixtures of monopoles and electrically charged matter (intertwined, like links of a chain), but we're out far enough on this limb for now.

The second idea concerns time travel without violating accepted physical laws. The innovations here are mostly psychological and philosophical.

TIME AND ALTERNITY BY COMPUTER

Time travel is a familiar concept in science fiction, and often brings with it the concept of alternate worlds. The mechanism of time travel is usually some extrapolation of modern physics—certainly fertile ground, with special relativity allowing communication to the past if faster-than-light particles could be found, general relativity allowing spacetime to be warped and twisted into temporal knots, and quantum mechanics seemingly founded on the temporary superposition of alternate worlds. Yet, if tachyons really don't exist, if Tipler vortex time machines are in principle impossible to build and black holes lead only to oblivion, if the alternate worlds in quantum mechanics are a mere mathematical artifact, or are truly inaccessible, are we stuck, helplessly drifting down the one-way river of time? Is there some way out, other than exotic physics? Here's how to do it with a philosophical leap and a lot of conventional future technology.

What Am I?

Let's suppose we have some method of reading out the contents of a human mind into a computer controlling a robotic body, in such a way that the machine behaves like the person it absorbed. Science fiction readers have encountered this concept many times, but often the stories and articles have been humorous in tone, masking, I think, a discomfort with the idea felt even by the authors. This feeling is sometimes articulated in statements such as: "Regardless of how the copying is done, the end result will be a new person." "If it is I who am being copied, the copy, though it may think of itself as me, is simply a self-deluded imposter." "If the copying process destroys the original, then I have been killed. That the copy may then have a good time using my name and my skills is no comfort to my mortal remains."

The point of view, which I will call the "Body Identity" position, makes a mockery of many of the supposed advantages of being "mind transferred" to a new body. I believe the objection can and should be overcome by intellectual acceptance of an alternate position I will name "Pattern Identity." Body identity assumes that a person is defined by the stuff of which a human body is made. Only by maintaining continuity of body stuff can we preserve an individual person. Pattern identity, on the other hand, defines the essence of a person, say myself, as the *pattern* and the *process* going on in my head and body, not the machinery supporting that process. If the process is preserved, I am preserved. The rest is mere jelly.

Matter Transmitters

Matter transmitters have appeared often in science fiction, at least since the invention of facsimile machines in the late 1800s. I raise the idea here only as a thought experiment, to simplify some of the issues in the mind transfer proposal. A facsimile transmitter scans a photograph line by line with a light sensitive photocell, and produces an electric current that varies with the brightness of the scanned point in the picture. The varying electric current is transmitted over wires to a remote location where it controls the brightness of a light bulb in a facsimile reciever. The receiver scans the bulb over photosensitive paper in the same pattern as the transmitter. When this paper is developed, a duplicate of the original photograph is obtained. This device was a boon to newspapers, who were able to get illustrations from remote parts of the country almost instantly, rather than after a period of days by train.

If pictures, why not solid objects? A matter transmitter might scan an object and identify, then knock out, its atoms or molecules one at a time. The identity of the atoms would be transmitted to a receiver where a duplicate of the original object would be assembled in the same order from a local supply of atoms. The technical problems are mind-boggling, and well beyond anything foreseeable, but the principle is simple to grasp. If solid objects, why not a person? Just stick him in the transmitter, turn on the scan, and greet him when he walks from the receiver. But is it really the same person? If the system works well, the duplicate will be indistinguishable from the original in any substantial way. Yet, suppose you fail to turn on the receiver during the transmission process. The transmitter will scan and disassemble the victim, and send an unheard message to the inoperative receiver. The original person will be dead. Doesn't the process, in fact, kill the original person, whether or not there is an active receiver? Isn't the duplicate just that—merely a clever imposter? Or suppose two receivers respond to the message from one transmitter. Which, if either, of the two duplicates is the real original?

Pattern Identity

The body identity position is clear: a matter transmitter is an execution device. You might as well save your money and use a gas chamber, and not be taken in by the phony double gimmick. Pattern identity gives a different perspective. Suppose I step into the transmission chamber. The transmitter scans and disassembles my jelly-like body, but my pattern (me!) moves continuously from the dissolving jelly, through the transmitting beam, and ends up in other jelly at the destination. At no instant was it (I) ever destroyed. The biggest confusion comes from the question of duplicates. It is rooted in all our past experience that one person corresponds to one body. In light of the possibility of matter and mind storage and transmission, this simple, natural, and obvious identification becomes confusing and misleading. Suppose the matter transmitted is connected to two receivers instead of one? After the transfer there will be a copy of you in each one. Surely at least one of them is a mere copy—they can't both be you, right? *Wrong!*

Consider the message "I am not jelly." As I type it it goes from my brain, into the keyboard of my computer, through myriads of electronic circuits and over great amounts of wire, and after countless adventures shows up in bunches of books like the one you're holding. How many messages were there? I claim it is most useful to think there is only one, despite its massive replication. If I repeat it here: "I am not jelly," there is still only one message. Only if I change it in a significant manner—"I am not peanut butter"—do we have a second message. And the message is not destroyed until the last written version is lost, and until it fades sufficiently in everybody's memory to be unreconstructable. The message is the information conveyed, not the particular encoding.

The "pattern and process" that I claim is the real me has the same properties as the message above. Making a momentary copy of my state, whether on tape or in another functional body, doesn't make two persons. There is a complication because of the "process" aspect; as soon as an instance of a "person message" evolves for a while, it becomes a different person. If two of them are active, they will diverge and become two different people, by my definition. Just how far this differentiation must proceed before you grant the two people unique identities is about as problematical as the question "when does a fetus become a person?" But if you wait zero time, then you don't have a new person. If, in the dual receiver version of the matter transmitter, you allow the two copies to be made and kill one (either one) instantly on reception, the transmitted person still exists in the other copy. All the things that person might have done, and all the thoughts he or she might have thought, are still possible. If, on the other hand, you allow both copies to live their separate lives for a year, and then kill one, you are the murderer of a unique human being. *But*, if you wait only a short while, they won't differ by much, and destruction of one won't cause too much total loss. This rationale might, for instance, be a comfort in danger if you knew that a tape backup copy of you had been made recently. Because of the divergence, the tape contains not you as you are now, but you as you were: a slightly different person. Still, most of you would be saved should you have a fatal accident, and the loss would be nowhere near as great as without the backup.

Intellectual acceptance that a secure and recent backup of you exists does not necessarily protect you from an instinctive self-preservation overreaction if faced with imminent death. This is an evolutionary hangover from your one-copy past. It is no more a reflection of reality than fear of flying is an appropriate response to present airline accident rates. Inappropriate intuitions are to be expected when the rules of life are suddenly reversed from historical absolutes.

Soul in Abstraction

Although we've reasoned from strictly reductionistic assumptions about the nature of thought and self, the pattern identity position has clear dualistic implications. Though mind is entirely the consequence of interacting matter, the ability to copy it from one machine or storage medium to another gives it an independence and an identity apart from its machinery. The dualism is especially apparent if we consider some of the variations of encoding possible.

Some supercomputer designs call for myriads of individual computers interconnected by a network that allows free flow of information among them. An operating system for this arrangement might allow individual processes to migrate from one processor to another in mid-computation, in a kind of juggling act that permits more processes than there are processors. If a human mind is installed in a future machine of this variety, functions originally performed by particular cell assemblies might be encoded in individual processes. The juggling action would ensure that operations occurring in fixed areas in the original brain would move rapidly from place to place within the machine. If the computer is running other programs besides the mind simulation, then the simulation might find itself shuffled into entirely different sets of processors from moment to moment. The thinking process would be uninterrupted, even as its location and physical machinery changed continuously, because the immaterial pattern would keep its continuity.

A process that is described as a long sequence of steps can sometimes be transformed mathematically into one that arrives at the same conclusion in far fewer operations. As a young boy the famous mathematician Friedrich Gauss was a school smart-aleck. As a diversion, a teacher once set him the problem of adding up all the numbers between 1 and 100. He returned with the correct answer in less than a minute. He had no ticed that the hundred numbers could be grouped into fifty pairs—$1 + 100$, $2 + 99$, $3 + 98$, $4 + 97$, and so on—each pair adding up to 101. Fifty times 101 is 5,050—the answer, found without a lot of tedious addition. Similar speedups are possible in complex processes. So-called *optimizing compilers* have repertoires of accelerating transformations, some very radical, to streamline programs they translate. The key may be a total reorganization in the order of the computation and the representation of the data. A very powerful class of transformations takes an array of values and combines them in different ways to produce another array. Each final value reflects all the original values, and each original value affects all the results. An operation on a single transformed quantity can substitute for a whole host of operations on the original array, and enormous efficiencies are possible. Analogous transformations in time also work: a sequence of operations is changed into an equivalent one where each new step does a tiny fraction of the work of every one of the original steps. The localized is diffused, and the diffused is localized. A program can quickly be altered beyond recognition by a few mathematical rewrites of this power. Run on a multiprocessor, single events in the original formulation may appear only as correlations between events in remote machines at remote times in the transform. Certain operations that don't matter in the long run may be skipped altogether. Yet the program is fundamentally unchanged. You know what's coming. If we thus transform a program that simulates a person, the person remains intact. Soul is in the mathematical equivalence, not in any particular detail of the process. It has a very ethereal character.

The Message is the Medium

If a mind can survive repeated radical restructurings, infusion into and out of different types of hardware and storage media, and is ultimately a mathematical abstraction, does it require hardware at all? Suppose the message describing a person is written in some static medium, like a book. A superintelligent being or a big computer reading and understanding the message might be able to reason out the future evolution of the encoded person, not only under a particular set of experiences, but also under various alternative circumstances. Existence in the thoughts of a beholder is no more abstract than existence as a transformed person-program described in the previous section, but it does introduce an interesting new twist.

The superintelligent being has no obligations to model every single detail of the beheld accurately, and may well choose to skip the boring parts, to jump to conclusions that are obvious to it, and to lump together different alternatives it does not choose to distinguish. This looseness in the simulation can also allow some time-reversed action—our superintelligent being may choose a conclusion, then reason backwards, deciding what must have preceded it. Authors of fiction often take such liberties with their characters. The same parsimony of thought applies to the parts of the environment of the contemplated person that are themselves being contemplated. Applied a certain way, this parsimony will effect the evolution of the simulated person and his environment, and may thus be noticeable to him. Note that the subjective feelings of the simulated person are a part of the simulation, and with them the contemplated person feels as real in this implementation as in any other.

It happens that quantum mechanics describes a world where unobserved events happen in all possible ways (another way of saying no decision is made as to which possibility occurs), and the superposition of all these possibilities itself has observable effects. The connection of this observation with those of the previous paragraph leads us into murky philosophical waters. To get even muddier, seriously consider the title of this section. If the subjective feelings of a person are part of the person-message, and if the evolution of the message is implicit in the message itself, then aren't the future experiences of the person implicit in the message? And wouldn't this mere mathematical existence feel the same to the person encoded as a more substantial simulation? I don't think this is mere sophistry, but I'm not prepared to take it any further for now.

Immortality and Impermanence

Wading back into the shallows, let's examine a certain dilemma of existence, presently overshadowed by the issue of personal death, that will be paramount when practical immortality is achieved. It's this: in the long run, survival requires change in directions not of your own choosing. Standards escalate with the growth of the inevitable competitors and predators for each niche. In a kind of cosmic Olympic games, the universe molds its occupants toward its own distant and mysterious specifications. An immortal cannot hope to survive unchanged, only to maintain a limited continuity over the short run. Personal death differs from this inevitability only in its relative abruptness. Viewed on a larger scale we are already immortal, as we have been since the dawn of life. Our genes and our culture pass continuously from one generation to the next, subject only to incremental alterations to meet the continuous demand for new world records in the cosmic games.

In the very long run the ancestral individual is always doomed, as its heritage is nibbled away to meet short-term demands. It slowly mutates into other forms that could have been reached from a range of starting points—the ultimate in convergent evolution. It's by this reasoning that I conclude that it makes no ultimate difference whether our machines carry forward our heritage on their own, or in partnership with direct transcriptions of ourselves. Assuming long-term survival either way, the end results should be indistinguishable, shaped by the universe and not by ourselves. Since change is inevitable, I think we should embrace rather than retard it. By so doing we improve our day-to-day survival odds, discover interesting surprises sooner, and are more prepared to face any competition. The cost is faster erosion of our present constitution. All development can be interpreted as incremental death and new birth, but some of the fast-lane options make this especially obvious; for instance, the possibility of dropping parts of one's memory and personality in favor of another's. Fully exploited, this process results in transient individuals constituted from a communal pool of personality traits. Sexual populations are effective in part because they create new genetic individuals in very much this way. As with sexual reproduction, the memory pool requires dissolution as well as creation to be effective. So personal death is not banished, but it does lose its poignancy because death by submergence into the memory pool is reversible in the short run.

Back to Time Travel

In the continuing struggle for survival, we've already acquired considerable control of time. Memory—genetic, reflecting our evolution; nervous, storing our experiences; or artificial, recording events and thoughts—gives us some mastery over the past. What of the future? A hallmark of intelligence is the ability to choose, from many possibilities, those actions that accomplish certain ends. In advanced robots, as in large-brained animals, there is the possibility of deliberation, in which alternatives are imagined and their outcomes weighed prior to the action. However imperfectly, such planning involves a prediction of the future, or, more precisely, of possible futures. The central goal of scientific inquiry has been the refinement of this skill. A good theory *predicts*. Theories and their predictions come to life in simulations, particularly on powerful computers. Such simulations have been especially accurate in the programs that predict the course of the planets and of spacecraft. More dramatically, if less accurately, modern weather programs simulate the action of the atmosphere over the entire globe. Increasingly powerful computation makes possible more accurate and longer range predictions. In a real sense, powerful simulators are time machines, giving peeks into possible futures, and thus the power to choose among them.

The laws of physics are quite symmetric in time. Simulations can usually be run in reverse as well as forward, and used to "predict" the past, perhaps guided by old measurements or archeological data. As with future predictions, any uncertainty in the initial measurements, or in the rule that evolves the initial state, will allow for a variety of possible outcomes. If the simulation is detailed enough, and is given all available information, then all of its "predictions" are valid—*any of the possible pasts may have led to the present situation*. This is a strange idea if you are accustomed to looking at the world in a strictly deterministic, Newtonian way. Interestingly, it closely resembles the uncertain world described by quantum mechanics, and perhaps hints at a mechanism underlying our world. Now, imagine an immense simulator that is able to model the whole surface of the earth on an atomic scale, and that can run time forward and back, and produce different plausible outcomes by making different random choices at key points in its calculation. Because of the great detail, this simulator models living things, including humans, in their full complexity. By the arguments above, such simulated people would be as real as you or I, though imprisoned in the simulator.

We could join them by linking up with the simulation through a telepresence interface, that connects a "puppet" deep inside the simulation with a physical "helmet" and "gloves" outside, allowing us to experience the puppet's sensory environment, and to naturally control its actions. More radically, we could "download" our minds directly into a body in the simulation, and "upload" back into the real world when our mission is accomplished. Alternatively, we could bring people out of the simulation by reversing the process, linking their minds to an outside robot body, or uploading them directly into it. In all cases we would have the opportunity to recreate the past, and to some extent the future, and interact with it in a real and direct way. Realistically simulating the future is more difficult because archeology cannot help, and because an advancing culture will produce fundamental new knowledge not found in the model, by research into new physical arenas or exploration of new geography. The same techniques, of course, allow visits to entirely novel situations and universes.

Finally, here's the core of an idea that, if correct, would put a radically new light on the fundaments of our space and time, incidentally explaining the most bizarre effects of quantum mechanics. Someone should develop it mathematically someday.

THE HARMONIES OF THE SPHERE

Quantum mechanics, a cornerstone of modern physics, has indeterminism at its heart and soul. Outcome probabilities in quantum mechanics are predicted by summing up complex valued "amplitude functions" for all the indistinguishable ways a given event might happen, then squaring the result. The amplitudes subtract from each other as often as they add, with the strange effect that some otherwise possible outcomes are ruled out by the existence of other possibilities. An excellent example is the *two slit* experiment. Photons of light radiate from a pinpoint source to a screen broken by two slits (Figure 1). Those that make it through the slits encounter an array of photon detectors (often a photographic film, but the example is clearer if we use individual, immediately responding sensors). If the light source is so dim that only one photon is released at a time, the sensors register individually, sometimes this one, sometimes that one. Each photon lands in exactly one place. But if a count is kept of how many photons have landed on each detector, an unexpected pattern emerges. Some detectors see no photons at all, while ones close to them on either side register many, and a little farther away there is again a dearth. In the long run, a pattern builds that is identical with the banded interference pattern one would see if two matched waves were being emitted from sources at the slits.

But waves of *what*? Each photon starts from one place and lands in one place; isn't it at just one place on every part of its flight? Doesn't it go through one slit or the other? If so, how does the mere existence of the other slit *prevent* it from landing at a certain place on the screen? For indeed, if one slit is blocked, the total number of photons landing on the screen is halved, but the interference pattern vanishes, and some locations that received no photons with both slits open begin to register hits. Quantum mechanics' answer is that during the flight the position of the photon is unknown, and must be modeled by a complex valued wave describing all its possible locations. This ghostly wave passes through *both* slits (though it describes the position of only a single photon), and interferes with itself at the screen, cancelling at some points. There the wave makes up its

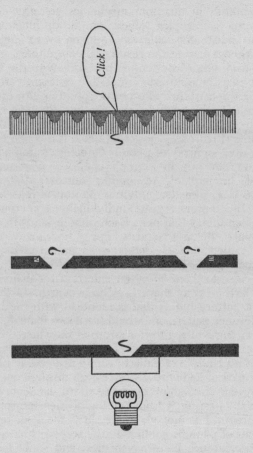

Figure 1: **Two slit experiment**. A photon picked up by a detector at screen S *might* have come through slit **A** or through slit **B**—there is no way to distinguish. In quantum mechanics the "amplitudes" for the two cases must be added. At some points on the screen they add constructively, making it likely that a photon will end up there; at nearby points the amplitudes cancel, and no photons are ever found.

mind, and the photon appears in just one of its possible locations. The undecided wave condition of the photon before it hits the screen is called a *mixed state* or a *superposition of states*. The sudden appearance of the photon in only one detector is called the *collapse of the wave function*.

This explanation profoundly disturbed some of the same physicists who had helped formulate the theory, notably Albert Einstein and Erwin Schrödinger. To formalize their intuitive objections they constructed thought experiments that gave unlikely results according to the theory. In some a measurement made at one site causes the instant collapse of a wave function at a remote location—an effect faster than light. In another, more frivolous example, called Schrödinger's Cat, a radioactive decay that may or may not take place in a sealed box causes (or fails to cause) the death of a cat also in the box. Schrödinger considered absurd the theory's description of the unopened box as a mixed state superimposing a live and a dead cat. He suggested that the theory merely expressed ignorance on the part of an observer—in the box, the cat's fate was unambiguous. This is called a *hidden variables* theory the system has a definite state at all times, but some parts of it are temporarily hidden from some observers.

The joke is on the critics. Many of the most "absurd" thought-experiment results have been observed in mind-boggling actuality in a series of clever (and very modern) experiments carried out by Alain Aspect at the University of Paris, and others. These demonstrations rule out the simplest and most natural hidden variables theories, *local* ones in which, for instance, the hidden information about which slit the photon went through is contained in the photon itself, or in which the state of health of Schrödinger's cat is part of the feline.

Non-local hidden variables theories, where the unmeasured information is distributed over an extended space, *are* a possibility. It is easy to construct theories of this kind that give results identical with ordinary quantum mechanics. Most physicists find them uninteresting—why introduce a more complicated explanation with extra variables, when the current, simpler equations suffice? Philosophically, also, global hidden variables theories are only slightly less puzzling than raw quantum mechanics. What does it mean that the "exact position" of a particle is spread out over a large chunk of space? This question was the subject of a lively controversy in the early part of this century among the founders of quantum mechanics. It's recently become of widespread interest again.

Quantum mechanical interactions have a "spooky" character clearly evident in the two slit experiment, and recently emphasized by physical demonstrations of the Einstein-Podolsky-Rosen paradox by Aspect and others. The ghosts can be exorcised, or at least elucidated, by proposing underlying mechanisms for the basic effects. These mechanisms often suggest radical new possibilities.

The "many worlds" interpretation developed in the 1950s by Hugh Everett and John Wheeler at Princeton, and frequently presented by John Gribbin in these pages (for instance, in the April 1985 issue), may be the most profligate non-local hidden variables explanation of this puzzle. In Everett's model, the two slit photon does go through both slits, *in different universes*. At each decision point the entire universe, or at least the immediate portion of it, splits into several, like multiple pages from a copying machine. Until a measurement is made, the different "versions" of the universe lie in close proximity, and interfere with each other (causing banded patterns on screens, for instance). A measurement that can distinguish one possibility from another causes the universes to diverge (alternately, the divergence is the definition of "measurement"). The interference then stops, and in each now-separate universe, a different version of the experimenter can contemplate a different unambiguous result.

Another possibility, outlined in the November 1986 *Analog* by John Cramer, is his "transactional" interpretation, itself based on an old explanation by Feynman and Wheeler for the lack of time-reversed waves implicit in Maxwell's equations. In it, observer and observed communicate with signals travelling both ways in time, so the outcome of the experiment is as much part of the initial condition as the experimental setup. Or perhaps the universe is a computation in some kind of machine. Quantum effects might be the result of limited accuracy and parsimony of calculation in its program. The equations of quantum mechanics implicitly state that the amount of information that can be extracted from a limited volume of spacetime is finite. Also, with proper encoding, the undecided state of a system contains less information than after a measurement. Only during actual measurements must the "universe computer" bother to choose one outcome from all the possibilities. Here, for the first time, I offer yet another, in some ways less radical (but half baked!) mechanism for quantum mechanics. I like it because it derives the spookiest consequences from a very concrete model.

One World, Not Many

Imagine, somewhere, there is a spherical volume uniformly filled with a gas made up of a huge but finite number of particles in motion. Pressure waves pass through the gas, propagating at its speed of sound, s. We assume no faster signal can be sent (the exact properties required of the medium will have to be developed elsewhere—here we deal only in generalities!). The sphere has resonances that correspond to wave trains passing through its entire volume at different angles and frequencies. Each combination of a particular direction and frequency is called a *wave mode*. There is a mathematical transformation called the (spatial) *Fourier Transform* that arranges these wave modes very neatly and powerfully. The Fourier transform combines the pattern of pressures found over the original volume of the sphere (V) in various ways to produce a new spherical set of values (F). At the center of F is a number representing the average density of V.

Immediately surrounding it are (complex) numbers giving the intensity of waves, in various directions. whose wavelength is so long that one cycle spans the diameter of V. Twice as far from the center of F are found the intensities of wave modes with two cycles across V, and so on. Each point in F describes a wave filling V with a direction and a number of cycles given by the point's orientation and distance from the center of F. Another way of saying this is direction in F corresponds to direction in V; radius in F is proportional to frequency in V. Since each wave is made of periodic clusterings of gas particles, the interparticle spacing sets a lower bound on the wavelength, thus an upper bound on frequency, and a limit on the radius of the F sphere. The closer the particles, the larger must be F. A theorem about Fourier transforms states that if sufficiently high frequencies are included, then F contains about as many points as V has particles, and all the information required to reconstruct V is found in F. In fact, F and V are simply alternative descriptions of the same thing, with the interesting property that every particle in V contributes to each point in F, and vice versa.

If the particles in V bump into one another, or interact in some other way (*i.e.* the gas in *nonlinear*), then energy can be transferred from one wave mode to another—*i.e.*, one point in F can become stronger at the expense of another. There will be a certain amount of random transference among all wave modes. Besides this there will be a more systematic interaction between "nearby" wave modes— those very similar in frequency and orientation, thus near each other in the F space. Such waves will be in step for large fractions of their length. Because the gas is nonlinear, the periodic bunching of gas particles caused by one mode will influence the bunching ability of a neighboring mode with a similar period.

Now consider the interactions viewed by a hypothetical observer made of F stuff, for whom points in F are simply locations, rather than complicated functions of another space. Keeping as many concepts from the V

space as possible, we can deduce some of this observer's "Laws of Physics" by reasoning about effects in V, and translating back to F. In the following list, such reasoning is in italics:

• **Dimensionality:** If V is three-dimensional, so is F. *Two of its dimensions correspond to angular direction of the wave trains; the other, the radius, corresponds to frequency.*

• **Locality:** Points near to each other in F can exchange energy in consistent, predictable ways while distant points cannot. *Two wave trains in V that are very similar in direction and frequency are in step for a long portion of their length, and the non-linear bunching effects will be roughly the same cycle after cycle. Distant wave modes, whose crests and troughs are not correlated, will lose here, and gain there, and in general appear like mere random buffetings to each other.*

• **Interaction Speed:** There is a characteristic speed at each point in F. Points far away from the center of F interact more quickly than those closer in. *An interaction is the non-random transfer of energy from one wave train to another. The smallest repeated unit in a wave train is a cycle. An effect which happens in a similar way at each cycle can have a consistent effect on a whole wave train. Effects in V propagate at the speed of sound, so a whole cycle can be affected in the time it takes sound to traverse it (which is also the temporal frequency of the wave train). The outer parts of F correspond to higher frequencies, and thus to faster rates.*

• **Uncertainty Principle:** The energy of a point in F can't be determined precisely in a short time. The best accuracy possible improves linearly with duration of the measurement. *The energy at a point in F is the total energy of a particular wave train that* *spans the entire volume V. As no signal in V can travel faster than the speed of sound, discovering the total energy in a wave train would involve waiting for signals to arrive from all over V, a time much longer than the basic interaction time. In a short time, the summation is necessarily over a proportionately small volume. Since the observer in F is itself distributed over V, exactly which smaller volume is not defined—and thus the measurement is uncertain. As the time and the summation volume increase, all the possible sums converge to the average, and the uncertainty decreases.*

• **Superposition of States:** Most interactions in *F* will appear to be the sum of many possible ways the interaction might have happened. *When two nearby wave trains interact, they do so initially on a cycle-by-cycle basis, since information from distant parts of the wave train arrives only at the speed of sound. Each cycle contains a little energy from the wave train in question, and a lot of energy from many other waves of different frequency and orientation passing through the same volume. This "background noise" will be different from one cycle to the next, so the interaction at each cycle will be slightly different. When all is said and done, i.e., if the information from the entire wave train is collected, the total interaction can be interpreted as the sum of the cycle-by-cycle interactions. Sometimes energy will be transferred one way by one cycle, and the opposite way by a distant one, so the alternatives can cancel as well as enhance one another.*

These and other properties of the *F* world contain some of the strangest features of quantum mechanics, but are the consequence only of an unusual way of looking at a prosaic situation. There are a few differences. The superposition of states is statistical, rather than a perfect sum over all possibilities as in traditional quantum mechanics. This makes only a very subtle difference if V is very large, but might result in a very tiny amount of "noise" in measurements that could help distinguish the F mechanism from other explanations of quantum mechanics. The model as presented does not model the effects of special relativity in any obvious way, and this is a serious defect, if we hope to wrestle it into a description of our world. There is something wrong in the way it treats time. It does have one property that mimics the temporal effects of a general relativistic gravitational field. Time near the center of F runs more slowly than at the extremes, since the interactions are based on lower frequency waves. At the very center, time is stopped. The central point of F never changes its "average energy of the whole sphere" value, and so is effectively frozen in time. In general relativity, the regions around a gravitating body have a similar property: time flows slower as one gets closer. Near very dense masses (*i.e.*, black holes), time stops altogether at a certain distance.

A few of modern physics' more exotic theories have possible explanation in this model. Although energy mainly flows between wave modes very similar in frequency and direction (*i.e.*, between points adjacent in F), non-linearities in the V medium should permit some energy to flow systematically between harmonically related wave modes; for instance, between one mode and another on the same direction, but twice as high in frequency. Such modes of energy flow in F provide "degrees of freedom" in addition to the three provided by nearby points. They can be interpreted, when viewed on the small scale, as extra dimensions (energy can move this way, that way, that way, and also *that* way, and *that* way . . .). Since a circumnavigation from harmonic to harmonic will cover the available space in fewer steps than a move along adjacent wave modes, these extra dimensions will appear to have a much smaller extent than the basic three. The greater the energy involved, the more harmonics are activated, and the higher the dimensionality. Most physical theories these days have tightly looped extra dimensions to provide a geometric explanation of the basic forces. Ten and eleven dimensions are popular, and hinted new forces may introduce more. If something like the F explanation of apparent higher dimensionality is correct, there is a bonus. Viewed on a large scale, the harmonic "dimensions" are actual links between distant regions of space, and properly exploited, could allow instantaneous communication and travel over enormous distances.

Big Waves

Now, forget the possible implications of the idea as a mechanism for quantum mechanics, and consider our universe on the grand scale. It is permeated by a background of microwave radiation with a wavelength of about one millimeter, slowly increasing as the universe expands. It affects and is affected by clouds of matter, and thus interacts with itself nonlinearly. If we do a universe-wide spatial Fourier transform of this radiation (that is, treat *our* world, as V), we end up with an F space with properties much like those above. The expansion of the universe adds a new twist. As the wavelength gets longer and longer, the subjective rate of time flow in the F world slows down. Any inhabitants of F would be ideally situated to practice the "live forever by going slower and slower as it gets colder and colder" strategy proposed by Freeman Dyson. By now they would be moving quite slowly—their fastest particle interactions would take several trillionths of a second. In the past, however, when the universe was dense and hot, the F world would have been a lively place, running millions or billions of times faster. In the earliest moments of the universe, the speed would have been astronomically faster.

The first microsecond of the big bang might represent eons of subjective time in F—perhaps enough time for intelligence to evolve, realize its situation, and seed smaller but eventually faster life in the V space. Though on the large scale F and V are the same thing, manipulation of one from the other, or even communication, would be extraordinarily difficult. Any local event in either space would be diffused to non-detectability in the other. Only massive, universe-spanning projects with long-range order would work, and these would take huge amounts of time because of the speed limits in either universe, so real-time interaction is ruled out. Such projects, however, could affect many locations in the other space as easily (in many cases more easily) as one, and these could appear as entropy violating "miracles" there. If I lived in F and wanted to visit V, I would engineer such a miracle that would condense a robot surrogate of myself in V, then later another one that would read out the robot's memories back into an F-accessible form.

The Fourier transform that converts V into F is identical except for a minus sign to the inverse transform that converts the other way. Given just the two descriptions, it wouldn't be clear which was the "original" world. In fact, the Fourier transform is but one of an infinite class of "orthogonal transforms" that have the same basic properties. Each of these is capable of taking a description of a volume, and operating over it to produce a different description with the same information, but with each original point spread to every location in the result. This leads to the possibility of an infinity of universes, each a different combination of the same underlying stuff, each exhibiting quantum mechanical behavior but otherwise having its own unique physics, each oblivious of the others sharing its space. I don't know where to take that idea.

Introduction

Speaking of fighting the Good Fight, remember Loyalty? Honor? Courage? Though we seem to be growing too sophisticated for such childish virtues, perhaps we can still admire them when they are displayed by other, lesser beings, we who no longer keep the faith.

LaToya is Wounded

Dafydd ab Hugh

I hear a sound. It is high-pitched and it hurts my ears. It sounds like something falling. I try to warn LaToya, but she does not understand at first. Now there is no time. I knock her down by jumping on her back.

There is an explosion. For a time I cannot hear or smell anything, or think. When I can walk again, I call out to LaToya. She does not answer. Something smells wrong, but I only smell what I have smelled before—TNT smoke, and some blood and urine, but not enough to panic.

Something sounds wrong, but I cannot hear anything I have not heard many times. After the explosion, the insects and animals have all become silent. Now they are starting up again, so I am not deaf. But something is wrong with LaToya because she does not answer my bark.

Now I notice something that makes me freeze. Just like hearing enemy voices, I do not move. But there is no enemy. I do not know what is wrong. Now I understand why I froze.

LaToya's voice inside my head is almost gone. I can

barely feel her—just enough to know that she is alive. But she is so close! I smell her thoroughly, up and down, and now I know. LaToya is badly wounded. I think she is near death. I wonder: did the mortar hurt her? I do not remember anything else that could have done it.

At first I panic. I run around and around her, calling to her. I try to wake her up. I want her to tell me what to do, for I am very afraid. I have never been alone before. I have never been without Captain LaToya Franklin, National Federation, United States Marine Corps, Military Identification Number 237-MM-9992.

No. I am a soldier. I must act like one, and not whine about what happened. I swallow panic, for I am in the Marine Corps too. I am a corporal, and I must not panic. I examine LaToya carefully, but she will not wake up. Her voice inside my head is saying nothing and is weak, but it is still there. It has not gotten weaker or stronger while I have waited. I do not know what to do.

I know what I must do now. I must get help. LaToya is wounded, and she needs my help. I will go. I tell LaToya that I am going to get help for her. I do not think she hears me, but I must report to her anyway. I nuzzle her, and tell her not to panic. I will get help. I will go get help. Then I leave. But it is like leaving my mother on the day LaToya took me away to become a soldier. I cry as I leave LaToya. I must get help for her. I must find a medic.

Very carefully I drag her into the brambles. They tear at my coat and hurt me; and I know they hurt LaToya even more because she has no fur. I cry at her pain. But they will keep many animals away, and maybe she doesn't feel the thorns. I make sure she is well covered, and then I run away.

The ground is dry and brittle beneath my paws. It makes too much noise as I run, but I do not care. Now I slow down and remember where LaToya said we are.

We are deep in the enemy's territory. The enemy defends its territory savagely. It has sharp ears and eyes. I must be silent. I must creep through its territory and rejoin my own unit.

I am afraid again, and I almost panic. Then I listen closely, and can barely hear LaToya's voice inside my head still. She is not saying anything, but she is alive. I do not know why I felt afraid just now. But LaToya always says to stop and think when it happens, until I know what frightens me.

I stop for a few heartbeats. I call up my map implant and find our position, and where I must go; and now I know what frightened me. It has taken LaToya and me many, many days to walk this far into the enemy's territory. There is a reason this is bad. I think and think. I try to think about time, but it gives me as much trouble as it always does. At last I understand. It will take many, many days for me to run back to my unit. Not as long as it took to come in with LaToya, because she is slow. But it will still be too late. I must go faster.

There is only one way to go faster. I must find a car or a boat or a plane or a helo. But the only ones close enough are the enemy's.

There is no choice.

I sneeze twice, and then lick my nose to clear out all the scents I have picked up since the explosion. Then I point my nose high up into the air to smell the faint scents up there. They are weak, but they are the truest. Animals do not run across them, and they do not mark the air with urine.

For many, many heartbeats I stay that way. I do not move. I take long smells from the air, first against the wind, and then with the wind, and then in the other directions.

I smell something. I smell water buffalo. At first I ignore it, because I do not want to hunt now. But then I remember that my pack sometimes puts sheep in a field with a fence. I know; there is a time before—I am very little . . . I herd them in and out of the field that has the fence. I keep them in the pasture where the tall ones put them. I protect the sheep from wolves and coyotes and animal-dogs. I scare away the cougars—now I am grown, and I am a soldier; now I remember.

I think that the enemy may do the same thing with water buffalo. There are no sheep in this place, so the enemy tall ones may use water buffalo the way my pack back home uses sheep. I smell again.

There are many water buffalo. I think there are more than I have smelled in a wild herd before. I think there must be enemy there too, to make the fences for the water buffalo. I smell once more to make sure of the direction. Now I run that way, and my heart beats fast like when I hunt. Maybe they will have a Military Transport Vehicle Pool.

I wait at the edge of the jungle, where there are many shadows. I think I see many tall ones walking around the buffalo. They are not as dark as LaToya, and not as light as the others of my unit. But they do not smell like enemy, so they must be civilians. And now I smell gasoline.

I creep from my place into the fields. I try to look like an animal dog. The scent of gasoline is strong in my nostrils, like a fire that I smell instead of feel. Now there is the scent of gasoline smoke, and I know that there is a vehicle here. The trail is fresh, and easy to follow.

The fields are like lakes. I sink up to my belly at times; I swim and walk and swim again, and smell rice and death in the furrows. Finally there is a walkway, and it leads me to the village. The tall pups run up to me and yap, and they pull my fur and my tail.

I smell them each in turn. There is something wrong; they are civilians. What did LaToya say about the civilians? It is important, I know—everything LaToya says is important. But I cannot remember; I am bad and stupid.

They are making a happy-noise, a laugh. But there is something wrong. They are not acting like the tall pups where I was before the war.

Then they grab. I yelp, and struggle, and try to bite. But one has me around the chest, and she is strong.

They say something. I do not know the words of the civilians here, but this word I learn everywhere: they say food, food. I am very afraid, and LaToya is wounded!

The tall pups take me away from the trail of the gasoline smoke. They drag me between their hutches and into another one. They lock me in a cage. They will eat me.

It is later. A civilian comes and looks at me. I act like an animal dog and lick his hand. But he stinks of the enemy. I wonder if his pack knows?

He takes my head in his hands, and pries open my jaws to look at my teeth, as if I am an animal. He offends me, but I dare not act to let him know that. Then he searches my body, maybe for disease, and he becomes careless.

Very carefully I reach my jaws down to his boot, as if I am biting a sleeping snake. I take hold of his knife very softly, just as LaToya taught me; and before he pushes me away, I have taken it out of his boot. He does not know I have it. Who suspects an animal?

I lie down and whine, sounding like I want him to come back. At the door he stops and brushes his boot. He is careful, this one! He finds the empty sheath.

Now he looks all around the room, under the table and the rug. Finally he makes angry-noises, and I catch his word "steal." He stamps out of the hutch making too much noise.

But he does not look under me.

He thinks I am an animal. But I am smart. I know about cut; LaToya teaches me many things when I hear her voice in my head. I know everything about knives—that they can cut.

I stand up again, and pick the knife up. It tastes like the enemy, and I feel good knowing it will be used to hurt him. The walls of the hutch are only thick grass. I can cut them. It takes many heartbeats, but now I am through. I push through the cut, and slink alongside the hutch in the shadows. When I get to water I drop the knife, and it joins the rice and the dead things.

I can crawl on my belly and be entirely under water,

except for my nose and my ears. When somebody comes, I duck all the way under. I cannot see under the water, but the tall ones see better than I. I do not know if they can see me. But maybe they think I am dead, and only there to make the rice grow. Nobody bothers me, and I do not have to fight.

All of the rivers in the fields are straight, and point the same direction. I have never seen anything like it. As I crawl, the odor of gasoline and smoke gets stronger; I still have the trail.

Now I leave the fields and follow the smell along a road. Much time passes. At last I find the truck.

It is stopped in another village, but this one is an armed camp. There are many, many enemies—too many to count. And then I smell something that makes all my fur stand up as straight as razorgrass. I have only smelled it once before, and for many scentings I try to say to myself that it is not what I think; it is only something else that smells too much like an Outsider.

But I know truly that an Outsider is what it is. It can be nothing else, even though the only time we smell it is in C-Tech School/Survreconintel. Then we K-9's smell it from a can.

This is not a can. But there are no Outsiders here! I lie silent on my belly and search carefully through all my Implants, and everything says they are not here on the ground. They are only in the sky. LaToya's memory-voice is telling me about the ground in the sky she says is a planet, but I cannot understand how there can be ground in the sky. It is not relevant to my mission and I do not have a need to know.

There is no doubt. There is an Outsider in this camp. There are also enemies, and animal-dogs. I must get away, to save LaToya.

I call up the map Implant and find my location. I know where the unit is, and I draw my line. But when I begin marking off days of travel I count up to five or six and lose track. After that it doesn't matter: her voice in my head is very weak; she sleeps too deep. I am afraid, and I know if I try to run all the way she will die. Already she is near death.

I get up and I trot into the camp. I must be bold. LaToya says boldness is the subtlest tactic. They will think I am an animal and ignore me.

There are no pups of the tall ones in the camp, or water buffalos, and there is no rice. There are many trucks and weapons. It will not be hard to sneak into a truck. But I do not know which one! If I choose wrong it might go the wrong way.

I keep in the shadows of the buildings, and scout the camp. There are only two roads besides the one from the other village. But my map Implants show only one road in this grid. At first I think I am counting wrong, but at last I realize my Implant is wrong! I am frightened again. The Implants are always right.

But they also say there are no Outsiders. I am confused.

The Outsider is important. I must save LaToya—but I have a mission, too. The Outsider's presence is intelligence, and I must tell the unit commander, who is now Colonel Trelloq, National Federation, United States Marine Corps, Military Identification Number 885-4L-7777. I must think about the Outsider.

It is very dangerous for it to be here. I know if it is found my unit is legally allowed to use the Big One to destroy it; that is the treaty, and LaToya knows all about the treaty. So it is also very dangerous to the enemy for the Outsider to be here. It must be doing something very important to risk so much!

I follow the scent of the Outsider and find the hutch where it is staying. It is talking to tall ones in the enemy pack, but I cannot get close enough to count how many. I must get closer.

There are animal-dogs here. They do not know I am watching because I am very quiet and I am downwind. But they are very close to the hutch. They are where I need to be. I adopt boldness and trot up to them as if I am an animal too.

At first they growl and I know they are saying stay

away from my territory. Then they scent me all over because I don't smell right to them—I'm not one of them. They are animals.

We walk around and around scenting each other and I act like I am no more than they; but the leader challenges me and is seconded by his sergeants. We fight.

It is a hard fight, but for a few moments I forget to worry about LaToya, and I feel good. Sometimes we withdraw and look at each other, and I can see the tall ones yelling and crowding around us. They are making laughter and are happy to see the fight.

The leader is bigger than I. He slashes—one, two! —with his teeth; he claws and tries to hold me with his paws. But though I am smaller, I am trained. I know how to fight. I use his size against him, and I attack where he does not defend. I bite his feet and claw his testicles, and then he is beaten. The other dogs turn on him too, and I am the leader of a pack of animals. The old leader limps away and licks his feet.

Now I can creep close to the hutch wall, and none of the enemy will stop me. They think I am only a dog, too. I am not worried about being food here. These tall ones are enemy soldiers, and so they are well-fed.

I do not know the speech of the enemy. I know some words. I listen for the words I know.

When the Outsider talks, my fur stands up, and ants crawl up and down my neck. I see the same happens to the dogs, and they don't want to be near it, so they leave me alone. This is good. I don't want to be the leader anymore. The Outsider makes some words that I know. I catch "demonstration" and "reciprocation," and now I hear the enemy word for "surrender," but it is spoken in the way they say he will surrender or they will surrender, not I or we.

At once, every danger sense I have is jangling. I search for LaToya's voice; it is there and I do not panic. It is not stronger, but it is not weaker. Something else scares me. Something about the Outsider and its demonstration.

Now I must think. Life without LaToya is unthinkable. She has always been inside my head since I first became a soldier. She is a soldier too, and she says we must always make pick-up. It is the law.

But she teaches me another thing too: first is the mission, second is the personnel, last is myself.

I lie on my belly and crawl without moving. I need LaToya. I think I must love LaToya. But LaToya is personnel. The intelligence about the Outsider is mission.

At last the Outsider is through speaking, and he leaves. I am crying. But I must follow. I only hope he is going closer to my own unit; otherwise, LaToya will die. And then I do not know what will happen to me.

The Outsider and four enemies get into the front part of a truck. They start the engine, and just before they drive away I run up and jump in the back. It is uncovered, and I am afraid I will be seen. But I hide behind a gasoline drum, and no one is looking. We leave; we do not drive along the road back to the village. We drive along the road that is not on my map Implant.

I listen well, but I cannot hear anything but the bang of the engine. I smell deeply, but the gasoline and the smoke fills my nostrils and the other scents are like rain on the ocean.

We are driving deeper into the jungle, and I am afraid. I can barely hear LaToya. Her voice is almost stopped.

Suddenly we are in a clearing. It is not on my map either. There are camouflaged tents here, and ammunition, and fast buggies armed with rockets and guns, and helocopters, and ground effect vehicles, and food and medical stores. I remember everything to make a full report when I talk to Colonel Trelloq, National Federation, United States Marine Corps, Military Identification Number 885-4L-7777.

There are many, many enemies here. I do not know how none of this could be on my Implants. Nothing is right anymore: the Implants are wrong, the enemy is massing where there is only empty jungle, and there is even an Outsider on the ground. Everything is wrong.

LaToya is wounded. If she were here, she would tell me what to do.

The truck jumps like a sheep over a fence that only it sees, and then we stop. The enemies and the Outsider get out and enter a tent. Soon enemies begin unloading the truck, and I must act! I rise up with a snarl, baring my teeth and saying death! Kill! I will eat you!

They jump back, startled by my appearance, and I jump over the sidewall and run between the tents. I escape them all. I am wise!

After some time, I can tell by their talk that they have forgotten me. I sneak around behind the tents until I find the one with the Outsider. It is easy; I can never forget that smell. The tent is large, and I must be bold. Very carefully, I squirm under a wall of the tent, and I am inside. Now I can hear, and see too.

It is dark inside, but they have a light at the table with the Outsider. They have a map, and they are pointing at it. I listen, and I hear the word for "landing site."

I swallow, and try hard not to whine. LaToya says I must never make a noise or be seen when I am surveilling, because the enemy has sharp eyes and ears. But suddenly I know I must violate something she says. I am surprised at myself, and afraid. I am afraid LaToya will walk through the tent flap and not love me anymore. I wish it were true, but LaToya is wounded, and I can only hear her voice now if I ignore everything else. It still says nothing. It just is.

I risk everything on one gamble. I walk forward slowly, quietly, but making no effort to conceal myself. Every instinct tells me I am wrong, that I must hide. LaToya says so! But I have only a moment, and I cannot waste it trying to hide where there is not a hiding place. I must hide in plain sight.

I am close now, and they notice me. At first they just stare, and do nothing . . . it is just what I counted on. I have barely enough time to look at the map, at where they are pointing, to Implant the landing site. Then the enemy major jumps up, and makes the most frightening word in his language, the word for "intelligence-enhanced animal." He knows me.

He pulls out his pistol and shoots me. The bullet burns like a whip, and I cannot move my left shoulder. But I still have three legs to his two, and I dodge him as he lunges for me. I run out the tent flap. He shoots many more times, but I am running and swerving as best as I can with a shot leg, and he misses every other shot.

He calls out words, and now many, many enemies are looking for me. They search around the tent, and the food, and out into the jungle. I know one place they will not look. I run deeper into the camp, to the place of the helocopters. The enemies are removing the camouflage from one of them, so I know they will fly that one next. When they run the camouflage away from the pad, I limp up and jump inside the helo. Again, it is simple to burrow under a tarp and hide.

Soon enemies jump into my helo, and the major tells them words about an "enhanced dog," so I know they are all on to me now. But they do not look behind them, in the helo itself.

My shoulder hurts terribly now, and I want to tell LaToya, but she does not hear me, and she cannot help me. I just close my eyes and try to let the pain pass through me, like LaToya says.

They start the turbos, and we are airborne. I do not know where we are going. I wait until we have been flying a very long time; now we are far away from their camp. We are not turning, so I know they are not the ones looking for me. I creep forward.

They cannot hear me, because of the rotors and their headphones. But I cannot hear anything either. The noise is like a waterfall in my head, and it is so loud it hurts, almost worse than my shoulder. I get close enough to the cockpit that I can see out. I see a river below us. It bends almost in a circle, and the shape looks familiar, so I recall my map Implants.

Now I know where we are. They have taken me a little closer to my unit, but they have taken me far east of LaToya, to a river that flows into Allied India. It flows right past my unit's base camp, far down-river.

Now is the time for bold action. I leap onto the pilot's back and bite savagely at his neck. His mouth opens, and I can just barely hear him scream. Then I shift my attack to the copilot, and now they are both too busy fighting me off to fly the helo. Many controls are bumped, and we spin uncontrollably.

We fall, the pilots still trying to fend me away. Then just as we brush the tops of the trees, I roll away and lie, belly flat, on the deck. The helo crashes through the trees and flips over on its back, and I am thrown around inside the cargo area. Finally it stops rolling. But now I smell spraying JP-8, and flames. I get out as fast as I can. I do not know if the pilots make it, but they are unimportant. They are enemies. I run toward the river. My shoulder feels like fire! Behind me, the jungle burns.

The trees grab for me. The vines catch at my wound, and the roots try to trip me up. They are enemies too! They are all enemies. I am dizzy. I smell animals, enemies. They will all try to kill me. All of the tall ones are enemies.

There is a fire in my head, where LaToya says my brain is. It is a fire inside. I am not on the farm. The Outsider is in my head, and when I find Colonel Trelloq, National Federation, United States Marine Corps, Military Identification Number 885-4L-7777, I will kill him; he is an enemy. LaToya is the enemy.

No! There is something wrong with my head. I am dizzy from my wound, and from the sound in the helocopter, and from the jet fuel vapors.

I lie down on the ground, panting. I have run for a long, long way. I can smell my own urine, but I do not remember marking. I am hurt.

LaToya can never be the enemy. When I think that, I know there is something terribly wrong. LaToya is not here; she is wounded. I must report to command—the

Outsiders will land! There is one here already! They will help the enemy. I do not know why.

And I must get help, and make pick-up of LaToya. She needs me.

When my head is calm again, I trot forward, trying to put more weight on my hurt leg to make better time. It hurts more than anything I can remember, but I tell myself it is for LaToya, and the hurt goes away a little. I do not think it is broken.

It is getting dark now. The jungle is waking up for the night. Far away I hear a tiger roar in fury. Maybe he has missed his kill. I remember what LaToya says: the jungle is much more dangerous at night than in the day. I keep limping toward the river. I have a mission.

Suddenly my danger signals fly off all at once, like crows from an approaching farmer. It is my most feared enemy, and my most familiar—cougar! No, this is different. It is a panther, and it is somewhere around me.

It is smart, for an animal. I do not smell it. I strain my ears, and two times I hear a slight, muffled, padded step. It is being very quiet. It is stalking me.

I think hard. If I cannot smell it, it must be downwind of me. I perk my ears forward and become still myself. At last it makes a misstep, and I hear the faint cracking of a leaf. I know where the panther is now.

But I know it is too big to fight. It would kill me, and I will not suffer the indignity of being killed by an animal. At the farm, I round the sheep together in a tight herd, and bark an alarm to the tall one. He comes with a rifle and shoots the cougar if it stays.

But I have no sheep to distract the panther, I have no rifle, there is no tall one, and LaToya is not here. I must fight for myself. The panther is creeping forward on hated cat feet.

I must think! I am afraid. My leg is stiff, and will not move right. I cannot fight the animal. But I can think; I am the smarter.

What kills animals? Tall ones; rifles; gas grenades. But we are only on a reconnaissance mission, and I carry no anti-personnel weapons.

Fire kills animals. It almost killed me in the helo. I know what to do now.

I still sense danger; the panther has not left. He wants me. I am afraid to take my eyes away from his direction, but I must. I still listen, and I bury my mouth in the thick, shaggy fur on my belly. There is a pouch where I carry things for LaToya. She teaches me many things, more than the B School does. But I have never worked the flare.

I know how LaToya uses it. I will do the same. Maybe it will like me and decide to ignite. I lay it on the ground, and now I hear the panther slinking forward. He will rush any moment now!

I hold the flare between my paws, even though I can barely feel my wounded leg. I bite the top, but nothing happens. I pull on it, and it opens! I can see the lever that LaToya pushes, but I cannot get at it with my mouth.

Now the panther has stalked into view at the edge of the clearing. It is showing itself. It wants me to run. Almost, I panic, and do what I must not. Urine trickles down my leg, but I ignore it, and the fear, and even the panther, and concentrate on the flare igniter.

I hit at the lever again and again with my hurt paw, trying to hold it upright with my uninjured one. One, two, three—I have lost count. Again, again, and suddenly a bright, welcome little flame appears at the top. The panther is almost close enough to rush now, and it does not even look at the flare.

I let it fall over, and in a moment the grass is burning, and the signal flare lights off. Now the panther sees the flames, and draws back hissing in a way that makes my ears lie back and my fur stand up. But it is not ready to give me up. It knows I am not a tall one, and it must think I am only an animal, like it. It does not know I know all about fire.

I pick up the burning flare in my mouth, and the panther pads softly around the fire. I walk the other way, keeping it between me and the animal. Now the grass fire is dying out in the wind. The panther sees an opening and springs!

I step back, avoiding its rush, and I thrust the burning flare deeply into its face!

The panther screams and backs away. It circles, licking its nose, and I smell burned fur. It pounces again.

Once more I roll back, and retaliate with my fire, and again the animal retreats. Now it is enraged. It charges wildly, trying to bat the flare away with its paws. This animal is smart! But I have been trained. I duck underneath the blows, and ram it with my unhurt shoulder, knocking the beast over. While it is on its back, I lay the flames right across its eyes and hold them there as long as my strength prevails against the panther.

At last, it bucks and heaves and throws me off, and runs away into the jungle, crying in agony. I have won! Now the fire begins to burn my mouth, and I drop the flare in the dirt and watch it burn until it goes out.

I whine and wish LaToya were here. She would be so proud! I am good; I am not an animal!

I hear more helos. They hover over the wreck of the first helo, where smoke still comes, but I am far away, and they cannot see me. I know that they are talking on the radio and alerting all of the enemies about me. Almost, I am glad about that. I know I have hurt them badly. I start once more for the river, and run many strides through the jungle.

I am at the river. The helos fly over me in the sky all the time. They know I am loose, and that I know of their plans, and they must stop me. I skulk along the edge of the river; I know they may think to look here.

I hear something ahead of me. It is voices. No, it is just the hiss of the wind through the trees, sounding like tall ones. No—it *is* talk; it is a pack of natives. I do not think they are enemies, but I am still dizzy, and my head still burns, so I do not know if I am good or bad.

But I must use them, no matter what they are. I limp up, and I let them see me. If they chase me, I will know they are enemies. They call to me. I do not know the words of the natives, but I recognize "dog" and "good boy." I approach cautiously.

Three of the natives are standing on a flat, wide tree that is floating in the river. I look and look, astonished. I have never seen a tree grow like that before. Then at once I understand. It is a funny kind of boat, without the sides or the white-hats to drive it.

I whine and crawl, and act like an animal. I do not like it. It is beneath my dignity as a Marine Corps non-commissioned officer, but it works. They find a treat, and entice me to board the boat as if I was a dog. They say "good boy" again.

I know which way we have to go on the river. It is downstream. Here, the current is swift, and I am sure we must go downstream. I do not know how the tall ones get the boats upstream again. Maybe they make them all here.

I limp forward, and now the natives notice I am lame. They are angry, but one of them pets me, so I know they are not angry at me for being bad and getting shot. They want me to go into a funny little house in the middle of the boat. I am happy to do as they ask, for I must get out of sight. I hear a helo coming.

The helo hovers overhead a while. The natives curse and make noises around the boat. Soon I watch the shore move away as we drift downstream. The helo flies away. I do not think the enemy really believes I am more than an animal; they do not even land and search the boat. I think about the enemy, and imagine what I will do if they come inside the little house . . .

Then at once it is morning. I have slept through day and night.

I stand up. My shoulder is very stiff, but there is a bandage around it, and it does not hurt much. But my pouch is gone! I have been discovered. I walk out onto the deck.

We are still moving down-river, but the water is so smooth it feels like we stand still. It is not like the English boat. The natives are talking excitedly, and they are waving my pouch around. I walk up to the leader, making my limp seem worse than it really is, and force my head under his hand. I have seen dogs do this.

He looks at my military ID, comparing me to the picture. But I do not think he can read English, and does not know I am a corporal in the Marine Corps. But he knows I am special.

They are talking, and I catch the word for "money." They must think to take me to a military unit for a reward. But which side?

A long time passes, and the flat boat keeps going farther downstream. The native men play with me, like I was a dog. I am so worried about LaToya I want to play, too. For a few moments I can stop thinking about her bleeding to death.

The jungle goes away now, and I see fields and animals. I see water buffalos and goats and cows, and I wish to be back on the farm, except with LaToya there too. It was so simple then! I fight off cougars and feral dogs, and frighten away coyotes, and nip and bark the sheep into line. There are no enemy tall ones, no intelligence reports, no Outsiders.

But there is no LaToya Franklin, either. Which is better? I cannot have her without the Corps, and without the war. She will fight until the war is over. Semper Fi. Maybe she will have to fight the Outsiders someday, if the treaty does not work. So will I.

I decide I do not want to be back on the farm. Life is nice there, but I know nothing about what it takes to keep it that way. Enhanced or not, I was an animal until I bled in the field. Now I am a corporal.

The sun is setting. The natives are worried; I can smell it. When one of them gives me food for the night, he looks over his shoulder at the black hills and whispers about "Sikh devils." I slink low; I do not want to be seen by the Sikh Khalsa, who fight for the enemy.

They all stop talking. For a long time, no one says anything, and we slip down the river as silently as a watersnake.

It makes no difference. I can tell them the enemy uses old LAMPS cameras to spot blockade runners, but I cannot speak the native talk and I cannot reveal myself for what I am. Either the Sikhs are watching, and we will be caught, or they are not.

I see a flash behind a hill. At first I hope it is a campfire; then I hear the noise of a rocket.

The first shot hits the water and explodes just below the surface. Then the laser spot appears on our house— the natives do not notice it or do not know what it is—and I jump over the side as the next rocket lands dead center. The boat explodes into flames, which fire the gasoline left by the first shot. Now the boat and the water both burn bright, and I can hardly breathe in the heat and the smoke.

I struggle to stay afloat, until I notice I am drifting straight into the flames. Machine gun bullets churn up the water all around me, but I ignore them; the enemy is shooting blind, since the fire will wash out their infrared. They will either hit me or they will not.

I am not afraid; I am well-trained. There is only one thing to do. I take a deep breath and swim beneath the surface. I swim and swim and swim, as long as I can hold my breath, and then longer. I know even when I think I will burst I still have air in my lungs. I have done it before, many more times than I can count, in IWEST school.

It is much harder for me than for LaToya; I have to claw downward to stay under the water. I swim and swim, and at last my eyes begin to see black, and I know I must come up or pass out. I break the surface—I am past the fire!

Debris is falling all around me, even now. I climb up onto a piece from the boat, shivering now that I drift away from the fire and the cold wind hits me. I wonder if the Sikhs are attacking because of me. I hurt inside; I think I am dying.

My heart leaps—something—I know now . . . LaToya is gone! Her voice no longer whispers within me! She is gone.

I am not proud of what I am doing. My brain is turned off like the switch on LaToya's computer.

Where am I? Where is LaToya? LaToya is dead! She is gone, she—

There is nothing. I am nothing. No LaToya. LaToya? Where are you?

Am I good? Am I bad? Oooooooohhhhh! Oooooooohhhhh! LaToya is not—

My brain tied to her brain tied to my brain tied

I cannot go on. I will die too. I am dead; LaToya is dead. The sky is black is not yet black, I don't understand . . . am I an animal now?

Wait—maybe it is okay. Maybe LaToya is here. I listen hard; I am good! LaToya . . .

LaToya where are you? LaToya I need you!

I am ashamed; I am not dead. But I am dead.

I am an animal.

I do not know how long it has been. I am still on the river. I no longer care about the intelligence. LaToya is dead; I know that. It is the only way that her voice in my head can stop.

LaToya is dead. I have a mission. I don't care.

Still river. Water. Have mission have LaToya mission.

dogthoughts animal not animal—I am not an animal, I am a

corporal marine dog enhanced thoughts LaToya

LaToya. LaToya. LaToya!

Hope—LaToya is not dead? Everything wrong . . .

The sky is black. It is night. I am not an animal anymore.

I am shivering; I am sick and afraid. But I am a soldier again.

I am Corporal Countryman Mandela Franklin, National Federation, United States Marine Corps, Military Identification Number 802-S8-8881. I have intelligence to report. An Outsider has landed and is collaborating with the enemy.

Can I live without her? We are a team. Our minds are one. When she is dead, I am dead!

But I must live. LaToya is dead; I know that now. It is the only way that her voice inside my head can stop. But I must go on, and return to my lines. I must report to the unit commander. I must speak with Colonel Trelloq, National Federation, United States Marine Corps, Military Identification Number 885-4L-7777.

I have another thought, but I am afraid to think about it. What if everything I know about the K-9s is wrong too, like the treaty and the Implant? Maybe something else can stop her voice in my head.

Maybe LaToya is still alive. It is desperation, not hope, I know.

I call up my map. I try to think how fast the river flows. I think I must be in Allied India now. My base will come soon, if it did not pass me while I was an animal.

I study my Implant. The river becomes two rivers, fifty kilometers south of my base camp. I will go onto the land then.

After much time, I notice my piece of the raft is sinking; I have to leave the river sooner. I have to leave now.

My belly aches, but I cannot stop and eat. I have a mission. I am scared of crocodiles, but I jump into the water anyway. I can feel my heart beating too fast, and I am bad. I am a non-commissioned officer; I must not be afraid of animals! I swim to the bank and shake myself dry. I run alongside the river bank, smelling for crocodiles.

The sun rises. Now it is late in the morning. I come to the road that leads to the base camp. I will be home before another sunrise.

But now I stop again. I don't know why. What is wrong? What is wrong?

LaToya is dead! I cannot think of anything else. I run in circles, whining like a dog. I lie down, and I eat grass that makes me want to vomit.

I am lying on the grass thinking. It is so easy! I can

be an animal. I will not ever have to report to the commander again. I will not care about intelligence.

I do not even have to put my thoughts into talk; it makes my head ache.

But I cannot be an animal. From the day the MARMI medical team cut open my head, I have not been an animal. An animal does not suffer through ten weeks of basic, and B-School, and C-Tech Survival/Reconnaissance/Intelligence School to serve LaToya and his country.

I am not an animal.

And maybe she is still alive.

I am a Marine. I am a corporal. I have a mission. I make myself get up and start running again. My leg still hurts, but I have grown used to the pain.

I run all through the day, and through the night. Before the sun rises again, I reach the perimeter of the base camp.

I start to trot right past the sentries, but one of them calls out and tries to grab me. I dodge him, but the other one blocks my path. I am fast! I run, and I almost make it. But he catches me. He holds me and soothes me, as if I am a dog. He tells his shipmate to check me for bombs.

I am surprised. Don't they know I am a corporal? But then I remember that my pouch and my military identification were blown apart with the raft. Their search is bad anyway; they do not even find the bullet hole. I am careful not to limp.

I talk to them. "Colonel Trelloq," I say, and "take me to the colonel." But they do not understand. I'm not even sure they know I am talking; they did not go to K-9 Recon/Intel Officers School. They are enlisted.

"Colonel Trelloq!" I bark, as loud as I can. They still do not understand. "TRELLOQ!"

One of them pets me, saying okay, take it easy boy, you're all right now, we're not going to eat you.

I am confused. What do they mean, eat me? Do they think the Marines have turned cannibal now? I should think it is a violation of the UCMJ to eat a non-commissioned officer, even a corporal.

Then I understand. They think I am a dog, and that the natives or the enemy might eat me. But if they think I am an animal, why are they talking to me? It makes no sense, but they are only a PFC and a lance, so I don't get angry.

"TRRRRRRRELLLLLLLLLLOOOOOOOQ!" I howl. At last one of them listens. It sounds almost like he's saying Trelloq, he says to the lance. Don't be silly, the other one answers. I speak again, pronouncing carefully like LaToya taught me. I am good.

"TRRRRR-ELLLLLL-OOOOOOOQ!" I decide that National Federation, United States Marine Corps, Military Identification Number 885-4L-7777 is a lost cause with these two.

Let's take him to the colonel, says the private. I am all for this plan, and I yip and lick his hands to let him know he is good. Why should he have all the fun, asks the other guard. We found him, so we should get to keep him. I just want Colonel Trelloq to hear how he says his name. Aw don't be silly, you know we'll interrupt the old fart's dinner and the dog won't do it.

"Trelloq!" I bark. "Trelloq! Trelloq! Trelloq!" I do not even care about what they called the colonel.

Oh come on, says the private; see, he keeps doing it. He'll do it in front of the old man, I'm sure. We need a break from the war anyways. Okay, says the lance corporal, as soon as Gueterra and Franklin arrive.

For a moment my heart leaps—but then I remember LaToya is dead; it must be another Franklin. Besides, LaToya is a captain; she would not pull guard duty.

LaToya is dead!

I wait and wait, and every so often bark "Trelloq!" just to keep them interested. Finally the other watchstanders arrive, and the private and the lance turn the duty over. At last they leave.

I have to wait again while they visit the messhall. Hurry up! I want to tell them. How can you eat when I have a mission to complete? But they are only a private and a lance corporal, they don't understand me, and they would stop to eat if their house was on fire. So I say nothing, but wait. At last they finish, and they finally take me to see the colonel.

I stand at attention, ignoring the pain and what the guards say.

"Corporal Franklin for debrief, sir!" I say, and the colonel's mouth opens in surprise. Of course the colonel understands me, because he has been through K-9 RIOS.

"Where is Captain Franklin?" he demands, and I tell him LaToya is dead. I tell him about the enemy, and the map, and the Outsider.

The colonel and the Marine Intelligence Unit debrief me for a long time. I draw a map as well as I can of the Implant I made showing the village where I smelled the Outsider, and where LaToya was hit. One of them tells me I traveled three hundred miles in four days. It's impossible, he says, and I finally know that I am good, even if it is true, and LaToya is really dead.

I know she would have said I am good.

At last they finish the debrief. The medics take out the bullet, and they bandage my leg. They spray it, and it does not hurt anymore. I sit and wait in Colonel Trelloy's office, and he finally comes back from the C3I tent.

"What do you want, corporal?" he asks. I am surprised.

"When do we leave, sir?" I say. "I am ready any time."

"Leave for what?"

I cannot believe he is stupid. He must just be testing me.

"To make pick-up, sir," I answer. "To retrieve Captain LaToya Franklin, National Federation, United States Marine Corps, Military Identification Number 237-MM-9992."

He waits a long time. Then he says, "Son, I can't risk any more men to pick up a body."

I am taken aback. I have never heard of such a thing.

"Respectfully, sir," I say, "Captain Franklin is a Marine. The Marines always make pick-up. What if she is still alive?"

"She's dead!" he says. I can see he is angry. Many times my two-legged shipmates become angry when I argue with them. I know they are smarter, but I am not bad. "Corporal, it's been too long; even you know she's dead. Your mindlink with her is gone."

"Sir, even if she is dead, Captain Franklin knows she will be retrieved. She is a Marine. A Marine is loyal to the Corps, and the Marine Corps never forgets."

"I CAN'T DO IT!" I know LaToya never backs down when she knows she is right. All right then, neither can I.

"Semper Fi," I say. "Sir."

For a long time he just looks at me. He is thinking about what I have said. Then he gets very angry and says all right—one helo and a med-evac team. He calls in his aide and gives the orders.

The trip back over the jungle takes hardly any time at all. We fly just over the treetops, and when we get close I guide the men through an interpreter—a trainer from the K-9s. The helo can't land, so we have to go down a line, with me in a basket.

We hit the deck, and something funny is in my head. For a little bit I run around in circles, whining and trying to catch the scent of whatever has me stirred up. But then suddenly I know what it is.

I can hear LaToya's voice!

LaToya is not dead! She is alive! She is very weak, and her voice is wandering; it does not say any words. But it is still there!

LaToya is only wounded. When I can speak at last, I tell the medics, and the interpreter translates. Then I lead them through the jungle until I pick up my own urine markings. I follow my trail and find LaToya again. She is where I left her, and there is the smell of many animals near her.

But none of them found her in the thorny brambles.

The med-evac team calls the helo, and they load her on board with a stokes litter. They tell me she will be all right, but she may be shipped stateside.

I don't care. I'm tired of the war anyway. We have

done our part. It is somebody else's turn to fight the
Communists and the Sikhs and the Outsiders and the
natives, and the colonels who need to be taught the
second rule of the Marine Corps by a corporal. I hope
she is sent home.

On the way back LaToya moans. It is the first sound
she has made since the mortar hit us. I lay my head on
her lap, and talk to her in my head. It's okay, I tell her;
I am good. I carried the intelligence to the brigade;
they know about the Outsider. Sleep now, LaToya, I
say; we're going home.

I listen very close on the way back, inside my head. I
can hear LaToya; she is dreaming. I know she will be
all right.

Semper Fi, mac.

Here is an excerpt from the new collection "MEN HUNTING THINGS," edited by David Drake, coming in April 1988 from Baen Books:

IT'S A LOT LIKE WAR

A hunter and a soldier on a modern battlefield contrast in more ways than they're similar.

That wasn't always the case. Captain C.H. Stigand's 1913 book of reminiscences, HUNTING THE ELEPHANT IN AFRICA, contains a chapter entitled "Stalking the African" (between "Camp Hints" and "Hunting the Bongo"). It's a straightforward series of anecdotes involving the business for which Stigand was paid by his government—punitive expeditions against native races in the British African colonies.

Readers of modern sensibilities may be pleased to learn that Stigand died six years later with a Dinka spear through his ribs; but he was a man of his times, not an aberration. Richard Meinertzhagen wrote with great satisfaction of the unique "right and left" he made during a punitive expedition against the Irryeni in 1904: he shot a native with the right barrel of his elephant gun—and then dropped the lion which his first shot had startled into view.

It would be easy enough to say that the whites who served in Africa in the 19th century considered native races to be sub-human and therefore game to be hunted under a specialized set of rules. There's some justification for viewing the colonial overlords that way. The stringency of the attendant "hunting laws" varied from British and German possessions, whose administrators took their "civilizing mission" seriously, to the Congo Free State where Leopold, King of the Belgians, gave the dregs of all the world license to do as they pleased—so long as it made him a profit.

(For what it's worth, Leopold's butchers *didn't* bring him much profit. The Congo became a Belgian—rather than a personal—possession when Leopold defaulted on the loans his country had advanced him against the colony's security.)

But the unity of hunting and war went beyond racial attitudes. Meinertzhagen was seventy years old in 1948 when his cruise ship docked in Haifa during the Israeli War of Independence. He borrowed a rifle and 200 rounds—which he fired off during what he described as "a glorious day!", increasing his personal bag by perhaps twenty Arab gunmen.

Similarly, Frederick Courteney Selous—perhaps the most famous big-game hunter of them all—enlisted at the outbreak of World War One even though he *wasn't* a professional soldier. He was sixty-five years old when a German sniper blew his brains out in what is now Tanzania.

Hunters and soldiers were nearly identical for most of the millennia since human societies became organized enough to wage war. Why isn't that still true today?

In large measure, I think, the change is due to the advance of technology. In modern warfare, a soldier who is seen by the enemy is probably doomed. Indeed, most casualties are men who *weren't* seen by the enemy. They were simply caught by bombs, shells, or automatic gunfire sweeping an area.

A glance at casualties grouped by cause of wound from World War One onward suggests that indirect artillery fire is the only significant factor in battle. All other weapons—tanks included—serve only to provide targets for the howitzers to grind up; and the gunners lobbing their shells in high arcs almost never see a living enemy.

The reality isn't quite *that* simple; but I defy anybody who's spent time in a modern war zone to tell me that they felt personally in control of their environment.

Hunters can be killed or injured by their intended prey. Still, most of them die in bed. (The most likely human victim of a hungry leopard or a peckish rhinoceros has always been an unarmed native who was in the wrong place at the wrong time.) Very few soldiers become battle casualties either—but soldiers don't have the option that hunters have, to go home any time they please.

A modern war zone is a terrifying place, if you let yourself think about it; and even at its smallest scale, guerrilla warfare, it's utterly impersonal.

A guerrilla can never be sure that the infra-red trace of his stove hasn't been spotted by an aircraft in the silent darkness, or that his footsteps aren't being picked up by sensors disguised as pebbles along the trail down which he pads. Either way, a salvo of artillery shells may be the last thing he hears—unless they've blown him out of existence before the shriek of their supersonic passage reaches his ears.

But technology doesn't free his opponent from fear—or give him personal control of the battlefield, either. When the counter-insurgent moves, he's likely to put his foot or his vehicle on top of a mine. The blast will be the only warning he has that he's being maimed. Even men protected by the four-inch steel of a tank know the guerrillas may have buried a 500-pound bomb under *this* stretch of road. If that happens, his family will be sent a hundred and fifty pounds of sand—with instructions not to open the coffin.

At rest, the counter-insurgent wears his boots because he may be attacked at any instant. Then he'll shoot out into the night—but he'll have no target except the muzzle flashes of the guns trying to kill him, and there'll be no result to point to in the morning except perhaps a smear of blood or a weapon dropped somewhere along the tree line.

If a rocket screams across the darkness, the counter-insurgent can hunch down in his slit trench and pray that the glowing green ball with a sound like a steam locomotive will land on somebody else instead. Prayer probably won't help, any more than it'll stop the rain or make the mosquitos stop biting. But nothing else will help either.

So nowadays, a soldier doesn't have much in common with a hunter. That's not to say that warfare is no longer similar to hunting, however.

On the contrary: modern soldiers and hunted beasts have a great deal in common.

APRIL 1988 * 65399-7 * 288 pp * $2.95

To order any Baen Book by mail, send the cover price to: Baen Books, Dept B, 260 Fifth Avenue, New York, N.Y. 10001

Have You Missed?

DRAKE, DAVID
At Any Price
Hammer's Slammers are back—and Baen Books has them!
Now the 23rd-century armored division faces its deadliest
enemies ever: aliens who *teleport* into combat.
55978-8 $3.50

DRAKE, DAVID
Hammer's Slammers
A special *expanded* edition of the book that began the
legend of Colonel Alois Hammer. Now the toughest, mean-
est mercs who ever killed for a dollar or wrecked a world
for pay have come home—to Baen Books—and they've
brought a secret weapon: "The Tank Lords," a brand-new
short novel, included in this special Baen edition of *Hammer's Slammers*. **65632-5 $3.50**

DRAKE, DAVID
Lacey and His Friends
In Jed Lacey's time the United States computers scan
every citizen, every hour of the day. When crime is de-
tected, it's Lacey's turn. There are a few things worse than
having him come after you, but they're not survivable
either. But things aren't really that bad—not for Lacey and
his friends. By the author of *Hammer's Slammers* and *At
Any Price*. **65593-0 $3.50**

**CARD, ORSON SCOTT; DRAKE, DAVID;
& BUJOLD, LOIS MCMASTER**
(edited by Elizabeth Mitchell)
Free Lancers (Alien Stars, Vol. IV)
Three short novels about mercenary soldiers—never be-
fore in print! Card's hero leads a ragtag group of scientific
refugees to sanctuary in Utah; Drake contributes a new
"Hammer's Slammers" story; Bujold tells a new tale of
Miles Vorkosigan, hero of *The Warrior's Apprentice*.
65352-0 $2.95

DRAKE, DAVID
Birds of Prey

The time: 262 A.D. The place: Imperial Rome. There had never been a greater empire, but now it is dying. Everywhere its armies are in retreat, and what had been civilization seethes with riots and bizarre cults. Against the imminent fall of the Long Night stands Aulus Perennius, an Imperial secret agent as tough and ruthless as the age in which he lives. But he stands alone—until a traveller from Earth's far future recruits him for a mission so strange it cannot be disclosed.

> 55912-5 (trade paper) $7.95
> 55909-5 (hardcover) $14.95

DRAKE, DAVID
Ranks of Bronze

Disguised alien traders bought captured Roman soldiers on the slave market because they needed troops who could win battles without high-tech weaponry. The leigionaires provided victories, smashing barbarian armies with the swords, javelins, and discipline that had won a world. But the worlds on which they now fought were strange ones, and the spoils of victory did not include freedom. If the legionaires went home, it would be through the use of the beam weapons and force screens of their ruthless alien owners. It's been 2000 years—and now they want to go home. 65568-X $3.50

DRAKE, DAVID, & WAGNER, KARL EDWARD
Killer

Vonones and Lycon capture wild animals to sell for bloodsport in ancient Rome. A vicious animal sold to them by a trader turns out to be more than they bargained for—it is the sole survivor of the crash of an alien spacecraft. Possessed of intelligence nearly human, it has two goals in life: to breed and to kill.

> 55931-1 $2.95

DAVID DRAKE

"Drake has distinguished himself as the master of the mercenary sf novel."—Rave Reviews

Here is an excerpt from the new novel by Timothy Zahn, coming from Baen Books in August 1987:

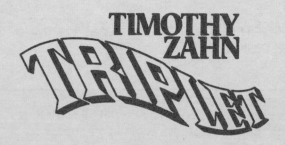

TIMOTHY ZAHN

TRIPLET

The way house had been quiet for over an hour by the time Karyx's moon rose that night, its fingernail-clipping crescent adding only token assistance to the dim starlight already illuminating the grounds. Sitting on the mansion's garret-floor widow's walk, his back against the door, Ravagin watched the moon drift above the trees to the east and listened to the silence of the night. And tried to decide what in blazes he was going to do.

There actually *were* precedents for this kind of situation: loose precedents, to be sure, and hushed up like crazy by the people upstairs in the Crosspoint Building, but precedents nonetheless. Every so often a Courier and his group would have such a mutual falling out that continuing on together was out of the question ... and when that happened the Courier would often simply give notice and quit, leaving the responsibility for getting the party back to Threshold in the hands of the nearest way house staff. Triplet management ground their collective teeth when it happened, but they'd long ago come to the reluctant conclusion that clients were better off alone than with a Courier who no longer gave a damn about their safety.

And Ravagin wouldn't even have to endure the

usual froth-mouthed lecture that would be waiting
when he got back. He was finished with the Corps,
and those who'd bent his fingers into taking this trip
had only themselves to blame for the results. He
could leave a note with Melentha, grab a horse, and
be at the Cairn Mounds well before daylight. By the
time Danae had finished sputtering, he'd have alerted
the way house master in Feymar Protectorate on
Shamsheer and be on a sky-plane over the Ordarl
Mountains . . . and by the time she made it back
through to Threshold and screamed for vengeance,
he'd have picked up his last paychit, said bye-and-
luck to Corah, and boarded a starship for points
unknown. Ravagin, the great veteran Courier, actually
deserting a client. Genuinely one for the record books.

Yes. He would do it. He would. Right now. He'd
get up, go downstairs, and get the hell out of here.

Standing up, he gazed out at the moon . . . and
slammed his fist in impotent fury on the low railing
in front of him.

He couldn't do it.

"Damn," he muttered under his breath, clenching
his jaw hard enough to hurt. "Damn, damn, *damn*."

He hit the railing again and inhaled deeply, exhaling
in a hissing sigh of anger and resignation. He couldn't
do it. No matter what the justification—no matter
that the punishment would be light or nonexistent—
no matter even that others had done it without
lasting stigma. He was a *professional*, damn it, and
it was his job to stay with his clients no matter
what happened.

Danae had wounded his pride. Deserting her,
unfortunately, would hurt it far more deeply then she
ever could.

In other words, a classic no-win situation. With
him on the short end.

And it left him just two alternatives: continue his
silent treatment toward Danae for the rest of the trip,
or work through his anger enough to at least get

back on civil terms with her. At the moment, neither choice was especially attractive.

Out in the grounds, a flicker of green caught his eye. He looked down, frowning, trying to locate the source. Nothing was moving; nothing seemed out of place. Could there be something skulking in the clumps of trees, or perhaps even the shadows thrown by the bushes?

Or could something have tried to break through the post line?

Nothing was visible near the section of post line he could see. Cautiously, he began easing his way around the widow's walk, muttering a spirit-protection spell just to be on the safe side.

Still nothing. He'd reached the front of the house and was starting to continue past when a movement through the gap in the tree hedge across the grounds to the south caught his attention. He peered toward it . . . and a few seconds later it was repeated further east.

A horseman on the road toward Besak, most likely . . . except that Besak had long since been sealed up for the night by the village lar. And Karyx was not a place to casually indulge in nighttime travel. Whoever it was, he was either on an errand of dire emergency or else—

Or else hurrying away from an aborted attempt to break in?

Ravagin pursed his lips. "*Haklarast*," he said. It was at least worth checking out.

The glow-fire of the sprite appeared before him. "I am here, as you summoned," it squeaked.

"There's a horse and human traveling on the road toward Besak just south of here," he told it. "Go to the human and ask why he rides so late. Return to me with his answer."

The sprite flared and was gone. Ravagin watched it dart off across the darkened landscape and then, for lack of anything better to do while he waited, continued his long-range inspection of the post line. Again he found nothing; and he was coming around to the front of the house again when the sprite returned. "What answer?" he asked it.

"None. The human is not awake."

"Are you sure?" Ravagin asked, frowning. He'd once learned the hard way about the hazards of sleeping on horseback—most Karyx natives weren't stupid enough to try it. "Really asleep, not injured?"

"I do not know."

Of course it wouldn't—spirits didn't see the world the way humans did. "Well . . . is he riding alone, or is there a spirit with him protecting him from falls?"

"There is a djinn present, though it is not keeping the human from falling. There is no danger of that."

And with a djinn along to— "What do you mean? Why isn't he going to fall?"

"The human is upright, in full control of the animal—"

"Wait a second," Ravagin cut it off. "You just told me he was asleep. How can he be controlling the horse?"

"The human is asleep," the sprite repeated, and Ravagin thought he could detect a touch of vexation in the squeaky voice. "It is in control of its animal."

"That's impossible," Ravagin growled. "He'd have to be—"

Sleepwalking.

"*Damn!*" he snarled, eyes darting toward the place where the rider had vanished, thoughts skidding with shock, chagrin, and a full-bellied rush of fear. *Danae*—

His mental wheels caught. "Follow the rider," he ordered the sprite. "Stay back where you won't be spotted by any other humans, but don't let her out of your sight. First give me your name, so I can locate you later. Come on, give—I haven't got time for games."

"I am Psskapsst," the sprite said reluctantly.

"Psskapsst, right. Now get after it—and *don't* communicate with that djinn."

The glow-fire flared and skittered off. Racing along the widow's walk, Ravagin reached the door and hurried inside. Danae's room was two flights down, on the second floor; on a hunch, he stopped first on the third floor and let himself into Melentha's sanctum.

The place had made Ravagin's skin crawl even with good lighting, and the dark shadows stretching around the room now didn't improve it a bit. Shivering reflexively, he stepped carefully around the central pentagram and over to the table where Melentha had put the bow and Coven robe when she'd finished her spirit search.

The robe was gone.

Swearing under his breath, he turned and hurried back to the door—and nearly ran into Melentha as she suddenly appeared outside in the hallway. "What are you doing in there?" she demanded, holding her robe closed with one hand and clutching a glowing dagger in the other.

"The Coven robe's gone," he told her, "and I think Danae's gone with it."

"What?" She backed up hastily to let him pass, then hurried to catch up with him. "When?"

"Just a little while ago—I think I saw her leaving on horseback from the roof. I just want to make sure—"

They reached Danae's room and Ravagin pushed open the door . . . and she was indeed gone.

August 1987 • 384 pp. • 65341-5 • $3.50

HE'S OPINIONATED

HE'S DYNAMIC

HE'S LARGER THAN LIFE

MARTIN CAIDIN

Martin Caidin is a bestselling novelist, pilot *extraordinaire*, and expert on America's space program. *He's also a prophet of technological change.* His ability to predict future trends verges on the psychic, as when he wrote *Cyborg* (the novel which became "The Six Million Dollar Man") and *Marooned* (which precipitated the American-Soviet Apollo-Soyuz linkup mission). His tense, action-filled stories are based on personal experience in fields such as astronautics, aviation, oceanography and the military.

Caidin's characters also know their stuff. And they take on real life, because they're based on real people. Martin Caidin spent a stint as a merchant seaman in Europe and Africa, worked for Air Force Intelligence in the U.S. and Asia, and has flown his own planes to many parts of the world. His adventures can be yours in these novels from Baen Books.

— — — — — — — — — — — — — — — —

EXIT EARTH—Just as the US and the USSR have finally settled their differences, American scientists discover that the solar system is about to pass through a cloud of cosmic dust that will incite the Sun to a paroxysm of fury. All will die. There can be no escape—except, possibly, for a very few. *This is their story.* 656 pp. • 65630-9 • $4.50 ————

KILLER STATION—Earth's first space station *Pleiades* is a scientific boon—until one brief moment of sabotage changes it into a terrible Sword of Damocles. 55996-6 • 384 pp. • $3.50 ————

THE MESSIAH STONE—"An unusual thriller . . . not only in subject matter, but in the fact that the author claims that the basic idea behind the book is real! [THE MESSIAH STONE] concerns the possession of a stone; the person who controls the stone rules the world. The last such person is rumored to be Adolf Hitler. . . . Harrowing adventure and nonstop action."—*Science Fiction Review.* 65562-0 • 416 pp. • $3.95 ————

ZOBOA—It started with the hijacking of four atomic bombs, and ended with the Space Shuttle atop a pillar of fire. . . . "From the marvelous, cinematic opening pages, Caidin sweeps the reader along in a raucous, exciting thriller."—*Publishers Weekly* 65588-4 • 448 pp. • $3.50 ————

To order these Baen Books, check each title selected and return with a check or money order for the combined cover price. Send to Baen Books, 260 Fifth Avenue, New York, N.Y. 10001.

Distributed by Simon & Schuster
1230 Avenue of the Americas • New York, N.Y. 10020

ROBERT A. HEINLEIN

"Heinlein knows more about blending provocative scientific thinking with strong human stories than any dozen other contemporary science fiction writers."
—*Chicago Sun-Times*

"Robert A. Heinlein wears imagination as though it were his private suit of clothes. What makes his work so rich is that he combines his lively, creative sense with an approach that is at once literate, informed, and exciting."
—*New York Times*

Seven of Robert A. Heinlein's best-loved titles are now available in superbly packaged new Baen editions, with embossed series-look covers by artist John Melo. Collect them all by sending in the order form below:

REVOLT IN 2100, 65589-2, $3.50	☐
METHUSELAH'S CHILDREN, 65597-3, $3.50	☐
THE GREEN HILLS OF EARTH, 65608-2, $3.50	☐
THE MAN WHO SOLD THE MOON, 65623-6, $3.50	☐
THE MENACE FROM EARTH*, 65636-8, $3.50	☐
ASSIGNMENT IN ETERNITY**, 65637-6, $3.50	☐
SIXTH COLUMN***, 65638-4, $3.50	☐

*To be published May 1987. **To be published July 1987. ***To be published October 1987. Any books ordered prior to publication date will be shipped at no extra charge as soon as they are available.

Please send me the books I have checked above. I enclose a check or money order for the combined cover price for the titles I have ordered, plus 75 cents for first-class postage and handling (for any number of titles) made out to Baen Books, Dept. B, 260 Fifth Avenue, New York, N.Y. 10001.